THE FINAL CURSE
OF
OPHELIA CRAY

CHRISTINE CALELLA

PAGE STREET YA

PAGE STREET YA

First published in 2024 by

Page Street Publishing Co.

27 Congress Street, Suite 1511

Salem, MA 01970

www.pagestreetpublishing.com

Distributed by Macmillan, sales in Canada by The Canadian Manda Group.

28   27   26   25   24   1   2   3   4   5

ISBN-13: 978-1-64567-872-4

ISBN-10: 1-64567-872-5

Library of Congress Control Number: 2023936743

Cover and book design by Rosie Stewart for Page Street Publishing Co.

Cover illustration © Sabrina Gabrielli

Printed and bound in China

DEDICATION

For Mom and Dad,

Thank you for always making sure I knew how much I was loved.
This book would never have been written without you.

A NOTE TO THE READER

This is a story about ostracism, about loss, cruelty, and disaster,
and about learning to love yourself even when other people
spit at you. I hope my readers protect themselves as they
journey forward—and if you need a hand, I have a
lighter to lend you.

ONE

The morning of the execution dawned as hot as any other, with only a shadow of gray clouds on the horizon to hint that hurricane season was barreling ever closer. Betsy Young had spent the night tangled in her sheets, tormented by the heat and her anxious dreams. Ophelia, who was already fully dressed in her best lilac gown, shook Betsy awake.

"I've changed my mind," Betsy said, dabbing at the wet back of her neck with her nightgown sleeve. "Th-this is an awful idea."

Ophelia stripped the sweat-soaked sheets away from her half sister's legs and tossed them to the polished wood floor. "You promised me."

Betsy straightened up. "I did. But Papa outright said we shouldn't go. That the crowd could get angry at you. Hurt you, even."

Ophelia perched herself on the end of the bed, a grim smile on her face. "I don't see what makes today particularly special. Last week, some little brat threw a rock at my head and drew blood. If I hid every time a neighbor glared at me, I'd never leave the house."

"Doesn't sound too bad to me," Betsy mumbled, heat rising in her chubby cheeks.

"Look," Ophelia said, fixing Betsy with a measured stare, "I know it's a big favor I'm asking. I know you don't like crowds, or violence, but—" She paused.

Betsy knew that her sister was taking special care not to let her voice tighten. Ophelia hated to look weak in front of anyone, even Betsy.

Eventually, Ophelia lifted her chin, calmly finishing her statement. "But I have never seen my birth mother in the flesh. Never. And this is my one and only chance. Papa and Eliza can give all the dire warnings they want, but I'm going. Now, are you coming with me, or shall I go alone?"

Betsy swallowed heavily, her throat as dry as if she'd gulped down hot sand. In truth, she was desperate not to go along. Betsy did not like leaving the house at the best of times. That was not to say she did not do it—she ran errands if necessary—but it was always stress inducing. The city was too crowded, too loud, too chaotic. But going to a *hanging*, of all things? This was a worst-case scenario.

Hangings repulsed her. And although the accused—the notorious pirate queen Ophelia Cray—may have been her sister's birth mother and namesake, she still seemed wicked and dangerous. Wicked and dangerous things made Betsy panic. But if she forced Ophelia to watch her mother die alone, then Ophelia was sure to think her a selfish coward.

Slowly, and against all her fainthearted instincts, Betsy reached out to take her sister's hand. Ophelia didn't seem to mind that Betsy's hand was clammy with sweat. She squeezed it.

Betsy scrambled to dress as quickly as possible, with Ophelia lending a hand to lace her stays vise-tight, as Betsy preferred. Betsy returned the favor by braiding back her sister's hair, deep enough brown that it was almost black, so that it could be tucked neatly beneath a silk cap. This was always a difficult task, as Ophelia's rebellious curls constantly fought against all means to restrain them.

It would have been hard for most people to guess that Betsy and Ophelia shared a father; they were both tintypes of their respective mothers. While Ophelia had inherited those famous flashing eyes, wild curls, and a constellation of freckles leaping out from a light olive face, Betsy had her mother's demure looks: fine-textured blond hair, rosy cheeks, and a figure that tended toward an appealing roundness. Betsy's stomach cramped with anxiety, knowing that today Ophelia's appearance would be a dangerous liability as they navigated the city streets.

The house was as silent as the city docks before dawn. Ophelia hitched up her skirts and crept down the stairs with ease, but Betsy felt one traitorous floorboard creak beneath her foot. This step had long been loose, and Betsy had not taken the required care to step on it noiselessly.

"Betsy!" Ophelia whispered from the base of the stairs, "You're not even trying!"

There was probably some truth to that, Betsy had to admit. Some small, treacherous part of her secretly wanted to be caught, and thus avoid the hanging altogether.

Roused to attention by Ophelia's voice, someone stirred in the kitchen. Their ears were greeted by the sound of leather boots tapping smartly against mosaic tiles, growing ever closer until Valois, the butler, rounded the corner into the foyer.

Valois seemed shaken. His meticulously groomed mustache twitched, and a lit cigar dangled from his left hand. "You two!" he said, shaking the cigar at them.

Ophelia whirled around, her hands clasped in desperation. "Let me start by saying—"

Valois flicked ash in Ophelia's direction. "Not a word out of you, deceiver!"

Betsy, still at the top of the stairs, gazed intently, almost hungrily, at the glowing cigar tip. She gave a timid cough to catch Valois's attention. He watched her, wary of tricks, as she descended.

"W-we're asleep," Betsy said when she had reached the landing. "We're asleep in our beds—which is good, because it means we couldn't possibly be awake to see you smoking one of those terrible cigars that Mama hates so. You know how she always says they leave an awful smell."

Valois blinked, looking almost impressed. "Very well then." He reached out his free hand to shake Betsy's. "We have an accord. I don't want to know what you're up to—and *when* you get caught, I was never here."

Betsy returned his solid handshake, and Valois vanished to go finish his cigar. Ophelia was off almost immediately, striding out the front door. Shaken by her own success, Betsy scurried to follow.

Ophelia slammed the door shut and they sprinted down the street, alight with victory, the hems of their dresses brushing against cobblestones.

THE FINAL CURSE OF OPHELIA CRAY

The hanging was scheduled for seven in the morning, with the gallows erected in the square in front of the jail, an ill-kept edifice that leaned precariously to the side like a squat, drunken sailor. There were odd bricks missing from its face, having been blown away in the storms of previous hurricane seasons. The crowds stretched farther than anybody might have guessed, with spectators packed in from the front of the hangman's platform all the way to the marble gates of the governor's mansion in the east; there were many squeezed in between the colorful booths of the western marketplace, and all the way down to the northern-most docks, where the planks must surely have been creaking and straining under all the weight. To her right, Ophelia noticed a father hoisting his son up onto one of the crooked palm trees that lined the square, the better for the boy to get a clear view of the gallows. The mob—the audience, rather—cheered in anticipation, their roars shaking the ground as much as any earthquake.

Ophelia resisted the urge to pinch her nose against the overwhelming smell of so many people crammed closely together, their perfumes and oils mixing with the tang of sweat and urine.

"We should have gotten here earlier," Betsy said, looking feverish and ashamed. "We're too short to see anything from the back." Although Betsy was relieved that she wouldn't be able to see Cray die, she knew that it was her own selfish hesitation that had held Ophelia up. If her sister never got to lay eyes on her birth mother, it would be Betsy's fault.

"No," Ophelia said, wrapping her strong, slender fingers around Betsy's wrist, "it'll be fine."

Ophelia shook the brimmed cap from her head, throwing her

shoulders back into a regal posture. Without the hatpins restraining her wild hair, it began to escape the white ribbon Betsy had used to tie it back. With minds of their own, Ophelia's curls began expanding, trying to reach up toward the sky.

"Your hair," Betsy said, reaching out a hand to flatten it.

"No," Ophelia said, pushing Betsy's hand away. She untied the ribbon altogether, and the curls sprang up, framing her head like a lion's mane. Ophelia tapped the elbow of the nearest man, who was standing on his tiptoes to get a better view of the distant platform. "Excuse me," Ophelia said, raising her voice over the babble of the crowd. "I need to get to the front."

The man turned, irritated, his bald head beaded with sweat. "Look, girl, everyone wants a better—" But the moment his eyes met Ophelia's, he saw the echo of a face he had often seen in wanted posters. His mouth tightened as if he'd suddenly contracted lockjaw, and he pulled back from her in revulsion, quickly pushing deeper into the crowd—desperate to put space between himself and Ophelia.

Everyone in the immediate area turned around with curiosity, only to grimace when they realized who exactly had come to watch the pirate queen die. The crowd split open as people shuffled away from Ophelia, treating her like a swarm of disease-carrying mosquitoes. She moved in the newly empty space, walking steadily toward the platform, with Betsy following in her wake. Ophelia kept her chin high as the sea of people parted for her, a straight-backed queen, apparently unconcerned by the way they averted their eyes the moment she got near.

This is no different, Ophelia told herself, *from any other day walking to the market. I am just walking to the market.*

Unlike Ophelia, Betsy was an outward mess of nerves, fiddling with the edges of her hat, tilting it down so fewer people could look her in the eye.

They made it to the front of the crowd easily.

A drum's rattle split the air as the clock in the jail steeple struck seven. The heavy door creaked open, and two officers in smart, palm-green uniforms exited. They marched the thin body of the accused between them, a hood covering her head. A crier with a squirrelly face walked briskly behind the group, holding a heavy wooden stick. A band, squeezed onto the steps of city hall, launched into an off-key rendition of a funeral dirge.

Now that the moment was drawing close, Ophelia was starting to question why she had come at all. To see her mother? To be seen by her? As she stood at the base of the platform, panicked, regretful thoughts tumbled over themselves inside her skull. *Why come here just to watch a stranger die?* Because that was all Ophelia Cray was: a stranger. A stranger who had wanted nothing to do with her daughter. There was no affection here, no relationship.

And yet, Ophelia had seen hangings before. Those criminals had been strangers too. No more or less than Cray was. Still, this felt different. So different that Ophelia's heartbeat had sped up to keep pace with the drumroll.

Ophelia's jawline hardened as she watched her mother be escorted up the gallows steps, Cray's well-shined boots absurdly at odds with the shabby sack covering her face. Ophelia had drawn her hands into such tight fists that her fingers were going numb. She couldn't understand why people were cheering.

Most everybody on the island of Peu Jolie, as well as the rest of the String Islands, was descended from a criminal or two—that was why their ancestors had been sent to populate the penal colonies built on these worthless, previously uninhabited islands. How would they feel if they saw their grandparents being marched to the hangman's platform? Would they cheer then?

Ophelia did not understand why some people were given second chances, respectability even, and others weren't. Weren't they all guilty?

The small pocket of people around Ophelia and Betsy may have been thinking along similar lines, because they were uncomfortably silent, some scowling as if Ophelia's presence had ruined their day out. But outside of that small bubble, the crowd was chanting and jeering. Betsy curled her lip in disgust at a man a few yards over who was shouting something vulgar at Cray and grabbing at his crotch. Betsy could not see what point there was in this. It wasn't as if Cray could see anything through that sack anyway.

Behind the officers, two more figures strode out of the jail and down the path to the gallows. One of them was a lean, angular man wearing a black suit and waistcoat, but with his face obscured by a sack-like mask of his own—the hangman. The other was a full-bodied woman with jet-black hair and a golden complexion, whose bright red uniform jacket was adorned with glimmering medals of service: the famous Commodore Lang. At the sight of this intimidating pair, the crowd fell mostly silent, with only the odd shout from the far back, seeming to come from miles off.

The hangman and the commodore ascended the platform— their thumping steps in perfect unison.

The commodore stopped and stood, facing out toward the crowd, just a foot from the top of the stairs. Ophelia's eyes combed her face. Lang was completely impassive. No emotion of any kind was visible: not pride, not happiness, not anxiety, not even mild interest. Ophelia wasn't sure what she expected to see in the arresting officer's expression—but it certainly hadn't been blankness.

The hangman continued on to stand behind Cray, looping the noose around her neck and tightening it. He forced the pirate to stand on a tall, wooden stool, and when Cray was positioned, he took a single, solid step backward, and inclined his head to the crier.

Giving a watery smile, the crier banged the end of his staff against the wooden floor. The sound echoed impressively through the square. Ophelia somehow couldn't imagine that a man that small would be able to speak above a whisper, but when he opened his mouth, his words made her eardrums ache.

"WE STAND HERE IN THE PRESENCE OF THE VILLAINOUS OPHELIA CRAY, OR AS SHE IS BETTER KNOWN, THE PIRATE QUEEN OF THE SOUTHERN WATERS. THE SIREN OF THE EMERALD SEA. THE WITCH OF THE WAVES."

The crier knew how many people came to these things for entertainment, and he was milking his moment.

"CRAY'S VESSEL, _THE BLACKFISH_, WAS CAPTURED BY THE NOBLE COMMODORE ANNE LANG AFTER PILLAGING THE TOWN OF COEUR-JOLIE. OPHELIA CRAY IS A WELL-RENOWNED KILLER WHO HAS BEEN APPREHENDED FOR HIGH CRIMES AGAINST THE

STRING ISLANDS NO LESS THAN ELEVEN TIMES BEFORE, ALWAYS TO BE RELEASED WITHOUT TRIAL."

A murmur of discontent rustled through the crowd, along with a few raucous laughs. Betsy turned to Ophelia, mouthing the words, "released without trial?" Ophelia ignored Betsy's question. She knew the answer as to why. Her father had explained it to her once. Something about an old law regarding pregnant women. But she didn't have time to walk Betsy through it now— and she had a feeling the crier was about to explain it for her.

The crier continued, nodding with apparent delight,

"OPHELIA CRAY'S VILLAINY IS NOTORIOUS. SHE STALKS THE CONTINENTAL COAST FOR GOLD, WHICH SHE HOARDS AT HER ISLAND HIDEOUT. SHE HAS LEFT THE BONES OF COUNTLESS NAVAL SHIPS TO REST ON THE OCEAN FLOOR. BUT HER GREATEST AUDACITY HAS BEEN IN HER ABUSE OF OUR MOST JUST AND MERCIFUL LAWS. A KNOWN SEDUCTRESS, SHE PREYS UPON INNOCENT SAILORS IN ISLAND TAVERNS, PROWLING FOR VICTIMS TO FILL HER BELLY WITH SEED, SO THAT SHE MAY NOT BE HANGED FOR HER CRIMES."

The crowd began to boo Cray, their profane taunts drowning out the crier for the first time. A woman to her back gave Ophelia a hard shove forward.

"BUT ON THIS DAY," the crier shouted, banging his staff to bring the crowd to a semblance of order, "INJUSTICE WILL BE SUFFERED NO MORE. AFTER BEING CAUGHT ON THIS TWELFTH OCCASION, A THOROUGH MEDICAL EXAMINATION CONFIRMED THAT OPHELIA CRAY IS

AT LAST ELIGIBLE TO BE PUNISHED TO THE FULLEST EXTENT OF THE LAW. SHE WAS ON THIS OCCASION INDICTED FOR OVER TWO HUNDRED PAST CRIMINAL ACTS OF MURDER, MUTINY, PIRACY, AND HIGH TREASON. SHE WAS CONDEMNED TO THE GALLOWS BY THE RIGHT HONORABLE JUDGE WESTERLING, CHIEF JUSTICE OF PORT JOLIE. TODAY, SHE IS TO HANG BY THE NECK UNTIL DEAD."

The crier took a deep, shuddering breath, and nodded at the female officer. **"COMMODORE ANNE LANG WILL NOW READ A MESSAGE FROM THE GRAND-QUEEN."** The jeering from the crowd momentarily turned over, becoming tumultuous cheers for this female officer. Ophelia felt her breath catch in her chest. How the townspeople loved the commodore! Almost as much as they hated her mother.

The commodore withdrew a scroll from her jacket pocket and began to read in a cold, clear voice, which carried some distance over the heads of the crowd, if not with the same earth-shattering volume as the crier.

"It is the honored duty of all citizens of our empire to live in righteousness. A soul lost to piracy is a soul lost to human mercy. The Queen begs that her subjects continue to despise such crimes and to dedicate their efforts to the eradication of these pirates, who threaten the harmony of our realm above all others."

These final words played in Ophelia's ears like a familiar tune. They were printed at the bottom of every pirate's wanted notice. She had been reading them beneath sketches of her mother's face—practically Ophelia's own face—for her entire life. Ophelia glanced over at Betsy, whose arms were wrapped around herself, contorted with discomfort.

Ophelia looked away from her sister again, back up at the platform. She let out a soft gasp. The anticipation that had been building up in her chest had been released, not out of any kind of surprise, but out of a strange relief. Ophelia didn't have to wait for the moment anymore. It had arrived, and would soon be over. The hangman had removed the sack from Cray's head.

Cray was laughing. She had a wide, wicked cat's smile. Ophelia knew she had never smiled like that in her life—but the pirate queen's hair, now stretching toward the sky, looked identical to her own, yet somehow even darker, so that it absorbed all nearby light. It seemed like something from an old magic story: a wig fashioned from black storm clouds.

Ophelia clutched tightly at her skirt as she stared up at her mother for the first time. She was beautiful. Beautiful and terrible.

Ophelia did her best to commit her mother to memory, knowing this would be her only opportunity. Her fine leather boots resting on the stool top. Her flashing eyes. The gold necklace that shimmered at the neckline of her tunic. She memorized every inch of her mother's skin: her calloused hands, bound at the wrists; the light freckles across her face; how her tan from years sailing under a hot sun had not yet been diminished by a few days in an underground prison cell. Ophelia knew, on a logical level, that she looked just like her mother, but she felt in her gut that her mother was something apart from her—apart from anyone she'd ever met. Her mother was a howling void. She didn't seem afraid. Perhaps she lacked the capacity to be.

Ophelia was both fascinated and deeply unsettled by her.

The crier banged his staff against the platform again, startling Ophelia.

"THE FINAL MERCY OF THE CROWN IS THIS. DOES THE ACCUSED, OPHELIA CRAY, HAVE ANY LAST WORDS?"

Cray's terrible smile grew wider, as if the edges of her mouth were threatening to snake their way past her cheeks and wrap around to the back of her head. The crowd lurched forward, everyone craning their necks to better hear what the pirate queen had to say. The audience for her death hadn't really come to hear the crier pontificate, or to listen to the queen's lecture by proxy. They had come to hear a pirate's final taunts, and then to watch her dance.

Cray's voice was as smooth and slow as molasses. The noose, tight around her throat, didn't seem to inhibit her ability to project much. "You're all fools," the pirate crooned sweetly, as if singing a lullaby to an infant. "You may burn my ship, hang my crew, and leave my body to rot in the sea like driftwood, but you will never be rid of me. I'm the Witch of the Waves, aren't I? I've already left you a thousand curses." Her dark eyes flitted downward, and her gaze connected with Ophelia's, as if she had always known her discarded infant would be standing there. She touched a light, fluttering hand to the golden necklace resting on her chest, and mouthed to her daughter, "For you."

Ophelia found herself mimicking her mother's action. She pressed her hand to the bare skin above her dress' neckline. She bit her quivering lower lip hard enough that it bled. She couldn't bear to look like a whimpering child in front of her mother, not when Cray herself was so calm in the face of death that her knees didn't even shake as she stood on that stool.

Cray blew Ophelia a kiss, then broke eye contact with the girl, laughing softly. She directed her steely gaze at the commodore and demanded, "Go on. Do it. I'll be the admiral of a ghost fleet, sailing back to haunt you. Send me on my way."

Lang might have smiled then, and no one would have blamed her for doing so in the face of Cray's arrogance, but she kept her face serene and professional. She assured Cray, "We'll honor that request." Lang nodded at the hangman, who placed the hood back over Cray's head, obscuring her face for the last time.

The hangman gave a swift, savage kick to the stool beneath Cray's feet.

The crowd burst into cheers and singing as the pirate's boots started to jerk. Ophelia wanted desperately to close her eyes, but she couldn't stop watching, somehow. Next to her, Betsy had hidden behind her fingers.

Cray's neck hadn't been broken from the short drop—necks rarely did break from this sort of hanging. As the noose slowly strangled her, the pirate queen's feet continued to convulse. The man who had earlier been showing off his crotch cried out, "A fine jig, bitch!"

Against her will, Ophelia began to sniffle as her mother's swinging legs slowed down to a mere twitch. She didn't want to cry, to show weakness as she was trapped by this jeering crowd, but she couldn't stop her nose from running. Betsy peeked out from between her fingers in time to see the final flutter of

Cray's feet. Ophelia tried to brush away all evidence of her tears as Betsy wrapped her trembling arms around her.

Most pirates were left to sway on the noose for a few days, or at least a few hours, but not Ophelia Cray. Rumor had it the constable was certain that if the pirate queen were left hanging, her body would be cut down and stolen before sundown. After checking Cray's pulse, the hangman freed her limp body from the noose, and carried it, still hooded, back into the city jail.

Immediately, an enraged roar shook the square. The crowd didn't want to dignify Cray with a proper burial—they wanted to see her body rot. As the crier and the officers followed the hangman inside, the mass of people surrounding the Young sisters grew increasingly restless—drawing too close to Ophelia, shouting the same vile things they had shouted at her mother. Torn from Betsy's arms, Ophelia fought to shield her face as the strangers descended on her. They were a dizzying swarm, pushing her this way and that, tearing her dress and snatching at her hair. Ophelia felt something hot and wet—her own blood— bubble against her skin as a woman dug sharp fingernails into her forearm. Her head struck the cobblestones. Once. Twice.

Betsy was shrieking somewhere not far away—the vulgar man had tried to grab her by the shoulders, and now she was on her knees, crawling toward Ophelia.

But Commodore Lang, who had clearly noticed Ophelia at the front of the crowd during Cray's last words, had not returned to the jail. She shouldered her way toward the conflict, a crusading splash of red in a sea of mocking townspeople. "Disperse!" she shouted. "Disperse now!"

The crowd fell back, shamed by the woman they adored, revealing Betsy and Ophelia to the commodore again. They were both crouched on the ground now, once again holding each other tightly.

Lang held out her arms to warn the people to stay back. To Ophelia, she said, "Cray's daughter, I presume?"

Ophelia peered up, and quickly shook off the safety of Betsy's embrace. "Yes?"

No pity registered on Lang's face, but there was no disgust either—which already seemed to Ophelia a welcome change. The commodore's response to Ophelia was brisk. "Is that an answer or a question?"

Betsy's arms had fallen limply at her sides, and she watched from below as Ophelia rose to her feet, brushing loose dirt from her gown.

Looking Lang hard in the eye, Ophelia repeated, "Yes."

At last, the corner of Lang's mouth gave a little spasm that might have been mistaken for a smile. "Better. What's your name, girl?"

Ophelia's eyes were every bit as hard as Lang's. "Ophelia Young. Why?"

Lang gave a barking laugh. "Why?" she asked, incredulous. She was smiling properly now, but even the smile made Betsy feel nervous and cold inside. Lang crouched a bit, putting her hands on her knees to look Ophelia in the eyes. "Your mother was a wicked woman, Ophelia. You don't have to be. Do you know that?"

Ophelia blinked. "I do." It was unclear as to whether she was responding to the former or latter statement.

"Where do you live?" Lang asked.

Ophelia gave their address.

Lang glanced at Betsy for the first time. "And you?"

Betsy stuttered. "Th-the same."

Ophelia seized Betsy's wrist, and pulled her to her feet. "We're sisters," Ophelia announced. She sounded almost proud, though Betsy couldn't imagine a single credible reason as to why.

Lang nodded. "Ah. Then you'd better both come with me. It would be safer for you both to be escorted home." Lang's dark eyes flickered around at the crowd, which was growing more restless by the minute.

After a moment, Ophelia agreed with Lang, choosing her words carefully. "I believe you're most likely right."

Lang walked the girls home. She banged the copper knocker on the front door, which was opened by Valois, feigning utter astonishment. "Madam," he said, dabbing at his bald head with a handkerchief, "welcome to the home of Master Nathaniel Young, of the Whitman-Young Company. Are you perhaps here on business?" He shrugged at Betsy and Ophelia, as if to say he had never seen them before in his life.

"There'll be no trouble," Lang said, raising a hand and waving away Valois's poor acting. Betsy scurried in through the front door, but Lang held Ophelia back. She removed the smallest medal from the front of her red jacket, a golden star with a purple stone in its center. She pressed the star into Ophelia's palm. "Stay straight on the path, girl," Lang said.

Ophelia seized the cuff of Lang's sleeve as the commodore turned to leave. She felt breathless; her voice was like cracked porcelain. "Let me join," she said. "The navy, I mean. Help me leave this place behind."

A shadow of mistrust crossed Lang's face. She tugged her sleeve away and left without another word. Ophelia's chest swelled with emptiness as Valois ushered her into the house and the front door clicked shut behind her.

In the days to come, she would stare at the medal in her cupped hands until she saw stars even when she shut her eyes.

TWO

One month after her mother's execution—with hurricane season nearly upon the island—Ophelia twirled the handle of her parasol as she crossed Port Jolie's main square. Suddenly, she felt a pinch on her waist. Ophelia immediately snapped her parasol shut and swung it at the tiny boy giggling on her left. She struck him in the back as he tried to dart away.

Ophelia preferred the adults of Port Jolie, were someone to make her choose. At least they merely turned away from her in the streets nowadays, talking behind their hands and glaring at her back. But the kids—always trying to sneak up on her and snap her stays, or put their filthy little fingers somewhere they didn't belong—were truly unbearable. Ophelia had never really liked being touched, and especially not by strangers.

The boy's friends had been hiding behind one of the nearby palm trees. They'd probably dared him to tweak the witch. Now, seeing their comrade's distress after being rapped with a frilly umbrella, another ran forward, aiming a kick at Ophelia's shins.

She was ready for him, again swinging her parasol like a saber. She didn't try to hit the boy this time, she merely made him jump back before his kick could connect. "Want to rethink this?" Ophelia asked as he stumbled back from her, pulling at his blue suspenders in an attempt to look tough.

The street was mostly empty. Ophelia craned her neck to look around at the surrounding houses. Here in the heart of the city, these were all prettily constructed two-levels, with curving iron balconies and outer walls painted in colors like wrapped candies, some mint green and others taffy blue. Ophelia wondered if someone might be looking out a window, perhaps a parent who could come collect their wayward child. But no luck—Ophelia thought she had even seen one set of front curtains rustle closed out of the corner of her eye.

The original boy came to stand behind his friend, watching Ophelia like a wary cat. "Witch," he spat at her. "Cursed."

Ophelia raised an eyebrow. "Do you think your mother will thank you for making a scene in public? I doubt she raised you to pinch strange ladies. Shall I tell her what you've been getting up to?" She glared at the kicker as well, adding, "Shall I tell both your mothers?"

"What would my mother care?" The kicker asked, sticking his tongue out at Ophelia. "She was the one who told me you're a witch."

"Your mother's very rude then," Ophelia told him, face cool. The woman was stupid to boot. If Ophelia were a witch, wouldn't she have deservedly turned someone in this city into a mule by now?

Ophelia reopened her parasol and began to stalk away, back straight and nose in the air. "What would you know about mothers?" one of the boys called after her, before turning tail to run like a coward. "Your mother was a murderer!"

"That she was," Ophelia muttered, but so that only she could hear.

As she continued along the square, Ophelia resettled her face into a smooth, blank expression. She had taken care to dress especially well that day, clothing herself entirely in white from her linen skirts to her curve-brimmed hat. To an outside observer, she would have seemed perfectly serene—and indeed this peaceful countenance was probably what had drawn those boys' ire—but in truth, Ophelia had only been fidgeting with her parasol in the first place because she needed something to do with her hands.

This was her last chance, she knew. It was obvious now, that the people of Peu Jolie would never stop loathing her. That they'd never stop throwing rocks and snatching at her hair. They had always despised her, even as a small child, for her mother's sins, but since the execution, the tension was rising. The children taunted her today—but their parents might bring pitchforks tomorrow. Ophelia was becoming increasingly certain that her only way off this island would be on a ship or in a noose. She couldn't afford to be rejected by the commodore again.

She had just reached the grand steps of the naval office when she heard a confident voice ring out behind her. "Miss? Pardon me, but I think you dropped something."

Ophelia turned on the spot, resisting a sigh, and found herself facing a tall young man with a strong jaw and a suntan that made him appear glowing and healthy. He was wearing a cocky grin that told Ophelia he was acutely aware of how well his naval officer's jacket had been tailored to his frame. He gave her a smart half bow and extended a white handkerchief to her. "Yours, miss?"

Ophelia gave a polite smile. "No, I don't think so."

The officer's eyes ran up and down Ophelia's body—taking in her parasol, her hat, and her boots—but primarily lingering on her chest. "Well, aren't you just a vision in white," the officer said. He had a clipped, continental accent. From the Gordon province, maybe. "On your way to some fine ladies' tea, I suppose?"

"Hardly," Ophelia said. "I have an appointment."

"I'm sorry," the officer said, still with a smile twisting at his thin lips, "I hope I'm not making you late."

"Not at all," Ophelia said, giving him another intentionally distant smile, hoping to bow out of the conversation quickly and gracefully. "I should probably get going, however." She didn't need another pointless distraction right now. What she needed was to concentrate on her meeting with Lang rather than on some strange officer's flirtations.

The man's eyes lit up. There was something genuine in his expression for the first time. He had ignored Ophelia's farewell and clearly misread the intention of her smile. "I'm sorry, but your teeth—"

Ophelia was flustered now. Had this sailor been raised by wild monkeys? Not enough manners to fill a thimble. She pressed her lips together tightly, hiding the gap between her two front teeth.

The officer laughed, and shook his head. "No, no. Don't hide them. They're lovely." He touched his hands to the fine lapels of his blue jacket. "I'm a midshipman on a beautiful little rig that goes all over the world——" He had at last said something that was of interest to Ophelia. Jealousy burned in her throat at the mention of his ship. If her emotions showed on her face, the officer didn't notice, as he kept right on talking. "——We just came back from Carthay, you see. And do you know what people over there call teeth like you've got, with that pretty little space? Lucky teeth. And I'd bet just anything that you're a very lucky girl."

Ophelia smirked, but did not show her teeth again. "That would be a first."

"What, miss?" the officer asked.

"Someone calling me lucky."

The officer bowed again, and snapping out his hand to take her free one, he brushed his lips lightly against Ophelia's lace gloves. "Edgar Ludlow, miss."

"Ophelia Young." Ophelia quickly drew her hand back and wrapped it around the handle of her parasol. She was always opposed to being touched, and that certainly included this Edgar person. He might as well have been one of the nasty little boys from before, only stretched out and squeezed into a uniform.

"Ophelia Young," Edgar seemed to turn her name over in his mouth. "I like that. A pretty name for a pretty girl."

Ophelia's eyes briefly closed in frustration. Her instinct about him being continent-born had proved right. She almost laughed at the absurdity of it. He was certainly not a local boy, or he wouldn't like the sound of her name one bit.

People only ever seemed to recognize her as Ophelia Cray's daughter when they were looking for a Cray—expecting a pirate created in her mother's image. When they were not primed to see a criminal's face echoed in hers, they did not see one. It was such a shame that Port Jolie was a small city, slotted into the few miles of jungle the earliest colonists had managed to carve away, before being undone by hunger and mosquitoes and disease. Perhaps in the larger cities of the continent, the gossip of her origins—of an infant abandoned on Nathaniel Young's doorstep—wouldn't have swept the streets like a plague. Perhaps she might have blended in.

She tried again to leave Edgar in her wake. "Thank you for the compliment, sir, but I'm afraid I must leave you."

"Of course," Edgar said. He held up the handkerchief again. "And you're sure this isn't yours?"

"Quite sure," Ophelia said. "Mine looks rather different." She withdrew her handkerchief, which Betsy had embroidered with lilacs, from her sleeve. The small golden medal was pinned in its corner.

Edgar's face fell. "Ah," he said, his voice suddenly theatrical and a touch mocking. "So you have a beau. And one who's earned the Star of Merit too. Can't say that I'm terribly surprised. Though I am, of course, disappointed."

Ophelia's eyes flickered toward the top of the steps. She had more important places to be, and more interesting things to discuss. As long as Ophelia could remember, she had never cared about romance of any kind. It was a dreadfully boring subject, and she could not see why it fascinated people so. "What makes you think that a boy gave me this medal?"

Edgar cocked his head to one side, but Ophelia turned away before he had a chance to reply. She began to climb the steps again, running her left thumb over the purple stone in the star's center.

Ophelia breezed through the heavy wooden doors at the top of the steps and into a marble foyer. A blade-thin middle-aged man with impeccable posture stood by the back wall, wearing the sand-colored uniform of a naval man with no officer position. His hair was heavily powdered in a way that had gone out of fashion a few years earlier. Ophelia stopped in front of him.

"I'm here to speak with Commodore Lang. I have an appointment."

The man gave a stiff nod. He had been seeing a lot of Ophelia recently, and he clearly didn't like it. "The hallway on your left. All the way down. Knock first."

"Of course," Ophelia said, dropping into a shallow curtsy, despite knowing that there was nothing she could do, no politeness she could observe, to make this stranger like her. "Thank you." Trying uselessly to swallow the lump in her throat, Ophelia took the hallway to her left.

The hallway was cool and empty. She could hear her cream-leather boots tapping against the marble with every step. Her fingers tightened around the parasol handle, and Ophelia reminded herself that this meeting was nothing to be worried about. Lang might be cold, but she wasn't like the other people on this tiny, backward island. She would understand Ophelia's need; she would see reason.

With the final door in the hall in sight, Ophelia closed her eyes and imagined that her boots weren't tapping against marble but rather against the wooden floorboards of a ship deck. The skies were clear, the wind was blowing through the sails, and Ophelia was wearing a beige uniform of her own—with her handkerchief tucked into the breast pocket.

Ophelia knocked on the final door.

"Enter."

Ophelia did as she was told, quickly lowering her head and trying to convey more respect with a single curtsy than she had in all sixteen years of her life combined. "Commodore Lang. I want to thank you very much for taking the time to speak with me." Ophelia rose from her curtsy and looked at the woman who had condemned her mother to swing—but who, nonetheless, might be her savior.

Lang was sitting behind a heavy wooden desk, in a severe, hard-backed chair. "Miss Young," the commodore said, gesturing to a seat in front of the desk. "Please sit. I trust you're well."

Ophelia sat, propping her parasol against the desk, and gave the admiral a slight smile. "Very well. I hope you can say the same."

"Yes," Lang said, raking her dark eyes across Ophelia's face. "I'll admit that I was intrigued when you scheduled a meeting with me. I can't imagine the reason for it."

Ophelia opened her mouth, then closed it again. She unfolded her handkerchief and placed it on the shining surface of the black mahogany desk. The star medal glimmered in the light. "I've kept this safe," she began, "and close to my heart ever since you gave it to me." Ophelia's eyes, previously fixed on the star, now darted upward to Lang's unmoved face.

Lang put up a calloused hand. "I have no time for pretty words or dancing around matters. Tell me your business."

But Ophelia was armed only with pretty words. She had perfected her speech weeks ago, and blazing forward despite all signs of reticence from Lang, she now rattled it off by heart—with each pause and inflection exactly where she knew they would be most effective.

"What I mean is that a great impression has been made upon me. I didn't know my mother, but I believe she did me a fine service in showing me precisely how *not* to lead my life. I don't want to end it swinging on the gallows. I'd like to be better, to make amends. I am only sixteen, and that may be young, but it's old enough to enlist in the navy. I have not changed my mind from what I said to you that day. It was not a whim, or a flight of fancy. I want to spend my adulthood undoing the damage my mother did. Let me be of service."

Lang leaned back in her chair, shifting her weight. "A noble aim, for sure," she said, a smile playing at the corner of her mouth now. "But why come to me? I believe there is an office in the basement of this building where locals can enlist. It's hardly something for a commodore to become involved with."

Ophelia pressed her lips together, looked down at her hands clenched in her lap, and then stared back into Lang's eyes. Attempting to strike a delicate balance between bold and deferential, she said, "I understand your time is very valuable, ma'am. I came to you, you see, because they won't allow me to enlist, although I've been petitioning to do so for the last month."

Lang blinked. A small laugh escaped her. "You don't strike me as sickly. Did you fail your health examination?"

"No, ma'am," Ophelia said. "I'm in perfect health. I fulfill all the necessary qualifications to enlist."

"Then why, may I ask," Lang said, "would they reject an able-bodied youth for service? The Imperial Navy is not usually in the business of turning down willing applicants."

"They think I'm cursed, ma'am." Ophelia felt like she hadn't blinked in a year. Her eyes burned, but she wouldn't break contact. "They believe that because my mother marooned me on this island at birth, I am the worst kind of luck. They believe I should never be allowed aboard a ship."

Ophelia suspected that Lang was actively intrigued now but trying not to show it. "Sailors are often superstitious," was all she said.

Ophelia raised her chin high. "They told me at the enlistment office, ma'am, that if I wanted to enter the navy, I would have to go over their heads. And I did. Over their heads, and over their superiors' heads. They've all told me no. They agree that I'm cursed. But I think we both know that I'm not."

"And here you are," the commodore said.

"And here I am," Ophelia agreed.

Lang smiled. "I don't believe you're cursed, no. But I also don't believe it's my place to force a shipful of sailors to work alongside someone whom they believe—rightfully or not—will cause the ship to sink."

"I don't think the whole ship will believe that," Ophelia replied, her tone calm but firm. "I met a young officer just outside. He had never heard my name before. He didn't blink twice at it. It's just the folk of Peu Jolie who know I'm her daughter. I could start a new life if I were given the chance."

Lang's fingers drummed against the desk. "And you'd like me to throw my weight around to terrorize the sailors of Peu Jolie for the sake of one little girl's desire to do good?"

"With all due respect, commodore," Ophelia said, choosing her words carefully, "you are the one who encouraged me to do good in the first place. If you have changed your opinion on the way I ought to live my life, then by all means, I insist you allow me to return this medal to you. But if you think there's a chance that I could help a single soul out there—if I could save one drowning man, protect one woman or child from piracy—then give me the shot I deserve."

Lang shook her head gruffly. "No, I'm sorry. I can't." She slid the handkerchief back across the table to Ophelia, star and all. "And I won't take back that star either. I gave it to you for a reason."

Ophelia reached out for the handkerchief, pressing the purple stone into the pad of her thumb again. She ought to leave. She knew that. She'd been dismissed.

But she didn't want to leave. She wanted to press harder. She couldn't give up on her best and only chance to get out of Port Jolie, off this stifling island—not now when she was closer than she'd ever been. Who was Lang to stop her?

Ophelia felt her cheeks get hot, and she was grateful that her complexion was not as traitorously see-through as Betsy's, or Lang would have been able to see her blush. She counted herself lucky to be able to hide her emotions. Her temper was like a storm gathering strength, but she pushed it farther out to sea. Carefully arranging her face into a delicate smile, she said, "I'm glad to hear you say that, commodore. But I'm afraid that if you will neither assist me in my goals nor take back this medal, I will simply return tomorrow. And I'll return the day after that, and so on, until you either allow me to serve my empire or to return this valuable gift."

Lang's upper lip twitched—it could have been from anger, since Ophelia knew that she was being impertinent, but her instincts told her the commodore was restraining another laugh. "You know," Lang said, with the air of someone offering a riddle, "if it is only the people of Peu Jolie that fear you, you could always go to the next island and enlist under a pseudonym."

It's a trick, Ophelia thought. *I'd have to get false papers. She's testing me.* But Lang wouldn't get her that easily. Out loud, she told Lang, "I would not. That's fraud against the empire. A crime. No, I'll do this legally, if you please."

"I see," Lang said, eyes cool. "Then shall I present you with a scenario?"

"A scenario?" Ophelia asked, suddenly hesitant. She had not expected this.

"To see if you have what it takes," Lang said.

"Oh!" Ophelia said, almost shocked at this sudden turnaround. "Of course. Proceed, please."

"What would you do," Lang asked, running her thumb against the sharp corner of her desk, "if the crew called you a witch, gave you only the dirty work?"

It took all of Ophelia's composure to hide her delight. This would be easy. All she had to do was say what Lang wanted to hear. She raised her chin, and said, projecting humility, "Then I would do the dirty work with pride, and try to prove them wrong."

In truth, this was not even a lie. Ophelia was confident that she could endure anything if only she was not on Peu Jolie.

"What would you do," Lang fired back, "if you came across someone who was harmed by your mother?"

Ophelia gulped. She supposed she should have expected more than one question. Slowly, she said, "I would apologize on her behalf, and make amends as best I could."

"If you were a captain," Lang asked, "how would you react to a ship in distress? Consider as if you thought the passengers might carry disease. Would you pass them by for the sake of the crew, or would you stop?"

Ophelia thought for a moment. She calculated, running her thumb over the star medal in her handkerchief as she tried to figure out what Lang wanted to hear this time. What was this question meant to gauge? Chivalry? It wouldn't do to leave citizens of the realm in danger when she could have helped. But maybe . . . common sense? It also would be poor decision-making to possibly infect an entire crew. Perhaps, self-sacrifice?

Ophelia pressed her thumb especially hard against the purple stone in the medal as she answered. "I would stop to help, no matter what. I'd go over alone to check what caused their distress, and if it was sickness, I'd let the crew leave me behind."

"Pretty words," Lang said, "but not quite so easy to back up."

"You only say that because you don't know me yet."

"No," Lang replied, hard lines appearing around her mouth.

"I know you better than you think. You're not a gifted liar, Miss Young. If I were you, I would avoid it altogether and keep my mouth shut, rather than uttering falsehoods."

Ophelia bristled, grinding her teeth together. "I'm no liar."

Lang let out a rare laugh. "That's even worse! You don't realize you're lying to yourself. You give me your well-practiced speeches and your calculated answers. But I'm not looking for a martyr, Miss Young. I'm looking for an honest, hardworking sailor, and you refuse to be honest."

Ophelia's lips felt numb, she wanted to protest, but she couldn't form words.

Lang kept going. "You're not unlike your mother in that respect. She had pretty words too." Ophelia's shock must have registered on her face because Lang gave her a severe nod. "Are you surprised I knew her? She wasn't just a woman I hanged. She was a naval woman too, once, until she mutinied and betrayed us all. And she said all the right things when she started out, until she went and did the wrong thing."

Ophelia rose from her chair, rattled. Her voice was thick. "I know the right thing to do, and I swear I will do it. What you don't understand is—what you don't—I have followed the rules all my life. I never break them. I don't lose control. I watch myself every second."

Lang didn't stand, and even sitting, she held the power in the room. She drummed her hands on the desk and said nothing.

Trying to impress Lang felt as useless as trying to scream at a storm to roll back to sea. "I follow the rules," Ophelia repeated, desperate.

"I appreciate that," Lang said, her face softening, but somehow becoming no kinder. "But there aren't rules at sea, you know. It's a wild place. And I don't want to know what you become out there—without the rules of society to keep you on the straight path. It's destroyed more people than just your mother, though that's reason enough to keep you on land."

"That's not fair," Ophelia said. The words were venom on her tongue, but once hanging in the air, she saw them as what they were: childish. Lang's response confirmed her fear.

"You're a child yet," Lang said. "Perhaps come see me again in two years."

But Ophelia couldn't wait two years, she knew that. She couldn't stay on this suffocating island for one more week. She seized her parasol and left the room, back arched and proud. She made a point not to slam the door, however. She left it hanging wide open—so that Lang would have to rise from her seat and close it herself.

THREE

The omens were not good. First, Valois burned the sweetbread. Then Papa misplaced his cufflinks. All day, Mama had put her nerves to the side, the better to help Betsy keep calm—compartmentalizing her own anxieties was not yet a skill that Betsy had managed to learn—but Mama's worries had finally caught up with her, as they always did. Now she was darting around the house like a woman on fire, muttering to herself and dusting any object within reach.

Ophelia was nowhere to be found.

Betsy felt dizzy and sick, like the world was swaying violently from side to side. The neighbors had always said their house was cursed, and with everything going wrong at once before such an important dinner, Betsy felt inclined to believe them. Of course, the neighbors also said it was Ophelia's presence that caused the curse, though Betsy didn't believe that part. If Ophelia was the cursed one, wouldn't things be running smoothly now that she was off gods-knew-where in the city? No, there was something else, some other type of malignant luck lingering over the Young household, Betsy was sure of it.

Half-convinced she was going to vomit, Betsy scrambled out the kitchen door and into the alleyway. She stood there, panting with her hands on her knees, willing herself to keep her lunch in her stomach. When she looked up, she saw Valois, leaning against the side of the house and flicking cigar ashes into the gutter. "You and your mother have the same hysteria, I think," Valois said. He took a long puff and exhaled a chimney's worth of smoke.

Betsy didn't doubt he was right. Mama often claimed that she had inherited her "excitable temperament" from her own grandmother, who had been an arsonist, banished to the colony at the age of fifteen after burning a barn to the ground.

"Here," Valois said, offering Betsy the cigar. "For relaxation. Don't breathe it in."

Betsy sucked on the end of the cigar too quickly, and ended up choking on a lungful of smoke. "I said not to breathe it in," Valois said, raising his hand to the bridge of his nose and sighing. "I live in a house without culture."

When her hacking coughs had subsided and she had wiped the wetness from her lips, Betsy straightened up, holding her sides. "That hurt."

"Of course it would," Valois said, his graying mustache twitching with laughter. "If you do it wrong."

The kitchen door swung open to reveal Mama, glowering at the pair of them. She began hitting Valois with the end of her dishrag. "Are you *absolutely* mad, giving my daughter that filthy thing? You're supposed to be watching the chicken as it roasts!

You've burnt one dish already this evening!" She grabbed Betsy by the arm and tugged her back into the house. "And you! You'll stink of smoke, tonight of all nights. Go up to my bedroom and douse yourself in lily water. Honestly, I don't know what you were thinking. I said, go!"

As Betsy scrambled back upstairs, she heard a tremendous crash from the dining room. "And what was *that*?" Mama shrieked.

"I broke a wine bottle!" Papa shouted back. Betsy's father didn't take hosting guests half as seriously as his wife did, and he was audibly laughing at his mistake. "It's to be expected: 'out of the fire, into the flood,' and all that." This was one of Papa's favorite expressions.

After applying a great deal of her mother's expensive perfume to cover the flinty smell of the cigar, Betsy was in a rush to get back on schedule. In her haste, she tripped over the hem of her nicest dress. It tore. She seized her sewing kit to stitch it up again, but her hands were shaking so badly—like a palm leaf in heavy rainfall—that she pricked herself with the needle, staining the fabric with her blood.

She screamed for her mother to come help her, and Mama came sprinting up the stairs, her cheeks pink with agitation and her pale blond hair completely disheveled.

"It's a disaster down there!" Mama announced, throwing open the doors to Betsy's armoire and rifling through its contents. "I just smashed one of the good plates—we won't have a full set now. We'll have to use the second-best . . ." She gave a little laugh and, pulling a cream-colored gown from the wardrobe, said, "Well, at least we can salvage your outfit." Mama ran a finger against the textured blossoms that had been stitched into the brocade. "I really do think this is one of the loveliest gowns you've ever made, dear. And these embroidered roses will bring out that pretty color in your cheeks."

It hardly matters whether I look lovely or not, Betsy thought to herself, sulking. *I'm unlikely to attract a suitor so long as I'm too scared to speak in front of strangers.*

Betsy wasn't sure when she'd first become afraid to leave the house. Perhaps it was when she was six—the year a man first spat at Ophelia in the street. Or when they were nine, and her grandfather died of the Mosquito Fever. Or at ten, when one of her father's many ships was sunk by a hurricane, taking the whole crew with it to the watery depths. Or perhaps at thirteen, when two fully grown men followed her all the way home from the market, catcalling her for the length of five city blocks.

Whatever the death knell had been, Betsy now preferred to stay at home as much as possible. Terrible things happened outside this house. People were wrong about there being a curse here; this was the one place everyone in their family could be safe.

But it *was* a small life. Betsy knew that. Ophelia, Mama, Papa, and Valois. But perhaps tonight she could add a fiancé to her small circle. Someone who would love her just as she was, and *where* she would always be.

She wanted that more badly than anyone could know.

Mama gave Betsy a quick peck on the forehead. "It's going to be all so wonderful. Now, I have to get back downstairs." Mama started to wring her hands as she hurried out of the room. "No doubt without me hovering around, Valois will sabotage something to spite me. Now, where's Ophelia? *Ophelia, come help, won't you!*"

Ophelia came sauntering into Betsy's bedroom a few minutes later, alone among the house's occupants not in a flutter. "Where have you been?" Betsy asked. But Ophelia didn't appear to hear the question, instead offering to help lace Betsy's stays.

"Make it tight as you can," Betsy said. "It's just going to go terribly, I can tell."

Ophelia did as she was asked, knotting the stays so tightly that the breath caught in Betsy's chest. Betsy was relieved by the corset's support—it would stop her from slouching, one of her instinctive defense mechanisms when meeting strangers. "Well, with that attitude, it just might," Ophelia said. "Don't oracle up a self-fulfilling prophecy for yourself."

Betsy merely pouted in response.

After Betsy had stepped into her gown, she sat still as Ophelia braided her fine blond hair and pinned it at the top of her head. When Betsy glanced in the mirror, she found that she looked quite elegant. Her dress had done its job, highlighting her natural *embonpoint*—a word she had once overheard in a dress shop to describe the governor's wife: another fat, fashionable woman whom Betsy admired greatly and often wished to emulate.

"You're beautiful," Ophelia told her, in that firm way that indicated this was just one inarguable fact, among many. "And not just beautiful. You're clever and sweet. If he doesn't like you, he's an absolute fool."

Betsy took a deep breath, staring dully at her reflection. "I'm not sure how I'll convince him of those good qualities," she said, "when I can barely speak my own mind half the time."

"Bah," Ophelia said, dismissively, fixing Betsy with an iron gaze. "Then if you can't talk, I'll sing your praises *for* you. He will not leave here tonight unacquainted with your virtues."

"Where have you been all day?" Betsy asked again, a tinge of desperation in her voice. She feared she knew the answer— that Ophelia had been off begging to join the navy again. Why couldn't she be satisfied at home, where they could all be safe and happy together?

Betsy pressed on for answers. "Did you see the commodore? Did something happen?"

"Yes, something did," Ophelia said, and Betsy's heart dropped into her stomach. "But nothing good."

"Oh!" Betsy couldn't stop the delighted exclamation from slipping out of her. She course corrected. "Oh no."

"She told me not to come back for two years. I want to apologize—to try to make it right, but—"

"No, don't do that," Betsy said, rather too quickly. "I—what I mean is—you'll only make her angrier if you bother her again too soon."

"No," Ophelia said, shaking her head and absentmindedly adjusting the lace at the cuff of Betsy's sleeve. "I can't accept that. I'm going to sea. I'll find a way, whether Lang likes it or not. And when you're a happily married woman, I'll send you letters and presents from all over the world. We're both going to get exactly what we want, starting tonight."

Betsy felt as if the floor had dropped out from under her. That wasn't at all what she wanted.

A floor below, the front door chimed. With a gasp like a wounded animal, Betsy spun around and hugged her sister tightly. Tears pricked at the corners of her eyes. Ophelia shook Betsy off, laughing. "Don't be silly! This is your night!"

The girls descended the stairs and entered the dining room. The small cedar table was heavy with china and crystal, and Betsy gave a relieved sigh. The preparations had come together just in time. Two unfamiliar men—the Whitmans—were laughing with their parents, oblivious to the chaos that had been raging in the house minutes earlier.

The taller of the two guests was a distinguished, older gentleman with a thick head of silver hair and noticeably slumped shoulders. He was sipping from a nearly overflowing glass of wine as he spoke with Papa. The shorter man was still technically a teenager, carrying the slight build of adolescence. They both had the cool white skin tone that was common in the Northern continental provinces.

"Girls!" Papa said, his voice booming. He had his own glass of red wine in hand, half-empty. Alcohol always went easily to his head, and he drank quickly when he felt there was something to celebrate. He'd probably smashed that first wine bottle while sneaking an early drink. Ophelia hid a giggle, but Betsy was far too queasy to find anything funny. She was also too busy taking in Matthew Whitman.

Matthew wasn't particularly tall, but Betsy was quite short too, so they might appear a fine, well-matched couple. His brown hair was pulled back into a ponytail, and he wore half-moon glasses. Betsy smiled weakly. She had always liked men in glasses. She thought they made them look kinder. He was definitely the type she was drawn to. This was a promising start.

"Girls, girls," Papa said again, crossing to put a hand on each of his daughters' shoulders and guide them toward the guests. "May I introduce my partner Jakob Whitman, and his son Matthew? They've come a long way. Jakob is teaching Matthew the ways of the business. I'm afraid we two old men can't be lively and productive forever."

Betsy and Ophelia both fell into curtsies. "Good evening," Ophelia said. Betsy tried to greet them too, but she only managed a tiny squeak. Both of the Whitmans returned polite smiles.

"Sit, everyone," Papa said, gesturing toward the table. "Valois should be out with the food at any minute. Sit." Betsy made her way to the table, where her mother directed her into the seat beside her, and directly across from Matthew. Betsy did her best to smile at him, but she was still blushing from the shame of having squeaked. Matthew gave her a watery smile back. His hands, the hands of a scholar, were clasped, but shaking.

Betsy wondered if he might be as nervous to meet her as she was to meet him. She hoped so. That would be a nice change of pace.

Betsy started to smile in earnest. With a discreet nudge from Ophelia, sitting next to her, Betsy managed to force out a few sentences of conversation. "It's a long way from the Cornwallis province. You must be exhausted."

As Matthew nodded, his glasses flashed in the lamplight. "Yes," he said. "Quite."

Mr. Whitman burst out laughing at his son's response. "Hardly!" he said, smacking Nathaniel's arm. "You mustn't let my son speak for me, he's just getting used to a hard day's work. He hasn't found his sea legs yet. You should have seen him, constantly leaning over the rail to—" Mr. Whitman laughed, glanced at the ladies around the table, and then coughed. "Never mind," he said. "I suppose it's not palatable dinner conversation. Anyway, we've just come from Peu Lorraine—"

"Not Peu Lorraine, father," Matthew corrected, pushing back his glasses. "Peu Toulouse."

"No, I'm certain it was Peu Lorraine!" Jakob fired back, his weathered cheeks flushed with embarrassment at being corrected. The old man's hands were trembling now, making the merlot he held slosh dangerously close to the rim of his glass. He hurried to place the wine back on the table, and the crystal clinked loudly against the cedar.

Betsy saw the porcelain plate in front of her vibrate ever so slightly—and she was certain that Matthew was nudging his aging father beneath the table, warning him to stop talking. But Jakob couldn't be stopped.

"Don't correct me, Martin—I'm certain it was Peu Lorraine!"

Betsy glanced over at her father, who flinched visibly at Jakob confusing his elder son's name. Papa seized an opportunity to move on from the uncomfortable exchange, pointing to the doorway as Valois entered. "Ah—food at last! I hope you both enjoy the meal. Valois and Eliza have worked very hard on it."

Valois began serving the food, but Betsy barely registered what had been placed in front of her. She picked at her meal with the rest but spent all her energy trying to work up the courage to join the conversation again.

"I'd like to hear a bit more about your son," Papa said, wiping his mouth with a cotton napkin. "What are your interests,

Matthew? How has your education progressed?"

Suddenly Matthew was talking so quickly that even Betsy could hardly follow. He seemed very passionate, and about nearly everything too. About locksmithing, the history of Cornwallis, his childhood tutors, his love of arithmetic, and keeping books. He also enjoyed riding and was teaching his much younger brother, Martin, to ride as well. This last interest worried Betsy. She'd never sat on a horse in her life—such a thing sounded terrifying. What if he wanted to go riding together?

"Always good with business, this one," Mr. Whitman chimed in. Betsy noticed another tremor in the old man's hand as he tried to cut his meat. "If he only can learn to keep his stomach settled on a boat, he'll surpass us both in these ventures of ours, Nate."

Papa smiled. "I'm glad to hear it." He took another sip of wine, now grinning slyly. "I'd hope that any future husband of my daughter would be able to make a good living."

Across the table, Matthew beamed. Betsy almost choked. Future husband! Her father had said the words. Of course, this dinner was intended to scope out a union between the families. With Papa having only daughters, and having been Jakob Whitman's junior partner for years, even from across the sea, it seemed natural for the family lines to combine to keep the business between them. But Betsy hadn't expected her father to be so candid about it so quickly. Perhaps it was the influence of the wine. Still, Matthew didn't seem upset about the intended arrangement.

Betsy felt a warm glow rising in her cheeks. A rush of delight and relief.

Stumbling a bit over his words, Matthew rushed to indicate Betsy and Ophelia. "All this talk about me. We should like to hear about your, uh, lovely daughters."

Ophelia looked at Betsy expectantly, who felt her jaw lock up, betraying her now that it was time to hold her own at this dinner. Next to her, Mama smiled and gave an encouraging nod.

"I, um. I—quite like to sew."

Matthew nodded, only once.

"She's marvelous at it!" Ophelia said, quickly and a little too loudly. Embarrassed, Ophelia lowered her voice and said again, "Betsy's marvelous at it. She sews almost everything Eliza and I wear. She's better than any seamstress on Peu Jolie, I'd wager."

Matthew seemed more interested now. He fixed his eyes— and their flashing lenses—on Ophelia. "Truly? Did she sew the gown you're wearing now?"

Ophelia glanced down at the pale blue dress she was wearing, as if to check she wasn't about to lie, and then nodded. "Yes. She did. Isn't it something?"

"It is," Matthew agreed. He looked at Betsy. "You must be very talented, to create something so"—here he glanced back at Ophelia and the gown—"beautiful."

"Thank you, sir," Betsy said, glancing down at her half-eaten plate, too bashful to keep staring him in the face.

"Ophelia is going to be quite the sailor herself," Papa said, a hint of bragging in his voice now. "She plans to sign on with the Imperial Navy." He lifted a glass and nodded at Ophelia, swelling with pride. He elbowed Jakob and teased, "I'd place good money betting that she finds her sea legs before your boy does."

It was Ophelia who looked overcome by praise now. She beamed with gratitude. "Thank you, Papa."

"But how can that be?" Matthew asked, his voice sharp.

"How can what be?" Nathaniel asked.

"How can Ophelia plan to join the navy if we're to be married?" Matthew clarified, suddenly haughty. "I'd never allow it. That kind of career is all well and good for *low-class* women. But it's unseemly in a proper lady, especially a wife."

Unthinking, Betsy let her silverware clatter to the table. Of course he would want to marry brave, confident Ophelia, and not her. What could be more natural? Mama stared at her, then gestured to her husband, open-mouthed but unspeaking.

Betsy felt as if all the air had gone out of the room. She was dizzy. For the second time that day, she was overcome with nausea.

"You're mistaken, sir," Ophelia said, an unmistakable coolness etched into her words, her cheekbones, her posture.

"In what way?" Matthew asked, rather rudely. "About the nature of a sailor's profession being unsuitable for a woman?"

"About you and me," Ophelia said, poison dripping from every syllable. "I have no plans to marry you, nor do I think that was my father's intention." Her tone softened now, as she glanced toward Betsy. "You were mistaken."

Matthew's lenses seemed to flicker back and forth between Ophelia and Betsy. "Ah. I see there has been a miscommunication."

All of the amiability had left Papa now. He looked to his business partner. "Jakob, I thought I made it clear that I was speaking of Betsy in our letters."

Jakob had gone very pale. His shoulders slumped yet lower as he gestured to Betsy. "A thousand apologies, miss." He glanced down the table at Mama. "And to you, Madam Eliza. It seems that"—he laughed uncomfortably—"my old memory is not what it used to be. I think I may have confused your daughters when I explained the purpose of this visit to my son." He put his hand on Matthew's shoulder, whose face looked hot, and his mouth slack-jawed. "But it is no matter, I hope? Forgive an aging man's failing mind. One sweet daughter or another—what is the difference? I'm sure that Matthew couldn't be more blessed, regardless of which daughter you intended him to court."

"Actually, father," Matthew said, grinding his teeth. "I think it matters quite a lot. This is mortifying."

"I agree," Betsy said quietly. She looked at Matthew earnestly, and in a moment of boldness, extended her hand across the table. "B-but we're all friends here. Let's move past it."

Matthew looked at her for a long time, tilting his head as though he was really seeing her for the first time.

"No," he said. He looked plaintively toward his father. "You said that we were doing your partner a favor in picking up his cursed daughter." He jerked his thumb at Ophelia, who made a noise of violent indignation.

"I was mistaken," Jakob said, out of the corner of his mouth. "Now would you please be civil—"

"No!" Matthew said, pounding the table and interrupting his father. "I will not be civil. Your rotting brain misled me. I don't believe in silly superstitions, so I was happy to take a pretty, vivacious bastard off your partner's hands! But I am not marrying some fear-ful girl who smells of an ashtray and never leaves the house."

Betsy flinched at Matthew's declaration of her frailties, and its implication. The Whitmans could only know of this quirk of hers if, over the course of years of friendly correspondence, Papa had confided in Jakob about his concern for her. This brief moment of quiet, shameful introspection felt much like hovering in the eye of a storm.

A moment later, it was as if a hurricane had hit the cozy dining room, the sudden outburst of rage from Betsy's family was so great. Papa's wine glass thudded against the table so hard it splintered at the crystal stem. Mama squawked like a parrot in indignation; Betsy could hear her feebly protesting on her behalf that she "does leave the house, *sometimes*." It was Ophelia, though, who commanded everyone's attention. She smacked both palms against the table and said, in a voice that made Betsy think of a city bell frozen over, "You have insulted us. You have disgraced yourself. I demand that you leave our home at once."

After Ophelia's declaration, the only sound left in the room came from the soft clinking of the glass chandelier, which hung from the low ceiling above the table.

Betsy herself couldn't speak. She was experiencing a muteness more profound than any other she had felt in her life—and Betsy Young was intimately familiar with being too upset, or too frightened, or too anxious to talk. Though she knew she should try to stick up for herself, to wrest some dignity from this humiliation, it seemed the only dignity left in the dining room belonged to her sister.

Matthew stood up, his lip curling as he stared at Ophelia. Ophelia stood up too. She was two inches taller than him.

"We will leave," Matthew said, tugging at his father's sleeve. Jakob, for his part, seemed apoplectic with misery and shame. "But we will only go because there is *nothing* here I want." He cast another cruel, dismissive look at Betsy, whose lower lip was wobbling traitorously as she tried to hold back tears.

For a long time, everything was still and silent—a tableau of unwieldy emotion. Matthew had announced his intention to leave but couldn't seem to move his feet. Finally, the weight of the silence became too much, pressing in too heavily on Betsy's chest. Words were rising unbidden from the angriest part of her gut—words Betsy knew she shouldn't say aloud. Betsy scrambled from her seat so quickly that she toppled the chair over. As she tore from the room, a spiteful, bitter curse escaped her lips, even though she knew it was wicked: "Just go, already! You're a nasty, terrible little boy, and I hope your stupid ship sinks!"

In the hall, Betsy was struck by the way that the stairs seemed to be stretching, becoming steeper. Her chest hurt. She couldn't breathe. Betsy knew that if she tried to race upstairs in this state, she would trip. A painful hiccup bubbled from her mouth. Besides, if they all wanted her to leave the house so badly, she would oblige them. Some fresh air, that's what she needed.

Betsy seized the handle of a hallway drawer, where they kept spare candles and matches. Her fingers gripped the matchbox like it was the antidote to poison. She tried to throw open the front doors, which were so heavy that she couldn't open them as far as she'd have liked. She hit her shoulder against the left door as it swung shut, but still managed to slip away into the cool island night.

FOUR

Ophelia's jaw clenched as she heard the front doors slam, and she knew Betsy was gone. She stood from her seat and hid her hands behind her back so that the Whitmans couldn't see that they were shaking. "You ought to be ashamed," she said, lifting her chin high again. "You've driven my sister from our home. Leave now before I return the favor." Matthew's feet started working again, and he practically sprinted from the dining room. Ophelia stared at his back with a small, hard smile.

The Whitmans disappeared into the night as quickly as Betsy had. Jakob Whitman shuffled out of their house with slumped, defeated shoulders, mumbling apologies to his partner that Papa refused to acknowledge.

Ophelia watched the two men retreat down the avenue, her fingers fumbling as she knotted the tie of her cloak. When they had turned a corner and were out of sight, she too went out into the street, prowling the cobblestones and calling Betsy's name. Papa and Eliza followed in her wake, like smaller fish behind a shark, but Ophelia wasn't sure how much good it did to have them there. Her father was muttering hotly under his breath, distracting Ophelia and stoking her own anger.

The pretty bastard. That's what he'd called her. Right to her face.

It was easy to come up with the places Betsy might go in the daytime—the sweet shop, the milliner's, the yarn store—but all those places were closed now.

"Surely Betsy wouldn't go to a tavern," Eliza asked, twisting nervously at the fabric of her skirts, and clearly hoping someone would assuage her worries. "She knows to stay away from rough crowds like that . . . doesn't she?"

"Betsy hates people," Ophelia growled. Papa had first met Ophelia's mother in a nearby tavern, which no doubt spurred Eliza's disdain for them. Usually Ophelia could tolerate that opinion, but tonight, she was irritated, just wishing both adults would stop talking. "She hates crowds. She hates loud noises. She wouldn't go where anyone else—"

Then Ophelia knew. Betsy had been gasping as she left—clearly in need of open air.

Ophelia led them toward the docks, and from there, she could see a pinprick of light along the endless stretch of sand. There was also a faint smell of smoke. She pressed forward and discovered Betsy sitting close to the waves. Her hair hung limp and disheveled, free from its braided crown. She had somehow created a meager—almost pathetic—bonfire, but what the kindling was, Ophelia couldn't immediately tell. She just knew that driftwood wouldn't have worked—it was too wet to light. Worse yet, Betsy's dress was unbuttoned down to the waist, its top half folded over, the empty sleeves flapping like twin flags in the night breeze. Her stays were nowhere to be seen, but—of course. She'd burned them for warmth and to illuminate the pitch-black night.

Eliza let out a little cry of horror and despair upon seeing her daughter completely undone. Ophelia was very nearly as shocked as Eliza—Betsy in this state reminded her absurdly of an unraveling ball of yarn, frayed and pitiable.

Low waves were rolling in, and Betsy stared out to sea, sitting in the stretch where higher tides had made the sand wet and silky. Ophelia kicked off her shoes to run out onto the beach, calling Betsy's name.

Papa and Eliza, unable to keep up with Ophelia, doubled over with their hands on their knees, breathing heavily.

Ophelia crouched on the sand next to Betsy but wasn't acknowledged. Betsy's small gray eyes were unblinking, reflecting the orange flames of her small bonfire as it struggled to stay alight. Ophelia waved a hand past her sister's pallid face, and got no response. "Come now, Bets," Ophelia urged. "Come back to me." Betsy still didn't move.

Then a mosquito landed on Betsy's neck, and she instinctively reached up and squashed it flat. Ophelia raised an eyebrow. If Betsy could move for the mosquito, she ought to have the energy to answer when spoken to.

"What were you thinking?" Ophelia asked, her voice stiff. "We didn't know where you went, or what had happened to you—"

"You're one to talk," Betsy said, so low it was almost inaudible. Her red, swollen eyelids slid shut. Ophelia felt her temper rising again—why didn't Betsy just look her in the eye?

"*What* did you just say?" Ophelia asked.

"I said you're one to talk," Betsy repeated, matching Ophelia's harsh tone. "Better get used to not knowing where I am, Ophelia, because you're leaving me. You're going to sea. You're going *out there*." Betsy jabbed a finger out at the waves. "And I'm going to be stuck here all alone."

Ophelia blinked back tears, and she felt rage flare up, white-hot, at Betsy for making her weak this way. "Bets, I didn't know you felt that way. I thought you wanted me to join up."

Betsy gave a lazy roll of her shoulders and wiped her streaming nose on her bare, exposed forearm. Her voice was a croak. "I didn't think they'd let you, not really. I thought you would have to stay with me, and I'd never have to tell you not to go, and you wouldn't think I was selfish to ask it. But now you've set your mind to it"—here she let out a pathetic hiccup—"and you're going to leave . . ."

"I haven't even gotten the yes yet."

"But you will. You always get what you want. I never do."

When had she ever gotten what she wanted? Ophelia balled her slender fingers up into a fist but hid her hands in the folds of her dress. There had been times before this—not constantly, but every so often—when Ophelia had thought she'd quite like to hit Betsy. She loved her sister, but this whining, *this indulgent self-pitying*—well, it was revolting in the way that small, quiet weaknesses so often were. Usually, when Ophelia felt like this, she would be able to hold back from striking, knowing what people would say. Wouldn't it be just like Ophelia Cray's daughter to hit her sweet, timid sister?

Today the only reason Ophelia was able to hold back from hitting Betsy was because Papa and Eliza had finally struggled their way across the shifting dunes of the beach to stand beside them. Eliza looked like she had just recovered from a week's fever. Their father's face was glazed with sweat. He had stripped off his blue jacket and rolled up his sleeves as far as they could go. His breathing hadn't completely slowed yet. Still, he offered a hand to Betsy to help her up.

Betsy didn't take Papa's hand, and Ophelia was hit with another crashing wave of anger. She stood up, violently batting stray sand from her pale blue dress like she was beating out a dirty carpet. "Don't just sit here and feel sorry for yourself, Betsy. Do something to make yourself feel better, but don't wallow. It's beneath you."

Betsy finally snapped her head around to look at Ophelia. Her full cheeks were wet and raw with tears. "How am I supposed to make myself feel better? By being selfish, like you? By leaving? Or *maybe*"—Betsy's nostrils flared as she breathed deeply—"maybe I'll just stand up and make a huge scene at the dinner table. Maybe I'll make my sister feel worse by sticking my nose where it *doesn't belong*."

Doesn't belong. The words were like a punch to Ophelia's chest.

Ophelia arranged her face into an unconcerned mask and gave a derisive laugh that sounded even to her own ears like the cawing of the crows. "So now it's my fault you can't defend yourself?"

"Well," Betsy said, scrambling to stand up and tripping over the hem of her dress, "you didn't exactly give me a chance to!

I should have been the one to tell Matthew off, not you. How will I ever learn to speak for myself if you're always doing it for me?"

This was madness. Ophelia let out another high-pitched laugh. She was to blame for being a good sister, now? All she ever did was protect Betsy's soft feelings.

Papa tried to interject, to calm the girls down. "You girls shouldn't talk to each other like this!" But Ophelia spoke over him. Betsy hadn't done a thing to help herself, after all. No one should pretend she had.

"Go on, then! Speak!" Ophelia said. Spittle flew from between her lips. "What do you have to say, but complain and wail and convince yourself of doom? You need me. You follow me around like a second shadow, waiting for me to act first. Who's to blame for that, Elizabeth? Tell the truth now. You're angry that he liked me and not you. Well, I didn't ask for that! I never ask for anything, and if you're so selfish that you want to-to sabotage my going away to make yourself feel better—"

Betsy burst into tears, weeping into her palms. Eliza had run to hold her daughter, rubbing Betsy's shoulder comfortingly. This was so typical, Ophelia thought. Betsy always did this, on the rare occasions that anyone fought with her. She would cry and moan, and make everyone else look the villain.

Ophelia was tired of playing the villain. She was tired of having to rein herself in so that she'd never lose control. It wasn't fair that Betsy could wish a sinking ship upon the Whitmans without anyone second-guessing her. Not when Ophelia was held responsible for ships her mother sank before she was even conceived.

Finally, Betsy choked out the words, "S-say you're right. Say

I'm your shadow. What am I supposed to do then, now that you're leaving for no good reason? This is your home, you know! R-right here, with us! You'll never find something better."

Ophelia turned around, her red cloak whipping behind her. "It wasn't just you he insulted, Betsy. Maybe I want to find someplace where people don't talk to me like that." Ophelia hitched her skirt up around her ankles and picked her way back through the sand and up to the high street. She was silent on the long walk back to the house, and she forced herself to think only of her budding plan—and of the safe in her father's study.

Betsy had to be wrong. Peu Jolie *couldn't* be the best home she would ever get. It simply wasn't good enough.

Ophelia crept into the study an hour to midnight, when everyone else was asleep. When she was a little girl, Papa would sometimes let Ophelia build a tent out of bedsheets in this room, and then she and Betsy would play there while he did the ledger books at his desk. When the front door creaked open, and they knew Eliza had come home from her errands, Papa would raise a finger to his lips and urge the girls in a conspirator's hushed tones, "Don't you dare tell her the password. She might be an enemy spy."

And then Eliza would come upstairs, and tickles would be applied to the right places, and the girls would always tell her the password anyway.

Now Ophelia had to come up with a password herself: the code to open the safe beneath Nathaniel's desk. It wasn't hard. Her first guess—Betsy's birthday, the eighty-seventh day of the dry season—was correct. She dialed it in on the round lock, and she heard a click. She opened the safe's door, and found a porcelain shepherdess statuette, a box of jewelry Eliza had inherited from her mother, Papa's ledger books, and two birth certificates.

Ophelia hardly spared a glance at her own certificate, with its blank line where her birthday should have been. Nathaniel had lobbied for nearly seven years before the stooges down at city hall had allowed him to fill out a certificate for his bastard daughter, and even then, they refused to let him record the day of her birth. As they said, Nathaniel knew only the date that Ophelia Cray had come to Nathaniel's door and deposited an infant in the arms of his household maid. He knew nothing of the true date the younger Ophelia had come into the world.

But Betsy's certificate—*that* one carried all the information Ophelia needed to convince a member of the Imperial Navy that her name was Elizabeth Young. She folded the certificate gingerly and tucked it into the sleeve of her blue gown. Sitting below the certificate, she found an ink sketch of Eliza, with a four-year-old Betsy sitting in her lap. Betsy was smiling with a row of pearly teeth much smaller than her adult set. Her father must have commissioned an artist for this image to always be able to look at the faces of the people he loved most. Ophelia's hand, insistent and greedy for affection, dug deeper into the safe, waiting to discover a picture of herself.

She found none. Her chest swelled with pain, her eyes with tears. She sniffed, resealing the door to the safe and exiting the household through the kitchen door.

It was refreshingly easy to sneak from the house without

Betsy holding her back.

A light rain was falling outside, dampening Ophelia's red cloak but feeling cool and pleasant on her face. The tall, stately houses in their own neighborhood were utterly silent, as they were full of respectable people who went to bed at respectable hours. But as Ophelia swept through the darkened streets toward the northern docks, the sound of drunken revelry, muffled through stucco walls and glass windowpanes, reached her ears. The tavern-goers never slept.

As she passed The Blue Bonnet—the very bar where Papa had first stumbled across the pirate queen, resulting in Ophelia's birth—she pulled on the hood of her cloak, making sure it obscured her face. Ophelia knew she had less than twenty minutes to catch her ferry to Peu Nadal, one of the smaller, less populated islands on the edge of Peu Jolie. The ferry ran every five hours. If she missed this one because drunks waylaid her, she'd never have time to carry out her plan without being missed. She rounded a corner, and to her infinite relief she saw a gangly ferryman ringing his bell, calling out in a bored voice, "Peu Nadal. All aboard for the midnight ferry to Peu Nadal."

Ophelia gave him the money for her passage and walked up the gangplank.

The ferry, quite unlike the grand many-sailed frigates belonging to the Imperial Navy, was a flat-bottomed boat that made its way from Peu Jolie to Peu Nadal not by catching favorable winds but by traveling along winding iron chains, which were anchored on the shores of the two islands. Ophelia couldn't help but look at this little boat with pity—such a shame for it to be chained in one place, touching the sea but never free to sail where it wanted.

The ferry made its slow, steady voyage away from Peu Jolie's docks, until eventually the city faded into the darkness. It was replaced by the endless jungle that separated the main city from the smaller, less prosperous villages on the far side of the island. They'd once been farming settlements, until early colonists had discovered how thin and infertile Peu Jolie's earth was. Most had scampered back to the city and the steady supplies imported to feed its population. She wondered if the island's natural flora had slowly reclaimed the abandoned farmland. Was it Ophelia's imagination, or could she hear monkeys chattering in the distant trees?

She slumped against the bow, closing her eyes, and although Ophelia thought she had only shut them for a moment, she soon heard the clanging of the ferryman's bell. She had dozed off standing up. Rubbing her eyes, Ophelia stumbled off the ferry and onto the unfamiliar docks of Peu Nadal. It was so much smaller than she had expected. Papa's business sometimes took him to Peu Nadal, when he arranged for his ships to shove off from the smaller island's less busy docks, but Ophelia herself had never visited before. The buildings were all shorter, a bit shabbier than those from home, the paint on their outer walls less vibrant.

She wandered through the streets, going inward, assuming that their naval office would also be in the town square. Probably an hour from sunup, now, fishermen were already taking leave of their homes and drifting past Ophelia toward their tied-up dinghies.

Ophelia found the naval office just as an orange tint was appearing on the horizon. Unlike Port Jolie's, it was made of stout red brick, rather than marble. On the front steps, a teenage boy with ginger curls was sitting with his arms wrapped around his knees. At the sound of Ophelia's footsteps, he looked up, blinking sleepily at her. Ophelia braced herself for him to recognize her face—but no recognition came.

"Oh, hello," he said, a vacant, pleasant look on his face. "Are you here to join up as well?" He pulled at the front of his shirt, proud of himself. "It's my birthday. I'm fourteen now—finally old enough! Wanted to put my name down the first second they opened."

He stuck out his hand for Ophelia to shake. She laid down her parasol, stiff all over, and gave his hand a pump.

"I'm Fitz Durant," the boy said, grinning ear to ear. "And you?"

Ophelia's voice was hoarse. "Young," she said. "Elizabeth Young."

Fitz jerked a thumb at the locked front door to the office, as if that slab of wood would spring to life and personally hand him his enlistment documents. "We're going to end up heroes, aren't we?"

The ferry drifted back into Port Jolie at ten in the morning. Ophelia's heart pounded in her chest. She was dizzy with excitement and lack of sleep. She had two beige uniforms slung over her arm, and instructions to report to a rig called the *Bluesusan* in three days' time. The navy was quite happy to have an able young woman like Elizabeth Young in their ranks, it turned out. Ophelia shoved their front door open so forcefully that it banged against the hat rack, knocking Betsy's bonnet to the foyer floor.

"I'm in!" Ophelia cried out, whirling into the dining room as her family was eating breakfast.

"There you are!" Eliza said, throwing down her napkin. "We were worried sick about you!"

"Where have you been?" Papa demanded, standing up.

Ophelia rushed to grab her father's arms, forcibly waltzing him around the cedar table. "I'm in! Didn't you hear? Meet the newest member of the Imperial Navy."

Eliza let out a gasp of surprise, clapping her hands over her mouth. Papa broke away from Ophelia, stumbling a bit. "Is that so? The commodore said yes?"

Ophelia shrugged, grinning. "Sure."

"Sure?" Papa asked, his brows furrowed.

Ophelia unclipped her red cloak and threw it over the nearest chair, not making eye contact with her father. "I leave in four days." She glanced over at Betsy, who did not appear to have been eating but rather picking at her food. Now, she laid down her utensils altogether. She glared at Ophelia, saying nothing.

"Gracious," Eliza said, standing from her seat, her hands fluttering. "I should cut some blue ginger." She laid her hands on Ophelia's cheeks, her palms so warm against Ophelia's skin, and gave her stepdaughter a quick kiss on the forehead. "To celebrate with your favorite flower."

"Thank you," Ophelia said, laughing as Eliza scurried off into the hall, muttering about ginger's "protective properties." Betsy was not the only superstitious one in the family.

"Well," Papa said, suddenly looking older than Ophelia had always pictured him. He ran his fingers through his red-brown hair, and she could have sworn it looked rather thin. "If you're leaving that soon, there's a lot to be done. Come up to the garret with me. I'd like to show you something."

Ophelia followed him, leaving Betsy alone at the dining room table. They ascended the main stairs and then climbed the rickety ladder that led to the cramped, dusty attic. She had never spent more than a few minutes at a time here before— Betsy had always been afraid of it, as if something evil was lurking there.

And perhaps there was. The attic was, after all, where people kept the unwanted things they'd rather not see on a daily basis. Broken things, secret things, and painful memories. Ophelia wondered if when she had arrived on their doorstep, the Youngs should have just shut her up in this attic and been done with it.

Ophelia brushed a cobweb from the rafter overhead while her father pushed a shabby black trunk toward her. "Sit," Papa said.

"What's this about?" Ophelia asked, her eyebrow shooting upward. "I thought you wanted to show me something."

"I do," Papa said, curious eyes roaming her face. He sat down on a trunk of his own and coughed into his hand, trying to dislodge dust from his throat. "But not just yet. First I want to ask you why you're running out of this house like it's on fire."

Ophelia blinked. "I don't know what you mean."

"Darling girl," Papa said, raising a hand. "You are good at a great many things, but lying isn't one of them. For a moment, try to pretend I'm as clever as you, and respect me enough to be honest." A long silence fell between them, as Ophelia stared down at her cupped hands. "Go on," he pressed. "I know you've decided this is the path for you. But you're still very young. We don't need the money from your wage. So, why the terrible rush to leave your family and your home?"

Ophelia looked determinedly forward at a seamstress's dummy with stuffing peeking out of a rip in its stomach. She ground her teeth together, but somehow the truth seemed to slip out, as if through the gap in her teeth. "This isn't my home, Papa."

She had expected him to protest. To wave this statement away, tell her she was being stupid, that *of course* this was her home. But all he did was lace his fingers together, mimicking his daughter's pose. "Tell me more."

Ophelia looked back at him, encouraged enough to meet his eyes again. "Don't tell Eliza and Bets."

Papa crossed his heart to ward against evil. "Gods forbid it."

"They hate me here, Papa. I don't have any friends. They glare at me in the street. And I could hide indoors, like Betsy, but I don't want to live in the dark. It's not living at all."

"And the sea has a certain allure. I know that as well as anyone."

Ophelia's head bobbed up and down. "It does! I just want to do something—go somewhere they don't know me!"

Papa frowned, and Ophelia noticed how lined his face had become. "Ophelia, you have to know, wherever you go someone will know who you are. It's in your name."

Restraining the urge to roll her eyes, Ophelia looked away, muttering, "And whose fault is that? You didn't have to name me after her."

Papa shrugged. "She asked me to. How could I break that vow?"

"So honorable," Ophelia murmured. "But anyway—it doesn't

matter. I *am* going away. I'm carving out a place for myself. And that place isn't here."

At this, Papa rubbed at the corner of his eye. Ophelia sighed, feeling guilty. "I mean, I'll come back sometimes. I'll visit. But I'm not going to be chained to any one place. I'm going to keep moving. I've got to be free."

He gave her a curt nod. "Stand up. Go in that trunk. It's the one I used to take on every voyage for the company. Your presents are in there."

Ophelia gathered her skirts, rolling over the black trunk onto its correct side and unlatching its buckles. A cloud of dust emerged as she flipped the lid open. She reached in blindly, and her hand closed around the smooth surface of a glass bottle. She pulled it out, brushed away a layer of grime with her sleeve, and let out a soft, appreciative noise. "It's lovely," she said.

"You like that?" Papa laughed. "It's a model of my first ship. My favorite too. It was called the *Moonskimmer*."

"Who wouldn't like it?" Ophelia asked, taking in the long, slim hull of the miniature vessel, still gleaming and clean inside the bottle. And then there were the starch-white sails, which looked like they had forever captured a strong wind. She ran her fingertip along a hair-thin crack in the flat of the bottle—not even large enough to compromise the structural integrity. "I think I remember this, actually," she said, grinning. "You used to keep this on the mantel in your office when we were little."

Papa nodded, and gave the cracked bottle a bittersweet look. "But Betsy knocked it over, and after that, I thought it might be better to keep it in storage."

Ophelia turned the bottle right side up. "Oh, we loved it though." She remembered the way she and Betsy had pretended to make the ship fly across invisible waves. Ophelia had always seen an absurdity in it, though, that the bottle which protected the miniature ship also rendered it useless. The ship was safe inside the bottle, naturally, but ships weren't meant to stay safe. No one builds a ship to keep it anchored in port.

Ophelia looked up at her father, but he wasn't meeting her eyes. "Papa, what's wrong?"

"No," Papa said, smiling thinly. "It's nothing. You girls really did love that ship. And I did too. Perhaps it's time to put it back on display."

Ophelia glanced back down at the miniature ship, and something occurred to her. She had been to the docks, and watched her father's ships leave port from time to time. But she had only ever seen the *Moonskimmer* as a toy. Never the real thing. "What happened to it? You said it was your first, but I've never seen it."

Nathaniel gave a light shrug. "It sank."

Ophelia's eyes snapped wide as her stomach was gripped with cold fear. "Pirates sank it? Not my mother, you mean!" She couldn't bear to think that her villainous mother had destroyed a rig so beautiful as the little thing in her hands.

Nathaniel burst into a hearty laugh. "Gods no! That ship was sunk by Billy 'the Brute' Burnham, back when you were three or so. Burnham was caught and hanged about six months after that." The smile drifted away from his face, covered up by concern— like the sun obscured by storm clouds. "It's a dangerous profession you're going into, seafaring. I'm proud of you, but worried for you too. That's why you're getting these gifts."

Ophelia let the air she'd been holding in escape from her lungs, relief flooding her body. It was a few seconds before Ophelia realized how tightly she had been squeezing the bottle while waiting for Papa to either vindicate or condemn her mother. She set it aside before it shattered in her hands.

Papa directed his attention back to the box, removing a leather pack, half-full and heavy. Inside, Ophelia found a slender wooden box. Nestled in velvet was a brass compass. Ophelia's face split into a grin as she snapped the compass open and shut several times. She tilted it from side to side, watching its needle recalibrate toward Papa, who was sitting at true north.

"My father gave me that compass when I first went to sea," Papa told her. "Hasn't seen much use lately, but it's yours now. Use it to find your way on the waves—and find your way home again." Ophelia shut the compass again and pressed it to her heart.

She didn't have the spine to tell her father how long it would be before she planned to return to Peu Jolie.

Papa reached into the pack for the second object, passing it to her carefully. Whatever it was, the thing was long, and wrapped in a plain cotton handkerchief. Ophelia pulled the fabric away. She was gripping the barrel of a flintlock pistol with an ivory handle.

"That pistol," Papa said, "was bought with the wages from my very first voyage. The navy will provide you with a saber, but a gun is surer protection. I want you to have mine." Ophelia didn't dare move her fingers to wrap them around the handle, but the temptation was undeniable.

"It's empty now," Papa told her, his dark eyes gleaming. "But later today, we're going to get it checked, cleaned, and stocked up on bullets for you. From then on, you're going to carry it with you always. And when you meet someone who means you harm, don't hesitate."

Ophelia nodded, rather hoping she'd never have occasion to use this gift.

Papa squeezed her shoulder, and kissed the top of her curly head. "Good. Now, there's one last thing." He was holding a black silk bag, small enough to fit in the palm of his hand. He didn't pass it to her. "This is from your mother," he said.

"Eliza?"

"No. Your other mother."

"Oh." Ophelia shook her head. "I don't want it."

"You might," Papa said. "One day. When you tire of your nomadic lifestyle. The hangman sent this to me, after her execution. There's a letter in there, but I haven't read it. I don't know what it holds. It's not my business, it's yours." He seemed to be turning over words in his mouth, before committing to saying them. "But . . . you say this island can't be your home. Maybe there's another that could be. Surely you've heard the rumors."

Ophelia laughed out loud. "Papa, you can't be seriously suggesting—"

"Cray Island. Yes. The place where she anchored her fleet. Stored her loot."

"Cray Island isn't real," Ophelia said, smirking at her father. "That's just one of the old rumors. You should know better than anyone—Cray didn't really eat babies, she wasn't a siren in disguise, and she certainly didn't live on a magical island."

Papa scratched absentmindedly at a raised, red bump on his arm. "I *do* know better than anyone, actually. I never saw the island, but I heard her crew talking about it, back when—well, when we met."

A heavy weight seemed to be pushing against Ophelia's chest. She started opening and shutting the compass to distract herself. "Magic is dead, Papa. Islands can't be magic because magic is dead."

"You don't sound like much of a sailor to me," Papa said, "if you don't understand the power of superstition. Out on the sea, strange things happen. And the danger lies in people thinking they happened for a reason."

Ophelia nodded. "A lazy sailor brings a bad tide. Witches sink ships. A stowaway cat means the water will run out. Things like that."

"Yes," he said, wringing his hands together. "Things like that. It can be hard to disprove whether accidents happen by coincidence or by fate. And sometimes, as a sailor, you go wild with the isolation and the heat, and lines can blur. Even I could never really be sure whether some things were chance or if I made them happen by force of expectation and intent. Don't discount willpower, Ophelia. Don't discount belief. Trust in yourself, but be wary. You'll be in a tough position out there, and I'd be lying if I said I wasn't worried about the crew distrusting you."

Ophelia lifted her chin defiantly. "I'll win their trust, Papa." In actuality, however, she wouldn't have to. She would start in their good graces and remain so, by virtue of her sister's name. Her father had nothing to worry about.

Papa closed his eyes, looking tired and old beyond his years again. "Just please, please, don't lose yourself on those waves." He tapped the compass, and his fingernail against brass made a soft *plink*. "And who's to say? Maybe you'll navigate to Cray Island with this old thing one day."

Ophelia tried to force out a dismissive laugh, but it died in her throat. "Even if I found it," she said, "even if it is real. I would never set foot on it. I don't want anything of my mother. And I certainly don't want that bag, or what's in it."

Papa closed his fingers around the silk bag, swallowing heavily. "Maybe not now. But eventually—"

"No!" Ophelia insisted, cutting him off. "Never."

Papa nodded. He slipped the bag into his pocket. "Then I'll put it in a safe place for you, shall I?"

Ophelia's heartbeat sped up. If he meant that literally, if he went to lock that bag in the safe beneath his study desk, he would surely notice Betsy's missing birth certificate. "Actually!" she said, her arm extending out jerkily. "Perhaps I will take it with me. Just in case I do end up wanting it."

Surprised but pleased, he pressed the bag into Ophelia's palm. "Alright then. Now why don't we take that pistol downstairs, get you some shot, and do target practice?"

"Sounds wonderful," Ophelia said, balancing her new possessions in her arms.

Her father folded his arms around her, kissing her curls for the second time. "I love you very much, you know that?"

Ophelia was trying not to think about how her father might look even older the next time she was home. "I love you too, Papa."

FIVE

In the past, when she and Ophelia had argued, Betsy was always the one who apologized, whether she thought she was at fault or not. This came naturally to her. Betsy apologized to her family, to strangers, to inanimate objects. But not this time.

Chilly silence settled over the house in the short days before Ophelia's announced departure, with each sister being too proud to break it. Papa and Mama began making increasingly frantic overtures toward forgiveness, preaching about conflict mediation and generally scheming to get the girls reconciled before Ophelia was long gone.

It was Mama who suggested that Betsy assist in tailoring Ophelia's horrid beige uniform. After all, Betsy's mood often improved with a needle and thread in hand, and Mama hoped this might be the change in the wind the girls needed to forget their rift. Betsy grudgingly went along with what her mother wanted, but not without loudly announcing that she was always willing to help around the household, *unlike some.*

Betsy refused to make eye contact with Ophelia through the task. Instead she ruminated bitterly on how stupid Ophelia would look in this sand-colored uniform rather than in a nice dress. It had legs, of all things! When she was close to finishing the second uniform, Betsy accidentally-on-purpose jabbed Ophelia in the hip with her needle.

"Ouch!" Ophelia cried out, squirming away from Betsy and jumping off the ottoman she'd been standing on. "Watch where you're sticking that thing!"

Betsy sniffed loudly, maintaining her dignity, but didn't respond. She returned her thread and needle to her sewing kit and snapped the lid shut.

"Hey," Ophelia said, grabbing Betsy's wrist and squeezing tight. "Hey. Can't you just be happy for me?"

Betsy licked her lips, which felt particularly dry that day, willing herself to do the right thing. To tell Ophelia to go, even if she didn't mean it. But her selfishness reared up again: a monster from the depths of the sea.

"No, I can't."

Ophelia's nostrils flared. She flicked a curl out of her eyes and stomped out of the parlor without another word.

Regret twisted like an octopus tentacle in Betsy's stomach.

The next morning, Betsy dressed before dawn. Ophelia had told them she would be leaving the next day. There wasn't time to be stubborn any longer. She felt a bit like a piece of paper thrown on smoldering coals—she was burning at the edges of her consciousness, bitter that once again, she needed to humble herself to achieve peace . . . but the larger part of her knew this was for the best. And, well, she knew Ophelia was right—at least in part. Betsy didn't want Ophelia to be made happy by leaving. She wanted her to be content to stay.

Mama had draped several yards of braided ginger over the archway to Ophelia's bedroom door. It was called blue ginger, but truly its color was almost purple, not unlike the hue of Ophelia's favorite gown. Betsy inhaled the sweetness, briefly calmed by it. But when she reached for the doorknob, planning to wake her sister gently and beg for forgiveness, she found the door was locked. Ophelia had never locked her bedroom door before. Betsy knew it had been done to keep her out.

It was a hot, muggy day, and Betsy's left cheek stuck to the door as she pressed her ear against it. She rapped on the wood, over and over again, until her knuckles started to hurt, then switched to the other hand. "Ophelia," she called, quietly at first, and then louder, "Ophelia! Please. Open up. I want to talk to you."

Unlike Betsy herself, Ophelia wasn't a heavy sleeper. She would have heard someone calling right away. "Please, Ophelia. We need to talk." Still, there was no sound of movement on the other side of the door. Betsy imagined Ophelia sitting up in bed, slender arms crossed against her chest, smirking with satisfaction as Betsy called out. "I was wrong, Ophelia. I'm sorry."

The sound of her plaintive calls must have woken Papa, because he came shuffling sleepily out of the main bedroom. He made a grunt, as if to ask, *Did she lock it?* He ducked into his office and returned with a skeleton key. It clicked in Ophelia's lock, and the door swung open. Betsy, who hadn't bothered to remove her cheek from the wood, felt it peeling away from the humid-sticky side of her face.

"You go," Papa said, his eyes still half-closed as he waved Betsy in. He looked a bit feverish. "It should be just the two of you." He made his slow, halting way back toward his bedroom, and Betsy stepped through the now open door.

Ophelia was not in her room. The window was open, and a breeze ruffled the sheer white hangings on the four-poster bed. The blankets were neatly tucked into the mattress—as if no one had slept there at all.

"Ophelia?" Betsy asked, in a hoarse voice.

There was no answer.

Betsy walked toward the empty bed as though walking to the gallows. She didn't feel as if she was inside her body. There was a note on Ophelia's pillow, written in a curving hand and signed with a flourish.

> *Goodbyes are hard for me.*
> *Can't we just pretend I said them?*
> *With love,*
> *Ophelia*

All the air had been knocked out of Betsy's chest. "No," she muttered. "No, no, no." She ran to the wardrobe. It was packed with dresses—dresses Betsy had sewn as gestures of devotion and love—but those hideous uniforms weren't there.

Betsy turned, pushing inward at the soft folds of her stomach, trying to replace her sudden anxieties with physical pain, and came upon Ophelia's slant-top writing desk. She threw open the drawers, finding her pen and ink, her stack of letter paper, all gone. And where was that pistol that Papa said he had given her? The compass? Gone! All gone, and Ophelia with them!

Betsy's jaw felt as if it had unhinged. She let out a long, agonized cry that was at first wordless but gradually transformed into a renunciation. "Ungrateful!"

She kept kneading at her gut, desperate for some kind of relief. She felt hot. She wanted to loosen the straps of her stays, but her fingers were too numb and useless to get the job done.

Betsy glanced inside the desk drawer again. Of everything that had once been there, all that remained was the box of matches Ophelia used to light her bedroom hearth. Betsy seized them. She struck the first, staring at the lit flame until white spots danced on her eyes and the heat traveled downward toward her fingertips. Betsy quickly blew it out, then struck another. This one she threw into the fireplace and began stoking the flame with an iron.

The fire spluttered to life and began to grow.

Now Betsy was back at the wardrobe, throwing the gowns she had constructed onto the floorboards. The white one, which Ophelia had worn visiting Lang! The green one, which she'd worn on their parents' anniversary! The ice-blue one, worn on the beach just a few nights before—the one that had made Matthew Whitman think she looked so pretty. Betsy couldn't bear to toss this one away—no, this abomination required worse. She tore at the silk of the waist, feeling it slowly tear along the seams. The fire crackled merrily in the hearth—like laughter. Taunting laughter.

Betsy cried out again, wordlessly this time. She would give the silk to the flame. She felt disconnected from her body as she threw it into the hearth, prodding it deeper into the logs with the iron poker. Silk did not burn quickly and left little smoke. It began curling at the edges as flame licked the material, wreathing the blue silk in a living, dancing orange.

Betsy stood watching the flame, her arms limp at her sides now, and slowly felt herself come back into her body. The silk gradually collapsed in on itself, turning into a dark, gritty ash. The room reeked of burnt hair, stinging the insides of Betsy's nostrils. Mama, ever sensitive to strange smells in her house, came barreling into the room, Papa moving sluggishly behind her.

"What is—what's going on here?" Mama asked, her gray eyes popping, her hands already wringing. She took in the scattered contents of the wardrobe, the open box of matches flung to the floor, and Ophelia's note, which Betsy had discarded on her bed. Mama put it all together easily fifteen seconds before any sign of recognition registered on Papa's face.

"No, darling," Mama said, seeing the red rims of Betsy's eyes and moving forward to embrace her, "no. Don't burn the lovely things you've made. Don't waste your talent." Betsy pressed her face into her mother's shoulder, inhaling deeply the smell of lily water. It did not mix well all together with the acrid scent of the burning silk.

Betsy clutched to her chest, Mama's eyes darted from the wardrobe to the hearth, doing mental tallies. "The blue gown," she said, "and the lilac one. Ophelia's favorite. Did you burn them both?"

"The—the lilac?" Betsy asked, blinking back hot tears. She had forgotten about the lilac gown. She broke away from her mother, checking the wardrobe again. The lilac gown, *the blue ginger gown*, wasn't there.

Ophelia had taken a piece of Betsy along on her trip, after all. No matter how angry they were with each other, Ophelia hadn't chosen a dress crafted by another seamstress to spite her. She'd taken her sister's handiwork.

This thought briefly steadied Betsy, but then her anger surged again, all the worse for the momentary respite. She would not let Ophelia off this easily. She would not.

From the moment he realized Ophelia had taken her leave early, the weary, pale look hadn't left Papa's face. He coughed through dinner, hacking into a handkerchief that Betsy had embroidered with little sailboats. Papa blamed the coughing on Valois's cigar smoke. Betsy blamed it on Ophelia.

Three mornings later, Papa didn't get out of bed at all, and Mama barreled her way around the house like a tropical whirlwind. Betsy followed the sound of her mother's frantic sighs to the kitchen—past the dining room table, where more blue ginger sat, wilting in a vase. Mama had set them out to please Ophelia, but now she was gone, without thanking a single soul.

Betsy leaned against the kitchen doorway, watching her mother shake a finger at Valois.

"If I catch you with another one of these filthy things," Mama threatened, tossing the whole of Valois's cigar box into the gutter outside the kitchen door, "I will dismiss you for damaging your master's health."

Valois paused to suck on his teeth, making a few noises that sounded like *tsk* and *tut*. Then he gave his mistress a half-apologetic smile and extended his long body into a bow. "A thousand apologies, madam."

Mama nodded briskly, and turned. Seeing Betsy in the doorway, she fished into her apron and pulled out a few folded bills. "Could you be a dear and run down to Baudin's? Get your father those lemon drops that ease a cough." Then she went twisting and sighing out of the room again.

Betsy looked up at Valois, whose thin mustache twitched in amusement. He said, "Your mother exhausts me, you know that?"

"Give her a break, will you?" Betsy said. "She's upset. Everything's falling apart in this house. *We're* all falling apart. Now Papa's sick, on top of Ophelia leaving . . ."

Valois gave a theatrical snort. "We all ought to count that as a blessing. The town isn't wrong, you know. That girl is cursed, and this house with it. Things *always* go wrong here."

Betsy looked down, playing with the strings of her apron. "Don't say that," she mumbled. "It's not true."

"It is!" Valois insisted. "But look, I don't mind. Your parents pay me twice as much to put up with this house and its reputation than I'd make in the same job elsewhere. That's why I don't care so much when your mother throws my luxuries into the mud. But still—I wouldn't have to explain one damned thing to my next employer if I left this house. They'd think I'd finally had enough of the curse. Plenty of us have come and gone.

I'm the only one who's ever stayed. Partially because I've come to care about you two little devils as I watched you grow up." Then, as if this admission was too much vulnerability for him, he added, "And I should not like to think about how this chaotic house would fall apart without me."

Betsy didn't know what to say to any of that, so she nodded.

Valois winked, pressing a heavy metal rectangle into her palm. "My lighter. Keep it safe, and away from me, eh? Otherwise I'll just go buy more cigars."

Betsy stared up into Valois's brown eyes, the skin around them crinkled with age and goodwill. She nodded again, tucked the lighter into her apron pocket, and went out.

Betsy was conflicted about Mr. Baudin's sweet shop. She loved the candy but hated going there. It was constantly packed tight with customers and much too loud. She'd be brave today though—face it for Papa.

Betsy dug her fingers deep into the curving glass jar that held the lemon drops, scooping out two large handfuls of the wax-covered candies. They slipped out of her fingers like water at the front counter, and Mr. Baudin slowly counted them up, making casual conversation as he did.

Betsy liked Mr. Baudin even less than she liked the tight squeeze of his shop. He was known as the friendliest man on Peu Jolie, due to his breezy manners with his customers, but Betsy thought this was all facade. He had always been subtly nasty to Ophelia.

"Have you seen the new posters they've hung around the corner?" Mr. Baudin asked.

Betsy shook her head, tilting the brim of her hat a little bit forward.

"Horrible stuff," Baudin told her. "Ought to be of interest to your family. I heard that sister of yours has gone to sea. She's being careful out there, I trust?"

Betsy's eyes narrowed, but she doubted Baudin noticed. She took the money from her apron and slapped it down on the table. "Thank you. Have a nice day." She pushed the wrapped lemon drops off the counter and let them pour into her apron pocket, where the little yellow bulbs filled the empty space around Valois's lighter.

She hurried out of the sweet shop, but the crowd outside wasn't as easy to escape. The corner wall was heavily plastered with wanted posters of the two leering faces. Onlookers formed a thick mob that stretched all the way to the sweet shop steps. Betsy shouldered her way through the group, apologizing profusely with every half step of ground she gained.

The first face on the posters was that of a young man with a square, heavy jaw. He would have been classically handsome if not for the fact that one of his front teeth was chipped into a deep diagonal line, stretching almost to the gum. The writing beneath his name declared, "The scourge of the southern seas! Deadly as a rabid dog, beware the bite of Jack Copeland, 'the Violent Bastard,' born in the slums of Peu Ankirk! This remorseless wretch is captain of a ship called the *Bloody Shame*. Copeland's crimes number in the thousands—may the Crown's justice, and the noose, be his."

Betsy fiddled nervously with the lace at the edge of her sleeve.

Violent Bastard? She didn't like the sound of that at all. She shook her head and turned to get a glimpse of the other sketch.

This one was of a woman, with a bob of fine, silky hair that framed her delicate bone structure. She had a set of pouty lips and eyes the sketch artist had imbued with a terrible, taunting glimmer. Her teeth too were the stuff of nightmares: visibly rotting from the root.

"Fiona Wall: Temptress of the Red-Flame Hair! The faithful accomplice of the Violent Bastard, no less his equal in lethal rage. The most committed murderess on the seas since the likes of pirate queen Ophelia Cray. Her point of origin is unknown."

Betsy couldn't bring herself to read their long lists of crimes. It was all too horrible. She wiggled Valois's lighter from inside her apron pocket. She flicked the lighter's switch, and loosed a brief, harmless spurt of flame.

Betsy turned to go. Hardly two months had passed since Ophelia Cray had swung, so naturally, they were being given new villains to worry about. Betsy made a gesture across her chest to ward off evil. She hurried home—back to safety.

As angry as she still was at her sister, Betsy said a quick prayer to every god that while Ophelia was out on the sea, she wouldn't cross paths with Jack Copeland or Fiona Wall.

SIX

Ophelia was leaning over the rail as the boat shoved off from the Peu Nadal harbor, gliding out from the docks, where the little ferry was still anchored, still trapped. Above her, the *Bluesusan*'s many straight-backed masts were shooting toward the heavens. Their sails, whiter even than the clouds above them, were full with a merry wind. First seeing them, Ophelia was immediately struck with the image of a pregnant woman's belly—swelling, full of promise.

She closed her eyes, listening to the cheers from the docks—*Port Nadal is cheering me, or at least cheering my comrades*—and the shouted orders from senior members of the crew. Soon, she would be assigned a role on the ship, and she would be obliged to help as their rig left port, but until she had her orders, all Ophelia had to do was stay still and feel the wind blow through her hair.

"Miss? Pardon me, but I think you dropped something."

Ophelia opened her eyes and straightened up, her back tense. She turned around to find herself staring up into the crooked grin of Edgar Ludlow, the officer she had met several days earlier outside of the naval offices. He was exactly the way Ophelia had remembered him—down to the handkerchief he was holding outstretched to her.

Ophelia arched an eyebrow, not immediately certain if Ludlow was teasing or if this was just something he did to ladies on a regular basis. Her question was answered when Ludlow got a good look at her face and, realizing his mistake, winced in embarrassment. "Ah," he said.

"As before," Ophelia said, fishing her embroidered handkerchief out of her breast pocket, "I have mine right here."

Edgar raised a hand as if to cover his boyish grin. "You have no idea how mortifying this is for me."

Ophelia crossed her arms, shrugging. "No, I think I have some idea. So, what is it? You carry around a handkerchief just so you can force women to talk to you?"

Theatrically withdrawing his hand from his face, Edgar pulled himself to his full height. "How else can I start a conversation with a proper lady? One usually needs a formal introduction."

Ophelia looked around the ship deck, with its quick-moving sailors dodging around each other and swearing as they tried to get everything done. "But this isn't exactly polite society, is it?"

Edgar shook his head, blue eyes twinkling. "Not once the land is out of sight." He pointed out over the rail, back in the direction they'd come. "And wouldn't you know?"

Startled, Ophelia swung around to catch a last glance of the tiny island. Her chest ached with an expansive, bitter emotion she wanted to name but couldn't. She had never been one for feelings: They were no easier for Ophelia to quantify than it would be to catch water in her fist.

But whatever feelings twisted at her now, she knew she could not imagine coming back here. To tiny, superstitious islands buffeted by storms, bad crops, and airborne disease. A place where no one would want to live—except criminals who were told it was a choice between the colonies or the noose.

Ophelia was moving on. To something better.

"What was your name, again?" Edgar asked her, reaching out to take her hand and bending to kiss it.

Ophelia's stomach twisted into a knot. *Her name.* She had told him her name that day in the square! She snapped her hand away from him, too quick for Edgar's fingers. She evaded his question, saying, "I prefer not to be touched."

Edgar's eyebrows furrowed. "I see?"

"Ludlow!" A brassy, female voice reverberated across the deck. "Does the Crown pay your sorry ass to flirt? Get to your station before I drag you there!"

Edgar barked a laugh, swinging around to face the stout woman who had shouted at him. "Come off it, Jo! I outrank you!"

Jo brushed her short fringe of black hair out of her eyes and placed her hands squarely on her wide hips. "Only 'cause you've a rich daddy to buy you an officer position! Now, are you gonna help us leave port or not?"

Edgar knocked an arm playfully into Ophelia's. "In truth, escaping Jo's wrath is the only incentive anyone on this ship has to do their jobs properly. I'd do it for a promotion, I suppose, but our captain wouldn't notice if I took an axe to the mainmast, much less if I was doing commendable work."

Ophelia raised an eyebrow. Was it true that the captain didn't notice hardworking sailors? If so, how was she to prove herself?

Jo let out a grudging chuckle and waved a finger at Edgar. "It's not just my wrath you've got to fear, pretty boy. Worry about Ames and the rod up her ass, as well."

"You've got me there, old girl. I'm on it." He sent a parting wink in Ophelia's direction and swaggered off, hands tucked in his uniform pockets, presumably to attend to his actual duties.

Ophelia was relieved to see the back of Edgar Ludlow. This was the hour of her victory. The moment they hoisted anchor, she'd become a woman of the Imperial Navy. It was too late for the ship to turn back, to insist that they didn't want her. And they did want her—there wasn't a soul on the *Bluesusan* who hailed from Peu Jolie. No one knew her face.

So long as no one learned her name, Ophelia was free.

She tilted her shoulders back, arms outstretched and her face upturned toward the rainy-season clouds—illuminated in the sun, all orange and flat and gray above her, and breaking in the distance, farther out to sea, where they yielded to blue skies.

A door to the inner cabins slammed shut. "Oy, new recruits!" A brisk, cracking voice sounded like the shot from a pistol. It belonged to a lean woman with limp, mouse-brown hair, fading to gray at her temples. She was not handsome, but her blue uniform, with its stylish red piping, was impeccably neat. The eyes behind her glasses were sharp and clever. "Assemble here, by the mainmast!"

Ophelia scrambled to obey, trying to move as quickly as possible toward the center deck without looking undignified. She assumed this woman was her captain, and she didn't care what Edgar said—she wanted to make a good impression.

"Don't be stupid, Ames!" A man stumbled through the same door, holding a bottle of whiskey. This man was small and chubby-cheeked, with a scruffy beard, and every piece of his uniform was a bright, striking red, the same color as Lang's.

No, Ophelia thought, *it can't be.*

The woman, Ames, had her hands clasped delicately in front of her. "How was I being stupid, sir?"

"That's not the mainmast," the drunk man insisted. "That's the mizzenmast. There's no such thing as a mainmast."

Ames gave a thin, polite smile and dipped into a shallow bow to the staggering drunk. She responded, but made irritated eye contact with one of the recruits. "I'm afraid that's not correct, sir. The mizzenmast is the one in the back, and the mainmast is the one in the center."

Five other new recruits, dressed in their sand-colored uniforms, came to stand beside Ophelia. Fitz, the ginger boy she had met on the stoop of Peu Nadal's naval base, was among them. He took his place directly to Ophelia's left, catching her eye and shooting a broad grin in her direction.

The drunk scratched at his nose. "Are you sure, Ames? If that one's mizzen, then what's the farmast?"

"Nothing, captain. You're thinking of the *fore*mast, which is at the front."

A ripple of confusion went down the line of recruits as they came to the same conclusion Ophelia had a moment earlier; this red-jacketed, full-cheeked man wasn't some drunk who had wandered aboard and put on a high-ranking officer's uniform by mistake. He was their captain.

The captain rolled his shoulders into a lazy shrug. "What does it matter?" He turned to the line of recruits and doffed his tri-tipped, feathered hat in a way that he clearly thought was stately and regal, but Ophelia could only see a caricature.

"My name, dear friends," the captain slurred, but nonetheless trying to strike a note of grandeur, "is Captain Augustine Hale, and 'tis I who shall steer you safely through the wild waves of the Emerald Sea."

Ophelia resisted the temptation to look over at Fitz and make doubtful eye contact, as the other new recruits were doing among themselves.

Beside Hale, Ames gave a small, restrained salute to them all. "And I am Victoria Ames, your first mate."

"And *that's* your first lesson!" Hale said, gesturing wildly at Ames. "How to snap a salute. Get at it, then, new ones. We've got to bring sobriety—sobrility—"

"Civility," Ames corrected under her breath.

"Civriety," Hale said, nodding with enthusiasm, "to this vast ocean expanse."

With varying response times, the six recruits raised their hands to their foreheads, and gave their chief officers due respect.

"Good 'em," Hale said, falling slightly into Ames as the boat gave a little shudder. He was blinking slowly, his eyelids heavy. Ames shuffled to the side, away from her superior.

"Ames here is a good one," Hale said, nodding sleepily as if he was burdened with ancient sage wisdom. "She'll see you all through your training, and soon you'll be——"

The ship shuddered again, a sensation that reminded Ophelia of riding in a coach and feeling a small rock be struck by one of the fast-turning wheels. Hale stumbled again, away from Ames this time, and burped. A small amount of green, pungent vomit bubbled up from his lips and fell into his unkempt beard.

Hale blinked. He waved a hand. "Dismissed," he murmured, and returned to his cabin, almost as if he hadn't noticed what he'd done to himself. But then again, maybe he knew perfectly well, and was just unconcerned by it.

Ophelia couldn't resist looking over at the other sailors anymore. Fitz looked positively horrified and was holding his hand to his mouth, clearly afraid his own gag reflex was about to be triggered. Ophelia tried to keep her face impassive, but a slow, inappropriate smile was creeping across her face. She had to bite back a laugh, like she always had to do at home when Eliza was being a bit silly—as though their dinner guests were actually invading marauders and not friends of the family.

It was just so deliciously, darkly ironic that Ophelia couldn't help but laugh at her own misfortune. It was only natural that when she'd finally freed herself of the small-minded people of Peu Jolie, she would wind up under the command of a drunken idiot. Papa's favorite saying popped into her head: *Out of the fire, into the flood.* Ophelia regained her composure only as the line slowly started to drift out of order, whispering among themselves.

"You are *not* dismissed," Ames said, her voice losing its polite meekness and back to sounding like a cracking whip again. "This is your *real* first lesson. Whenever the captain gives you an order, you check it by me first, or, the gods forbid, you could end up wrecking this ship on a sandbar. Luckily for us all, Captain Hale doesn't leave his cabin to give orders very often." She gave them all a shrewd once-over. "Your second lesson is to discard all thoughts of glory hunting. We're not here to slaughter pirates. We're here to deliver information and documentation faithfully and efficiently throughout her majesty's empire. Now, I'm going to do a roll call. You will respond in the affirmative, with the words, 'Present, ma'am.' Fitz Durant?"

Fitz gave his first salute: a haphazard affair. His response came in a squeak: "Present, ma'am."

Ames rattled through the other recruits' names, calling Ophelia's last. "Elizabeth Young?"

Ophelia's salute was crisp. "Present, ma'am."

In her first two weeks onboard the *Bluesusan*, Ophelia found that while she and her fellow crewmates kipped on hard, thin mats, the officers slept in private rooms on comfortable cots, or hammocks at the very least. They all ate hardtack, a sort of biscuit that could last for years—and had, which meant that their supply had gone moldy long before Ophelia came into the scene. There was only fruit to eat in the days immediately following their arrival at a port, and the situation with meat was even worse—in her first week, Ophelia found a maggot wriggling in the center of her potpie.

No wooden ship could have been watertight, and Ophelia hadn't been expecting that—but she was shocked at how much water, and really all kinds of excrement, would leak through the various layers of the deck before falling in with the bilge at the lowest level of the ship. As one of the new recruits, Ophelia was constantly assigned to the bilge pump, which required a team of six people to operate, pulling endlessly on an iron chain to haul water out of the ship. It was long, exhausting work, but there was a comforting rhythm to it, the way the team became a single entity as they pulled. It took a while to acclimate to the smell of the work, however. Eventually the scent of shit, salt, and acidic urine became as much a part of Ophelia as the expanding sinew in her arms. The smell had clung to her skin from the moment she first entered the bilge, never really letting go. Ophelia fell onto her mat each night, muscles aching and sore, her uniform stiff with sweat, and she would be solidly knocked out for as long as her sleep shift would allow.

She was happy.

Ophelia didn't mind the maggots in the meat, not really, or the biscuits that could crack a tooth. She ate fruit when she could get it and the moments she was above deck more than made up for the time when she was confined below. Up there, under the stars, sea salt would settle in her hair, and her fellow sailors would joke with her about the captain's drunken antics. They didn't know she was Ophelia Cray's daughter—to them, she didn't belong to anyone. "Elizabeth Young" might as well have sprung out of thin air for the sole purpose of helping to empty the bilge.

For the first time in her life, Ophelia had become a part of something larger than herself. Here with her fellow new recruits, she learned to hoist a sail, ran drills with her saber, and even once wrapped her hands upon the ship's wheel and felt a spark of divine inspiration tingle in the skin of her palms. On this ship, she was neither special nor odd. It confirmed what she had always secretly believed—she didn't have to hide from the world in her parents' house, like Betsy did. She just needed to sail far away, until nobody was left that could pick her out from the crowd.

One night, while Ophelia lay awake on her hard mat, listening to the creak of the ship and the snores of her fellow crew, her mind turned to her mother's black silk bag, still lying at the bottom of her pack.

Quietly, her fingers shaking with anticipation, she untied the bag's laces and tipped it upside down. A golden necklace tumbled into her palm.

A jolt like lightning sent a tremor through Ophelia's arm. She immediately closed her fist around the piece of jewelry, and dropped her hand into the gap between her legs. She looked over her shoulder to see if anyone was awake.

No one was.

Ophelia peeked back into the little bag, and found a folded scrap of paper lining the inside. She wiggled it out, opening it to find a letter written in thin, arching handwriting.

I know you'll come to my hanging. I knew it all along. I willed it so, and so it shall be.

Force of will is magic, my child, and I will this for you. I also will that you'll return to the sea, and soon. My hangman will send this necklace to your father's address when I'm dead, along with my final request to pass it on to you. I trust that your father will oblige, because he's the sort who keeps his promises. This is the only thing you'll inherit from me, apart from your looks and your blood. Nothing else is left. These are the only things they can't take from us.

All my children have my face, some have my ships, and you, the daughter who will stand at the base of my hangman's platform, shall have this necklace. Let it serve as a reminder that our only home is the sea. Child, return to the tides and leave the city behind. It is no safe harbor for you. Be bound no longer by the petty laws and pettier superstitions of the soil. I know they think my daughters are cursed. But you are not. You are lucky, as I have been lucky. It is their fear of us that gives us our greatest strength.

Join your sisters. They will call to you, as I have called to them. I would say goodbye now, but we both know that my death isn't the end. I remain in this world so long as my kin do. Don't let them shame you for your blood. Theirs isn't clean either.

The note wasn't signed.

Ophelia didn't know why her father thought she'd want this trinket, or this note from Cray. Perhaps he thought obliging her final request was respect due to the dead—but what due did a monster like her deserve, after all? Cray's shadow had lingered over her too long. *I ought to throw this horrible thing into the sea,* Ophelia thought, and then immediately reconsidered the idea. Someone might spot her tossing it, and have questions. Instead, she shoved the necklace and note back into her pack, and left them there, all evidence buried.

Soon after setting off from Peu Nadal, Ophelia was given her first shift of the night watch. This four-hour shift above deck was not hard because of the duties themselves—it mostly had to do with keeping an eye out for ships in distress, approaching storms, or anything they could run aground on—but it was occasionally difficult, depending on what time of night you were assigned, to stay awake after so much time spent on physical labor during the day. Luckily, Ophelia's shift that evening only extended to a little before midnight, and there was so much novelty to her first watch shift that she didn't have trouble keeping her eyes open at all, unlike some of the veteran sailors.

With less than thirty minutes left in their shift, of the five sailors meant to be patrolling the deck, only Ophelia and Edgar, the officer in charge, were doing their duty. Two beige-uniformed sailors by the names of Allan and Weber were napping against the starboard rail, while another was nowhere to be found. After Weber gave an impressive, throat-rattling snore, Edgar saun-tered over to Ophelia with his hands in his uniform pockets. "Incredible, isn't it?" he asked. "Falling asleep with no regard to what Ames would do if she caught them. Takes talent."

Ophelia took care not to let her teeth show as she smiled. "I don't know how they're not awake right now."

Edgar gave a lazy shrug. "The ride's not exactly smooth."

"That's not what I meant," Ophelia said. She gestured around her, indicating the billowing sails overhead, the gentle cry of the waves as they turned over, the twinkling stars which were scattered in the night sky like diamonds stitched onto black satin. "I mean, how could anyone sleep on a night like this? A ship like this?"

"You're liking your first outing with us navy dogs, then?"

"Of course," Ophelia said, her voice soft, almost fervent. "I used to dream about this. When I was little, I mean. I'd close the hangings on my bed and pretend I was below deck on a ship. I would—well, it's silly."

"No," Edgar said, "not at all." He plucked at his blue uniform. "I was the same way. I always wanted this. Not since I was a child, maybe, but for a long time." He tilted his head to the side and began talking out of the corner of his mouth in a jaunty display of self-deprecation. "My father decided early on I wasn't fit to serve in the family business, so I needed to find another way to make him proud of me. Couldn't tell you if it's working."

Ophelia couldn't help herself. A giggle escaped her mouth.

"Ah!" Edgar said, pointing at her. "She laughs!"

Ophelia shrugged. "I suppose I—" She cut herself off, noticing a large, hulking man round the side of the captain's cabin. This was Ronan Doyle, the fifth member of their night-duty shift, who had been missing in action all this time. He came swaggering into view, clearly a little drunk. He lifted one of his long, muscular legs up against the rail, stretching it. "Isn't that just the most?" Ophelia asked, making a tutting sound that wouldn't have been out of place coming from Valois's mouth. "He hasn't been here all night, and here is, swanning in at the very end, right when Ames is about to come back and check in with us." She smacked her hand against her thigh. "You know what? I'm going to give him a piece of my mind."

Edgar seized Ophelia by the arm. "Don't do that. Ronan isn't someone you want to piss off. He hasn't been on this ship more than a few years, you know. He got transferred here after he was accused of killing his last commanding officer. Trouble is, no one could prove he did it, so he couldn't be court-martialed. And they only couldn't prove it because everyone on his old ship was afraid of standing witness against him."

Ophelia's eyes snapped wide. She was so surprised she didn't even bother shaking Edgar's hand away. "Is that true?"

"Very," Edgar said, lowering his voice conspiratorially. "So play nice. In fact, you'll find it's in your best interest to stay on everyone's good side while on this ship. If you ever want to be promoted out of the rank and file, that is. I assume you *do* want to be promoted someday?"

Visions flashed through Ophelia's mind—visions of herself in a red jacket, an array of medals flashing on her chest, as Peu Jolie cheered themselves hoarse for her. "Yes," she said, reaching out reflexively to check if Lang's medal was still safely pinned to her handkerchief. "I do."

"Then take my advice," Edgar said, releasing her arm at last. "Make as many friends as you can, especially in the lower decks. That's what I try to do. You never know who'll speak for you when it's time to hand down promotions. Hale won't help you, and Ames can't. She only cares for efficiency. Plus, she has no wealthy connections and her personality's so dry she hasn't any friends in the upper brass. That's a woman who'll labor the rest of her career under a captain far stupider than she." Edgar gave Ophelia an appraising look. "Heard such a thing can happen all too often, especially to female officers. Not everyone's a Lang. Stay a loner, and you'll end up an Ames."

"Huh," Ophelia said. She suddenly became aware that the night wind had made her fingers very cold. She flexed them. "Making friends has never been my specialty," she admitted.

"Don't worry about it," Edgar said. "You'll do fine. After all, we're already friends, aren't we?" He leaned in to whisper. "That's why I haven't told anyone about your real name."

Ophelia almost gasped, but she caught herself just in time. "I—I don't know what you're talking about."

Edgar straightened up, chuckling. "Come on. Don't be coy about it. I had to run names in my mind awhile. Amelia, Olivia . . . whatever. I knew the name you gave me wasn't Elizabeth Young."

"Perhaps I gave you a fake name in the square," Ophelia suggested, a puckish look on her face. "Perhaps I didn't appreciate your prying, improper attitude."

Edgar bit his lip. "Alright, Lucky Teeth. If that's how you want to play it. I'm sure you've got your reasons, and I've got no motive to throw cold water on you. We're gonna rise through the ranks together, you and I. Only natural"—his tone became teasing and flirtatious again—"two ambitious people like us, both young and pretty? You, literally, in the former case."

Ophelia turned her head away from him, unwilling to give Edgar the satisfaction of seeing her smirk.

"Let's do something fun," Edgar said, taking Ophelia's hand and guiding it to her holster, to rest on her pistol handle. "Has anyone taught you to duel? By South Sea rules, not what you see of gentlemen dueling in festival plays."

Ophelia grinned, surprised. "That actually does sound fun."

"Alright," Edgar said, buoyed by her positive response. He spun her around like a courtier dancing with a lady at her debut, so that they stood back-to-back. "Now draw your weapon and walk ten paces back—and don't actually shoot me, now. Remember, this is just for fun, Lucky Teeth!"

Ophelia gave a helpless grin, and made the sign to ward off evil. "I swear by all the gods."

"So," Edgar announced, bouncing on his heels as he reached his mark, "despite what the plays tell you, it's not two shots and it's over. Standard pistols hold three bullets before reloading. Until both contestants have emptied their chambers, or one is dead, the duel continues." Here, he gestured with the tip of his gun to a spot twenty paces down the deck from himself. "Go on then, Lucky Teeth." Belatedly, Ophelia made her way to her mark with a skipping gait that she suspected would make him laugh. When she twirled around on her spot to look at him, she was pleased to find him chuckling. She'd been right.

"Alright," Edgar said, recovering from his fit of laughter. "You've got your mark; I've got mine. You can move forward from your mark in a straight line as far as you want to, but once you take a step forward, you can't step back again."

"Unless you want your head blown off!" Ronan called out from his spot by the rail. He elbowed Weber awake, and the sailor's snores transitioned to a brief yelp of fright as he was unceremoniously roused from his nap. Allan dozed peacefully on.

"Wha's going on?" Weber slurred. "We've got a duel?"

"Hardly," Edgar smirked, as if to say that if this was a real duel, he would win. He looked back at Ophelia while inclining in a little bow to Ronan. "Our friend here is quite right. If you step back mid-duel after going forward, my hypothetical second would unload his gun into your head." He wagged a finger at Ophelia. "Which would be a waste of your pretty face."

Ophelia snorted, turning her back to him. "Come off it."

Edgar made a great show of ignoring her objection. "*But*," he said, pressing doggedly on, "At the farthest end of your mark, my pistol will be least reliable, so if you want to play it safe, don't give up ground. Don't move forward."

"But at the farthest end of my mark, my shots will be least reliable too," Ophelia retorted, spinning back around to bare the gap in her teeth.

Edgar's eyes glimmered with amusement. "Not one to play it safe, eh?"

Ronan and Weber watched the pair of them mime out a few mock duels, splintering the silent ocean air with comic heckles and catcalls, calling Edgar's purported skill at aiming into question and loudly speculating whether the rich boy would have the spine to fire in a real duel. They also offered, quite to Ophelia's surprise, the occasional bit of helpful correction to her form: never to cross her thumbs on the ivory handle, and if firing one-handed, to keep her elbow straight.

At last, Ames finally came above deck, and—after giving the still sleeping Allan a harsh dressing-down and threatening to have him flogged—released the five from duty. "About time!"

Ronan cried, rubbing his great, meaty hands together as they crossed the deck toward the hatch. "No more playacting, you two—now for some real ruttin' fun."

The moment they had all descended the ladder, and were once again in the dark lower deck, where the crew huddled in their sleeping quarters, Ronan produced several bottles of expensive whiskey from his canvas pack. He passed them around, encouraging everyone to drink as much as they liked. Ophelia was scandalized to see young Fitz take a tentative drink—it must have burned going down, because he immediately started coughing like a cat suffering from a hairball.

"Good on you, Ronan!" Edgar had called out upon taking his first swig. "Mighty price to pay though, I'm sure." Ophelia agreed with Edgar—she couldn't help but think this was oddly generous of Ronan. She guessed that buying liquor of this quality would have taken a huge percentage out of his wages.

Ronan gave a booming laugh, clapping Edgar on the shoulder. "As *you* well know, Ludlow, goodwill among the crew is priceless." He stretched out his arms, shouting to his comrades. "Notice this one! Ludlow's the only officer who doesn't think he's too ruttin' good to drink with us poor folk down here!" A cheer rang out from the drunken sailors.

Edgar steered Ronan over to Ophelia. "Then make sure to count my new friend in. Elizabeth Young, meet Ronan Doyle."

Ronan was at least a foot taller than Ophelia, and when he clasped his massive hand around hers for a shake, Ophelia's was completely swallowed up. "Go on then, gilly," Ronan said, shaking the bottle at her. "Drink up. Let this be a lesson to you. It's the lower crew you've got to count on. Not the captain and them blue-jacket bastards up there. Solidarity."

Ophelia usually didn't drink much, apart from maybe a glass of wine at dinner, and even then only when her parents had guests over. She didn't see the use in getting herself all fuzzy. And she really hadn't had any experience with strong liquor, as Ophelia had never stepped foot into a bar. Still, she was inclined to accept. Everyone else was doing it, after all, and she didn't want to be rude. Besides, she believed what Edgar had told her about Ronan's murderous temper. The long white scar that traced his bald skull implied a man who'd survived several nasty fights.

Ophelia smiled up at Ronan, and she noticed his eyes flash down to take in the gap between her teeth. "I've never actually had anything this strong before," she admitted.

Ronan let out a barking laugh. "Then it's about time you get started. You've got a lot of catching up to do if you're going to fit in with this crew." He shook the mostly empty bottle again.

Ophelia took the bottle, pressed her lips to the cool glass, and drank. She prepared herself mentally for the burning sensation in her throat, not wanting to look inexperienced like Fitz. To ensure no one could think less of her, she took several large gulps. "Thank you," she coughed, trying to pass the bottle back to Ronan, but he was looking at the leaky ceiling above them, his face sharp as he listened intently for something.

Ophelia thought that Ronan, an experienced sailor, must have known something she didn't, because suddenly, the amiable atmosphere was split by a guttural yell from above deck. Ophelia leaped to her feet. Was this their first sign of action, at last, after weeks of hauling dirty water into the sea?

"Is it pirates?" Ophelia called out, a quavering note in her voice that she hoped sounded to the others like excitement rather than fear.

The clattering of footsteps on the wooden stairs quickly answered her question. Ronan dove to the floor, making to recline casually against the wall, as Captain Hale came stomping down the steps, roaring like a wounded dragon. "My whiskey! Which one of you bilge rat bastards took my whiskey?"

Ophelia looked down at the bottle still clutched in her hands. Ronan had never taken it back. Edgar's eyes met Ophelia's, urging her to do something, and quick.

The world swayed, though Ophelia could not be sure if that was the onset of drunkenness or simply the lurching ship. She did the only thing that made sense to do—get rid of the evidence. She threw the bottle to the side, hoping to get it as far away from her as possible before the idiotic captain noticed she had been holding it at all.

Even as she let go, Ophelia winced, realizing the flaw in her plan a split second too late.

The bottle shattered against the deck. Captain Hale's head swiveled toward the mess, the feather on his hat bobbing like the head of a particularly stupid chicken.

"Did you just throw that?" he demanded, staggering up to poke Ophelia violently in the chest.

Ophelia did not like to be touched, and this captain was only a few inches taller than she. She reached up a hand to slowly guide the captain's finger away from her. "I prefer not to be touched, sir," she said.

The captain let out a loud, terrible laugh. "Oh, do you? You prefer not to be touched, you rutting thief? We'll see if you like the touch of the cat."

Ophelia glanced over at the rest of the crew, in confusion. *The cat?*

"I thought cats were bad luck aboard a ship," she muttered.

"Not a real cat, gilly," Ronan growled under his breath.

Captain Hale seized Ophelia's wrist and tried to drag her toward the rickety stairs. "Why don't I introduce the two of you? It's been years since the cat met a proper lady, and not the drift-wood wenches who wash up here."

"Pardon me, Captain, but don't you think this is a little rash?" Ophelia hadn't realized that Ames had descended the stairs behind the captain, as she'd been so quiet until this moment. But there she was, standing with her spine straight and her hands folded. "The girl is a new recruit. I highly doubt she would be bold enough to steal from her captain. The thief is surely one of the others. She was just caught in an unfortunate position."

Captain Hale released Ophelia's wrist. "Good point, Ames." He crossed his arms and stared the short way down at Ophelia. "Now you'll tell me who gave you my booze, girl, or I swear to all the gods, you *will* make the acquaintance of the cat."

Ophelia's skin prickled, but she kept her chin high. She didn't know what "the cat" was, but it certainly had the cadence of a punishment. And yet, Ophelia didn't see any value in betraying the trust of a member of the crew. She was angry that Ronan had stolen the alcohol—but he had been right about solidarity. The crew members would be the ones who would watch her back if they ever did come to tangle with pirates, not Captain Hale. He would probably just hide in his cabin until the fighting was done.

Ophelia had just gotten used to fitting in. She wouldn't give up the taste of it yet.

"I don't know the name of the person who gave it to me," she said.

Ames's eyebrows lifted. "Are you stupid, girl? Just give us the name, and you'll be spared punishment. This is our last mercy."

Ophelia shrugged, careful to keep her eyes from drifting toward anyone else, especially not Ronan. "I don't know their name. I don't remember their face either."

Captain Hale inched closer to her face until his rotten liquor breath was oozing into Ophelia's nostrils, worse than the smell of the bilge. "And how is that possible?"

Ophelia gave another wild shrug—the whiskey was already making her shoulders looser. She let out an unrestrained laugh, which was only partly put-on. "I dunno," she said, "I guess I've had too much to drink." It took all of Ophelia's willpower not to let her next thought slip out from her lips: *Something I'm sure you know plenty about, Captain.*

"The cat it is, then," Captain Hale snarled, pulling Ophelia toward the stairs again. "Five good lashes to the back."

Before Ophelia knew it, she was up on the main deck, the stars gleaming above her and the wind whistling all around. It was just like how she'd imagined it would be when she was young and she would play pretend all alone in her bedroom. The liquor was even giving the world some of that dreamy quality she'd thought only a child's mind could produce. But the dream didn't last long; Ames stripped Ophelia's jacket off her back, and she was tied by her hands, facing the mainmast.

Most of the crew had gathered around the mast to watch her punishment, mumbling discontentedly. She heard someone sniffling—she suspected Fitz—but no one moved to comfort that person. Ophelia wondered if Ronan would give himself up before she was actually punished, but his baritone voice never rang out. However, she could hear one voice—a female one she didn't know—calling for mercy. None came.

Ophelia heard Captain Hale's labored breathing behind her, but all she could see was the grainy wood of the mast. There was a cry from the assembled crew, and Ophelia screwed her eyes shut, ready for the pain of the first blow—but there was only a sharp, whistling sound, and a flutter of air against her back. Captain Hale was too drunk to aim the whip properly.

"You do it then, Ames," Hale demanded. There was a smack of leather against palm as Ames took the whip—the cat-o'-nine-tails, as Ophelia would later learn it was called—and delivered the first lash to Ophelia's back through her undershirt.

Ophelia cried out. Tears immediately sprung to her eyes as her shirt tore and her skin opened. She was glad she had been tied up in such a way that none of the crew could see the anguish on her face. When the next lash came, Ophelia bit her lip until it bled, but kept herself from shouting again.

When the third lash came down, Ophelia was mostly concentrating on keeping tears from spilling out over the brim of her eyelids. She might have red eyes when she turned around—but she would not abide having wet cheeks.

Do not cry. Don't you dare cry.

To get through the remainder of her punishment, Ophelia let herself go to another place.

Once, when the girls were five, Eliza had taken Ophelia and Betsy to the sweet shop. The owner, Mr. Baudin, was famous for being the friendliest man on the island. Ophelia was starry-eyed upon entering the bustling shop, hypnotized by the great glass vials of candy curving like fishbowls on their shelves. But Betsy had been overwhelmed by the store, frightened by the tightness of the space and the roar of the excited customers. The sight of this chubby little girl shaking with nerves had prompted Mr. Baudin to emerge from behind the counter. He reached into the sleeve of his striped silk shirt and produced a piece of marzipan, which he presented theatrically to Betsy.

A shy smile broke out on Betsy's face. Ophelia opened her palm hopefully. She'd expected the kind-faced man to produce another piece of candy, but instead he winced, brushing Ophelia's hand away. "None for you, she-cub. If you want candy, go out to the street corner and ask your mother's wanted poster for some. She sank my last shipment." Baudin rose from his kneeling position, wiping his sugar-dusted fingers on his apron, and went to ring up a customer's purchase at the register.

Tears stung at the corners of Ophelia's eyes. This was the first she had heard that Eliza was not her birth mother.

Betsy, seeing the miserable look on Ophelia's face, embarked suddenly on the first daring moment of her life. Spiteful, she grabbed a handful of chocolate from a nearby jar, took Ophelia by the hand, and pulled her outside, the shop bell tinkling behind them. They didn't stop running until reaching the street corner where the wanted posters hung.

"What are you doing?" Ophelia had asked, eyes streaming despite her best efforts. "You haven't paid!"

"He was rude," Betsy said, her own eyes burning with an uncharacteristic rage. "He should be punished."

Curious, Ophelia peered up at the faces on the wanted posters. She had never really looked at them before. Her stomach gave a jolt, and her heart ricocheted up to her throat. She had seen herself on the wall. She'd only just learned to read, but she could make out her own name too. She sounded out the words below it. *Mur-der. Theft. Ass-ault. Mu-til-a-tion.* It seemed that any sin Ophelia could name, this woman had committed.

Wordlessly, Betsy held out her cupped hand, which had already become a sinkhole of melting chocolates. As if she thought sweets might help.

Betsy, she thought, the corners of her eyes stinging, *I miss you.*

They were untying her from the mast. She could barely stand, and fell into Edgar's arms. "You sure know how to take a hit." He pulled her closer to whisper into her ear, "Smart not to give up Ronan's name. You're learning fast."

Strong hands pulled her away from Edgar. "Oh, give her here," that unfamiliar female voice said, "she doesn't want anything from you right now."

"Or possibly ever." Ophelia was pretty sure that one was Jo.

Blood trickled down her back. The world was hazier than ever—if she could have thought straight, she'd have been grateful for the numbing effect of the booze. She lifted her head up to the woman now holding her. She had a sallow, pale face and thin brown hair. She looked almost as tired as Ophelia felt.

"I'm the ship's medic," the woman said, "Emily. You did well. Only yelled out the once—no swearing, even. It was all pretty dignified, everything considered. Now let's clean up these cuts."

With Jo's help, Emily lifted her down the wooden steps, and gently placed her facedown on her mat. Jo pushed Ophelia's curls away from her shoulders, and Emily crouched over her. She peeled back the blood-stained undershirt from Ophelia's skin. Its removal stung like she'd received a sixth lash from the cat.

"It's not too bad," Jo said, leaning close to get a good look. "Ames went reasonably light on you. The stripes sting, but these aren't too deep. They should heal without scarring if you don't touch them."

Ophelia could only groan in response.

Someone else had come to stand beside her. He knelt on the deck floor so he could whisper in her ear. "Damn respectable, kid," Ronan said. "It's good you already know the truth of this ship. It's the poor folk below deck against those bastard officers more than it's us against them pirates out there. And now that I know you've got my back, I'll be sure to have yours."

He stood again, probably knowing Ophelia didn't have the capacity to respond, and walked away, his footsteps loud and rhythmic, like the throbbing in Ophelia's back.

SEVEN

Betsy had to admit, at last, that the neighbors were right. Their household was cursed, and that curse had come to roost in the form of a wide, raised lump on her father's forearm. Brilliantly red.

There was a reason no one had ever lived on these damn islands before the colonists. The mosquitoes were always trying to kill you. Now it was her father who had caught the Mosquito Fever, and Betsy knew that these things could go one of two ways: Either the medicine would take or Papa would die. Betsy had watched her maternal grandfather linger with this illness for months, growing steadily weaker, the light receding from his eyes. She wasn't sure she had the strength to watch her father suffer like that.

Papa was now bedbound, drifting in and out of consciousness. His face was always glazed with perspiration. Betsy had now caught him several times talking gibberish with complete confidence.

"Papa, quit that," Betsy said. She laid a cold washcloth on his forehead and tried forcing him to lie back down on his pillows. "Just rest awhile." The bedclothes stank of sweat and cod liver oil, and Papa must not have wanted to nestle in them either. He fought Betsy's grip, wriggling and trying feebly to sit up.

"I don't want to!" Papa spat the words like a petulant child. "I won't, Ophelia! I won't!"

His hand was straying toward his bitten arm, trying desperately to scratch at the red bite, and Betsy smacked it away. "Stop that!" Her father drew back his hand, blinking up at her in surprise.

"Betsy?" he asked.

"Yes," Betsy said. "Of course it's me." Who else would it be? He had one daughter who tended the family plot, and one who didn't. Betsy was the one who was loyal to this family. How could he ever mistake her for Ophelia, even momentarily?

A wave of guilt passed over her. She took her father's hand, gently this time. "I'm sorry, Papa. I didn't mean to be sharp. But you mustn't scratch." She glanced down at his arm and found that it was too late—blood was already oozing from the inflamed stretch of his arm, smelling sharply of copper.

Mama bustled into the room carrying a clay pot full of freshly cut nettle. She placed the pot at Papa's bedside table, and stroked her husband's hair back lovingly. To Betsy, she said, "My mother always said a pot of nettle invigorates the unwell."

Betsy went to fetch Papa another cup of water, ready to hold vigil alongside her mother for as long as it took. When she returned, Mama stood with her back to the door, throwing a piece of paper onto the fire.

"What was that?"

Mama gave a start. She clearly hadn't heard the door reopen. "Nothing," she said, unable to look Betsy in the eye. She sat on the wooden stool by her husband's bedside, producing a tiny pair of silver scissors. They flashed in the firelight as she began to carefully trim Nathaniel's nails short. "We can't let him scratch it any worse," Mama muttered. "It could get infected so easily."

Betsy nodded, trying to concentrate on getting her father to drink. But there was a doubt needling at her mind—an old island superstition that made Betsy wonder if it wasn't Ophelia's curse that had hurt their household, after all. *She who casts a curse unwisely will see it rebound on herself.* Betsy couldn't help but think . . . she had wished death on the Whitmans, shouting that their ship ought to sink at that terrible dinner. Could it be that her ill wishes had rebounded to kill her father instead?

"Mama," Betsy said, "I'm so—"

Eliza cut her off. "I'm worried too, dear." She ran her fingers along her husband's graying hairline. "But I'm sure it will be okay."

Betsy knew her mother was lying. Mama was no better at hiding her emotions than she herself was. The previous day, she'd heard Mama whispering frantically to herself as she folded laundry. Superstitious to a fault, Mama had even taken Grandfather's portrait off its nail in the parlor and turned her father's unblinking eyes to face the wall, afraid his lack of regard for his son-in-law had stretched all the way from the Cities of Death to jinx his health. After all, Grandfather had always despised Papa, and if he'd had his way, no marriage would have ever taken place between him and his beloved daughter. Though of course,

Betsy had to be grudgingly grateful that Grandfather had hated Papa—if it weren't so, Ophelia would never have been born.

The way the story had been told—the afternoon before Ophelia was conceived, Papa had been on his knees in Mama's childhood home, begging Grandfather to allow them to marry. Betsy's grandfather, sent to the island for embezzlement, looked down on the son of a highwayman and refused. Ophelia had been born from Papa's utter dejection, his low tolerance for alcohol, and his need for female comfort. He and Mama would never have married if her stomach hadn't begun to unexpectedly swell with Betsy, leaving her father no choice but to allow the marriage. Mama had been delighted at the *two* surprising babies, the surprising marriage, and the surprisingly happy ending to their star-crossed tale.

But Mama did not look happy now.

"Look," Betsy said, reaching out to place her hand lightly on her mother's shoulder, "I know it's not good."

Mama couldn't meet Betsy's eyes. Her lower lip trembled, and then she let out a sudden gasp and burst into tears. Snot bubbled from her nose. "Oh, my love," she said. "I don't know what's going to happen. To your father or to us."

Betsy gulped. "What do you mean? Is this about that letter you burned?" She glanced over her shoulder at the paper that had been tossed in the fire. It was already ash.

Mama clutched at the folds of her skirt. Betsy watched as her mother's knuckles went increasingly white and bloodless. With a little gasp, the explanation tumbled out of her mouth. "I suppose I should tell you. Word reached the Whitmans of your father's illness. They were on the edge of the String Islands when they heard, and now they want to double back." Mama gave a harsh laugh, and glanced up at the ceiling as if hoping some sympathetic god might intervene. "I think that terrible boy intends to pressure me into signing over your father's half of the shares. He kept saying that business should be the least of our worries in these troubled times, and that he could take care of our assets until—until your father recovers."

Betsy stood up violently, turning her back to her mother.

She hadn't thought about what would happen to them if her father died. She assumed her father had placed money in a trust for her and Ophelia and her mother, but who knew how much? The Whitmans certainly couldn't be trusted to provide any support to keep her family off the streets. She couldn't even give them the benefit of the doubt that they wouldn't cheat them out of their share of the business. They needed a strong personality to stand against Jakob and Matthew if they didn't want to lose any of their assets to shady double-dealings.

"What did you say to him?"

"Nothing. I burned the letter for a reason. He won't get anything from us."

"How long can we ignore them?" Betsy turned back to her mother, and sat down again, tears stinging at the corners of her eyes. Her father understood the business. She and her mother were homebodies. Afraid of the sea, afraid of risk-taking, afraid of everything. They needed a guiding hand in these matters. Someone bold.

Betsy was supposed to have fixed all that. If Matthew had

wanted her, they would have been secure, and they could have focused their attention entirely on her father now.

"I'm so sorry," Betsy said, pressing her hands against her mouth to muffle her moans. "It's all my fault. What happened with the Whitmans . . ."

Mama swung around, a fierce look transforming her soft, round face into stone. "Exactly none of this is your fault. Don't ever think that. It's not your fault that Jakob didn't raise his son right."

"But my ill wish," Betsy choked out. "What if this illness is my doing?"

Mama gave a quiet laugh. "Don't be daft, my love. It's alright to be superstitious, but we must draw the line at paranoid. Curses do not happen by accident. They need *intent* behind them. That's what my mother always said she'd learned about witches in the old country, and I believe she was right." She laid aside her tiny scissors on the bedspread. "We're going to get through this." She seemed surer now. She stood up, and kissed Betsy on the top of her head, where her hair parted. "We just need to have faith, and a bit of luck."

"A bit of luck," Betsy murmured. Then it suddenly became obvious what had to be done. They needed a strong personality to battle with the Whitmans. Ophelia was that personality. And even though Betsy was still furious, even though the mere thought of going running to Ophelia for help made her stomach churn—Betsy prided herself on being the unselfish sister.

"We need Ophelia to come home," Betsy said. "We need everyone here to deal with all that's happening. Her little naval dream is just going to have to wait, isn't it?" Betsy stood from her stool and announced, in a sharp, falsely cheery tone, "I'm going to write her a letter." And what a letter it would be! Betsy was going to give Ophelia what for—really let her have it for her selfish exit. By the time Ophelia read Betsy's signature, she would be tripping over herself to assuage her guilt. Ophelia would board the next ship home.

Betsy knew *she* couldn't save the family—but she could drag Ophelia back to save it, and that was the next best thing.

"Darling," Mama said, her blond eyebrows furrowed. "I'm not sure you've thought this through. We don't even know where Ophelia is right now. She could be anywhere on the Emerald Sea."

Betsy wasn't to be deterred. "Then I'll visit Commodore Lang, won't I? She'll tell me where Ophelia is. She owes us that much, after letting her leave."

Mama gave a nervous little laugh, twisting and untwisting her handkerchief—one that Betsy had bordered with yellow daisies when she was twelve. "But won't it be awfully silly if we pull Ophelia away from her first voyage—and then your father's perfectly well by the time she comes home? He may well be, you know. Perhaps your father will get better on his own—perhaps we're overreacting. Billy Norton, you know, that strong lad from Locust Street? He shook the fever off two years ago. One day he was on death's door, and the next—"

Betsy reached out to grip her mother's wrists, to stop her from fidgeting with the embroidered cloth. "Billy Norton was a hale eighteen-year-old, mother. He had his health, and the gods on his side. But Papa needs all the luck he can get, and Ophelia's his lucky charm. Besides, we need her for the Whitmans. I'm writing. When all's done, she can sail off into the horizon—see if I care."

Betsy kissed her father on the forehead and practically raced downstairs, full of fiery intent. She seized a hat from the rack by the door, and a parasol propped by the mirror in the hall. She rushed into the street—not caring how many people stopped to stare, not caring how many people she needed to shove out of her way to get to the naval offices faster.

The town houses around her quickly became a candy-colored blur as she wove through the crowds, smacking sluggishly moving people in their ankles with her parasol, the way she had seen Ophelia do to people who accosted her on the street.

She came barreling up the marble front steps of the naval office, her skirts hitched too far up her legs for her to look in any way respectable or ladylike. Betsy could just imagine tripping on a hem now, of all times—tripping on these grand steps and knocking out her front teeth. Betsy pushed open the office's front doors, huffing and puffing like her mother in the middle of a frantic episode, shouting the commodore's name.

A door at the end of the long hall opened, and Betsy caught sight of the commodore's plump silhouette, shadowed on the doorway. Lang drifted into the hall, the heels of her boots clicking. "I believe someone is calling for me?"

"Yes," Betsy said, skidding to a halt in front of her. "My name is Bets"—she shook her head reflexively—"I mean, *Elizabeth* Young. We've met once before. You know my sister, Ophelia."

If anything, Lang's eyebrow eyebrow arched at her sister's name. "I might have guessed," she said.

"Our father is dying," Betsy said, her eyes imploring. "I need to contact my sister. To bring her home. The illness came on so suddenly—she didn't know he was ill when she left. She needs to see our father, to say goodbye."

Lang's expression was politely puzzled. "I beg your pardon, but why are you coming to me with this?"

Betsy tilted her head to the side, as baffled as Lang. "Well— you're the one who got her an appointment. She left early, without telling us where she was headed. I need you to tell me where she'll next come into port, so I can send her a letter and bid her home."

The confusion slid from Lang's expression to be replaced by a chilly stiffness. "When did she leave your home?"

Betsy supplied the date, and soon Lang had turned her back on her. She reentered her office and began rifling through her desk. Betsy followed the admiral inside just as she pulled out a letter and made a clipped sound of triumph. "Aha! A letter from Victoria Ames, first mate of the *Bluesusan*. Included is a list of her new recruits for bookkeeping purposes, and on that list"—she gave a wry laugh, making eye contact with Betsy again—"can you guess the name?"

Betsy felt she was at least three steps behind, but her heart knew enough to be thumping in panic. "Ophelia Y-Young?"

Lang paced toward Betsy, her boots still clicking steadily like the drum at Ophelia Cray's hanging. Her lip curled as she said, "Wrong."

She held the letter to Betsy's face, so close that the ink might have rubbed off on her nose if it were wet. Betsy took the letter from Lang's hands, going almost cross-eyed as she scanned intently for a familiar name. And the final name on the list was very familiar indeed.

"Elizabeth Young," Lang said, her voice soft as a snake's hiss. It occurred to Betsy for the first time that calm Commodore Lang might be very angry indeed. "And what did you say your name was, my dear? Now, this might be a wild guess, but it seems to me that your sister has stolen your identity and lied to the empire."

Betsy tried to speak, to protest, to defend Ophelia—but her tongue felt suddenly swollen.

With a sound like a lightning clap, Lang slapped her palms down on the surface of the desk. Her back was turned to Betsy with her shoulders hunched. Silence lingered in the room for some time, and then Lang said, yet more quietly, "I have to assume that one does not commit fraud for noble reasons. Ophelia's mother was a mutineer, and now she has conned her way onto a naval boat. A revenge seeker, perhaps? I could sense dishonesty in her from the moment she stepped through that door. It would be irresponsible for me not to see her clapped in irons."

Acting solely on instinct, Betsy scanned the letter in her hands for any pertinent information—before neatly folding it and tearing it first in half, then into quarters, then into tiny, tiny shreds.

Lang straightened her back, smoothing down her bloodred uniform jacket. She revolved, and looked at Betsy with a stern eye. "What exactly do you think you're doing?"

"I think you should let my sister be," Betsy said. The voice emerging from her mouth was somehow both hoarse and shrill—entirely unlike her own.

And then Betsy sprinted down the long hall before Lang could shout at her for tearing up the letter. Hot blood pounded in her ears. A fire had been lit in her belly.

Lang was calling after her. "Come back here! Come back, you foolish girl! *Sentry!*"

But Betsy didn't so much as slow down when the lobby's sentry tried to put himself between her and the exit. She plowed straight at him, giving him a mighty shove. He was knocked bodily to the ground as Betsy made her daring escape.

EIGHT

Ophelia's scabs itched. There were no mirrors in the lower decks of the ship, so she couldn't see them, but it was impossible to forget that they were there, the tingling ridges stretching up her back like tiny mountain ranges. Emily had instructed her not to scratch them, but sometimes when she slept, she did it unconsciously.

"Lass! You're doing it again!"

Jerking out of a doze, Ophelia sat up and brushed fine grains of sand off her lilac skirt. She turned to blink at Emily, sitting on a burlap blanket a few feet behind her. She was picnicking with Jo, who had bought them all some of Orana's local dishes for a meal on the beach. Emily's head leaned against Jo's shoulder, forcing her long neck—reminiscent of the giraffes Ophelia had seen in paintings of the great continent's savannahs—to bend at an odd angle. Still, both women looked quite comfortable with the arrangement.

"Sorry," Ophelia said, voice hoarse from her nap. She blinked up at the sun and squirmed. The healing cuts had been more comfortable in her uniform, which was looser than having stays pressed into her skin. But they had landed in Orana six days ago—and once a female sailor disembarked her ship, she was meant to hold up certain societal expectations. One of those expectations, Ophelia knew, was dressing like a proper lady. Stays had never chafed Ophelia before, but now that she'd gotten a taste of freedom, she wanted it back as soon as possible.

Ophelia rubbed at her eyes, and asked, without thinking, "Would you loosen my ties a bit, Bets?"

Jo gave a barking laugh. "What'd you just call me?"

Ophelia swung her head like she was trying to shake water from her ears. "No, sorry. I didn't mean that. Bets, *Betsy*, is my sister. I was just dreaming about her. Won't happen again."

Ophelia chastised herself for her stupid mistake. Thank the gods she had only stolen her sister's given name, Elizabeth, and not her nickname! A few minutes dreaming of Betsy had made her foolish, given her a sense of false security—and a bit of wistful sadness too. But she stubbornly refused to be homesick, especially as she didn't really have a home.

Emily and Jo shared a brief look, but smiled indulgently at her. "No trouble," Jo said, gruffly. "Come over here, now, and we'll see what we can do about those stays."

She pushed her curls to one side of her shoulder and Jo slowly loosened the crisscrossing laces of the stays. Air trickled into the space between the starched fabric and Ophelia's skin, bringing relief with it. She sighed happily, settling back onto the blanket.

"Do you think Ames will want us back on the ship tomorrow?"

Ophelia asked. There had been some question of when they were all due back to the *Bluesusan*—they'd had a good stretch of fair weather with the wind at their back, and that meant they'd landed in Port Orana four days earlier than they'd expected. Jo had explained that when this sort of thing happened, it was usually up to the captain to decide when the rig would set out again: either after fulfilling the only scheduled week of leave or on the date originally projected for their departure. Since Hale hardly knew one day from another, it fell to Ames to make the call.

"It's hard to say," Jo said, scratching her chin and looking out at the steel-gray waves. "Ames knows morale has been low recently. It's not wise to ignore discontent among the crew. That's how mutiny happens. But she loves efficiency more than anything, including her own mother. It'll probably be decided based on weather."

She shook a finger at Ophelia. "Remember this, though. Never be tempted to linger too long after we're called back. Ames has been known to leave tardy sailors behind, and people who overstay their leave don't get paid."

Emily snorted, and rolled her eyes at Ophelia. "They don't just lose their pay. They also get court-martialed. Jo always seems to forget the most important part."

Jo grinned, throwing her arm around Emily's shoulder. "I don't care about stuffed-shirt officers handing down punishments. I care about the coins in my pocket." She kissed Emily's cheek.

Ophelia reclined on the blanket, staring up at the sky, which was almost as gray as the waves. "Why did we have to take our leave in Orana, though?" She pouted. "There are hundreds of beautiful ports in Carthay, as you'd expect from the grand-queen's native province, but this isn't one of them. If I'm going to be on land, I'd like the city to be less dirty than the boat."

Emily burst out laughing. "That's a feminine perspective if I've ever heard one," she said. "I quite agree with you. But the menfolk in the navy? Orana's a real favorite for them. I can't work out whether it's the cheap liquor or the busty tavern wenches."

Jo's face took on an impish smirk. "I don't see why it can't be both. I used to be fond of the drinking and the barmaids around here. That was before I was a taken woman, of course." She winked at Emily, who hid her face so that Jo wouldn't get the satisfaction of seeing her smile.

Ophelia moaned in frustration again. "I do wish Ames' beloved documents could have been delivered anywhere but here. I know we need to 'do our duty for the empire,' but all Orana has of any real value are the beaches." She gestured out in front of her, where the fine white particles of sand settled in swirling patterns, looking like strips of lace that stretched for miles. "I wanted a good marketplace—somewhere I could buy presents to send back. But nothing here is worth buying."

"I'm not sure about that!" A buoyant voice called out across the dunes behind them. Ophelia looked up to see Edgar Ludlow stomping his way through the drifts of the beach, waving at the three women as if he'd been marooned on an island and was signaling for help. "Have you even entered a bar yet, Lucky Teeth?"

Ophelia wrinkled her nose and laughed. "No, of course not! I was raised not to go to seedy taverns." For the thousandth time since coming ashore in Orana, Ophelia imagined the sound of horror that Eliza would have made if she spotted her in such a place. It was a funny picture—but that didn't mean Eliza wasn't right about bars and the people who drank in them. Her own last experience with alcohol had certainly proved that no good came of such things, and Ophelia was determined not to mix with drinking again.

Edgar had reached their blanket now. He had his hands on his hips and was blinking down at Ophelia like a disappointed father. "Did your mama also raise you to avoid dancing and fiddle players? I've come to rescue you from boredom. While you've been here sunbathing, the rest of the crew has been off raising hell. Gods above, you should have heard young Fitz—he's been serenading the crew. Had all the tavern patrons tossing coins at him. You have to join, Lucky Teeth. I'm telling you—you haven't lived 'til you've done a jig on a bar top and kissed a local."

Ophelia looked up at him, raising a hand to keep the sun from her eyes. "I'm not really interested in kissing."

Emily chuckled, pointing at Edgar. "You hear that? She's not interested. Now piss off."

Edgar gave a dramatic sigh, and talked out of the side of his mouth to Ophelia. "Our fair Emily's never liked me much. Can't imagine why."

Emily's tone was placid as she replied, "I can't be the first to dislike you, rich boy."

"The first I've known about!" Edgar laughed. He turned his attention back to Ophelia. "Fine, forget the kissing. But I really do want you to catch that fiddling. You'll miss the local color if you don't come. Give me a mere hour of your time and I promise you'll be utterly captivated." He gave a courteous bow in Emily and Jo's direction. "Everyone should come along, actually. I know Jo likes her liquor, and you won't find a cheaper place for it on the southwest coast."

"Cheap and dirty," Ophelia said, giggling into her hand despite her better instincts. "You really know how to paint an enticing picture. But I won't abandon Jo and Emily. I'm not coming if they don't."

Jo threw Emily a wide-eyed, pleading look. "He's not wrong about how cheap the liquor is. That more than makes up for his lack of charms, doesn't it?"

Emily sighed. "Fine. But just for one hour, and I'm holding you all to that."

Edgar stuck out a hand to help Ophelia up. "I figured that since we're back on land, I ought to treat you ladies like a gentleman again."

Ophelia ignored the offered hand as she clambered to her feet. "I'm fine."

"And you're no gentleman," Emily added.

Edgar pouted. "Why don't you like me, dearest Emily?"

Emily brushed past Edgar as she headed up the beach, the cheap red fabric of her skirt trailing in the sand. "You remind me of my father."

"Oh," Edgar said, a polite note in his voice, but a cocky smirk plastered on his face. "Was he devilishly handsome too?"

"There was certainly devil in him. He's why I went to sea."

Jo threw back her head and cackled. "It's been seven years,

and that son of a bitch still doesn't know where Em really went when she said she was headed to the milliner's."

"The point is," Emily said, casting a particularly eloquent glare in Edgar's direction, "I can see through all kinds of horse-shit, but yours is a brand I'm particularly familiar with."

Unperturbed, Edgar only gave Ophelia a lazy grin. "Well, you like me at least, don't you, Lucky Teeth?"

Ophelia smoothed down the panels of her silk dress, not really thinking about Edgar's question. If Emily had joined up to flee her father, that meant she wasn't the only person who'd gone to sea to leave something behind. Still—it had been so sweet to dream of Betsy again, if only for a few minutes. It occurred to her that she was glad to be wearing her lilac dress again, after all, whether the stays pinched her wounds or not.

Edgar led them through Orana's grimy streets—with its shit-filled gutters and its squat houses of yellow stucco—to a tavern with cherry-red shingles on its roof. He opened the front door and ushered his companions into the dimness inside.

The tavern was low-ceilinged, its walls bearing years of water stains. There was a small chandelier of visibly dirty glass hanging above the bar, but Ophelia didn't think it lent the tavern the air of class they were hoping for. Someone renting out one of the rooms upstairs was making quite a racket, and the banging from above made the chandelier shake, spilling dust and ceiling particles onto the bar surface below. A thick-hipped woman in an apron kept having to produce an old rag to sweep the fallen bits of plaster off the counter.

The whole building was packed; full of loud, contented

chatter and the occasional drunken shout. Edgar was right—someone in the corner was standing on a chair and sawing away at the strings of his fiddle. The fiddle's song was sweet, bouncy, and somehow *golden*. It seemed to ricochet off every surface in the bar, and Ophelia suddenly didn't regret coming.

"Come on," Jo said, grabbing Emily by the hand and pulling her toward the bar. Jo hip-checked anyone who got in her way as she crossed the tavern, and a few men pointed at her and jeered. It wasn't clear to Ophelia if these white-bearded lushes were jeering at Jo because of her pushing or because, unlike Emily and Ophelia, she hadn't bothered to dress like a respectable lady for her time ashore. Jo was wearing breeches and a belted tunic stained with sweat. Ophelia was half-certain that Jo had joined the navy just so no one would ask her to act like a "proper woman" ever again. There were different rules at sea. Better ones. No one looked at Jo, or Ames, or anyone like a woman when they were on the ship.

Well, except perhaps Edgar. But as Emily had once put it, he was just "desperate as a lustful schoolboy" for ladies' attention.

Edgar reached out to grab Ophelia's hand the way Jo had seized Emily's, but Ophelia quickly crossed her arms. Edgar kept grinning anyway. "At least let me buy you a drink, Lucky Teeth. And let me see that pretty smile."

"I'll just have water," Ophelia suggested, turning to Edgar and smiling with her mouth pointedly closed. Edgar's face fell, though he tried to hide it. "Ah, of course. Refreshing water coming up." He cut his way through the crowd, less aggressively than Jo had, but still making a path for Ophelia to follow him, and banged on the counter to place his order.

The aproned woman at the bar glanced up at Ophelia while she pumped water into a mug. Ophelia gave a shy smile, and in return the woman gave her an approving head nod. "Good teeth," the woman said, her accent thick. "They bring you luck?"

Ophelia gave a bashful shrug, as Edgar elbowed her and said, "I told you about those teeth and Carthay!"

When the water came, sliding across the bar from where the aproned woman stood, Edgar caught it and passed it to Ophelia. She sipped and coughed. "It's a little dirty," she said.

Edgar chuckled. "That's pretty standard for Orana. Come, sit with me." He pointed across the bar to where a few members of the crew were huddled together, including some of her fellow workers on the bilge line, and Ronan, who rose to his feet, gesturing at Ophelia and roaring in approval. On their tabletop, Fitz stood with a tankard of ale in his hand, singing a mournful, tremulous Peu Nadal ditty with Leah, another bilge rat some ten years his senior, who wore her blond hair in a crown of braids. They had their arms thrown over each other's shoulders and swayed with the melody, both obviously quite drunk. Their voices went rather nicely together: young Fitz's voice hadn't quite dropped yet, so he sang the high harmonies while Leah's husky alto went low.

"Who gave Fitz ale?" Ophelia demanded. "Look how small he is! He oughtn't have it."

Edgar threw back his head and laughed.

"That wasn't rhetorical," Ophelia said. "What genius had that idea?"

Edgar smirked. "Who really knows?"

Ophelia's eyes narrowed, canny. "It was you, wasn't it?"

Given over to laughter again, Edgar protested through his hysterics, "Well who could help it? It's so funny!"

At that moment, throwing up his tankard to toast at the song's rousing climax, Fitz slopped half of what remained in his drink down his front. This did not seem to dampen his mood one bit, and he kept on singing as loud as he could manage. Ophelia's crewmates roared their approval, obviously very fond of their young comrade.

Edgar shared a knowing look with Ophelia as she tried to suppress a guilty giggle. "See? I'm not wrong. And don't look at me that stern way, Lucky Teeth. At least I bought the damn drink for him and didn't let him waste his scant wages. I am nothing if not generous." He knocked his knuckles against the bar, signaling for an ale for himself and, successful in his goal, slid off into the crowd.

Ophelia made to follow Edgar as he shouldered his way back through the sea of patrons, but she'd hardly begun to move before a bony hand snapped out from the crowd to close around her wrist. Her mug of water slipped from her grip and smashed— water soaking into Ophelia's boots and leaving shards of glassy clay scattered on the moldy floorboards.

Trying to break free, Ophelia swung around to stare the stranger in his face, wishing she had her trusty parasol to give him a few hard raps. She immediately recognized him as one of the nasty, bearded men who had shouted profanity at Jo. His shock-white hair was wild, his eyes bloodshot, and his nose a shape that could only come from having been broken on several occasions. He smelled like urine and stale ale.

"Get off me!" Ophelia said, twisting her wrist in an attempt to break his grip.

"It's you," the man said, holding tight despite her best efforts. His eyes were popping and mad. "It's you. After all these years. I'm not letting you get away this time."

Ophelia spat in the man's face. "I don't know you! Unhand me, or you'll regret it."

Edgar, who had successfully reached the crew's table, turned around expecting to see Ophelia directly to his back. "Hey!" he shook his fist at the old man, shouting over the heads of the crowd. "She doesn't like to be touched, you know! Especially not by bone-ugly curs like you!"

The strange man wasn't distracted by Edgar's outburst, or even Ophelia's saliva on his cheek. If anything, his grip grew stronger as his pale blue irises began to dance, moving in his sockets so quickly that they seemed to mix with the redness in his sclerae. "Ophelia Cray," he murmured. "We meet again."

Ophelia, who'd still been struggling hard, suddenly froze. "I'm not Ophelia Cray."

"You are," the man said. "You're Ophelia Cray."

Ophelia just shook her head over again, silently begging him not to say the name any louder. No one could hear. They couldn't hear.

Blinking, the man stared at her frightened face and softened a bit. He squinted, now skeptical. "No tricks. You're Ophelia Cray. Or . . . are you the Young one?"

Ophelia could hardly breathe, turning over possibilities in her head. How could he know about her? They were so far from Peu Jolie. She'd come such a long way. Ophelia's left hand crept down to the belt she had slung over the waist of her silk dress, her fingers resting on the handle of her father's pistol. "You let go of me." Maybe she could scare him off before anyone heard something they shouldn't.

"You took my ship," the old man said, his eyes boring into Ophelia's now, not remotely bothered by her implicit threat. "And my ruttin' crew too. They stripped me of every medal I ever earned. All I got to keep was the jacket." The stranger began to laugh, stretching out his free arm to display the tattered red jacket that hung from his thin, twisted frame. It was covered in years of grime, but underneath everything, Ophelia knew that its shade of red was precisely the same as the jackets worn by Lang and Hale.

She could almost hear Lang's soft, measured voice in her ear, and it raised goose bumps on Ophelia's skin as if she had been hit with a cold breeze: *What would you do if you came across someone who was harmed by your mother?*

Ophelia started to tremble. She dropped her hand to her side, knowing the pistol was no option at all. She couldn't hurt this man. Her mother had already hurt him.

But then she glanced at the far end of the bar, where Jo and Emily were sitting, absorbed in each other's presence. They hadn't seen or heard anything yet. The bar was too loud, with the shouting and that lovely fiddle. She had time. But then Ophelia looked over at the table where the rest of her crewmates waited for her. Edgar and Ronan were making their way back toward her now, shoving people out of their way as they tried to come to her aid.

They couldn't know.

"I don't know you, old man," Ophelia snapped, managing to tear her arm away from him at last. "You're crazy."

"Do we have a problem here?" Ronan growled at the stranger, the veins in his neck particularly noticeable as he clenched his jaw. "Because this here's my crewmate. If you've got a problem with her, you've got a problem with all of us."

The old man whirled to face Ronan. He was easily a foot shorter than his challenger, but he wasn't cowed. He bared his yellow teeth and announced to the bar at large, "You're the one who's got the problem! There's a witch snuck onto your ship." He jabbed a gnarled finger in Ophelia's direction. "She'll steal your crew, your rig, and leave you to burn and starve on an island somewhere, like she did me."

Edgar curled his lip and let out a haughty laugh. He pulled at the front of his blue uniform as if trying to be impressive, winking at Ophelia. "My, my, Lucky Teeth, you have been busy. When did you find time to earn that medal on your handkerchief between all the marooning and killing?"

Ophelia couldn't quite find this joke of Edgar's funny, but she faked a laugh that came out higher and colder than her genuine one. "He's mad," she said, looking entreatingly back and forth between her allies.

"Obviously," Ronan sneered, shoving the old man's shoulder and sending him stumbling back several paces.

"You've been warned!" the old man cried, throwing his elbows into any rib he could to get attention—even just bystanders who happened to be near him. "A witch! A murderer and a she-wolf and a whore!"

Edgar gave a wordless shout and gripped the old man by the shoulders to stop him inflicting any more collateral damage. "Hey! You stop that. You're lucky we don't break your jaw." His eyes drifted downward to take in the man's jacket, and its true hue under all that dirt. A disdainful smile twisted his handsome features. "Ah, I see what this is about. Some pathetic, disgraced captain. Past your prime, old man? Suppose you thought to take your bitterness out on my friend. Make way for the younger generation, why don't you?"

Ophelia swallowed heavily. Her tongue was very dry, like it had been coated with the fallen dirt from the tavern ceiling. "It's okay," she whispered to Edgar. "Let him go. I can fight my own battles."

"Rut that," Ronan said, his voice like thunder. "You're our crewmate, and when someone in our crew gets into a fight, we make sure they have a second. Or a third, if necessary."

"Yeah, Lucky Teeth," Edgar said, not meeting Ophelia's eyes, but still glowering down at the sad, strange man in his tattered jacket. "I'm your second."

When Ophelia was seven, she had once choked on a cherry pit at the breakfast table. Eliza, shrieking in fright all the while, had bent Ophelia over and struck her hard between the shoulder blades until the pit dislodged and rolled from her tongue. Now, looking at this fallen officer, glaring at her with so much hatred in his eyes, Ophelia could have sworn there was another cherry pit trembling in her throat.

She knew this was guilt, and that there was no way to shake it free but to do what she'd promised Lang she would: apologize on her mother's behalf and try to make amends.

But then Ophelia thought better of it. Why should she have to go around on her hands and knees, begging people not to hate her for her mother's crimes? Why should everyone else get amnesty at birth and not her?

"Let him go," Ophelia ordered Edgar again. "He's just mad, that's all. He can't help it."

Edgar shoved the man away. The stranger's face had become blank, his eyes hard. Ophelia turned her back, the hem of her lilac skirt kicking up dust from the floor. "Let's go," she said. "There are other taverns in Orana."

Ronan threw up his arm to tell the crew members across the room they were leaving. Ophelia watched coldly over her shoulder as the others knocked back their drinks and pushed out their chairs. She walked away, though the man continued to shout at her back, his voice breaking in anguish now. "One day, I'll find me another crew! I'll find some good men, and we'll sail to your rutting island. I will take what is owed me!" He let out a wild sob. "You count on that, Ophelia Cray!"

A cold hand seemed to close around Ophelia's heart—seizing it, tightening.

She looked back at Edgar and Ronan. Edgar's gray-blue eyes, twinkling merrily, met Ophelia's, as if to suggest that the truth of her identity was an amusing joke they alone shared. Ronan's face, though, had gained a shadow.

"I'll be on the ship," Ophelia said.

In the end, the *Bluesusan* shoved off the next day, exactly one week after they had landed, and four days before they had been scheduled to depart. Ophelia wasn't sad to leave Orana—and that horrible old stranger—behind, but Fitz pouted to her about their bad fortune. "Apparently whenever we leave places early, letters get lost. People can't find you until the travel projections make it back to your home city's base. My parents were trying to send me a late birthday gift too. Finally saved up enough money for one."

Ames had erred on the side of efficiency rather than generosity, despite the crew's protests and Edgar muttering to anyone who'd listen that "someone ought to teach our second-in-command to appreciate her crew." It was true that Ames might have been willing to give the crew four extra days off, but a large storm was headed toward the coast, and if it hit them while they were still anchored in Orana, they might be stuck in port long past when the navy expected the *Bluesusan* back en route to deliver missives again. Ames would allow the crew to relax if it cost her nothing, but not if it chanced her superiors questioning her own job performance. And beside all the other considerations, it appeared that Ames thought she could outrun the storm.

She was wrong.

NINE

Betsy returned to her home with her chest full of fire. *Ophelia is in danger. She needs my help. Lang is going to have her thrown in prison—or worse.* The gears in Betsy's brain whirred as she tried to stitch together all she'd learned. Ophelia had joined the navy, that much was clear. But she'd joined without Lang knowing, and using Betsy's name. How could she accomplish such a thing? The answer hit her like a collapsing ceiling: Ophelia must have taken *her* birth certificate.

"Mama!" she shouted up the stairs. "Mama, what is the password to Papa's safe?"

"Why, it's your birthday, dear," she called back. "But why?"

Betsy was already thundering up the stairs, too out of breath to answer. Upon reaching her father's office, she had to enter the combination twice because her shaking hands had ruined the pattern the first time. After what seemed an eternity, the door swung open. Betsy took quick stock of the safe's contents: Mama's porcelain shepherdess, Grandmother's jewelry box,

Papa's ledgers, and *yes*. Ophelia's birth certificate. But not hers.

Betsy didn't trust her memory for long, so she seized paper and pen from her father's desk, scribbling down all the contents she remembered of the ruined letter from Lang's office that had held Ophelia's next location—Port Orana.

So now Betsy knew the facts, but what to do was another matter entirely. Ophelia was half an ocean away! She could write her a letter to warn her—but who was to say a letter would get there in time? She had to hope that Lang did not memorize the contents of the letter before handing it to Betsy. She'd be on a fact-finding mission first before drafting a letter of her own, warning the navy in Orana to arrest Ophelia on sight. Still, Betsy would need luck to ensure her letter reached Orana before Lang's did. And luck was the one thing Betsy never seemed to have.

"Darling, what's going on?" Mama had ambled into the study. Her head tilted curiously to one side as she caught sight of a shining glass bottle on the mantel. "I haven't seen this in years. What's it doing back down from the attic?"

Betsy had finished her mad dash to re-create the letter. She felt as breathless as when she had been running. She pulled the bottle from her mother's hands, bringing her attention back to the matter at hand, and stuffed the glass miniature carelessly into her apron pocket. "That's not important right now."

Mama opened her mouth to ask another question, but Betsy waved her confusion away. She staggered out into the hall to peer down the stairs, expecting the bell to ring at any moment. "Ophelia's done something terrible," Betsy said. They were both extremely fast talkers. Betsy explained the situation faster than a mosquito could flit across a room. By the end of the story, Mama was clutching at her heart, making the ward against evil.

"Gods preserve us . . ."

A rigorous clanging echoed up the mahogany steps. Someone outside was ringing the bell furiously. All Betsy's joints locked up at once. "That'll be the navy come to arrest me."

Betsy practically tumbled back down the stairs, tripping over the ornate rug that lined them as Valois loped toward the door. She shoved him out of the foyer and threw open the door herself, shouting, "She didn't do anything wrong, I tell you! She's simply run away, someone else must have—"

The fire blazing in Betsy's chest was smothered out by a blast of cold water. It wasn't anyone from the navy at their door, but Matthew and Jakob Whitman in their best suits—Matthew extending a thin bouquet of orchids toward her with a limp arm.

Betsy blinked. Her tone became flat. "What are you doing here?"

Matthew Whitman crossed the threshold without being invited. He doffed his hat. Jakob followed, mumbling an incoherent apology. His hands were shaking horribly.

Matthew's voice drowned out Jakob's. "We finished our tour of the String Islands, miss, and my father insisted that we return here before we left, to make a proper apology." His eyes flashed behind his glasses. "My father is an old man. He cannot afford to have a strained friendship weighing on his mind. And when we came back to Peu Jolie, we heard the unfortunate news about Nathaniel."

Mama came tentatively down the stairs, and Betsy saw her

own confused expression echoed on her mother's face. She opened her mouth, but didn't seem to have words.

"Madam Eliza," Matthew began, dropping into another bow, "might I extend my sincerest sympathies for your husband—"

Betsy swung away from her mother, focusing on Matthew. Her lip curled, her hand snaking into the pocket of her apron to wrap around the lighter for courage. "Keep my mother's name out of your mouth. And stop acting like my father is already dead. The real islanders know this disease. It can linger on for months, so just—just stop talking."

Mama slowly lowered herself farther down the stairs, nodding. Her face was stony, but her voice was a squeak. "I agree with my daughter's sentiments."

Betsy sent an adoring look in her mother's direction, but Matthew Whitman wasn't easily silenced. "But the fact remains that your father's death is imminent." He paused for breath, recollected himself, and added unconvincingly, "So if there is anything we can do to help . . ."

"Nothing," Betsy growled. "Besides, we have business to attend to," she muttered. "You'll only get in the way."

Jakob, his eyes filmy with tears, nodded. Responding to Betsy's firm tone, he shuffled out immediately. Matthew was far less penitent. The cool look on his face was that of a person who was amused but had no sense of humor to speak of. He reached into the inner pocket of his jacket. "Business, you say? Well, we sail for Cornwallis tomorrow at noon. You can find us at this address until then if you change your mind about needing our assistance."

Valois, still glaring at Betsy for having shoulder-checked him, locked the front door behind the Whitmans. "Is someone planning on telling me what's going on?"

The women ignored him. Mama was twisting at her apron. "And what is the plan now?" she demanded of Betsy. "The commodore will still investigate Ophelia and find her in the end!"

Betsy steeled herself. "I guess I'll have to sail to Orana first and bring Ophelia home before they find her."

Mama gave that parrotlike squawk again. "Ridiculous!"

"I d-don't exactly love the idea either, but I don't see another option."

Mama unlaced the back of her apron and threw it to the floor. "You girls will be the death of me. Elizabeth, I forbid you to leave this house. Haven't we enough problems, with your father so ill?"

"So what do you suggest—we abandon Ophelia?"

Mama's face bloomed red. Her lip wobbled. "Abandon her!" she cried. "She's the one who went half a sea away, and told us nothing." She sank onto the stairs, her cheeks already wet. Valois stooped to pick up his mistress's apron and hand it to her. Mama mouthed her thanks and wiped her nose on the cotton. She looked up at Betsy, who was hovering nervously by the hat rack. "I thought I had two daughters," she said, gulping. "But one has flittered off without so much as a thank-you, and now you decide to do the same? I'm sorry—you know I love that girl. But Ophelia broke the law, and if you go chasing after her, you'll be an accomplice, and get jailed alongside her."

Betsy glanced behind her, staring at the solid wood of the front door. She had always liked staying inside in the quiet and the dark—but jail was hardly the same as hiding in her room, sewing. Her brief moment of bravery flickered and died. "You're right, Mama. I don't know what I was thinking."

Ophelia would have to get herself out of this trouble, as she'd gotten herself into it.

She withdrew the bottle from her apron, studying it. She recognized the hairline fracture on its base—remembered dropping it as a child. Betsy let out a rueful laugh. How could she help Ophelia? She'd only ever made things worse. She deposited the damaged bottle on her father's bedside, hoping it would cheer him somehow.

It had been sweet, for a moment, to imagine taking up the mantle of the older sister, which was rightfully hers—and be the one to save Ophelia for once. But it was better for her to stay home, where she was useful. Yes, Betsy would do as she always did. She would remain at home, in the dark, and stoke the hearth. Tend to her father. Calm her mother's nerves.

But then—midnight. Betsy was woken from fitful sleep by her mother screaming and raced to her father's bedside.

It was true. The islanders did know the Mosquito Fever, and how it often kept its victims lingering for months. But with Nathaniel Young that wasn't the case. He had died quietly in the night.

Betsy squeezed her father's fingers. They were stiff.

Mama collapsed in the corner of the room, weeping into her hands. A shaft of moonlight fell across the floorboards, stopping just short of where Mama was crumpled in a heap. All the heat had been leeched from Betsy's body, not just her father's. She wrapped her arms around herself, surprised that she had not begun crying yet. But she couldn't cry—this didn't feel real. The house was too quiet, the end too sudden.

She was numb. Betsy hadn't thought he would die yet. She'd thought he had time. That he might even get better.

It was the silence that disturbed Betsy most. She'd always liked the quiet, but now she wanted to scream as Mama had screamed when she found the body. Her mother sobbed noiselessly now. Betsy could not stay here in the quiet and the dark. She knew she must flee from this cold body and into the warmth.

Betsy stepped into the line of moonlight, letting it stream onto her face and bare arms. It did nothing to thaw her frozen skin. She closed her eyes, opening her mouth to tell her mother how she had to break her heart once more.

TEN

The ship shuddered, leaning this way and that. Two nights after their departure from Orana, Ophelia was fighting to simply keep her stance wide enough to remain upright. The wind had knocked her face-first once already. Rain fell with such force that it felt like being whipped with the cat again, but this time, it wasn't just her back absorbing the blows.

"We've got to get that sail down!" Edgar roared, pointing up at the mainmast's sail. The storm had hit them fast, unexpectedly. If the sail didn't come down to deck, it would be mangled by the vicious wind and rain. Should that happen, the crew might as well say their prayers, because their next destination wouldn't be any port—but the Cities of Death. They would drift aimlessly on the seas until the water ran out, and then the sun would bleach their bones.

Not that Ophelia could even really imagine the sun in a hurricane like this. It already seemed like something from a past too distant to remember.

Her boots couldn't grip the flooded deck anymore, and the line was fighting her, slipping away and burning her wet palms. Over the roar of the storm, she could still hear the ship creaking—she feared the thrashing waves would tip the *Bluesusan* on its side.

Edgar, the only officer anyone could currently find on deck, had taken control of the situation, tapping Fitz to scale the mast and bring down the sail. He had two things in his favor for this assignment: He was small and he was brave. Fitz seized the lines to hoist himself up as he climbed the pole—all Ophelia and Edgar, behind her and anchoring the rope with his weight, needed to do was hold the rope steady for him. The rest was up to Fitz.

The clouds above them were so dark and thick that Ophelia couldn't rightly call them clouds anymore. Ophelia's chest heaved with exhaustion and cold and fear. Panic gripped her and an absurd thought entered her mind: This was the sky now. No light, no mercy. Forever. It would be dark forever, and she was going to die under this sky.

The line pulled away from them again, ripping out of their hands and flying upward. Fitz, drenched with water, screamed out—but his cry was lost in the howling wind. Panicked, he tried to seize the escaping line but was dragged along with it, flying upward above the deck, and then fell with a terrible wet crunch when he could hold on no longer. Ophelia dove toward him. "Fitz!"

She turned the boy over. He'd broken his nose. His face was sopping and covered in blood. "It's okay," she told him. "It's okay. Just stay down. I'm gonna get you below deck. Hold on."

Fitz moaned, holding his nose and trying to stem the flow of blood. His reply came out muffled: "I'b bine, you go."

Edgar had also been thrown aside, but he scrambled up and helped Ophelia seize the rope again. Her muscles strained to keep her standing and to operate the pulley. Edgar gestured to another crewman, sliding across the deck, and he came to join them.

Edgar clasped Ophelia's shoulder, and she blinked at him, confused. "You go!" he mouthed. He pointed up the mast, all the way to the whipping sail.

She would die under this sky. She really would.

Water streamed off her curls, into her eyes and down the back of her neck. Her sopping uniform felt like a lead weight, pulling her downward, even as she tried to hoist herself up. Ophelia pulled, screaming with the pain of fighting nature. She balanced where the ropes knotted together, gasping for air that wouldn't come—water poured into her mouth and she spat it out again.

Ophelia made the mistake of looking down, to see if Fitz was still moving. Then it hit her how high up she'd already gotten above the deck.

Dizzying.

Ophelia felt her eyesight had abandoned her, like she was already falling and partway to unconsciousness. But no—that was just how dark the world was now. Below, Edgar was gesturing for her to keep climbing, but fear choked her.

She was all tangled up in these ropes, with so far to fall. The drop would kill her. Break her neck. Was this how her mother felt on the gallows?

The lines strained against her, their shaking resounding down to the very core of her bones. She couldn't breathe—if that wasn't a symptom of hanging, she didn't know what was.

She was stuck; halfway between the swirling storm clouds and the flooding deck. She knew she had to stop looking down if she wanted to ever get unfrozen. *She had to look up*—but that wasn't a particularly pleasant thought either.

Below, she saw a massive beige blur circling a red and blue dot. It felt like a hallucination, but when she shook some water out of her eyes, she realized that it was Ronan and Ames. Ronan looked like a roaring bull who, try as he might, couldn't get any sound to come out. He pointed past the captain's cabin, and Ames followed the gesture, sprinting as best she could to the bow of the ship, where she was blocked from Ophelia's sight. Ronan followed, pulling something from beneath his jacket.

A burst of lightning seared through the sky above her— momentarily turning the night to day. She screamed in fear, but the wind swallowed the sound.

She had to get down. But to do that, first she needed to go higher. She steeled herself, knowing that she was all that stood between her ship and annihilation. She would succeed today, or die trying. Perhaps she would succeed and die for her trouble. But she would succeed. There was no other option. She redoubled her grip on the rope in her palms, closed her eyes, and heaved herself up. It was much like pulling the iron chain to operate the bilge. It was just as dark, though wetter, but she was already stronger than she used to be. Her boots slipped against the slick wood of the mast as she went higher, higher.

Her arms ached. She was drowning. She was going to die under this sky.

Then the rain stopped pouring. She stopped to look out over

the deck, almost fearing she'd gone mad. Out yards beyond the deck edge, beyond the ship, the storm was raging on all sides, swirling and encasing their rig, but not touching it. The eye of the hurricane had turned the *Bluesusan* into a ship in a glass bottle. Everything was quiet for a moment.

Ophelia's wet fingers reached the sail. She was not sure exactly how she did it, in hindsight, but she loosened the mainsail from the mast, and it fell to the deck with a thump.

She began to lower herself. Slowly, carefully.

Not carefully enough. Buffeted by the wind, she lost her grip on the rope.

She was falling. Screaming a scream that could at last be heard, echoing across the ship and ringing in ears. She screamed until she ran out of breath and couldn't find the strength to inhale again. She couldn't breathe, *couldn't breathe*. Her hand had been burned by the rope.

Was the rope around her neck?

They exited the eye, and the storm hit them again, just as Ophelia smashed into the deck.

ELEVEN

etsy pressed her face into the crook of her mother's neck, inhaling. Her mother hadn't bothered to put on perfume since the day her father had first been unable to leave his bed. Now instead of the familiar scent of lily water, Betsy could only smell the sharp odor of the antiseptic Mama had been faithfully applying to her father's broken skin. No need for that anymore— but still, the smell lingered.

Mama was usually enthusiastic in her affections, her embraces tight, drawing Betsy so close that they might have been one organism, sharing one heartbeat. Not so now. Betsy had thrown her whole weight into the hug, but Eliza's arms hung limply at her sides. She was as stiff and cold as Papa.

"I forbid it," Mama whispered. Her pretty eyes were closed, her mouth barely moving as she said, "I will never forgive you."

"Yes you will, Mama."

"No. Not for this. Not for leaving me alone. Not now." She opened her eyes, holding Betsy's gaze. She seized Betsy's wrists and dragged them from her shoulders. "I will not lose my daughter, as well as my husband. I will not be alone."

Betsy twisted, breaking the weak grip on her wrists. Now she held her mother's hands and was kissing each finger—as Mama had when she was a child woken by bad dreams. "I am doing this for our family. I will be back. Your daughters will *both* come home."

Mama squirmed away, staggering backward until she hit the bedside table, rattling the pot of nettles and the glass bottle. She gasped for air. Sobs wracked her body and her pink face had gone purple with distress. "You've broken my heart." She turned, gripping the small table to remain upright. She stood still, breathing heavily—and her gaze drifted to her husband's face.

A soft, yet wild, laugh burst from Mama's mouth. She wiped the wetness from her lips, and leaned over Nathaniel's body. She caressed his hairline. "How could you leave me too? You weren't traveling anymore. We were finally safe, after—after—"

She glanced back at the bottle. She took it in her hands, as gently as if it were a baby bird. Her thumb traced the hairline fracture. She lifted the bottle over her head—Betsy cried out—and smashed the bottle against the floor. The glass shattered, shards bursting outward. The ones that landed in the shaft of moonlight glinted like melting ice.

A shame, Betsy thought, *no bottle to protect it anymore.*

Mama sank to the floor again, horrified by herself. She clapped a hand over her mouth to stifle her sobbing.

Betsy knelt. She picked up the glass bit by bit. Finally, she took the tiny model ship in her palms. The mainmast was crooked.

"This was Papa's ship, wasn't it?"

Mama nodded repeatedly, her hand still on her mouth.

Betsy straightened the mast and crossed to the bed. She peeled her father's stiff hands apart, and placed the little ship between his palms, so that he could hold on to it forever.

Ships weren't meant to be in bottles, anyway, Betsy supposed.

Betsy must have packed. She must have read the note from Matthew Whitman and gone to find her father's partners in their hotel accommodations. She must have cried. She must have told them what happened, and begged them to let her board their ship, the *Sunshearer*, and to drop her in Port Orana on their way back to Cornwallis.

But she did not remember doing any of it.

She could only hold on to one thought: that she needed to get to Ophelia before Lang sent word that she was a mutineer, a pirate. The last time the sun had risen on Peu Jolie, the Young family had held four members. Now it had three. Betsy would do anything to keep it from becoming two. She wasn't sure how she could board a ship and not remember doing it—but her grief had succeeded in doing what no kind words from her family had ever accomplished. It had numbed her anxiety. She was sailing across the Emerald Sea—in hurricane season!—and she wasn't afraid. She was asleep.

The first thing that roused Betsy from her dreamlike state was a sharp rap at the door to her room in the lower decks of the ship. "Miss Young?" Betsy shuddered at the sound of Matthew

Whitman's voice through the wood. Neither grief nor gratitude for his assistance had dulled her hatred of him.

Betsy stood from her cot. It squeaked. She cracked the door open to peer out on his thin face. "We're taking tea above decks. My father and I. Would you like me to escort you up?"

"No," Betsy said. She made to close the door, but he stuck his boot in the crack. "Are you quite certain?" he asked. "There's a rather remarkable noblewoman traveling with us as well. Perhaps you'd like some feminine company?"

Betsy glanced down at Matthew's intruding shoe, moving to slam the door. He only pulled his foot back just in time. "The only company I want is my sister's," Betsy said. "Tell me when we're close to Orana."

She had done the math. It took a week to sail from Peu Jolie to Port Orana. Lang's letter had mentioned the date Ophelia was due to arrive at the port, and she had already been there for four days. The leave was meant to last a fortnight—and then Ophelia would set sail again for regions unknown to Betsy. This meant Betsy's window was not large. If everything went perfectly, she would only arrive in Orana three days before the *Bluesusan* was scheduled to weigh anchor again.

Matthew could talk about tea and noblewomen all he liked, but the math was all that concerned Betsy. He didn't seem to see it that way, though. "Are you certain there is nothing you need from me?" he asked, his words muffled through the heavy wood of the door.

"There is nothing I require," she spat. "Nothing from you."

Matthew sounded confused and hurt. "Now, Miss Young.

Surely we can make amends. I have apologized, you know. Besides, any novice sailor—"

Matthew was a novice sailor himself.

"—will tell you that you need to get fresh air, or you'll become terribly ill. You've been crying for days."

Betsy considered this. It would be an awful thing if she was incapacitated when it came time to dash through Orana, tracking down Ophelia. Besides, her eyes were sore and weary from weeping. Feeling a breeze might do her good. She gave a grave nod, allowing Matthew to lead her to the upper decks of the *Sunshearer*.

The lurching of the ship was far more drastic above. Betsy refused tea, worrying that if anything went into her stomach, she would immediately throw it up. She lingered by the hatch, squinting at her surroundings. Her eyes were not accustomed to the light after several days' journey in the dark. Matthew hovered by her elbow, pestering her with offers of assistance. He was a far more attentive butler than Valois ever was—and also far more annoying.

Sipping tea at a small foldable table with Jakob Whitman was a woman clad in a spectacular pink traveling gown adorned with a sweeping train. If Betsy had been in better spirits, she might have been consumed with sartorial envy at the sight of such a creation. It made the woman look like a fairy queen—but as it was, Betsy had turned emotionless and calculating. Her sharp eyes immediately zeroed in on a ripped stitch in the hem. A scoff jumped involuntarily from her throat, her fingers itching for a needle, to make repairs.

"Who's that woman? In the gown?"

Matthew followed Betsy's line of vision, and Betsy couldn't miss the hunger that flared up in the boy's eyes when they landed on the noblewoman. "Ah, that's Lady Ruza Eden. She's a dowager from Carthay. She paid us a fine fee for passage home. She was vacationing in the String Islands, you see."

Betsy had been so preoccupied by the woman's outfit that she only now noticed how lovely the woman was—how Matthew watched her like she was a piece of delicate china, beautiful to gaze at, but fragile and expensive enough that he dared not touch. Her skin tone was golden, and she had the same thick brown curls as Ophelia, which made sense, as they were common in Carthay—where old rumors had always placed the pirate queen Ophelia Cray's origins. This meant that until Cray's hanging, there had been two "queens" from the coastal province—the grand-queen herself had grown up as a noblewoman of Carthay, until she was selected from among all the continent's elite to rule in the Center City. The two might even be kin. Ruza's styling was grand enough to suggest such consequential status.

"She's pretty," Betsy noted, a curt edge to her voice. "But someone ought to fix that ripped stitch in her hem."

Matthew's head cocked to one side. He was looking at Betsy with sharpened curiosity, as if she were an attraction at a festival. Betsy glared fiercely back at him, willing him to say what he was thinking. That for the first time, and far too late, he was seeing that she had some value. She'd cursed him at that dinner table, and if she were a witch like from the old stories, she would curse him all over again. She wrinkled her nose in determination, waiting for him to respond with an insult or, worse, a demeaning compliment. But as she stared into his pale, pointed face, it began to twitch.

An algae-green color washed over his cheeks, and Matthew's calculating look was lost as it morphed into one of shame and terror. Abandoning Betsy entirely, Matthew lurched across the deck to catapult the contents of his stomach over the rail and into the sea. Something jumped upward from Betsy's stomach too—a booming, nasty laugh. The woman in the pink gown, Lady Ruza, glanced across the deck at the sound. Betsy was frozen in embarrassment for a moment—furious with herself for allowing a fine lady like that to witness her making such an undignified noise—before she composed herself enough to turn and flee back to the darkness of the hatch.

On the sixth day of the voyage, only a single day out from their arrival in Orana, there came a knock at Betsy's door. She tried to ignore it, knowing there was only irritation waiting outside.

When she was below deck, huddled up in her private room and sitting on her cot, Betsy could almost forget that she was at sea at all, and that was how she liked it. She embroidered for distraction, her thread dipping and bobbing through cotton like a dolphin breaching from the waves. It was easier below, where her stomach was far less troubled. When necessity demanded that she go above, she could hardly hold down her meals. And she would not make a fool of herself as Matthew regularly did. The firstborn daughter of Nathaniel Young would not vomit over the rail.

Matthew still came knocking on the door to her private room at least twice a day, and Betsy found him to be both remarkably persistent and remarkably obtuse. It was difficult to turn him away, no matter how brusque she was with him. Then there was the other reason it was difficult to turn him away—no matter how well aware Betsy was of his true nature, there were still brief moments where Matthew's performance strayed toward the convincing. When he could conjure up softness in his tight facial features. When he stumbled upon a line of argument that was tactful, almost human.

The day before, when lurking in her doorway, he'd found the words: "Your father would be so proud of you. I know your mother is."

Betsy very nearly fell for his hollow sentiments in that moment. They'd only just dodged a storm that morning. She was weak, frightened, and nauseous. Words of kindness had been desperately appreciated. She'd almost invited him in, before seeing his satisfied expression. She chose to shut the door on him instead.

It was the insidiousness of his methods that infuriated Betsy most. He always came to her cloaked in the behaviors of a lover. *Won't you share a meal with me, Betsy? How pretty your dress is, Betsy. Tell me your deepest thoughts and fears, perhaps?* But Matthew Whitman had revealed his disdain for her far too early and forcefully for him to convincingly backtrack now. Did he think her so pathetic that she would believe him to have changed his mind about courting her? Did he think this was the way to secure her father's company shares?

The knock came again, and Betsy threw down her embroidery and stumbled off the cot as the boat swayed. "How many times do I have to tell you? I don't want to share a meal, I don't want to talk, and I don't—" She threw open the door.

"If you aren't in the mood for male company, may I offer an alternative?"

Lady Ruza was standing on the other side. She had her face cast downward, hiding a smile. Her arms were outstretched, her beautiful pink gown draped over them.

Betsy gaped up at her, clutching the doorframe to remain upright in her shock.

The lady's curls were piled artfully atop her head today, setting off her swan-thin neck to advantage. She was wearing a grass-green traveling gown that Betsy knew would perfectly match the rolling waves beyond them. She didn't quite know what to do with Ruza standing there. It was one thing to admire a noblewoman from afar—but the String Islands didn't have nobility. They had governors, who answered to the continent's grand-queen herself, but no families with titles. Only ex-criminals' descendants who had made money for themselves, and ex-criminals' descendants who hadn't.

Betsy was completely outclassed. Words and all known forms of societal procedure deserted her. Her tongue felt thick in her mouth.

Luckily, Lady Ruza seemed perfectly content to do the talking for her. "My dress has a ripped stitch," she said, offering out the gown to Betsy. "Now, I don't much care for that obsequious Master Whitman, but he mentioned that you noticed my situation, and that you had the skill to fix it. Might I impose upon you?"

Betsy nodded eagerly, giving a hoarse grunt, and moved to smooth out the blankets on her cot, tucking them in so that they would be stretched tight and flat. She motioned for Lady Ruza to sit on the now immaculate bed.

"I-I think—" Betsy said, accepting the dress from Lady Ruza's arms and marveling at the softness of the material. "I think I have some thread that's the right color in my kit."

In actuality, Betsy didn't *think* she had the right color. She knew. Opening her sewing kit was like staring at a relic of witchcraft—like an enchantress had somehow magicked a rainbow inside a box and trapped it there. Betsy had never yet found a project she wasn't prepared to meet. She pulled at the knob on the wooden box's lid, and the kit unfolded as if greased with butter.

"Oh, how lovely!" Lady Ruza said, peering in at Betsy's collection.

Betsy's fingers trembled as she searched through the box for the correct shade of rose pink to fix the lady's gown. She'd never been watched working before, at least never by someone who wasn't her mother or Ophelia. But she was feeling a rush, a joy, that she hadn't experienced since Papa's death. She was back at what she was good at, what she loved! And she was suddenly desperate for Ruza to see just how good she was. Betsy found the spool she had been looking for and began to examine the hem more closely.

"Do you mind if I wait with you?" Lady Ruza said. "I'm starved for some proper company. That old man doesn't seem to have his mind quite in order, and it takes all my energy not to slap his son. That greedy station climber keeps trying to inquire about my friends in Carthay and if they have need of a merchant contact. He even asked if I know the grand-queen! Can you imagine inquiring such a thing to a mere acquaintance?"

Betsy had to fight to keep her face unchanged, to show no interest in the answer to Matthew's tactless inquiry. Luckily, Ruza did not linger on the topic of royalty, as she was too busy listing Matthew's other failings—which immediately endeared her to Betsy. "And he needs a bath terribly," Ruza continued on. "Have you noticed? He has a bit of dried vomit on his neck that's been there for days."

A hearty *Ha!* rose up from Betsy's belly and exploded outward. Betsy wasn't sure she'd ever made such a loud, undignified sound in her life. Her face grew hot instantly, and she glanced at the lady, trying to cover her mouth and to summon the dreadful cackle back into her body. But the damage was already done. For a split second, Ruza stared at her. Her face blank, her mouth twitching. Then Ruza let out a shriek of laughter herself, clutching at her ribs. Ruza's laugh was even less pretty than Betsy's.

"Stay as long as you want, my lady," Betsy said, grinning broadly.

Ruza shook her head. "You're not a citizen of Carthay. I'm not your lady. Call me Ruza."

Betsy nodded. She pushed the pink thread through the needle. Her fingers weren't shaking anymore. "Alright. Ruza, then." She began to sew.

Ruza leaned against the wood-paneled wall and took Betsy's pillow into her lap. "Now, I have to admit something to you.

Among his other faults, young Mr. Whitman has been . . . indiscreet about your recent loss. That is part of the reason I came to see you. To provide what little solace I can. I understand, you see." She looked down into her lap, her jaw moving wordlessly, like she had to loosen it in order to push the painful words out. "I am newly widowed. And I decided to go traveling as a means of stepping away from that loss. To escape the places that held painful memories and, I suppose, all the friends and family whose good intentions only seem to hurt me more. I gather you're doing something similar?"

Betsy bit down hard on her lower lip, and nodded.

Ruza's eyes grew distant, her smile dazed. "The String Islands have been so lovely. It is a beautiful home you'll return to when you're ready. But I'm not ready myself. I'm avoiding Carthay for as long as I can. I can't wait to see—oh, just everywhere I can."

Betsy had found a rhythm with the needle now. Hot tears trickled down her cheeks, but she didn't brush them away, and Ruza had the manners not to point them out. This would be fast work—but she almost wished it wouldn't be. She liked Ruza. It wasn't just that she resembled Ophelia. Ruza had that same fire in her heart, and it caused Betsy to realize that Ophelia's abandonment of her probably hadn't been a mere whim. Maybe the burning coal in Ophelia's chest—the same as in Ruza's, as in her own when she saw their father's cold body—hadn't just given her wanderlust. It had been her means of escaping a painful trap.

A shout came from the upper deck. Betsy gave a jerky nod of the head. "I never wanted to leave home before. I prefer a safe harbor, generally."

More shouting. Betsy's heart was thumping faster now, irregular. Two thumps, and an offbeat. Three more in quick succession. She felt sick. What was going on up there? She craned her neck to look at the ceiling, as if she might see through it to the commotion above.

Ruza apparently noticed nothing. "Where then," she said, giving a phlegmy laugh, "do you think you'll go from here?"

Betsy laid down her needle. "I don't know."

Ruza laughed. "Well, who does, really?"

"I need to find my sister," Betsy said. "That's all I know. And we still have my mother. Or—I do." For the first time, it dawned on Betsy that Ophelia might consider herself an orphan now. She didn't know if she would. Mama had raised them both with love, but it was only Papa's blood they shared.

An ear-piercing shriek came from above. A high female voice was calling out in desperation. "Please! *Please* help us! Oh gods above, please help us!"

Ruza scrambled off the bed, apparently aware of the problems on deck for the first time. "Come on," she said, shooting Betsy a concerned look. "Let's see what's happening."

Betsy didn't pause to think, or even to place down the pink gown, before following Ruza out of her room and up to the main deck. She threw the lady's gown carelessly over her shoulder and climbed the ladder after her.

TWELVE

For a moment, before Ophelia opened her eyes, she forgot where she was. She might have been curled up in her four-poster bed at home, the sheets wrapped around her crisp with starch—the distant shouting that of drunk festivalgoers out in the street who had risen with the sun.

Then she stretched her arms, yawned, and sat up. She was back below deck, the dim lanterns swaying overhead. Her uniform was scratchy, stiffened from being drenched with salt water. Sunlight streamed in from the hatch, and noise rumbled from above.

They had made it through the storm.

Ophelia had never been so sore in her life—not even after Ames lashed her. She moaned, looking around to find that almost every crew member was gone, with only a few other sailors snoring on top of their mats. Joints aching, she stood up and slowly made her way up the ladder.

The full force of the sunlight was blinding. At first, all that

Ophelia could make out was the crowd of sailors huddled at center deck, which was still swampy with water from the storm. She
started to nudge her way toward the mainmast, and even before
she got to the front, she heard a hoarse voice calling out to her.
"Lucky Teeth, stay back!"

Edgar and the other officers in their fine blue jackets had been
tethered to the mainmast with long, thick ropes. They weren't
tied as Ophelia had been for her whipping, but face-forward, their
hands bound in front of their crotches. There—directly between
Edgar and a stocky, pimply-faced officer named Lawrence—was
Captain Hale. He was unconscious, his head dropping forward so
that his bearded chin slumped against his chest.

Ophelia looked around at her crewmates in horror. They were
rip-roaring drunk, almost to a man. Fitz was not far from her,
one of the few unrestrained people on deck not swimming in
drink. He shot her a worried look; his nose, broken and purpled
from his fall from the mast, was a vivid reminder of the previous
evening's pains.

Ronan stood triumphant, holding aloft another bottle of
stolen whiskey, the captain's tri-tipped hat covering his bald head.
Across the way, she saw Jo and Emily, white-faced and also dead
sober, clutching at each other. "What's—"Ophelia asked the
general crowd, "what's going on here?"

The response from the people beside her rang out in eerie
chorus: "Mutiny!"

Ophelia's stomach revolted, knowing what fate would befall
her as a mutineer. How could she ever return to Peu Jolie, or
her family again, if the first ship she ever boarded immediately

succumbed to mutiny? She would be blamed for inciting it, like her mother before her. No, Ophelia thought, grinding her teeth together, the curse will not do her in this easily.

"Ronan, come on now, old boy!" Edgar cried out. "We're friends, aren't we? Let's settle this like gentlemen. No need for further violence."

Ophelia wasn't sure what Edgar meant by *further* violence, although she supposed it would have taken significant force to round up the officers this way.

"You might be a gentleman, Ludlow," Ronan said, tipping his hat gracefully at Edgar. "But I'm not."

"Hey!" Ophelia shouted, stepping forward. "Let's at least be civil, as it befits men and women of the Imperial Navy." She reached out to untie Edgar's restraints but was met with a roar of objection from the forty or so crew members assembled on the deck.

"Don't touch that boy," Ronan said. "They're all tied up for a reason."

"And what reason is that?" Ophelia shot back.

Ronan spread out his arms wide, telling Ophelia to look around her. At the exhausted crew, at the flooded deck, at the masts stripped of their sails. "The officers put our lives in danger when they decided to sail into that storm." Ronan spat on the deck, and his saliva quickly melted into the rainwater. "They don't give a shit about our lives, or our safety. So why should we care about theirs?"

Applause and approving shouts from the crew. Ophelia's shoulders tightened, and a chill sank inch-deep into her skin.

Her voice shook with anger. "Two days ago, Edgar was your friend. He drank with you. You told me that crew members stick together. And these other officers don't have anything to do with us running into that storm! Ames made that choice." Ophelia glanced over at the men tied to the mast. The first mate was conspicuously absent. "Where . . . where is Ames, anyway?"

"Gone," Emily cried out. Her voice was trembling, but her eyes were sharp and accusatory. "She's been missing since the storm." Her gaze lingered on Ronan's back.

"What do you mean, she's missing?"

Ronan rolled his gigantic shoulders, unconcerned. His voice became a drawl. "Sometimes, in a storm, someone goes over the side."

"So," Ophelia said, her eyebrows furrowing, "did anyone see Ames fall over the rail? Or are we just assuming—"

"Look!" Ronan growled, cutting Ophelia off. He started pacing the deck, his teeth bared like a feral animal. He gestured gruffly at the rest of the crew. "The point is, she went over. Don't matter if no one saw it. She's *dead.* Gone. And do we miss her?"

The crew's reply came in thundering unison. "NO!"

Ronan threw back his head and laughed. "And with Ames gone, it's not like we're gonna let Hale stay captain. He'd run us aground within a week. Nor should one of these useless rich boys be captain just because their fathers bought 'em a post and a rutting blue jacket. One of us should be in charge now. Someone who knows how this rig ought to run." Ronan flashed Ophelia a grin that only lifted one side of his mouth. "Someone like me."

Ophelia's whole body ached from the previous night's fall,

and the sun was beating down mercilessly on the back of her neck. But she wasn't going to let this go—no matter how badly she felt. This wasn't right.

She was about to launch into a tirade—*"What about honor? What about our responsibilities? What about the chain of command?"*—but Edgar got there first.

He strained against his ropes, calling out, "We don't need to descend into chaos like this, friends! We were trained to protect the seas from pirate scum, not become pirates ourselves. Look, Ronan, if we need to settle this with violence, don't take it out on the other officers. Let's behave like men of honor. Untie me, and we'll duel for the captain's hat."

Ronan burst out laughing. "Interesting offer, Ludlow. Suppose a rich boy like you has been itching for action all your life. But a real duel isn't like in the stories. There's no glory. It's just six shots, and my lead in your brain."

Ophelia, frozen halfway between the mainmast and the crew, suddenly realized that Captain Hale, limp and unmoving, wasn't just unconscious from the drink. He wasn't breathing.

Silently, she drew closer to the mast, reaching out toward Hale.

"Don't," Edgar urged her, briefly distracted from Ronan's threats. "Lucky Teeth, stay back."

Ophelia pushed on Captain's Hale's waxy forehead, lifting his head upward until it rested against the mast. With his head up, his beard no longer obscured his injury. His throat had been cut to the bone.

Click.

Without thinking, Ophelia had drawn her pistol, aiming it at Ronan's chest. A shiver ran through the crowd.

Ophelia advanced on Ronan, her words hissing like air out of cracked ice. "Did you murder this man?"

Ronan put his hands halfway in the air, a mocking surrender. He was so large. Ophelia wasn't sure a bullet would immediately take him down. "Think about what you're doing, lassie. I've shown you the nice side o' me. You don't want the ugly."

"The whole of you is ugly," Ophelia snapped. "Now let me rephrase the question. Did you murder this man and *then immediately ransack his office for booze?* Have you no shame?"

The crew members were sidling slowly backward, away from Ophelia's drawn weapon.

Ronan's laugh was unexpectedly soft. A tickle against satin. "I call that a challenge where I come from, you bilge rat gilly-bitch. But it can't be a challenge—you oughta have heard the gossip by now 'bout what happens to people who challenge me. Isn't Ludlow here always whisperin' in your ear?"

Ophelia let her eyes drift up from Ronan's boots to the rope-like scar across his bald head. She bared her teeth, running her tongue across them. Her hand tightened on her gun. "I have heard the rumors," she admitted. "But you'll find I never back down from a challenge. Not when there's so much at stake."

Ronan gave a belly laugh. "And what's at stake?"

"Your honor or your neck," Ophelia said. "Take your pick."

Ronan's fingers twitched. "Enough words. Why don't you take pretty boy's spot in the fight?" His arm snapped behind him, and he'd drawn a gun of his own. "Duel me. Winner gets the captain's hat. Loser has their corpse thrown in the waves."

Edgar was trying to rip free from his ropes again, protesting. "No, listen to me—I'll handle this."

"Fine," Ophelia said, her eyes narrow and locked on Ronan. "I accept your challenge. But you'd best untie Edgar now. He's my second."

Ronan nodded, gesturing for one of his friends, a burly man called Clovis with black hair and narrow eyes, to join him as his own second. He gave the order to the crew. "Make some room!" Ronan's eyes danced with malicious delight. Ophelia knew that he had only accepted her challenge because he was so certain she didn't have a chance.

Jo came forward with a knife so large it could only be rightly called a saw, and began to cut through Edgar's ropes. "Listen to me now, girl," she hissed to Ophelia under her breath. "Don't be stupid. Stay far back and let him win without getting yourself killed. Honor isn't worth shit if you're dead."

Edgar's ropes fell to the ground, and he tried to shake out the stiffness in his muscles. He reached for the pistol at his waist. "I'm a real crack shot. Waive your right to the duel—I'll take your place."

Ophelia shook her head. "Sorry, Edgar. It might not be worth shit, but my honor's all I have. Just back me up, alright?" Jo shot her a worried, bloodshot glare, but Ophelia held her gaze. "And I'd rather be dead than a pirate."

"Hey!" Ronan shouted. "Are we at a duel or a tea party? Stop jabbering and get on with it."

Ophelia cracked her knuckles and went to stand back-to-back with Ronan.

As their seconds counted off time for them to begin the twenty paces, Ronan muttered threats under his breath. "I'm gonna blast your pretty little head open."

Ophelia merely smiled a smile he couldn't see.

She took twenty steps from Ronan's back, then spun around, pistol raised.

Edgar stood a few feet behind her, whispering advice. "Ronan's an alright shot, but you're tiny, and he's a big bloke. A shot of yours from far away might hit him. He's a wide enough target that Jo's quite right. Don't get close enough to him to cede your size advantage."

Ophelia could hardly hear him. The sound of the whole world had been dulled. Edgar's advice didn't matter. There was no one, nothing that meant anything except for her and her pistol, and Ronan and his.

Ronan has to fire first. That was the one thing Ophelia could concentrate on. She knew he wouldn't let her down.

Her moment of silence was ended by an echoing bang, as a burst of smoke and flame issued from Ronan's barrel. Ophelia stood stock-still as the bullet whizzed past her. Ronan's aim had only been off by inches. Someone in the crowd whistled with appreciation for the shot.

Ophelia took a moment to collect herself, to breathe deep. Her eye tracked the journey she wanted her bullet to make—to bury itself in the center of Ronan's meaty chest.

She fired.

No sound came. No smoke.

Her eyes widened in horror. A cackle of laughter floated over from the crowd. Ophelia's gun had misfired.

Ronan was laughing too. "Tough luck, that. You're still owed all three bullets, but you lose your turn to fire. You'll be dead before you get the chance to use 'em."

He shot again.

This time, Ophelia didn't register the flash or the smoke at all. A searing pain erupted at the top of her skull, a little right of center. Her ears rang like an off-key band at an execution, and hot blood trickled down her forehead.

Ophelia wasn't aware that she had begun to stumble backward until Edgar, who had caught her, heaved her to her feet. "You're okay, you're okay," he whispered. "It's just a graze. It'll be a hell of a lot worse if Clovis over there decides to blast you for leaving your mark. Gotta stand up, Lucky Teeth."

Ophelia steadied herself. She knew the ship was anchored, but she still felt it lurching.

Yet—she was alive. A dangerous overconfidence burned at her throat, a sensation not unlike gulping down whiskey. She took a step forward. Then another.

"What do you think you're doing?" Jo wailed from behind her.

"Lucky Teeth, cut it!"

But Ophelia kept walking ahead, unsteadily at first, and then with a rigid, tin-soldier stiffness. No retreat. No surrender. Her father had told her not to get shot. Her mother had told her there was power in her force of will. She was going to win. She willed it so.

Ronan, whose hulking body loomed closer with each step, squinted down at Ophelia like she was positively mad. "You're coming that close to me with a misfiring gun? One more bit of bad luck for you, girl, and I can put my gun straight to your forehead!"

Ophelia smiled wickedly. Bad luck, he said? What could bad luck do to her? She was the Curse. She brought the bad luck with her.

She was less than a foot from Ronan now. She raised her gun and stuck it in the soft flesh of his neck. Cocked it. "So this isn't against the rules? Lovely. Because it's my turn to shoot."

Ronan's response was soft, breathy. "*Rut* that."

He jabbed his gun into her stomach, and pulled the trigger.

Nothing happened.

Ophelia made a clucking sound with her tongue, smiling sweetly up at the large man. "Misfire, perhaps? Bad luck."

Panicked now, Ronan pulled the trigger again, and again, but each time, no bullet came.

"Or perhaps, worse luck even than that," Ophelia crooned. "Perhaps you don't have a third bullet in the chamber? Perhaps when I saw you pursuing Ames last night, you weren't going to assist her, but rather to shoot her point-blank and shove her body in the ocean. Maybe you were too busy cutting Hale's throat and getting drunk on his whiskey to remember to reload. Pity." Ophelia pushed the nose of her pistol a little harder against Ronan's throat. "Looks like I've got plenty of time for my next shot."

Ronan screwed his eyes shut, and a tear leaked unwillingly from the left. "You win. Just do it and get it over with."

"Aye-aye, mutineer," Ophelia crooned. "I will get this insubordination over with."

Faster than an island snake could strike, she dropped her gun-wielding arm from his neck and shot him in the knee.

Ronan howled and dropped to the deck, clutching the bloody mess that had formerly been his knee joint. Ophelia plucked the captain's hat off his head, sticking it on her own. Her ears still rang horribly. She didn't waste time watching Ronan squirm. She turned to the crew, which was struck with an appreciative silence. Even Clovis, the second, had lowered his gun. His sinewy muscles were relaxed, and he wore the calm look of a man who considered an argument well settled.

"There will be no more talk of mutiny," Ophelia announced. "We are a naval ship of the grand-queen's navy and we will continue to act as such. We will protect the seas from criminals of all stripes, and that includes disloyal sailors. The next crewman who suggests abandoning our responsibilities will be strung up and hanged from the mast. Ronan's knee was my last speck of mercy on that front. Am I understood?"

Ophelia's words were met with a mumbled chorus of "Aye-aye."

Emily broke free of the crowd and grabbed Ophelia's arm. "We need to clean that graze."

Ophelia pulled away. She wasn't done talking. "Someone cut the officers loose now. No harm is to come to them. They're to do their jobs, like everyone else. And if anyone is thinking that I'm not meant to be in charge, that you maybe want to challenge me, like Ronan did? Well, I can't wish you good luck. Because luck won't get you shit, you know?"

A smattering of whistles and grudging applause greeted her

statement. "You have work to do," Ophelia said. "Let's get this ship moving and back on course. Any questions? Direct them to Ludlow. He's my first mate." Finally satisfied, Ophelia let Emily lead her into the captain's quarters. Jo followed, as did Edgar, who was casting her a glowing look.

The air inside Captain Hale's cabin—*her* cabin now—stank of dried vomit. Emily sat Ophelia down on the bench behind the captain's desk and hurried away to fetch medical supplies. In the brief minutes she was gone, Jo nosed about in the captain's belongings, cackling as she produced yet another bottle of whiskey from beneath the cot. "Give me that," Emily snapped as she reentered, and Jo promptly handed the bottle over, looking besotted.

"You did a damn stupid thing with that duel. This'll sting a bit," Emily told Ophelia as she took off the captain's hat and pressed a bit of whiskey-soaked rag against the shallow, line-like wound on her skull. "And even though you won, you shouldn't take away the lesson that this was even a *decent* idea."

Ophelia wore a sleepy smile. "Sorry to have worried you."

Emily smacked the back of Ophelia's head, taking care not to hit the part that was wounded. "Don't be smart."

Jo took a long drink from the whiskey bottle and wiped her mouth with her forearm. "And don't think this captain thing will last longer than the next port. You might get a promotion, sure, for keeping this boat from mutiny, but you won't leapfrog all the way to captain. Enjoy being lord of the castle now, because the best position you can hope to get from this is midshipman." Jo gave a hollow laugh. "Imagine, risking your life, and you'll only end up Ludlow's equal. It's hard for merit to rise above petty cash."

Edgar's eyes narrowed. "Hold on, there, Josephine. I don't imagine I'll be staying midshipman. Lucky Teeth and I just quashed a mutiny and all. We're bound to be rewarded."

Jo cackled, pointing to Ophelia. "Even worse! You might have just gotten shot to secure *Ludlow* a promotion to captain. Those stiffs in the naval offices certainly won't promote a bilge rat like you over him when they come down to making a decision. The irony! You should have let him fight the duel!"

"Oh, be quiet," Emily admonished Jo. "She doesn't need to hear that right now." Emily tucked a loop of gauze beneath Ophelia's hair, and tied it tightly at the top of her head in order to keep pressure on the scrape. Ophelia glanced at the small tarnished mirror in the corner of the cabin. A laugh bubbled from her mouth. As dizzy and as tired as she felt, she looked more like a girl wearing a headband to a party than one who'd just walked straight into the barrel of a gun.

Emily gave Ophelia's hair an affectionate stroke, saying, "You rest a bit. Jo and I will grab your things from below."

Jo grudgingly put down the whiskey and followed Emily out the door, smacking her lover on the ass as she went. Seeing this, Edgar laughed out loud. "Now *they've* got the right idea of things." He slid onto the bench beside Ophelia. He reached up to adjust her gauze headwear, grinning. "How you feeling?"

Ophelia shrugged. "Alright, I guess. Could have had a bullet in my skull, but I don't. Suppose I can't complain."

Edgar's smile only got wider. He pushed his fingers through

his hair, slicking it back. "See, I knew you were lucky. First minute I saw you. And look what a team we've made. You, the captain. Me, first mate. And if Jo's right, and the navy ends up making me captain for good and all—I promise you I'll return the favor. I want you to be my second."

Ophelia snorted, not making eye contact. "First we have to worry about getting this ship back en route to a port."

Edgar stood up from the bench, making it shake. He started pacing the room, restless with happy energy. "Come on! Get some perspective!" He kicked at the air in triumph. "We've got to be—what?—the youngest captain and first mate on the Emerald Sea? That calls for at least a moment of celebration. Take a second to enjoy it!"

Ophelia leaned her cheek against her hand, laughing in spite of herself. "Interim captain and first mate."

Edgar gave a loose-shouldered shrug. "Close enough! Soon to be made official, and more than enough to rub my brother's *stupid face* in it when I write my next letter home!"

"You have a brother?" Ophelia asked.

Edgar came to a sudden stop, fixing a weary look on her. "A real trial of a brother. Older. Our father owns a hotel, and Teddy's the one inheriting it. Never lets me forget it. Convinced dear old Dad I was too much of a screwup to keep around, so he bought me a mid-level appointment with the navy and sent me out to sea where I couldn't bother anyone." His grin slowly returned, his eyes lighting up like a hearth fire that had just been stoked. "Wait until they hear."

He rejoined Ophelia on the bench. Her hands tingled as she

let Edgar's words soak in—realizing what it would mean to go back to Peu Jolie and tell them all that they were wrong. That she was a hero.

"You're smiling," Edgar said. "Not even hiding the teeth this time."

Ophelia clenched her hands together, willing that pleasant buzz to stop. "I suppose I am. But I need to keep calm, right? That's the only way to do this thing properly. Still, I'm thinking . . . yes. My first visit home will be *different* because of this." The roaring of a crowd on the Port Jolie docks filled her ears— maybe when she came back, they would cheer for her like they cheered for Lang that day on the gallows.

But these far-fetched daydreams embarrassed even Ophelia herself. She ducked her head, suddenly becoming very interested in the grains of the wooden desk. "They . . . don't exactly like me there."

"No kidding," Edgar laughed. "Ophelia Cray's daughter can't be a popular figure."

Ophelia gave a start. "You knew?"

Edgar moved closer to her, wrapping an arm around her shoulders. "Of course I knew. You're not exactly a skilled liar. But I don't care. Why should I? Family doesn't mean anything. If you ask my family, I'm a complete waste of space and resources. They'd prefer I didn't share their blood at all, so why should I care about yours?"

Ophelia couldn't bring herself to meet Edgar's eyes. "Thank you," she said.

"No trouble."

Ophelia quickly searched for a way to turn the conversation, preferring not to linger in emotion. "So, your family was that bad, huh?" She finally looked into Edgar's face, and found a storm brewing behind his eyes.

"They denied me my basic dignity," he said, voice thick. "You ever feel that way?"

A harsh laugh echoed from Ophelia's throat. Had she ever felt denied of dignity? She remembered how the crowd had looked at her the day her mother was hanged. Like she wasn't a person. She thought of how they laughed behind her back, poking and prodding her on the streets.

"Yes," she said. "I've felt that. No one's ever thought I was different from her. No one." Ophelia wasn't even sure if, deep down, Betsy had ever thought she was different from her mother. And Betsy had always been the person she could count on, no matter what. "Even my mother thought I was meant to become like her."

The room swam in front of her, and perhaps it was the blood loss or the head trauma, but Ophelia could have sworn she was standing at the foot of the gallows again. Her voice was hard. "That's why she gave me the necklace. And the note." She felt like she was choking. "I should just throw them into the sea. Maybe that would prove something."

Edgar's eyes gleamed. His face was very near hers now. "Chin up. You don't have to prove anything to me. It's they who are backward. But we're gonna show them they're all wrong, aren't we? Prove we're different than they thought. That you're a right little hero. That I was worth something from the beginning.

We'll be the team that cleanses the Emerald Sea of every last pirate. Make those bastards afraid to sail the waters we tread. That'll teach everyone what we're made of."

Ophelia nodded, smiling. She liked that proposition.

Then—her joy gone, all at once. Edgar had dipped his face closer to her own, pressing his mouth against hers, his hand gently cupping her chin.

She pulled away. "I'm sorry . . . but I'm just not interested in you like that. We're friends. That's all."

Edgar blinked. He seemed politely puzzled. "I thought we got on well enough. What is it, then? You're a woman-lover, like Jo and Em? I might have known. What other kind of girl goes to sea when she's rich as you?" He seemed completely baffled that someone could be disinterested in him for any other reason. But she had told him time and time again that she didn't like to be touched.

"No," Ophelia said, heat rising in her cheeks that she was glad he couldn't see. "I'm not. I'm a nothing lover, and I'd like to keep it that way."

Edgar hurriedly made to stand up, turning his face away so she couldn't gauge his expression. Ophelia was baffled that he could accept the pirate blood in her but be so ruffled over something as foolish as kissing. When Edgar spoke, his voice was sown with bitterness. "Aye-aye, *Captain*."

"Don't be angry," Ophelia said as he made for the door.

Edgar turned back around, his usual easy smile slightly wooden. "Who could ever be angry at you, Lucky Teeth?"

THIRTEEN

When they hit sunlight, it became immediately clear that something was terribly wrong. The crewmen—usually hustling around, attending to duties Betsy didn't understand—were standing stock-still on the deck, staring out across the water. Their silence terrified Betsy above all, and her heart began to race even faster as she followed their line of sight.

Not far away, no more than three hundred yards, Betsy spotted a shabby-looking ship. It was obviously very old and had recently sustained damage. Its mainsail bore a large, ominous-looking rip down its center. The name of the ship was painted on the rail of the hull in gold lettering, but it had mostly peeled away, and Betsy couldn't make it out, beyond the fact that it had been two words.

The ship was moored along the edge of a tiny lump of sand. It would have properly been called an island, but Betsy thought that was being generous. There wasn't even a tree on it.

"Help us! Help us, please! We were hit by a storm! We've run aground on a sandbar!"

Now Betsy saw who was shouting. A thin woman, the only person standing on the deserted deck. She was dressed entirely in white, with flowing petticoats and a flowered hat with a wide brim. Betsy moved toward the rail and squinted at her. Even from a distance, she seemed like a well-off lady. Betsy saw a string of pearls clasped around her neck.

The woman had very pale white skin, which made her almost appear sick. The only color on her at all was the shock of vivid red hair beneath her hat.

Matthew materialized from the crowd to stand at Betsy's side. He cried out to the woman. "Fear not, madam! We're coming to help you!"

The woman fell to her knees on the deck, clutching at her chest. "Bless you, bless you!"

Betsy felt a strange prickle on her skin. A warning, something about this redheaded lady was *wrong*, somehow. She shouted out across the water. "Are there other survivors?"

There was a brief moment of silence as the woman considered this. She offered up the response, "Perhaps one or two!"

Matthew made to turn and address the captain at the wheel. "Maneuver to assist, sir!"

Betsy seized Matthew by his forearm and whirled him back around. "Hold on. I'm not sure about this. Why doesn't she know the number of survivors? How is the mainsail torn, but so little other damage? This seems . . . s-suspicious."

Matthew rolled his eyes, and his glasses flashed in the midday sun. His smile was predatory. Gone was the meek facade he had worn when he attempted apology. "Oh, it's su-su-su-suspicious, is it?" He shook Betsy off him. "Don't let your woman's timidity stop us from saving this sweet young lady—and her compatriots, of course."

The *Sunshearer* began to swing slowly ever closer to the damaged ship, coming to draw in near to the other ship's rail. Five of the crewman rushed over to tie the two rails together. They leaped over to the foreign deck, where the redheaded lady was waiting. Her hands were clasped to her heart, with a sweet, close-mouthed smile stretching across her pale face. "My heroes!" she cried out. Then she pointed at the hatch to the lower decks. "You must go down there, and bring the other survivors up. They are weak from hunger, and can hardly stand, and I'm afraid"—here, the woman gave a girlish laugh, one that Betsy thought was patently absurd for the situation—"I'm just not strong enough to bring them up myself."

The crewmen at the woman's side hastened to follow her instructions and go below. Beside Betsy, Ruza's entire body had tensed. She called out to the redhead. "And how is that you are not equally weak from hunger?"

The woman's head snapped in the direction of the question, and her eyes widened when they landed on Ruza. She dropped into a curtsy, and said in a lazy drawl, "I see I'm meeting a member of the nobility. But of course, the men were so chivalrous. They made sure to give me enough to eat as the supplies waned, wanting to give me the best chance of survival." She reached up to wipe a tear from the corner of her eye with her index finger, which bore a nail as long and sharp as a claw.

The men of the crew were enraptured with the woman,

Matthew most of all. He shot out his hand to beckon the lady over onto the safety of their own ship. The lady graciously accepted Matthew's help to climb over the rail. Betsy thought she saw Matthew's hand, first on the woman's back, slip below her waist, but the woman apparently didn't notice. She threw her arms around Matthew's neck, embracing him tightly.

A pistol shot split the air. Betsy shrieked, and stumbled backward, only not falling flat on her behind because Ruza seized her arms to steady her.

There was a second shot, then three more in quick succession. Now Betsy could track where they had come from—only slightly muffled by the wooden hatch of the foreign ship.

Their own crew flew into outrage and panic, reaching for their swords and pistols.

The woman, still half embracing Matthew, twisted around him, at his back now with her elbow tightening across his throat. She reached down the front of her dress and withdrew a pistol. Its copper barrel glinted menacingly in the sun. She raised her gun for it to rest on Matthew's temple, and her delicate smile opened wide to reveal a mouthful of rotten teeth.

"I wouldn't make any sudden moves if I were you," she said, her voice still honeyed, but sharpened to a point. Their crew froze, unsure of what to do as their employer's son whimpered, his eyes tilting up to get a look at the gun.

Betsy was torn between the desire to vomit and the desire to cry out in exultation, "I told you, didn't I?"

The other ship's hatch was thrown open with a bang, and a flood of unfamiliar bodies swarmed out, all laughing and brandishing deadly weapons of their own. Ruza shrieked, turning to grab Betsy's hand.

Pirates.

Betsy knew their crewmen were dead. Bleeding on the floor, in the dark lower quarters of the other ship, probably each with a matching hole in his forehead. Ruza seemed about to faint, taking repeated shallow breaths. Betsy stroked her hair comfortingly and was shocked to see how steady her hand was.

A tall white man in a purple silk jacket emerged at the head of the swarm, swaggering out to push himself over to the deck of the *Sunshearer*. Even before he went to wrap his arms around the redhead's waist—creating a perverse train of embraces between himself, the woman, and Matthew—Betsy recognized him. The heavy jaw, the neat hair, the cracked front tooth. "Jack Copeland!" she gasped.

"Nice job, Fi," Copeland growled, slowly lifting the fashionable hat from the woman's head and giving her auburn hair a long, lingering kiss. He withdrew from her, one hand in the pocket of his luxurious jacket, the other turning a pistol over and over in his palm. He wandered, unconcerned, into the center of the deck, as his pet criminals all clambered over to join him, pistols raised and trained on the various members of the *Sunshearer*'s crew.

"I'm Jack Copeland," the pirate announced. "The Violent Bastard of Peu Ankirk. You may have heard of me." He threw his head back, giving a raspy laugh, and pointed a finger in Betsy's direction. "This lass sure has."

All the blood rushed out of Betsy's face, maybe out of her

body, because she was suddenly very cold from head to toe. She immediately shoved Ruza away from her, and away from the blaming direction of Copeland's pointer finger. How stupid she had been to cry out.

Jack Copeland surveyed Betsy with something approaching interest. "Tell me girlie. I'm handsomer in person than in the drawings, aren't I?"

Betsy squeaked, wrapping her arms tightly around herself. She sure hoped the question was meant to be rhetorical.

Now that their crew had joined them aboard, the red-head—Fiona Wall, the Temptress of the Red-Flame Hair, Betsy realized—pushed Matthew away from her, letting him land with a pathetic thump, face-first on the deck.

Fiona went to join her lover at the deck's center, drawing in close. "It's a trick question," she simpered. She was not yet looking at Betsy, far too occupied with making her fingers dance against the side of Copeland's neck. "If you say he's not handsome, he shoots you in the head. If you say he is, I shoot. I'm the jealous type." Then she lifted her head to grin at Betsy, and a strange, shrewd expression crossed her face. "You look awfully familiar," she said. "Have we met?"

Betsy shook her head so quickly and emphatically that she almost got a crick in her neck.

Fiona snorted. "Well, don't *lie*. That's very rude." She waved her gun dismissively at Betsy. "No, no, no, no, it's probably just that all colony girls look the same."

Jack was growing bored with Betsy. He stretched out his arms wide, turning to face the *Sunshearer*'s crew. "Who's the man in charge? Bring him to me. The faster you hop-to, the less bloody your deaths will be. I almost promise."

The captain stepped forward, his face stony and resigned. "That's me. I'm the captain. I'm the one responsible for this vessel."

"Good looking out," Jack said, training his gun on the captain's head. "Very honorable. I respect that. I always kill the person in charge first, you know. It's—what do you call it?—demoralizing. But at least you go quick."

Fiona reached out to squeeze Jack's shoulder. "Hold up, darling. If the captain's in charge"—she jerked her gun back at Matthew, who was still on the ground, apparently too afraid to move from the position he'd fallen into—"then why was this little stick insect giving him orders? He was the one who told the captain to maneuver in."

Again, Jack threw back his head and laughed. "Good catch, Fi." He moved to where Matthew had fallen quick as a flash, and brought his boot down on Matthew's right hand with a painful-sounding *crunch*. Matthew cried out as the bones in his hand snapped.

Now Jack's pistol was cocked toward Matthew. "So, are you the merchant, little man?"

The captain tried to run forward again, but was restrained by several snarling pirates. "No! He's just an apprentice. My employer's son. I'm the one you want to kill."

Jack's head swiveled back to the captain, his dark eyes alight. "Well, if he's the apprentice . . . where's the master?"

It was quickly sussed out that Jakob Whitman, not feeling well, had stayed in bed that day. He had been a little feverish, and had probably not heard the commotion above at all. Copeland sent two of his men to drag Mr. Whitman upstairs. Betsy felt a cold hand close around her heart. She heard the old man's confused shouts from below as he was woken and torn from his bed.

Ruza let out a sob, but it went unnoticed by anyone but Betsy, who dragged Ruza's mouth into the fabric of the gown still slung across her shoulder, muffling her sounds of fear before she drew the pirates' attention. Tears threatened to choke Betsy too, but she had experience being tormented by tears that would be embarrassing or inconvenient to shed, and she was able to hold them back.

Jakob Whitman emerged from below, his feet barely skimming the ground as the two burly pirates hauled him out and threw him bodily onto the deck before Jack Copeland.

Copeland grinned, lowering himself to crouch at the old man's level. "What's your name there, grandfather?"

Jakob Whitman's face was glazed with sweat. His eyes were darting around in their sockets as he tried to make some sense of the chaotic scene surrounding him. He looked thinner than the last time Betsy had seen him. Apparently sailing no longer agreed with his health.

Jakob muttered his name, and Copeland began to crow. "Now, that's the name of a man in charge! I've heard of you, now! One of the richest merchants in Cornwallis. But that's the thing about money—you can't take it with you."

Copeland stood, his gun still only inches from Jakob Whitman's face, and fired. Betsy had shut her eyes when Copeland's finger twitched, but that didn't stop her from seeing the mess left behind when she opened them again—so much brain and blood splattered across the deck.

Betsy couldn't keep her tears back anymore. Her knees gave out and she fell, Ruza falling with her. Across the way, Matthew vomited and began crying out in incomprehensible anguish.

Jack clapped his hand on Fiona's shoulder, and she wriggled closer to him, giggling again. He tweaked Fiona on her delicate nose, and said, "Well, that was good fun—who's next?"

Fiona gave this question serious thought, letting out a long *hmmm* sound while twirling at the string of pearls around her neck. Except, they didn't look so much like pearls up close. Betsy squinted at the irregular shapes of the polished, white decorations on Fiona's necklace. All the air was sucked from her lungs as Betsy realized the truth: Fiona Wall's necklace was strung with human teeth.

"I know what we should do," Fiona said, dropping her necklace so that it bounced against her bodice. She slapped playfully at Jack's chest. "Let's do it all at once. Slaughter everyone in a uniform. I love the chaos when they realize they're all gonna die at the same time."

Jack, obviously delighted by Fiona's suggestion, seized the sides of her head and kissed her deeply. Their lips parted with a distinct smacking sound, and Copeland waved an arm lazily at his crew. "You heard her, boys. Everyone in a uniform."

There was hardly a moment between the order and its execution. Betsy, still on her knees, dropped down to lie flat on the deck. Her cheek against the wood grain, Betsy opened her mouth to scream but no sound emerged—or perhaps the explosions of gunfire all across the deck covered her scream so completely that she herself couldn't hear it.

Every pirate emptied their gun into a member of the *Sunshearer*'s crew. The shots went on for an eternity. Betsy smelled ammonia first before realizing the smell was coming from the hot liquid trickling between her thighs. Next to her, Ruza was muttering and crying.

When the symphony of death ended, only Betsy, Ruza, and Matthew were left breathing, and the deck was awash with blood.

"Stand up," Fiona ordered, kicking her cream-colored boot at Ruza's shoulder. She glared down at Betsy. "And you as well. Let me get a look at those teeth."

Ruza's entire body shook with noiseless, convulsive sobs. She staggered to her feet, tripping over the hem of her dress. Fiona seized Ruza by the neck, her clawed thumb prying the lady's mouth open as she examined her teeth. "Good collection," Fiona sneered. "Pretty. Shiny. I bet nobles have the money to treat their teeth right, don't they?"

Ruza, her eyes closed, her mouth trembling, nodded. This was a mistake. Fiona struck like a snake, slapping Ruza across the face so hard that she stumbled back several paces. "Do you think you're better than me?" Fiona asked, laughing wildly. "You're not. And I'll prove you're not when I rip every one of those pretty little pearls out by the root. You hear what I'm saying, m'lady?"

Laughter burst out all around them as the pirate crew gave Fiona a round of applause. Ruza clapped her hands over her mouth, falling to the ground again. Fiona ignored Ruza, stepping past her toward Betsy.

Betsy opened her mouth immediately, not wanting to give Fiona any reason to bring her sharp fingernails close to her face. Fiona smirked in approval as she caught sight of Betsy's rather large front teeth. "Has anyone ever told you you've got rabbit teeth, bitch?" Fiona raised her middle and index fingers up to her lips and wiggled them mockingly. "They're so big they could crack a spoon in half. What's your name, Rabbit?"

"E-Elizabeth Young." Fiona's grin deepened in its wickedness, as if Betsy's stutter had revealed another weakness in her character, beyond her plainness and cowardice. But she did not speak her insight aloud. Fiona simply reached toward her. Betsy winced, but no strike came. Instead, Fiona had seized the pink gown—wet with Ruza's tears—and pulled it from Betsy's shoulder. It slithered off her like a snake. "Isn't this pretty?" she said, holding up the dress in front of her and turning to model it for Jack. "I want it."

"I'll get you a hundred pretty dresses, love," Jack said, drawing close to her for another kiss. "But this one's a bit too big on you."

Fiona pouted, pushing him away. "But I *want* it."

Betsy, who had still had her eyes lowered, snapped into a straight posture. She didn't know why she said it, but she said it even so: "I can fix that for you."

Fiona spun back around toward Betsy, her eyes hungry, but wary. "Is that right?"

Betsy nodded. "Y-yes. I make dresses for my mother and sister all the time. I was just fixing this one for her." Betsy gestured down at Ruza. "I could tailor it for you. You've—" Betsy paused, not knowing if her next statement would be the right tactic, but barreled on anyway. "You've got the perfect waist for dresses like this."

Fiona preened, clearly flattered. "I'm intrigued," she said, swanning forward to come close to Betsy. "And you're good at this?"

Betsy licked her lips. "I'm *great* at this. I could make you other dresses too. Ones even prettier. You could pick out the materials. Colors. Patterns. Tell me what you want. I'll make you the best-dressed woman on the Emerald Sea."

Fiona took Betsy by the hands and squeezed. She laughed airily. "How fun! I'll keep you as a little pet. But you know, one wrong move, one prick with a needle—and *boop!*" Fiona tapped Betsy on the forehead. "You'll get a bullet. Right between the eyes."

Betsy nodded, blinking to keep her eyes from watering.

Fiona drifted back toward Ruza, reaching into the front of her dress once again and pulling out a set of pliers. Even with her heart racing and the world spinning around her, Betsy had to admire the sturdy construction of Fiona's corset, that she could hide so many metal objects down there without them being visible.

Fiona pinched the handles of her pliers, and they clinked rhythmically as they inched closer to Ruza's mouth. Her lips were already swelling from the earlier blow. Ruza dropped to the deck again, shielding her mouth with her hands and begging, "No! No!"

But Fiona crouched down and dug her hand into Ruza's curls, wrenching her head backward and needling her pliers between Ruza's wet, trembling lips. Betsy felt vomit rising in her throat as Fiona got a good grip on one of Ruza's front teeth—and pulled.

There was a sickening noise as the tooth was ripped out from the root. It happened so quickly that Ruza didn't have time to howl until it was done. She staggered, but was still held aloft by her hair. Fiona let the first tooth fall to the deck, then reached for another.

"Wait!" Betsy cried out, scrambling over to pull back Fiona's reaching, grasping arms. Behind her, Betsy heard a chorus of metallic clicks, as thirty pirates cocked their guns at her back. She raised her hands in submission, glancing back at them warily. Fiona had turned back to Betsy, her lip curling into a sneer. But she had released Ruza's tooth, momentarily.

"I don't mean any harm," Betsy said. "It's just that . . . I've seen your posters, you know. On Peu Jolie. You're famous there. Everyone's heard of Fiona Wall and Jack Copeland."

Fiona was instantly mollified, and gestured at the men to lower their weapons. "Hold on. I wanna hear where she's going with this."

Betsy took a series of shallow breaths, taking in the look of self-satisfaction that Fiona was wearing. She was prideful. Vain. Betsy could work with that. "It . . . I-it's just that you're legends in the String Islands." Betsy glanced over at Jack, who was the only one with his pistol still aimed at her. "Both of you!" Turning her head back to Fiona, and licking her lips again, Betsy murmured, "With Ophelia Cray dead, you're poised to become the most famous pirates in the world."

Fiona's face split into a wide smile, showing off those horrible, mossy teeth. She stroked her red hair over her shoulder, blushing. "Really? You think so? I've always thought *pirate queen* would be a fitting title for me."

Betsy nodded, eagerly at first, then slower. "Yes. Absolutely.

But they don't know your names yet in Carthay like they knew Ophelia Cray. 'Cause, you know, Lady Ruza didn't know who you were. What's the point of scaring a bunch of criminals' descendants, when you could have the mainland nobility shaking in their boots?"

Jack's gun fell to his side. He stretched his arms lazily behind his back. "Now, I like the sound of that, Fi."

Fiona stood up, looking intently at Betsy. "Go on."

Betsy clenched her hands in supplication. "Don't you know who Lady Ruza is? She's the grand-queen's cousin." This was a lie, as far as Betsy knew, but it was a believable one, and something in both Fiona's and Jack's demeanor had changed the moment she said it. They were looking at Ruza in wonder, as if the grand-queen herself had floated down from the sky.

Betsy plowed on. "Send her back alive to have tea with the Queen, to tell of her narrow escape from you, and soon everyone on the great continent will know your names. You'll be the most famous outlaws ever born. People will sing songs about you. They'll make art of your faces that won't just hang on street-corner walls. But the first step to getting your immortality is letting the noble lady go with the rest of her teeth intact. She'll need them to tell the story right."

Fiona's eyebrows furrowed, just a tiny bit, just enough to let Betsy know that she was skeptical. Or maybe she just didn't understand the logic behind it.

Jack crossed to put his hand on Fiona's shoulders. "The girl is talking sense, Fi. Maybe we let this one scarper off, spread our legend a bit?"

Fiona nodded seriously, and pointed at Ruza with her pliers. "This here's your lucky day. We're gonna drop you in a rowboat, and fair's fair, if you make it to land you get to live."

Ruza, who had been kneeling stock-still and silent this entire time, simply nodded, as if incapable of finding words. She tried to mumble a "thank you," but it came out as a gravelly gurgling sound.

Matthew had crawled over to Jack's ankles, across the grim, messy expanse of the deck. The knees of his blue breeches were stained through with the blood of the *Sunshearer*'s crew. "With all due respect," he muttered, afraid of looking Jack or Fiona in the eye, but staring resolutely at the puddle a few inches from Betsy's feet, "You ought to put me on that lifeboat with her."

Jack let out a roar of laughter. "And why's that?"

"Because . . . because I'm the only son and heir of the Whitman-Young Company. You've got the other heir here, and you just said you're not letting *her* go. You shot my father. Her father just kicked the bucket. Some island fever melted his brain. If one of us doesn't live, the business won't get inherited by anyone. It'll dry up. No more ships going out for you to pillage. Just our money, getting dusty in a vault, and our goods sitting in warehouses. I'm thinking of your finances here. You can't rob ships that never leave shore, can you?"

"You cowardly son of a bitch!" Betsy shouted at Matthew, but Jack was already pulling the scrawny boy to his feet, giving him the world's iciest glare.

Finally, Jack said, "The boy makes a point."

Matthew grinned widely, and the moment his teeth were

exposed, Jack brought the handle of his pistol up to meet Matthew's mouth. Matthew's teeth instantly shattered like a porcelain teacup; Betsy didn't have time to look away. Matthew fell to his knees again, his one unbroken hand pressed against his ruined, bloody mouth—now a mass of weeping gums and sharp edges. Jack swaggered away, spinning his pistol from the trigger and chuckling to himself. "But I reckon you don't need good elocution to keep your company's books in order. You said it yourself—your survival is about sending ships out for us to loot, not being a good party guest like the lady here."

Fiona was overcome with giggles. Jack glanced at her, concerned. "You didn't want those teeth, did you, darling?"

Fiona waved him off, still laughing. "No, no. His weren't pretty enough."

A few minutes later, a lifeboat was lowered into the water, Ruza and Matthew on it. Ruza took the paddles and began to hurriedly row away—Matthew apparently in too much agony to help. Betsy felt dread consume her. Now she was left alone on a ship, with no one but a horde of pirates and fifty corpses for company.

FOURTEEN

The ship had been swept off course by the storm, and Ophelia knew that as captain, it was her job to get them en route to their next assigned port and deliver the empire's documents securely. Unfortunately, Ames hadn't bothered to fill the crew in on their next destination before meeting her demise. Emily sat with Ophelia in the captain's cabin, helping her to cross-reference Ames's journal entries with the star maps. "We know we're meant to cross the Emerald Sea, eastward," Ophelia said, consulting her father's compass, "and land somewhere in Cato by the end of the month. But I can't find record of which port we're supposed to anchor in."

Emily shook her head, frowning. "Ames kept a lot of official correspondence in her jacket pocket, where Hale couldn't spill booze on it. It might have gone overboard with her. Port Ibudo has the largest naval station in Cato, but we've no—"

A rapping came at the door. "Captain!"

"Enter," Ophelia said.

The door burst open and Lawrence, the pimple-faced officer, was standing there, breathing heavily. "Captain, there's a ship of unknown origin within sight. Two actually. Cannons are sounding."

Ophelia stood up so fast she almost went dizzy. *Pirates.* Either they were besieging an innocent merchant vessel, or another naval ship was in need of backup.

"Ready the men for a fight," Ophelia said, picking her captain's hat up from the back of her chair and throwing it on her head. "This is the first action we've seen in a while."

And the first action you've seen, ever, a needling little voice reminded Ophelia, as Lawrence ran to repeat her orders.

She touched her pistol on her belt. Emily handed Ophelia a saber that had been hanging on the wall. She looked tempted to reach out to Ophelia with some sort of comforting touch, but instead simply said, "It's part of the job." That was comfort enough.

"It *is* the job," Ophelia said.

Ophelia exited to the deck, where men were readying the cannons. The eyes of the crew were on her, so she raised her chin high and strode toward the wheel of the ship, slipping her compass safely into her breast pocket. Edgar was standing at the wheel when she approached, but the moment she was within reach, he stepped aside for her, casting his eyes down.

Ophelia wrapped her hands around two spokes of the wheel, and gave an odd shiver as a surge of warmth passed through her body. This was where she was meant to stand. She looked out at the deck, at the men and women, almost all older than she, more experienced than she was—all waiting for her to speak.

"Alright, sailors!" Ophelia called out. Her voice sounded

stronger than she had expected. "We're going to hit these bastards fast, and we're gonna hit them hard. Our first priority is rescuing civilians, understand? Before glory, before spilling pirate blood, before recapturing loot. We're gonna get the civilians to safety, on this boat if need be. Cannons at the ready. This fight will be over so quickly we won't have time to know fear."

Ophelia's speech was returned with a flutter of salutes and a chorus of "Aye-aye."

She turned the wheel flush to the left, and the boat began to turn. "Edgar!" Ophelia called out, tossing him a spyglass. "Figure out which ship is which. I don't want them aiming at the wrong person."

Edgar gave a brisk nod. "Aye-aye."

She steered into the fray.

Ophelia had never imagined that anything could be more dis-orienting than their night trying to pass through the storm. But this was worse. So often during the storm everything seemed to slow down—but now the world passed her by at three times the speed. From the moment the first of their cannons sounded, there were flashes of fire and smoke, and a symphony of shots. The pirates crossed over to their boat, some of her crew crossed over to theirs. Blue and beige uniforms merged with a swarm of pirates in tattered dress, everyone blurring together in a haze of gun smoke.

Someone darted at Ophelia. She raised her saber and parried. She knocked them down on the ground and moved on to a new opponent. When that one too laid at her feet, she left the wheel behind to follow her valiant crew onto the pirates' ship. Blood roared in her ears—but she was not afraid. Putting down attack-ers felt as natural to her as swiping her parasol at boys on the streets of Peu Jolie. She didn't think. She didn't feel. She was steel and blood and sinew and instinct.

And then everything quieted. The decks of three ships were still, except for the gasping of the wounded and sobs from the captured civilians. Her mind rushed back, her heart rattling in her chest, bringing with it human emotion. Relief? Regret? They had won—much more easily than Ophelia had expected. In fact, as she looked across the deck at the fallen bodies of the pirates, she counted no more than twenty among their number. They had been a meager crew indeed for a ship of this size.

A pirate lay at Ophelia's feet, not yet dead. He was spread-eagled on the deck, face pale, with a great, deep gash in his chest from a gunshot. She might have been the one who injured him, but she couldn't remember. Everything had happened so fast.

She didn't want to feel anything for this man. It was shameful enough that she had felt something for her mother, a murderess, the day she had hanged. Ophelia was determined to hold back the weakness of sympathy now. She was no longer a child, but a woman of the navy.

The pirate was coughing, weak and thick. Clearly, his lungs were collapsing, slowly filling with blood. He opened his eyes, fighting to stay awake. Ophelia knelt by his side, watching quietly. His vision wasn't quite gone, and he seemed to fully understand that she was there. His eyes widened, and his lips moved slightly, mouthing the words: "It's you."

A ragged breath escaped Ophelia's chest. She couldn't help the weakness. She knew the truth: This was just a man, not a monster. "How do you know me?" she whispered.

The pirate blinked. He shook his head. "End it. Please."

Ophelia's eyes had begun to burn. A confused storm was swirling in her brain as she started to emerge from the fog of battle. "No," she said, voice hoarse. "I won't kill you." It wasn't right. It was her job to kill pirates, and they had done wrong capturing these civilians, but it still didn't feel right. They were people. Flesh and blood like she was.

Ophelia drew the handkerchief from her jacket pocket, putting pressure on the man's chest wound. "Maybe we could heal you," she muttered, as breathlessly as if she were the one who was injured.

The pirate's lips moved again, but this time Ophelia couldn't make out the words. She had the absurd urge to put a hand on his cheek, but she needed both hands to stem the flow of his blood. The white fabric wasn't white anymore; her hands were stained, and blood had bubbled up to obscure the place where Lang's medal was pinned. The light was leaving his eyes. Ophelia had to keep him awake, conscious for long enough to get real help. She choked out the words, "Do you have a name?"

But he was already gone, somewhere far away. She couldn't imagine where. Ophelia averted her gaze, blinking rapidly.

She stood, looking out across to the merchant ship, which carried a large breach in the hull from the pirates' cannons. Perhaps eight civilians were huddled together on the ground, clutching each other and hiding their eyes from the massacre around them. Something had to be done for them, and she wasn't sure what. But they were looking to her, the girl in the captain's hat, with blood dripping from her hands. The crew was looking at her too, expectant.

She was studying her hands when she became vaguely aware of a quick but steady sound behind her—the thumping of heavy footfalls.

Edgar's voice. "Ophelia! Get down!"

Ophelia broke out of her fog and dropped to the deck, hearing a single shot. She flipped over onto her back and saw that, just to her right, another body was twitching and dying. A massive body. Ten feet behind it, Edgar held a smoking pistol.

His every limb shaking, Edgar lowered the gun. "It's okay now, Lucky Teeth. I got him."

Ophelia crawled toward the dying man. She recognized his head first. Bald, with a long scar arching across it—and a neat, fresh gunshot wound at the base of his skull. "Ronan," she breathed. "How did he get out of his cell?" Ronan's body stilled, and she saw that he had a pistol of his own clutched in his hand. She pried it from his fingers, and read the initials carved into the ivory handle. "C. L. Who in this crew has the initials C. L.?"

Edgar quickly pivoted to aim his pistol at Clovis. "Clovis Lee," he growled.

Clovis raised his hands into the air. "I didn't do anything!" he protested.

"Then, amuse us," Edgar said, pacing toward the surrendering giant, "with the tale of how your friend Ronan became freed from his cell in the heat of battle, supplied with your gun."

Clovis didn't have an answer. But he did have a question. He cocked his head to the side, looking curiously at Edgar. "Who's . . . Ophelia?"

Ophelia's numbness returned, as if the battle had begun

again. Edgar's mouth was agape, his usually handsome face now childish and pale. He turned away from Clovis and reached up to massage his jaw, hiding an embarrassed expression. In that blurred moment, in saving her life, he had blown her cover.

Ophelia needed to distract the crew from Edgar's mistake before anyone else caught on. She raised her chin high, her voice sharp as she reproached Clovis. "Stop asking stupid questions. You've committed a fool's crime. Did you think it was so certain that Ronan would kill me that you wouldn't need to come up with a convincing lie?" She glanced around at her crew. "Take this piece of refuse back to our ship, and tie him to the mainmast. I believe I mentioned I had no mercy left."

Jo gritted her teeth, coming forward. "Gladly," she said. Fitz, carrying a heavy chain, assisted Jo in binding Clovis's limbs and dragging him back over to the *Bluesusan*.

"As for the rest of you," Ophelia announced, trying to calm her own trembling hands, "these citizens can't get back to shore on their own ship. It's too badly damaged. We'll have to abandon our own course for now. We'll turn back to Carthay before we get any farther out to sea, let them off in Orana. There we'll reestablish our orders, and resupply. Likely get a new captain too, but until then, you've got me. Now, let's get everyone safely aboard, and shove on back in the direction we came."

The crew quickly hopped to follow Ophelia's instructions, ushering the trembling passengers over to the deck of the *Bluesusan*. She fought a quiver in her voice as she called out, "Now who was in charge of this sorry ship?" Pursuant to the empire's laws, navy ships were supposed to leave pirate captains alive, so that they could meet the empire's justice publicly in the next port.

"We've got him right here!" Emily called out. Her saber was pressed to the back of a man in a black tri-tipped hat. Lawrence, pointing his pistol at the captain's head for good measure, slowly warned him not to try anything funny. But Ophelia didn't think the man was planning any daring acts of escape. Were he standing, he might have been impressive, but as it was, he was blubbering so hard that his tears were dripping into his steel-gray muttonchops.

Lawrence was unimpressed by the pirate. "First enemy ship we've encountered in eight months, and this wretch is less frightening than the little girl we've got for our own captain."

Ophelia glowered at Lawrence's back. Did he think himself funny? A man had just tried to murder her while her back was turned. She looked around at the crew rushing to their duties. Could any of them be trusted? Had they noticed Edgar's slip? Perhaps they were all biding their time until they could put a bullet in Ophelia Cray's daughter.

She had to give them a good reason to stay loyal. A reason to respect her, *fear her*, too much to stab her in the back. It was time to let instinct kick in—do or die. After reading her mother's note, Ophelia knew just what she would say: *It is their fear of us that gives us our greatest strength.*

Her order had been obeyed. Clovis was bound to the center mast face-forward, his jacket and undershirt stripped away. Someone—she wasn't sure who; she was still incandescent with rage—pressed the cat-o'-nine-tails' leather handle into her palm. "He won't just get a taste of the lash," she muttered, half to herself, half to her crew. "He'll get his full of it." Ophelia measured the weight of the cat in her hand, and struck.

Clovis cried out in pain, but Ophelia hardly noticed. He had mutinied. She had fought Ronan with honor—even shown him mercy. She had tried to do right by the crew, yet Clovis had helped Ronan attack her. Were they all whispering behind her back, like the townsfolk of home? Clovis was more a pirate than she was. *He* was the mutineer, after all, not her. Ophelia would not be betrayed again. She would not flee this ship, as she'd had to flee Peu Jolie. She would make an example.

Ophelia didn't know how many times she struck him with the lash. She hadn't initially declared how many lashes he was owed. She had forgotten to do that, but it didn't matter. She felt she could hit him forever.

The front of Ophelia's beige uniform was splattered with blood. Clovis was still crying out, but weaker each time. Eventually he went slack against his ropes, and Ophelia knew he had passed out from the pain. But she couldn't stop hitting him. That day at the foot of the gallows, Ophelia had thought her mother was a void. She had been wrong. Her mother was like her—a wailing storm beneath skin, only barely restrained and waiting to burst free.

The storm was loose now.

Someone strong grabbed her wrist. "That's enough, lass," Jo whispered in her ear.

When it was all over, Ophelia couldn't bear to face the crew anymore. Her skin was cool marble, now burning from hot tears. She heard the whispers as she left the deck. She'd seen the disgusted looks on their faces. She'd proven herself to be exactly what they'd expected of her—exactly what everyone on Peu Jolie had thought her to be. She was dangerous. Prone to violence she couldn't control.

Before she opened the door to the captain's cabin, Edgar jogged to meet her. He stood so close to her, Ophelia nearly drew back, afraid he'd move in for another kiss. But he merely reached into the breast pocket of her jacket, fishing out her father's brass compass. He removed the whip from her hand and replaced it with the compass. "Good show, Lucky Teeth. But you can calm yourself now. Get centered. Find true north."

Ophelia could feel the eyes of the crew on them. She turned the brass compass over and over again in her hand. In a voice like a lost child, she said, "I lost myself. He told me not to."

"Who did?"

"My father. That's why he gave me this."

A thin, strained smile twisted at Edgar's lips. "Isn't that nice?" He clicked the compass shut for her, his large hands covering her own for a moment. "Well, it's a fine instrument you've got there. Now go. Get some rest."

Ophelia went into the captain's cabin and collapsed on her cot. Emily followed her, sitting down beside Ophelia at a comfortable distance. Edgar shut the door behind them, but stayed outside.

"I know you don't like to be touched, so I won't," Emily said.

"I don't like to be touched by strangers," Ophelia corrected.

Emily inched a little closer to her, understanding her meaning. "Is there someone you're missing right now? Not a stranger?"

Ophelia nodded, her face pressed into her pillow. She missed a thousand things about home now. The way Eliza would make her turtle soup when she was sick. How Papa had learned to braid her hair when she was little. But mostly, she wanted Betsy. She remembered the way Betsy had held her on the day her mother had died—her arms had been shaking, but she'd shielded Ophelia from the jeering crowd. She needed Betsy now, to keep the storm inside her chest at bay.

Ophelia's reply came out muffled, her mouth still pressed against cotton, afraid to let Emily see her wet face. "My sister. I don't like to cry in front of people. But with Betsy it's alright. She doesn't care if I'm weak. I'm sorry, I didn't mean to—"

Emily sighed. "I have to say, I don't know what you're weeping for. Clovis deserved what he got. You can't let things like that go unpunished."

"I was supposed to prove everyone wrong. To make folks like me. But I was a brute, and now the crew surely hate me."

Emily gave Ophelia a long, thoughtful look, blinking slowly. "Tell me, lass," she said. "What did you come to sea for, anyway?"

Without hesitating, the answer that Ophelia had prepared for Lang fell off her tongue. "I wanted to help people."

Emily's laugh was a short, harsh burst, not unlike a cough. "Listen, girl, the older you grow, the more you'll cultivate a sense for horseshit. Even your own horseshit. Tell me the real reason you came."

She'd wanted them to cheer for her.

Ophelia shrugged, not able to meet Emily's eyes. Her words came out in a mumble. "I don't know."

FIFTEEN

*A*n orange glow had settled over the endless horizon by the time the pirates successfully brought the *Sunshearer* farther out to sea and moved everything of value in its cargo hold into their own. They raised up a clean, functional sail to replace the ripped one they had used to lure in their prey. Then Jack Copeland ordered his men to fire their cannons.

Hot tears pricked at the corners of her eyes as Betsy watched the ship sink below the waves, sending the still bodies of its crew down with it. Betsy pressed her fingers together, dragging them across her heart to ward off evil. Not that it would do any good. Evil was already here.

The only things Fiona had allowed Betsy to remove from the ship were her sewing kit and her apron—the lighter still secreted away in its front pocket. Then Fiona had pointed her gun at the small of Betsy's back and forced her to scramble over the rail to the deck of the *Bloody Shame*. Blood coated the soles of Betsy's boots. She wondered how much of it belonged to Jakob Whitman.

Betsy hadn't allowed herself to look down at the faces of the fallen men on the *Sunshearer*'s deck. She couldn't. A realization hit Betsy, sending a tremor through every muscle in her body quite as strongly as if she'd been struck by lightning.

This was her fault.

She had wished this on the Whitmans, after all. She had laid a curse upon their ship, and then had the audacity to test the gods' sense of irony by climbing aboard with them. She remembered what Mama had said about curses—how their magic was really all about intent. Betsy had willed the ship to go down, and so it had. She'd sunk this vessel. Fiona and Jack were just the means by which her curse was carried out—fate's bitter, petty way of executing it. Betsy was every bit as much to blame as the people who shot the crew and fired the cannons. She had, as Ophelia might have put it, oracled up a disaster for herself.

But others had paid the price.

Fiona lit a lantern, dug her claws into Betsy's wrist, and dragged her below decks. Together, they moved along a dark, musty passageway. At the end there was a brig, separated from the rest of the ship by a thick, iron-barred door. Fiona lifted a key from a hook on the wall, unlocked the door, and pushed Betsy inside. "You'll stay there until I have need of you," she taunted. She and her lantern went bobbing back down the hall in the direction they'd come, leaving Betsy in darkness.

"I'd tell you that your eyes adjust eventually, but truthfully, they don't adjust as much as you'd hope."

Betsy squealed, dropping her kit in fright, and stumbled back until she hit the wall. She slumped to the floor. The voice had been only inches from her! Who was this, another pirate? Her jailer, placed in here to torture her?

"Oh, please don't be scared. I didn't mean—I didn't mean to scare you."

Betsy felt clammy and nauseous all over, but her breathing slowed. "Who are y-you?"

"My name is Ravi. Ravi Randawa." The stranger, Ravi, let out a breathless little laugh. Betsy was surprised by how crisp and posh his accent was. "Gods, it's been a while since I've gotten to introduce myself. It feels almost like being in society again."

Trying to calm herself down, Betsy reached into her apron to grip her lighter—and then realized that a lighter was a very useful thing to have in this darkness. She pulled it out, flicking the switch. A tiny golden flame burst in front of her eyes, and suddenly the stranger wasn't a mysterious upper-class voice in the shadows. He was a boy. Or rather—warmth blossomed in Betsy's cheeks—a young man.

Betsy took inventory of his looks within a millisecond—and yet savored them at the same time. Ravi Randawa was very tall and very thin. Betsy thought that "gangly" might be the right word for it. He had the stretched-out look of someone who'd grown a great deal very quickly. With that warm brown skin tone, she suspected he was from the Lalithan province. He was dressed in a shabby butler's costume: a sort of cheap, rumpled version of the black and white suit that Valois wore. He was sitting cross-legged on the floor and didn't have any shoes. The cuffs were much too short for him, exposing a significant stretch of bare ankles.

His ears stuck out a touch too far, although his shining black hair mostly hid that. And he had such large, expressive eyes, magnified by the loveliest pair of round glasses. Oh, he was *just* her type.

Best of all, while Betsy was admiring Ravi Randawa, Ravi was looking back at her with equal intensity. He smiled so widely and brightly, it felt like sunlight had burst into the room alongside her lighter's flame.

"Oh," he said, shaking his head in happy incredulity, "you don't know how good it is to see a friendly face. Not someone threatening me with a knife, or a gun, or some pliers."

"P-pliers?" Betsy asked. And suddenly she saw what Ravi was referring to. She had been so distracted by the look on his face, she hadn't noticed the state of his mouth. Two of Ravi's teeth were missing, the ones directly behind his canines. This made him look like a seven-year-old boy, still waiting for his adult teeth to come in.

Ravi self-consciously reached up to cover his mouth. "Sorry," he said, "I know that's not pleasant to look at." He blinked over at Betsy. "Please, miss, can I know your name? I promise, I'm not one of them."

Betsy blinked back at him. That much was obvious.

She wiped her left palm on her apron, since she was holding the lighter with her right, and stuck it out for him to shake. "I'm Betsy Young."

Ravi scrambled to his feet, went to meet her left hand with his right, laughed at himself, and then fixed his error by shaking her hand enthusiastically with both of his. Then suddenly, he stopped, his face freezing in a look of almost comical sadness. "No—pardon me. It just occurred . . . just occurred to me. I'm just awful, aren't I? Here I am, so pleased to see you, but you—

if you're here, then—then something terrible just happened to you. I can hardly believe how insensitive I am. Are you alright? Of course you're not alright. I don't know why I'm asking that. I'm so sorry, I'm babbling. I'm sorry and I'm babbling and I'm sorry *that* I'm babbling. I'm afraid that—I'm afraid. You must be afraid too. What can I do to help?"

He released her hand then, just realizing he'd been shaking it the whole time he was speaking.

Betsy smiled weakly. "You can tell me how long you've been here. It looks like they've got you playing butler. However long you've lasted, w-without, well, without them killing you. Then I'll know—then I'll know that if I'm smart, I can last at least that long too."

"Six months," Ravi said.

"Six months? You've been held on this ship for six months?"

"Yes."

"I was expecting more like six weeks. Now, I don't mean to be r-rude, but . . . why haven't they killed you yet?"

"Because of this," Ravi said, reaching into the deep pockets of his butler's uniform. He pulled out a thin leather-bound journal with yellowed pages. He opened it, and Betsy could see lines and lines of messy, fading writing in a language that Betsy didn't know. She supposed that it was the Lalithan dialect of West-Tongue.

"It was my grandfather's," Ravi said. He glanced nervously at Betsy, as if worrying he was boring her. "It's a bit of a long story."

Betsy suppressed a harsh laugh. "We've got nothing but time."

Ravi straightened his glasses, laughing too. "Well, yes! I suppose." He launched into his tale.

"When Grandfather was a sailor, he was a go-between for the gold industry. He was contracted to transport a large number of gold bullion blocks from Lalitha to Carthay. These bars were the purest gold Lalitha had to offer—their worth incalculable. But on the journey, they were struck by an unexpected storm and had to anchor on an uncharted island. They took on so much damage that they realized they would die at sea unless they lightened the boat's cargo. So they stacked the bars in a cave on the island with the intention of coming back for them again. But when they tried, it seemed like the island had disappeared. Long after everyone else cut their losses, my grandfather spent the rest of his life searching for those bars, with only the notes he had taken on the first trip to guide him. He never found them. He ended up building a mercantile empire, but never found the gold. Neither did my father." Ravi let out a heavy sigh. "And nor shall I, apparently."

"But I don't understand," said Betsy, "what has that got to do with you still being alive?"

"Well," Ravi said, "it's a family business now. And it's become a tradition for my kin that each of our first voyages at sea be dedicated to seeking out the lost treasure. It's a rite of passage: We serve as a sailor and a navigator, and when we come home again, we've earned our first ship." His face grows gaunt, haunted by memories. "Unfortunately, my maiden voyage hasn't gone exactly as expected. Fiona tortured one of my captured crewmates until he admitted what we were looking for. They can't make sense of my journal themselves, but Jack figures that by process of elimination my ancestors have already figured out most of the islands the gold *isn't* on. He thought I'd be able to lead him right to the treasure pile. But . . . six months on, and no luck. I would guess his patience is about to run out." Ravi looked down at himself, and seemed to suddenly remember that he was dressed like a butler. "Oh—and a few days before he captured me, Jack blew the head off his last servant, so he needed someone to fill in anyway."

Betsy whistled, like the air being let out of a teapot. This did not bode well for her survival odds. "A shame," she whispered, massaging the growing headache from her temples, "I don't have anything near as good as secret treasure." She took a deep, shuddering breath, and thought for a moment about what Ophelia would do. The answer was simple.

"Alright then," Betsy said, leaning in closer to Ravi to whisper yet more imperceptibly. "That settles it. We'll just have to escape."

Ravi straightened his glasses, looking at Betsy like she was a madwoman. "How?"

Betsy shrugged. Her heart was racing. She walked the length of their tiny cell, shining the light from her flame into all corners, looking for anything that could be useful. Nothing was on the ground. "Well, I-I-I don't know. But we'll find something." Her eyes had landed on the sewing kit she had dropped when she'd been startled by Ravi. "Maybe, you know, we, w-we could pick the lock with one of my needles, and get out of this cell!"

Ravi nodded, just once. He walked to the cell door, pressed his body against it, and squeezed his long, thin arm through the bars. When he stepped away, pulling his arm back into the cell, he was holding the key from the wall hook. "It doesn't matter if we get out of the cell," Ravi told her. "They're not hiding this key from us for a reason. It's because once you're out, you still don't have anywhere to go. You're still trapped on a ship with thirty pirates, in the middle of an endless sea."

Betsy's lower lip began to tremble. The momentary fire that had flared in her belly went out. So did the fire in her lighter as her thumb finally fell away from the switch. The strong shell she'd built up as she pretended to be Ophelia shattered. She broke into tears, choking and gasping.

What did it matter, she asked herself, if she cried in front of this handsome boy? So what if her face went blotchy, or if snot leaked from her nose? He couldn't see her face in the darkness anymore, and she probably already stank of piss anyway. More important, they were both going to die here. Her father was already dead. Her sister was going to hang at worst, and malinger in prison for decades at best. Her mother would be alone forever, blaming Betsy for breaking her promise to come back. It didn't matter what she did or what Ravi thought of her. She was going to die before she had really lived.

Ravi paused to put the key back on the hook where he'd found it. Turning back to Betsy, he took a hesitant step forward, then another. He wrapped her up in his arms, letting Betsy sob against his chest. "I'm sorry this happened to you," he said. "And I'm very sorry to crush your hope. But that's just it. We can't have hope here."

"Pessimistic," Betsy chided, voice tight with tears.

"*Practical*," Ravi countered. "The only way to survive is to keep our heads down and lay low. Maybe we'll live long enough to meet a naval ship. That's our only shot. Apologies, if I've upset you."

Betsy didn't know how to tell him that *he* hadn't upset her. She had upset herself. After all, she was going to die by her own ill wish. She had sent the *Sunshearer* to its demise, and she would soon follow it.

"It's alright to cry," Ravi said, rubbing her back in a slow, comforting way. "I cried a lot when I first got here. I just know that my family is out there, wondering where I am. Looking for me. And that's almost worse. As you can tell from how long we've been searching for that treasure, we're not particularly good at finding lost things."

Betsy gave a small, choking laugh into Ravi's shirt, which might have been mistaken for a sob. She had never known someone to present pessimism—and that *was* what it was, no matter what Ravi called it—so kindly. She'd also never been hugged by a boy before. Under a different set of circumstances, this might have been nice. Her nose was clogged from crying, but she wondered if Ravi smelled good. He seemed like the kind of person who would smell good.

"Do you have a family?" Ravi asked her. "I mean, of course you do, everyone technically does, but—"

A rhythmic clanking sound began down the hall. Betsy and Ravi immediately leaped apart, afraid of what would happen if they were caught, even for a moment, in any state but constant terror. The clanking continued, growing closer.

"What's with all the wailing?" drawled the voice of a pirate Betsy didn't recognize. "Better cut it out or Jack'll take one of your ears, one way or another. He always finds a reason, don't he? Now, budge along. You're being called to serve, the both of you." Betsy scrambled to pick up her sewing kit from the mold-covered floor.

The pirate turned out to be a hobbling old man named

Dawkins, who kept an empty tin mug that he used to frighten them with noises in the dark. He led them to a private room that was reasonably spacious for the below decks of a ship. Inside, Jack and Fiona were waiting: Jack, tapping the tip of his knife against a table that seemed to have been constructed out of driftwood, and Fiona standing on a wooden crate, dreamily swirling the skirts of Ruza's gown around her ankles.

"Oh, good!" Fiona said as they were ushered inside. She pointed a clawed nail at Ravi. "You'll bring us our dinner now. And you!" She turned her gaze onto Betsy as Ravi scurried off to the kitchen galley. She cocked a scarlet eyebrow. "Now we'll see how talented you really are. But I suppose it's not a total loss, even if you were lying to me. I'll just use your blood to dye one of my dresses red."

This threat was so ridiculous, and Betsy was already so terrified, that she found she just couldn't muster up the energy to be any more scared than she already was. She simply exhaled, moving to kneel beside the crate, so she could begin taking the hem of the dress up several inches. Her concentration was impaired by the sound of Jack slowly scraping the blade of his knife against the table edge.

"Well," Fiona snapped. "Aren't you going to say anything? This will be no fun if we do it in silence."

They were both children. Begging to be entertained.

The only thing Betsy could think of to say was, "I'm . . . I'm afraid you can't use blood as a true dye. It stains, y-yes, but brown, and it would get lighter every t-time you got it wet."

"Huh," Fiona said. "That's interesting." She plucked at the extra fabric around her chest. "You said this could be taken in, right? And could you lower the neckline too?"

Betsy nodded, willing to ruin any seamstress's elegant work to stay alive. She continued to adjust the hem, while Fiona stared down at her with a vicious gleam in her eyes. "So, tell me, did you go to the hanging?"

"The hanging?" Betsy asked.

"The hanging," Fiona snapped. "Cray's hanging. You're from Peu Jolie aren't you? And that's where she swung. You must have been there. Her gallows dance was practically the social event of the season, I hear. I would have happily watched her choke myself, the wretched bitch. No one could make a name for themselves as a pirate with her using up all the air."

Through gritted teeth, Betsy admitted, "I did go."

Fiona laughed gaily, with a shrewd glint in her eye, like she knew something about Betsy that even Betsy didn't know. "I thought as much. Who would miss the opportunity? I would've gone back for it if I could. And I'll say this for the old bat. She had style. I met her once—just the once. But it was like getting struck by lightning. And then I met up with this one." Fiona turned her head to beam at the back of Jack's head. "He was just a bartender by the docks then. But I told him about meeting Cray, and we knew at once what we wanted to be."

Betsy swallowed a dry lump in her throat. "Ophelia Cray inspired you to become pirates?"

Fiona tapped her index finger against her lips. "Well, I wouldn't say *inspired*. But I liked her clothes. They looked expensive. I wanted them. But I was just a maid then, and I couldn't afford expensive things by stealing knickknacks from the merchants whose underthings I washed. And now Cray's been hung . . . I'll finally surpass her. Dead folk have no use for lovely things. Now everything's wide open and mine for the taking." Fiona held Ruza's dress against herself to admire the effect. "And I'm going to look damn good as the Emerald Sea's next pirate queen."

Betsy narrowed her eyes, but didn't dare look up.

The door to the room creaked open and Ravi came back in, balancing two silver trays heavy with food, and two clay mugs. "Put that here," Jack demanded, finally laying down his knife.

Betsy, still stewing, felt the words slip out of her mouth before considering whether they would be wise: "So, you're from Peu Jolie too?"

"Excuse me?" Fiona asked. "I didn't say that." The fabric Betsy was holding grew less taut as Fiona dropped the extra satin she'd been holding tight.

At the table, Jack took a long draft from the mug, which was giving off the overwhelming, dizzying scent of cheap rum. He took a bite of meat and immediately spat it out. "This is overdone." He pointed Ravi out the door, saying, "Get me the cook. Tell him I want to give him my compliments."

"I j-just assumed," Betsy said, glancing away from Jack and back at Fiona. "You said you would have gone *back*. You can't go back somewhere you've never been."

Fiona immediately seized Betsy by the wrist and twisted, her face contorted in a snarl. "I am never going back to that filthy city. No one can make me. And I won't have a jumped-up merchant brat thinking she knows *shit* about my life."

"Please," Betsy gasped. "My wrist. I can't sew for you if you break my wrist."

Very suddenly, Fiona calmed—or appeared to. She released Betsy and let out a giggle. But the sound was too sharp, and went on too long to be comforting. "Sweetie," she said, "worry less about *me* seeing my hometown again, and worry more about whether I'll mail your mama your entire smile, one tooth at a time."

Heat burned in Betsy's cheeks. Anger, where there logically should have been fear.

"Leave my mother out of this," she muttered. Fiona didn't appear to have heard Betsy's comment.

Betsy did not dare look into Fiona's eyes. "We could take a break now for you to have supper," she said, raising her voice with a concerted effort to keep it from shaking. "I'll have this dress finished in no time. I could even take your measurements and work on it in my cell, if I could be allowed a lantern."

The door opened again, and Ravi, stone-faced and miserable-looking, showed a bald, one-legged pirate into the room. Jack pushed out his chair immediately. "Puget," he said, grinning. "I'm so happy you could come. Why don't you take a bite of the meat you served me?"

The smile dropped off the cook's face as he parsed that Jack wasn't actually going to deliver him any compliments. He hobbled over to the table, his wooden leg clunking against the floor with every other step, and took a bite as he'd been told.

"How do you find it?" Jack asked, leaning over to whisper in the cook's ear.

The pirate swallowed, looking at his captain in abject fear. "I—I suppose it's a bit tough."

"And having lost your leg," Jack asked, "do you now find your duties in the kitchen to be . . . a bit tough?"

The pirate gulped again, but there was obviously nothing left in his mouth to swallow. "I manage, sir. Most of the time. My apolo——"

"No apologies," Jack said, waving his left hand. "I'm glad to hear you're managing." The cook was still bent forward in an obsequious half bow. Jack struck quickly, slicing off the man's left ear and letting it fall to the floor.

The cook let out an unearthly scream, staggering over and holding the place where his ear used to be—now gushing blood.

"If you can manage without a leg, you can manage without an ear," Jack said, waving the agonized cook out of the room. He snarled at Ravi, pointing at the floor, "Clean that."

Then Jack turned to look at Betsy, and her veins ran cold. That look was almost enough to make Betsy abandon the idea of her fledgling plan by itself. Almost.

"You'll get no candle, you stupid bitch," Jack said.

Fiona made a whining, pouting sound, but Jack ignored her, still staring Betsy down. "You won't get so much as a lump of wax. Do you have any idea what damage an open flame can do on a wooden ship?"

Betsy ducked her head meekly. "Forgive me, sir. I hadn't realized."

The lie tasted like sugar on her tongue.

SIXTEEN

O phelia lit the lantern at the wall, allowing dim light to shine through the bars of the brig. Edgar stood a few feet behind her, watching quietly as the pirate, slumped against the wall, twitched in his sleep.

"We should wake him up," Ophelia said, "and brief our guest on what's going to happen when we reach Carthay."

"Fair enough," Edgar said. He removed a key from his jacket to unlock the brig door, and entered the cell. He appeared to consider bending down to shake the man awake, but then thought better of putting his hand on someone so obviously filthy. He kicked the pirate in the ribs instead.

The man jerked awake, looked from side to side like a frantic rat, and noticed Ophelia through the bars. He squinted up at her, and his face flooded with recognition. An angelic smile transformed his face. "You!" he said.

Ophelia leaned in closer, wrapping her fingers around the wooden bars. "Are you happy to see me, pirate?"

The man did a double take, and his smile flickered away. He looked like his tongue had become dry as sand. "You're the captain," he mumbled, looking down.

"Well," Ophelia said, "interim captain. And do you know where we're bringing you?"

Edgar peered interestedly down at the captive as he shifted himself forward and crawled toward Ophelia on his knees. "Please don't kill me. Please."

"Of course we have to kill you," Ophelia said. "You're a pirate. You've stolen. You've murdered."

The man reached through the bars to tug on her jacket. "Have a heart, ma'am. They need me, you know."

Ophelia shared a confused look with Edgar, who looked ready to kick some more sense into the man. "What?" Ophelia asked the pirate. "What do you mean? Who needs you?"

"My girls!" the pirate cried. "I've been their right hand since their mother swung. We were supposed to be back by now. They'll be alone without me. Have pity, Miss Cray."

Ophelia ripped her jacket out of his hands, staggering backward in disgust. "Miss *Cray*?"

The man closed his eyes and struck his own forehead against the bars. "Apologies. My apologies. *Captain* Cray."

Ophelia threw herself forward again. Her mouth twisted into a snarl. "My name is not Cray! And you ought to have thought about how your daughters would survive without you before committing to a life of crime."

The man pushed himself back, off his knees and into a sitting position. "My daughters? No, ma'am. Not my daughters.

Don't you know? Don't you know them?"

"What I know," Ophelia said, pounding her fist over her heart, "Is that I am Captain Young of the Imperial Navy. I've captured you for piracy, and I'm bringing you to port to face the Crown's justice. I don't care about your sob story." She glanced briefly at Edgar, before finishing with a quieter, "I don't care."

The pirate shook his head. "There must be something of her in you. You look just like her."

Ophelia crossed her arms. "Ophelia Cray? I've heard that before, let me tell you."

Edgar held up a hand to Ophelia. "Hold on. We've hit an interesting vein here." He nudged the pirate again with his foot, gentler this time. "I want to hear more about this Cray woman. Wasn't she executed months ago? Time for you to elect a new captain, methinks."

The pirate crawled back toward the wall, wrapping his arms around his legs and shivering violently. "My captain's not dead," he said, before letting out a pathetic sob that inspired instant revulsion in Ophelia.

"You're mad," Ophelia whispered. "I saw Cray die. I was in the crowd that day. I saw her boots kick."

Edgar fixed Ophelia with a thoughtful look. "I just bet you did."

"Look!" the pirate said, desperate. "Just let me go! You've killed my crew; we can ravage no more ships together. Just let me go home to Cray Island, to the girls."

Cray Island! Ophelia's heartbeat sped up. So, her mother's island was real. But she didn't want to reveal any weakness to the pirate, so she tried to keep her face as impassive as Lang's had been on the gallows.

"I'll take you there too," the man offered, looking canny and hopeful now. "If you set me free. I'll take you home."

Ophelia hurriedly turned her back on him. She left the brig, her boot steps the only sound in the world, apart from the quickening beats of her own heart. She tried to convince herself that he was lying. That there was no island, and if there was, he wouldn't know the way. He was just lying to save himself.

Ophelia Cray was dead, and the path to Cray Island was lost with her. It would stay lost. Edgar appeared behind her. "Hey, Lucky Teeth. Wait up."

Ophelia spun to face him. Her hands were fists. "He's just telling tales, Edgar. Spinning lies to win mercy. There's no use talking about it."

A cunning look crossed Edgar's face. "I'm not sure about that, friend. What's this Cray Island he talked about? Maybe he's right. Maybe there's a pirate haven out there, stacked to the heavens with your late mother's treasure. Or maybe the pirate queen *is* alive. We could bring her in, and the loot too. Imagine the promotion. We just need to find the place."

Ophelia raised her chin, casting Edgar a look of pure condescension. "She already went down, *Eddie boy*. I heard her final words, I watched her swing. That's all you get. Ophelia Cray is gone, and her treasure with her. I should know. I inherited the only gold left on her person by the time the navy was done with her."

"And the island?"

Ophelia shrugged. "I don't know where it is. It's probably a fiction."

"A damn shame," Edgar said, a teasing tone in his voice as

they reached the hatch to the upper decks. "You mentioned a necklace before. Is that the gold you meant? And is it *pretty?*"

"Pretty? Sure it is." Ophelia's hand traced the bare part of her collarbone. "But unlucky. The highest order of unlucky. Cursed, really."

And then, as if by speaking of the curse, she had invoked it, Ophelia climbed the ladder into the sunlight and found half the crew waiting for her, weapons drawn. Fitz was at the front of the crowd, unarmed, but rigidly holding out a shining necklace made of hammered gold. "Clovis was right, wasn't he? You're not who you say you are."

Ophelia's intake of breath was so sharp it hurt her ribs. She swallowed. She looked up at the sky, trying to buy time as she figured out what to say. Thick black clouds tumbled in from the horizon. Ophelia scanned the crowd, looking for friendly faces. Jo was there—by the mainmast. But her face was unreadable. She stayed silent.

There was nothing Ophelia could say. Except maybe the truth. "No," she admitted. "I'm not Elizabeth Young. My real name is Ophelia. Elizabeth is my sister."

"Ophelia?" Lawrence asked. "As in, *Ophelia Cray?* In all my years of service, the pirate queen's picture hung on every street corner from Cornwallis to Peu Katrin. And always in *that necklace.*"

Fitz, his eyes puffy and as red as his hair, threw the necklace on the deck at Ophelia's feet. "Put it on! Let's see what you really look like, *pirate.*"

Ophelia stayed frozen. Her right hand hovered at her pistol's holster, but she didn't draw the gun. Gently, she asked Fitz, "Did you go through my things?"

Fitz gave a splutter, reaching clumsily for his saber. "You joined with me!" he cried.

He pointed his blade at her, but it wobbled along with his shaking hand. "You stood there and lied right to my face. I wanted to help people—and you joined to betray us!" A dam burst behind his eyes, a trickle of tears turning into a flood. Ophelia had never had a younger sibling, not really, and she felt rather like Fitz was the closest thing she had to it. She hadn't meant to hurt him.

"I didn't join to betray you," Ophelia said. "I joined because I wanted a clean slate. I'm as loyal to the navy as any of you. That's why I haven't drawn my pistol yet."

Lawrence let out a short burst of laughter. "Ha! If you're so loyal to the navy, why'd you bring that damn necklace with you? That's proof enough you're no good."

Ophelia raised her hands in the air, surrendering. She could have told them that she didn't bring it knowingly. That she had thought of tossing it to the sea a thousand times, but was too afraid of being seen. But that wouldn't have been true.

She hadn't disposed of the necklace because she hadn't wanted to. Not really.

"Hey," she said, slowly crouching downward, hands still up. "I'll put it on if that'll make you happy. But I didn't come to betray you, no matter what you think of my mother."

"Put it on," a sailor from the back of the crowd hissed.

"Go ahead, witch!"

"Nowhere to hide now!"

Ophelia knelt and picked up the necklace. The crew was jeering, spitting. She half expected to see the gallows crowd from

Peu Jolie among their numbers. Ophelia laid the necklace on her collarbone, but her fingers fumbled on the clasp. She sensed someone at her back, and felt Edgar's breath hot on her neck. His voice was low, lilting. "Let me help with that, Lucky Teeth. Just play this nice and calm. See if we can soothe the crowd."

Ophelia nodded once, as Edgar fastened the necklace. She looked down—it was so odd to see it there on her chest.

Edgar raised his arms, walking out from behind Ophelia to stand between her and the crowd. His face looked artfully troubled. "Tell me, lads," he said, appealing to the crew. "When you ransacked Miss Young's quarters, did you find any evidence of witchcraft? Potions, herbs, ragdolls with pins sticking out of them? Things like that. Anything she could have used to sink the ship."

Lawrence gave a tiny shake of the head. "No, we didn't."

"Of course not," Edgar said. A slow smile spread across his face, forming a dimple in his left cheek. "That's because Ophelia Young doesn't need cursed items to sabotage the navy. She *is* the Curse."

Ophelia's heart gave an awkward thud, offbeat, but powerful. What was Edgar playing at?

Edgar pivoted gracefully, almost like a courtly dance move, to face Ophelia again. He bowed to her. "There's only one way to get rid of a pirate's curse. You have to drown it."

Still unsure if this was some kind of risky scheme, Ophelia widened her eyes at Edgar, whispering, "What do you think you're doing?"

Edgar straightened from his long, gentlemanly bow. "I'm saving this ship from you. After all—I was the one who told them to check your things." He winked. "Sorry, darling. Had to do it.

You bewitched me, and I took my first chance to break your spell and tip off the crew. Didn't I, Ophelia? Didn't I tell you to *duck*?"

Ophelia stopped breathing. Her eardrums shook, like he was shouting her name all over again. He hadn't called her real name on the pirate's deck by accident. He'd been setting a plan in motion to discredit her.

"Why?"

Edgar cocked his head to the side, all innocence. "Why?" he asked. "Because I was meant to be captain, not you. I tried to quell the mutiny first, you remember. But you lied and schemed your way here. I'm not surprised, of course. It's in your blood. No one could trust an ungrateful thing like you." His eyes flashed, and his lips took on a mocking pout. *"Don't be angry."*

Flashing visions of that first day in the captain's cabin. Edgar's wooden smile. His bitterness. And now he was taunting her with her own words. It felt like a punch to the gut. She wasn't sure if Edgar was punishing her for daring to fight his duel for the captaincy, or for not kissing him back, or both. But it shook her all the same.

Edgar turned away from her, and the crowd of sailors parted to let him get behind the row of guns. His next sentence was clipped. "Throw her overboard."

The crew chorused back. "Aye-aye, Captain!"

They rushed forward, enveloping her like the sea they would give her to. Ophelia might have had time to grab her gun, but she didn't bother. What would be the point? Sure, she could probably kill one man, two, even three. But then she would be out of ammo, and she would end up in the drink anyway.

Lawrence drove his knee into Ophelia's stomach, and she

collapsed, spit spraying from her mouth. There were roars of approval. Someone tore at her hair. She felt blood as someone scratched her neck. She couldn't breathe—couldn't think. She was back at the foot of the gallows, the mob trying to make her pay all over again. Except where was Lang to disperse them? Where was Betsy, to crawl to Ophelia on her knees and shield her and make it alright?

There was a shout from far away. "Stop that, stop it!"

But the blows kept landing. She was already on her knees, but a kick to her back sent her forward, smashing her jaw against the deck. Her vision swam, blotches of black and white. They left her down for a moment, her cheek pressed against wood. "Betsy," she murmured. "Betsy."

Someone hauled her to her feet, as easily as if Ophelia were made of straw. Her head bounced limply as they carried her to the rail. Her vision came rolling back like the tide. Jo was standing with her thick legs planted solidly, her arms outstretched. "No!" she roared. "I'll not have this! We are the Imperial Navy, not witch hunters! Let her face court-martial, not *drowning*."

Ophelia couldn't turn her head far enough to see him, but she heard Edgar's response, a lazy drawl. "Ignore Josephine. She's bewitched too, you know." His laugh was soft. "But she'll calm herself. Or I'll have Emily roundly whipped."

Jo's arms dropped to her sides. She scanned the heads of the crowd, her lips moving silently. "Emily?" she said at last. "Where's Emily?"

"Below," came Edgar's answer. "Which is where she'll stay, until I'm certain you'll cause me no trouble."

Jo staggered toward Edgar, out of Ophelia's sight. "You can't hurt Emily. You can't—"

Hands pushed against Ophelia's back. Someone was lifting her knees, forcing her to stand on the rail. Her breath came fast and sharp. Her head was in splinters. She grasped out to the rigging, steadying herself. Every nerve in her body sang with fear.

Jo must have been dealt with because Ophelia couldn't hear her protesting anymore. She couldn't understand why she hadn't been pushed overboard yet. But then she heard Edgar reciting some very familiar words—that was when she realized she wasn't being murdered. She was being executed. But Edgar's voice was full of self-satisfaction, no impartiality. He was much more a crier than he was a Commodore Lang.

"We stand here in the presence of the villainous Ophelia Young, or as she is better known, the Curse of Peu Jolie. She stands here, indicted for acts of falsehood, mutiny, and witchcraft. She is hereby condemned to the ocean by the honorable *Captain* Edgar Ludlow, in atonement for her crimes. It is the honored duty of all citizens—" As Edgar launched into the message from the grandqueen, Ophelia's mind wandered. What did she care about all of this? What could she care?

The waters below were choppy and gray. Far from the emerald beauty that surrounded Peu Jolie and gave the ocean its name. The sky was black with clouds. Thunder boomed in the distance. Thick mist extended in every direction. If she squinted, Ophelia thought she saw a dark shape moving in the mist beyond, growing larger, coming closer.

A ship?

"—who threaten the harmony of our realm above all others."

Yes, a ship. It was cutting through the mist now, a tiny sloop with red-paneled sails. And at the bow, a silhouette: tall, powerful.

"The final mercy of the Crown is this," Edgar said. Ophelia was barely listening. That woman—it couldn't be—but it was. Her mother.

"Does the accused, Ophelia Young, have any last words?"

He was barely a nuisance to her now, as ever. She was breathless; the world spinning. How could he expect her to devote energy to giving memorable last words when there was the ghost of her mother lingering across the gap?

"Well?" Edgar demanded.

Ophelia straightened up, letting out a cold, incredulous laugh. "Like what?"

Those must have been good enough last words for Edgar. Before she had the chance to continue, Ophelia felt a hard, sharp shove to the small of her back. She heard Jo cry out.

She was falling, falling; dropping down toward the storm-gray sea. The air was sucked from her lungs so that she couldn't scream, couldn't breathe. Her vision blurred as the fall lengthened, slowing into an excruciating, endless torture. In the instant before she struck the water, she reached up to try clawing an invisible noose from her throat.

She was going to die under this sky.

SEVENTEEN

In the dark of their cell, when she was certain that they were alone, Betsy whispered to Ravi, "I have a plan."

Ravi's tongue clicked skeptically. He removed his glasses and shined them on his shirt, looking weary. "Is it a good plan?"

"It's a very bad plan, in fact," Betsy said, a tiny smile quivering on her lips.

"Is it bad enough to get us killed?"

"Ravi," Betsy said, turning his name over in her mouth like a prayer, "it doesn't matter if the plan gets us killed or not."

Ravi's laugh came out choked. "Betsy, I rather think it does!"

Betsy crawled closer to him, to sit side by side with their backs against the same wall. She hesitantly reached out to place her palm atop his hand. He did not push her away. In fact, his eyes flicked toward her, sparking with hope—the very thing he'd once told her they weren't allowed to have.

"It doesn't matter if the plan kills us," Betsy whispered, infusing as much comfort into these terrible words as she could.

"Because if we don't try, Jack and Fiona will definitely kill us. We can't be inactive anymore. It's a matter of certain death versus only . . . probable death."

She didn't add that if they did not make an attempt soon, it wouldn't just be them who would die. The chance of Betsy catching Ophelia before she was apprehended by the navy grew slimmer by the hour. She couldn't afford to waste time.

Ravi sighed mournfully. Then he forced a smile, gazing at Betsy silently for several long seconds. "It has been over seven months since I held a pretty girl's hand. I can't tell you how much I missed it."

Betsy was so shocked that she spluttered. No man had ever been this forward with her before—but then again, no man had ever been locked in a tiny cell with her before. "W-what," she coughed. "Hold hands with a lot of girls back at home, did you?"

Ravi's smile, boyish with its missing teeth, turned rakish. "I did alright."

He turned Betsy's hand over by the wrist, studying the palm lines. "And maybe it's just that I like a madwoman holding my hand. Because as mad as you are, you're likely right."

"I'm right?"

Ravi nodded. "Certain death versus only probable death. Not great odds, but we might swing them in our favor if we work together. Now, tell me about this terrible plan."

Betsy told him.

Hardly a moment after she was done talking, Ravi laughed out loud.

"You're right. That *is* a bad plan."

Jack grew more restless by the minute, and every minute the *Bloody Shame* was skimming farther out into the expanse of the ocean, farther away from Orana. The next morning at breakfast, when Ravi set down the plates of food, Jack pounded the table with his fist, making the silverware and mug of rum rattle ominously. "Where's my gold, Lalithan? I was promised gold. There are things I want to buy."

Across the table, Fiona settled her chin into her hand, grinning. "And things to buy for me."

Jack gave Fiona an affectionate glance, murmuring, "Of course, sweetling."

Betsy, who had been instructed to stand behind Fiona and wave a cheap paper fan at her back to cool the air, felt queasy. The pirate couple was violent and mercurial with just about everyone else, but with each other they were sickeningly sweet. Earlier that morning, she had watched as Fiona gently, lovingly shaved Jack's face with his omnipresent razor, cooing sweet nothings all the while. She'd felt sick then too.

Jack turned to look at Ravi again, his hand drifting toward the hilt of the razor. "So—you were saying where my gold is hidden?"

Ravi swallowed, and Betsy could see a lump bobbing in his skinny throat. "Well, I did have a thought."

Jack gave a rumbling laugh. "That would be a first."

Ravi looked down at his feet, afraid to even look Jack in the eye. "I was thinking . . . my family has searched for years, combing the islands farther out to sea. But what if the reason they've been missing the island is because they were looking in the wrong sea altogether? They were headed for Carthay, after all. Maybe, after the storm, my grandfather got all turned around and never realized the island was in the center of the Boiling Sea, not the Emerald one."

Jack stared at Ravi for a long time, mulling over his suggestion. Ravi had his arms wrapped around himself and was still looking determinedly down at the floor. At last, Jack conceded, "The idea isn't completely ludicrous. It would explain why no one's found anything. All right then. We'll shift course. Head back toward Carthay."

Betsy's heartbeat picked up, but she tried not to let her delight show on her face. Back toward Carthay meant back toward Orana—and back toward her sister, if only she could manage to get away from this wretched boat. But that's just the sort of thing she couldn't think about, Betsy reminded herself as she redoubled her speed fanning the back of Fiona's head, or she'd jinx it.

Betsy had lost count of the days since she'd been torn away from the *Sunshearer*. She didn't know if Ophelia's ship was still meant to be in port at Orana or not. She'd heard the pirates whisper of a hurricane a while back—a storm like that might have kept the *Bluesusan* moored in Carthay longer than intended. That idea gave Betsy hope, although she knew hope was dangerous.

As the *Bloody Shame* circled back toward the great continent, the atmosphere on the ship grew tense—the crew always mimicked their captain's mood. When Jack was irritable and twitchy, more inclined to violence, they were too. Betsy didn't know how many times she'd been tripped by a restless pirate sticking out his boot. Ravi was hardly any calmer. He'd stuck his neck out, suggesting they look in a different geographic location. Unless Copeland's bad mood blew over soon, Betsy knew that Jack might shoot Ravi between the eyes if his idea didn't prove as brilliant as promised.

The only person on the ship unladen with concerns was Fiona. No matter how violent Jack got with his crew, he showered Fiona with attention and gentleness. She would be safe no matter what happened. For her part, Fiona spent the days finding little ways to torture people. Forcing Betsy to strip off her blue dress, and dress in rough-hewn men's clothing. Tossing said dress into the waves. Tweaking Ravi's ears, and suggesting that Jack use his razor to carve off their extra inches. Even the crew—which was drunk all day and all night—lived in fear of her turning her whimsical cruelties toward them, knowing Jack wouldn't dream of keeping her in check.

Fiona was delighted to twirl around the deck in dresses Betsy had tailored for her—but her avarice was never satisfied. Every night before dinner, Betsy found herself kneeling at Fiona's feet, bringing up a new hem.

Eventually, the trajectory shift brought them within spitting distance of Carthay's coast. The day they first saw a thin green line on the horizon, Betsy was at her work again, this time fixing a dress of scarlet velvet to fit Fiona's specifications. "Ma'am," Betsy said, not making eye contact, "might I suggest you take the pistol out of your corset while I fix the top? It will ruin the lines of the silhouette if we're not careful."

Fiona shrugged, reaching down her neckline to pull out the pistol. "As you say." She tossed the weapon lazily on the table, and Betsy flinched. She heard a creak at the door—Ravi's arrival with dinner—but didn't look up.

"Where's the *food?*" Jack snapped, leaping up from his seat at the table, his razor again clutched in his fist. Ravi was holding two mugs of rum in his hands, but had no plates to speak of. He was trembling. "I'm so terribly sorry. That old man—Dawkins, I think—he said he was hungry. That he couldn't wait to eat. He took the dish from me. I had Puget start making a new dinner, but it will be a half an hour—I thought you might like the rum while you wait?"

Jack's diagonal-cut tooth was digging into his lower lip. An angry, red vein throbbed in his temple. He drove the point of his razor into the tabletop. "You're lying," he growled, pacing toward Ravi.

Betsy tightened her grip on her needle, wishing it was something longer and sharper. She could have done with a blade of her own.

"I'm not lying, I swear," Ravi said, slumping to make himself smaller. "Why would I lie to you? You could take my ear if you wanted, sir. I like my ears."

Jack laughed, and reached for the razor's handle. He wrenched his weapon back out of the wood, and drew so close to Ravi that their noses were inches apart. Jack turned the blade over in his hand, breathing heavily. "You like your ears?" he asked.

Ravi nodded, his eyes shut tight. He made a slight whimper.

"Well, so did Dawkins." And Jack turned on his heel, stomping out the door to the lower decks, in hot pursuit of the sailor who had absconded with his dinner.

Fiona giggled into her palm. "Dawkins should thank him. Just like yours, Randawa, his ears always stuck out too far."

Betsy forced out a laugh. "Good one, ma'am. Could you come down off the crate for a moment? I want to check if the hem looks right at ground level."

Fiona descended from the wooden crate as Ravi took quick, shallow breaths to get over his narrow miss with Jack. He crossed to the table, still jerky with nerves, his eyes fixated on the ground. Then, out of nowhere, Ravi took a sharp fall to his knees, having apparently tripped over the leg of Jack's chair. Betsy stared, dead-eyed, as rum from the mugs spilled out in a wide amber arc, soaking the bottom of Fiona's velvet dress.

Fiona lunged at Ravi, her hands extended like feral claws, raking him across the cheek. "You bumbling idiot! My dress will be ruined now."

Ravi's long, thin body was extended in a half bow. He was mumbling fervent apologies. On the floor, Betsy was shaking in fear. This moment could end Ravi, and if it did, it would be her fault. This had been her idea. "N-not to worry, ma'am," she said, practically squeaking. "I can get that out. It won't stain."

Fiona relaxed. She backed away from Ravi, who was still stooped, and glanced over her shoulder at Betsy. "You think so?"

"Definitely," Betsy repeated, more confident this time. "It will not stain. Let me get a good look at it. It's mostly on the back here." Betsy pointed at the far corner, glaring at Ravi. She was dry, mocking. "Now you go over there and think about what you've done."

A gleeful, merciless laugh from Fiona. "I didn't know you were funny, Rabbit! Yes, stupid boy. Go stand in the corner." Ravi obeyed, his eyes wide and intense.

Fiona stretched, yawning like a contented house cat. Her blind rage had swept away as quickly as it had come. She adopted a conversational tone. "How do you plan to get the stain out?"

"Simple," Betsy said, flicking the switch on her lighter. "I'll burn it away."

Flames erupted from the bottom of Fiona's dress and surged upward toward her waist. Betsy tucked her sewing kit hastily under her arm and scrambled back before Fiona even registered the fact she was on fire. Then, she began to shriek.

White spots danced on Betsy's eyes; she couldn't look away for even a moment. She had done something horrific and miraculous. With her back to the table, Betsy reached out her free hand to feel for Fiona's discarded pistol. She seized it, and strode across the room to join Ravi. "Go on!" she said, shoving her sewing kit into his arms. "Let's start running."

Ravi nodded, and darted out the exit.

Betsy glanced back at Fiona one more time. She was screeching in agony, rolling on the ground, trying to snuff out the flame. It didn't seem to be working. Her dress was still being devoured, and the tasseled corner of the rug by the table had caught fire too.

Betsy's eyes were stone as she watched her captor burn. "Well, Fiona," she said, "at least now you'll never go back to Peu Jolie. But *I* just might."

She lingered for a moment for the sake of lingering, and then Betsy ran, following Ravi out into the hall and up the ladder to the main deck. They burst into daylight to find the crew gathered around the writhing figure of the pirate Dawkins, holding both sides of his head against the gushing of ruby-red blood. "I swear," he howled, "I didn't take it!"

Jack was standing over Dawkins's body, twirling his razor and looking satisfied. But having heard the hatch swing open, he looked up to see Betsy and Ravi blinking confusedly in the sun.

"What the bleeding cunny are you two doing above deck?" Jack growled, advancing on them.

Betsy raised Fiona's pistol, cocking it. In truth, she was certain that if she fired, she would miss—to say nothing of the havoc the kickback would wreak on her balance—but Jack needn't know that. "We're leaving," she announced. "And you're not stopping us." She walked forward, jerking her head at Ravi to indicate that he should follow right behind her, where another pirate couldn't easily shoot him.

"Like hell you are," Jack said, actually grinning. "It's almost sweet that you're trying—but let me speak so clearly even a stupid wench like you will understand. I'm going to cut out your tongue and feed it to the sharks."

Betsy ground her teeth together, saying, "You don't have time to banter with me. Your lady's on fire."

Jack blinked. "What?"

"I said," Betsy snarled, withdrawing her lighter from her apron pocket and allowing its case to shine in the light, "your lady's on fire." Her tongue, once threatened, had turned poisonous. "*Do you have any idea what damage an open flame can do on a wooden ship?*"

Jack became seized by fear and panic. The blood drained from his face as he sprinted toward the hatch, bypassing Betsy and Ravi completely. "Fiona!" he cried out, voice cracking. "I'm coming!"

With Jack out of sight, Betsy slowly began to step backward, toward the rail, the pistol in her hand still raised and poised to fire. "No one wants a gunshot wound," Betsy reminded the rest of the pirate crew. "So, let's play this smart. My friend and I are leaving on a lifeboat, and you're going to let us. In fact, if you were really smart, you'd all run down below and try to help your captain put out the fire."

Nobody moved. Then, a lean-muscled man with crisscrossing tattoos up his forearms made a sound of confusion. His brows furrowed as he asked, "But if the ship's on fire, why should we let you take one of the lifeboats? You're talkin' 'bout smart, but if we had any brains we'd riddle you with holes and take the dinghies ourselves." The pirates mumbled general assent.

"Bleeding cunny," Betsy said.

She turned around, grabbed Ravi by the hand, and fled. The pirates, drunk and unprepared for a fight, clumsily attempted to load their pistols. Betsy leaped over the rail and into one of the dinghies precariously suspended on ropes just below.

Ravi landed in the lifeboat a split second sooner than Betsy— his legs were longer. It tilted dangerously to one side, and then swung in the other direction when Betsy crashed into the other half of the boat. For a moment, she feared the ropes wouldn't hold, but while the boat swung in midair, they didn't fall.

Betsy righted herself. She and Ravi immediately scrambled to work the pulleys and lower the boat into the water. When they were bobbing in the ocean, Ravi withdrew a steak knife from his trouser pockets—he must have stolen it from the cook—and sawed through the ropes to free them.

On the ship above, pirates were peering down at them over the *Bloody Shame*'s rail, jeering and shooting at last, though their drunken aim was poor. Ravi and Betsy each seized an oar and started paddling away, out of the guns' range. Only one bullet got close to them—it chipped the wood at the very tip of Ravi's oar. The other bullets slipped into the sea.

As they glided away from the *Bloody Shame*, Betsy still heard shooting, but the bullets were no longer being wasted on them. She knew the pirates had turned on each other—there were only four dinghies to begin with, only three now. They would never hold the whole crew, and it was every man defending his own best interests as he tried to fight his way to comparative safety.

Betsy threw back her head and cackled. The rush of freedom was intoxicating.

Across from her, Ravi's smile was so wide that she could again see the empty gaps tucked behind his canines. The sun shone brightly in his dark hair, which was covered in a thin layer of dust. He sounded breathless. "Elizabeth Young, you are—you are—you're brilliant, aren't you? You did this! You saved us! Why, I could just kiss you!"

Betsy, not thinking for once in her life, and emboldened by their daring escape, simply asked, "Why don't you?"

She inched closer to him, and Ravi leaned forward to meet her. Their lips were just about to touch when a thundering *boom* rattled their bones, and sent the waves swelling uncontrollably to starboard, threatening to capsize the lifeboat. Betsy shrieked. Some pirate—too focused on revenge to fight for his own life— had aimed a cannon at them, missing by mere feet.

"Perhaps we'll do that later!" Ravi suggested, panicky. He seized Betsy's oar and told her, "Let me take care of this. We used to race boats on the river when I was back at academy. I'm quite good."

A warm, pleasant glow expanded in Betsy's lungs, making her feel like her body was no longer restrained by gravity. She nodded, smiling, and told Ravi, "I'm sure you are."

They rowed toward the green line on the horizon.

EIGHTEEN

A sharp pain in her ribs. Water bubbling from her mouth. She could breathe again, almost. She hacked salt water from her lungs.

Black storm clouds above. "Mother?"

"No," the tall woman said, "I'm not your mother."

Not her mother. Ophelia blinked upward, and the woman's face swam into view. She actually couldn't have been much more than five years older than herself. She was several inches taller than her mother had been, with a left eyebrow cut in half by a vertical, indented scar. Her hairstyle too was different, her dark curls restrained by elegant, coiled braids. The rest was her mother, though—the flashing eyes, the sharp profile, the air of authority and composure. She could understand how from a distance she'd believed her mother was staring out at her from across the water.

Ophelia coughed. A few stray flecks of water came out. "I see that now," Ophelia muttered. She shoved herself upright, ignoring the pain in her chest as it grew more intense.

Embarrassed, she muttered, "I don't know what I was thinking. Ophelia Cray's dead."

"Not entirely," the stranger said. "My name is Ophelia Cray too."

Ophelia narrowed her eyes. She felt blood pounding in her ears, and every rapid heartbeat came like a sharp ache. "You're a liar."

She scrambled for her pistol, her wet hands slick against its smooth ivory handle. She lifted it—her arm heavy as lead— aimed at the woman, and clicked the trigger. Nothing happened.

The woman gave a snarl. She raised her shining boot and kicked the malfunctioning pistol from Ophelia's hand. Ophelia cried out in pain and terror as her only weapon skidded away across the deck.

A new voice, also female, sneered. "Don't you know a pistol can't fire when wet? Or has the drowning made you stupid?"

Head aching, Ophelia was inclined to agree that drowning *had* made her stupid. She was cradling her right hand now, and her throat was still sore from the burn of salt water. She took slow notice of another girl flanking this "Ophelia Cray." The duo now crouched beside her, looking down. They both had Ophelia's gap teeth, her warm skin tone, her high cheekbones. The sneering one was almost a dead ringer for her own reflection, except that her waist was curvier and she bore none of Ophelia's freckles— but even her eyebrows arched like Ophelia's did when she was skeptical.

She must be hallucinating. It would be only natural, after the fall—*the fall*. She felt it all over again, the sharp push to her back, the visceral sensation of her stomach leaping toward her throat.

And she remembered who had done it. She had thought he was her friend.

It was then that she finally craned her neck to take a look at her surroundings. The *Bluesusan* was sailing away in the distance, which meant that the deck she was lying on, in a puddle of water from her own lungs, belonged to the sloop she had seen in the distance.

"But, but that's her name," she said, sounding stupid even to herself. "My name. You're—you mean you're called Ophelia too?"

Ophelia Cray let out a harsh laugh. "You didn't think you were the only one? Mother was vain. She loved naming babies after herself. I personally prefer going by Phe, though. Lessens the confusion. There's another of you fancy islander Ophelias living in Peu Ankirk. Ophelia Newsome, I think she's called."

The other girl stepped forward, tossing her mane of curls contemptuously over her shoulder. "Heard she just married a banker, and a fat, prosperous one at that." Then she ticked off a finger, adding, "Then there was the stillborn Ophelia. Probably there are other Ophelias out there living the high life on land and we don't even know it."

Ophelia could hardly process this information. "I'm—I'm just Ophelia."

Phe smiled mockingly. "Of course you are."

Now Phe pointed to the other girl, whose expression still suggested that a rotten fish had washed up on their deck. "And this is Cordelia. She used to be called Ophelia too, but she changed it."

Cordelia raised a hand, her fingers curling in a dainty way that clearly indicated disdain. "Charmed," she said, inclining her head to Ophelia, her every syllable dripping with sarcasm, "I'm sure."

"Cordelia's also a fair bit of a bitch," Phe added. She received a hard shove from Cordelia for her honesty.

Ophelia looked around the deck again. It was deserted, with no one else to be found. "Where are they?" she asked with growing suspicion. "Where is the rest of the crew?"

Phe snorted, turning her back to Ophelia, and Ophelia couldn't help admiring her magnificent red greatcoat. It was completely identical to the one her mother had worn on the gallows; it shone like silk, but seemed thicker, more durable. She couldn't guess what the material was. Betsy would have known.

"No crew," Phe said. "Just us. Some are out on a voyage at the moment, some were killed with mother, and the least loyal among our men—"

"And women!" Cordelia added, flatly.

"—scampered off for a cushy life ashore right after Mum got hung."

"Hanged," Cordelia corrected.

"Whichever," Phe snapped.

Cordelia was kneeling down now. Ophelia blinked at her, feeling like there was still water in her eyes. Cordelia wore a gauzy dress of white linen, completely unsupported by any corset or solid structure whatsoever. Ophelia, scandalized, felt a bit of Eliza stir inside her.

Cordelia reached out her tapered fingers to pluck at the chain around Ophelia's neck. "And what's this?" Her voice was an unsettling croon, the susurrus of a flowing stream. "Lalithan gold, I think. Hard to forget jewelry like this. Mum never took the damn thing off."

A snarl distorted Cordelia's pretty face. She wrapped her fingers around the necklace's chain, as if tempted to tear it straight from Ophelia's vulnerable neck. "Seeing as it's the only speck of treasure she didn't spend on the fleet, it seems like something to be inherited by her true daughters, doesn't it?"

Ophelia pried Cordelia's hand away from her neck. Her chest falling and rising with shallow, painful breaths, she demanded of the others, "What happens next? You take the necklace and you kill me?"

Cordelia stood, loosing a derisive laugh. She flicked her eyes sideways at Phe, unwilling to dignify Ophelia's question with a response.

Phe stood in a casual stance, inspecting her nail beds. "We're not going to kill you. We could use another crew member, to be sure."

"No!" Ophelia tried to push herself into a standing position, but the pain in her chest became too intense. It winded her, and she collapsed back onto the deck. "I can't stay here! Or, what I mean is, I can't go with you! I would never be a pirate. I *need* to get back to my crew."

The *Bluesusan* was supposed to be her new home. A better home. Now it was fading into the mist.

"Ha!" Cordelia said. "The crew that shoved you out to drown?"

Phe sent a withering look in Cordelia's direction. "Hush," she said, pointedly. She turned to Ophelia. "Rest yourself. I cracked one of your ribs getting the water from your lungs."

"I can't—I can't be a pirate," Ophelia protested weakly.

Phe ignored her, motioning to her sister and declaring, "Let's haul anchor and get us back home, alright?"

Ophelia staggered to the rail of the ship, her ribs feeling like they were splintering into a million pieces. She gazed uselessly out at the misty expanse of water between her and the long-gone *Bluesusan*. Ronan might have been a mutineer and murderer, and Edgar a traitor, but at least she knew where that ship was headed—and what it required of her.

Ophelia reached blindly for the handkerchief in her pocket, still caked with dried pirate's blood, and unfolded it so that she could see Lang's star medal. She clutched it until its stone dug into the soft skin of her palm. All her body weight on the rail of the ship, she cried out to her sisters' backs. "I could never be a pirate!" She spat out the words like poison, hissed them with infinite loathing. "I could never be like you. I'd rather die."

At these words, Phe and Cordelia drew their weapons in perfect unison, pointing them at Ophelia's chest; the gesture was as nonchalant as if they were passing the gravy at dinner. "If you don't cooperate," Cordelia said, her mouth twisting into a smile, "you might just."

Ophelia's eyes darted to the place on the deck where her sodden, useless pistol lay. She thought suddenly of her father's compass. A memory flickered to life; Edgar saying, "A fine instrument you've got there." She imagined him with his feet up on the captain's desk, snapping her father's keepsake open and shut.

That was two presents from Papa down, then. And she was

about to betray him entirely by joining up with pirates. What would he say to her when he heard? That is, if she ever saw him again to tell him.

She gripped her handkerchief tighter, until she felt the sharp edge of the metal star pierce her skin. Fresh blood blossomed against the ruined cloth. *Forgive me*, she thought, although she wasn't sure if it was Lang's forgiveness that she wanted.

She inclined her head, feeling her muscles loosen, as if in relief. She had realized there was no way out. She was going with the pirates. They would make her a Cray at last.

The curse had come to fulfillment.

NINETEEN

etsy had fallen asleep during the heat of the day, and she woke up with her head against Ravi's chest, tucked beneath his arm.

He was still dozing when she started to stir. Betsy let out a quiet laugh when she saw that his glasses were askew. They had rowed for hours—well, mostly Ravi had rowed. Betsy had pitched in whenever he needed a break to regain his stamina, but the progress she made was much more slow going. They'd been fighting their way toward shore for a day, at the very least. And there'd only been a small amount of food and water stored in the lifeboat.

Betsy slowly realized that the boat had become very still, although she could hear water lapping against the side. She sat up and looked around. They had drifted ashore on a beach covered with fine white sand that had settled in swirling patterns. *The white-lace beaches of Orana.*

Betsy nudged Ravi awake, straightening his glasses for him.

"Ravi, Ravi! We're here. We actually made it."

Ravi blinked dazedly up at her. "We're—we made it? We're in Orana?"

"Yes," Betsy said, laughing wildly. "We jumped ship at just the right time! Your calculations were exactly right!"

Ravi craned his neck to look around. His response was almost inaudible. "I can't believe it." A slow grin spread across his face. "I just gave my best guess for where to direct Jack. I really didn't think I'd get it."

Betsy stood up and scrambled out of the boat. "Yes! We got it right! Do you understand what this means? For once, nothing went wrong!" Overwhelmed with joyful energy, she stretched out her arms, her head thrown backward, and spun in the sand.

Ravi held out his right hand, and she took it, wheeling to a stop. Betsy stared at the hand. His ashy palm was now blistered from rowing. She laid her palm against his, and his graceful, long fingers extended far past the tips of her plump ones. This boy was beautiful.

He laced his fingers into hers. "May I?" he asked. "I mean—I mean—might I?"

Betsy didn't bother answering. She stood on her tiptoes, laying her free hand on the back of his neck. Their lips met, and her first thought was how soft his lips were—although a bit chapped after all the time they'd spent in the baking sun.

Betsy's perpetually anxious mind slowed its usual whirring down to a calm, contented purr. Then she felt Ravi's left hand caress the very end of her blond hair, where it gave way to a gentle curl, and everything went completely quiet at last. The only sounds she heard were the distant crying of birds and the splash of waves against sand—until a shout pierced the air. "Put your hands in the air!"

Betsy and Ravi broke apart, lifting their arms. Betsy turned to find a group of four city officers in palm-green uniforms, each with a weapon trained on her. The lead officer, a man with a thick brown beard, watched her with pinprick eyes. "Keep your hands where I can see them, lass."

"What have we done?" Ravi asked, his voice pointedly polite.

"We've received a report of pirates crossing the Boiling Sea," the officer said. He pointed at their dinghy, an eyebrow raised. "And you two just came ashore in a lifeboat with the name *Bloody Shame* etched on the side. I trust you're familiar with that ship's somewhat unsavory reputation?"

"Y-yes," Betsy said, "but we're not pirates."

"No," the officer said, his tone clipped and prim. "You're certainly not. I rather suspect that you are one Elizabeth Young, of Peu Jolie? Is that so?"

Betsy nodded, dumbly.

"We've been looking for you."

At this revelation, Ravi seemed rather pleasantly surprised. His face broke into a sunny smile, and—clearly under the impression they were all friends—lowered his arms, moving to clean his glasses on the front of his shirt.

Two of the four officers cocked their guns at him, and he gave a little jump, uprooting the sand by his feet. "Did we tell you to put your arms down?" the lead officer growled.

Blinking rapidly, Ravi shoved the glasses back onto his face and threw his hands upward again. "I—I'm afraid I don't under-stand. You know who she is. We were captives on the *Bloody Shame*. We've done nothing wrong."

Betsy sighed. She could hardly bear to look at him. She tried to say his name, to explain herself, but her voice came out only as a squeak. And still, Ravi was protesting their joint innocence.

"My name is Ravi Randawa," he said, the words tumbling over each other as he rushed to explain. "Look me up. My father is the head of the Randawa Company. The records will say I went missing months ago. We're not pirates! We're escaped captives."

The lead officer threw back his head and laughed. "We know well *you're* no pirate, boy! It's obvious by the mere look of you. But we do have a warrant for *her* arrest." He lowered his gun, although his men kept them raised, and produced a length of rough-hewn rope. He paced toward Betsy, dragging her hands behind her back and binding them. He leaned into Betsy's ear, speaking in a mocking stage whisper for Ravi's ben-efit, "Something about an accomplice to mutiny? And fraud too, wasn't it?" He pushed Betsy forward, and she stumbled in the dunes, righting herself only at the last moment.

The lead officer put his hand to his bearded chin, surveying Ravi for a moment. "We haven't a warrant for any Ravi Randawa, but you're with her, so I have to assume that makes you an accom-plice's accomplice." A nasty grin split over his face. "Seems best to arrest you as well, don't you agree?"

Ravi didn't fight the man. He just let out a confused, helpless bleat, like a dog whose tail had been trodden on. Soon they were being dragged up the beach—the scuffed, oversized boots Fiona had forced Betsy to wear kicking up the delicate white sand with each shuffling step.

"How did you even know we would be washing up here?" Betsy asked, in an exhausted, resigned sort of way.

The lead officer, who was the one pulling her forward, gave a barking laugh. "Now, that's a good one. There is a Lady Ruza Eden, who just found her way back to the Carthay coast, who promptly rushed to visit her brother-in-law, Orana's admiral-in-residence, entreating that the navy hurry off and rescue her friend Elizabeth Young from the clutches of Jack Copeland and Fiona Wall."

Betsy tried to make sense of this—she couldn't quite see how Ruza's kindness could have led to her destruction. But the officer kept going. "And, most unluckily for you, when Lady Ruza arrived, Admiral Eden was hosting an Admiral Lang, who recently arrived from Peu Jolie, looking to apprehend a young sailor masquerading under the name Elizabeth Young."

Betsy closed her eyes so she wouldn't have to see Ravi craning his neck to look at her.

"And then," the officer finished, all jauntiness, "it was a quick leap when our city watchmen noticed that a lifeboat, painted with Jack Copeland's ship name on the side, was coming into shore."

Betsy sucked on her teeth. She couldn't quite say, in all honesty, that she was surprised. This brand of unluckiness was the curse, through and through. She was mostly disappointed in herself for believing, just for a moment, that her streak of bad luck had been broken.

She couldn't bear to glance at Ravi as they were hauled through the grimy streets of Orana. Besides, with the way she was being pushed, she had to spend most of her time looking down, to avoid tripping over her own feet or stepping in horse dung. They soon reached the naval office and stepped into the cool shade of a marble lobby near identical to the one in Port Jolie. Despite the dreadful circumstances, after so many hours exposed to the merciless sun, the reprieve from the heat felt like a miracle.

They went through a side door, down a set of damp, dimly lit stairs. Betsy found herself staring at a single cell, where the air hung thick with humidity. She was relieved of her pistol, and even her beautiful lighter. She and Ravi were pushed inside the cell, inspiring Ravi to remark under his breath, "Feels just like old times, doesn't it?"

What was different from their time in the pirate's brig, however, was that they were no longer alone. Another man was already locked in there—a shriveled old coot who stank of alcohol, wearing a tattered red coat. He was rocking in the corner, his arms wrapped around his knees and muttering to himself.

"Enjoy yourselves," the lead officer said as he left. "We've left you with the most refined public nuisance in all of Port Orana. Should be good company." The officers swaggered away, laughing amongst themselves. Betsy stretched out both her arms, leaning her palms against the damp stone walls. She couldn't bear to see the look of betrayal on Ravi's face. She couldn't.

"Just say it, why don't you? Just say that I lied. That it's my fault we're in this mess. My bad luck that got you here and my selfishness for not filling you in on why I needed to land in Orana." It was unequivocal that she had done this to Ravi: helped him escape one prison only to be immediately thrown in another. It was exactly her father's favorite expression: *Out of the fire, into the flood.*

She heard Ravi's footsteps as he paced the stone floor. She could just imagine him, pushing up his glasses, his face all twisted up in frustration that was at once adorable and heartbreaking. "The thing is," he said, slowly, "I'm not sure you did lie. I don't remember asking you whether you were an accomplice to mutiny. If I had, and you'd said no, perhaps I'd be a bit more ticked off, but as it stands, I'm afraid all you've done is save me from certain death at the hands of the Violent Bastard."

Betsy had half a mind to check if there was water in her ears. She turned to him, not quite believing that he could be so calm.

Ravi's face was so neutral, so terribly polite. "I've never asked what brought you to sea before. I'm asking now. Please tell me the truth."

So, Betsy told him everything, from Ophelia Cray to the family curse, her father's death, Ophelia's deception. At some point, her knees gave out, and she slumped to the floor. Odd—because the rest of her felt so light after telling the truth. "I'm sorry, Ravi," she said. "This is all my fault. You just got caught up in my bad luck."

"You're not bad luck," Ravi told her, crouching to look into her eyes. "You're brilliant. That's why I like you so much. You're brave— and clever and pretty." He extended his hand to her. "We got out of one prison together, I'm sure we can find a way out of this one."

Betsy hated the way he was looking at her, with an uncharacteristic optimism. She had come up with one wild escape plan, but to concoct another was too much to ask. Especially now her lighter was gone; it had always given her an odd sense of protection, a courage substitute. Without it, she was back to her old self. To being nothing. She wasn't *Ophelia*, after all. She was just Betsy.

She stared at him, mouth half-open. She wanted to cry. "You don't have to lie, Ravi. I know I'm not brave."

"How can you say that?" Ravi said, looking perplexed in exactly the adorable way she had just imagined. "Betsy, you are the bravest person I've ever met. You saved my life just by showing up on that ship. Without you, I'd given up all hope. But you gave it back to me. You've got so much grit"—his eyes, behind the round glasses, were full of fire—"and you love your family so much, that you never considered anything but escaping. Of *course* you're brave. Don't sell yourself short."

Betsy's mouth, already slightly parted, fell open the rest of the way. How could it be that she, the girl with the worst luck in the world, had stumbled her way into finding this wonderful boy? Then she decided to stop questioning her good fortune. She grabbed him by the collar and pulled him into another kiss.

When their lips parted—this time when the moment seemed right—Betsy thought the ceiling might disappear, and she would float away. This altogether pleasant feeling didn't last long, unfortunately. Soon she became aware of a rather foul odor creeping nearer her, all fish and shit and ale. Then there was a firm grip on her wrist.

She shrieked, wriggling around, to find the red-jacketed vagrant had abandoned his corner to seize her arm. His eyes were popping and mad. "I believe," he said, "that you mentioned something about Ophelia Cray."

Betsy's first instinct was to deny everything—but of course, she had mentioned the name. What would be the point in lying? She raised her chin in her best imitation of her sister and said, "What of it?"

The old man bared his yellow teeth in a feral smile. "The bitch ruined my life, is all."

Ravi pushed up his spectacles and said, rather stiffly, "She ruined a lot of lives, as I take it, but that's no reason to manhandle innocent women. I'll thank you to keep your hands to yourself."

Wary eyes on Ravi, the old man slowly uncoiled his hand from Betsy's wrist, lifting one finger at a time. Then, pulling at the cuffs of his shredded, filthy jacket as if to retain his dignity, he added to Betsy, "Your sister didn't much like being touched, either. When we met. Stormed off to her ship, she did, and her pretty little boyfriend went and consigned me to this hellhole for ruffling her feathers."

Betsy, whose heart had leaped when the man first mentioned Ophelia, now grew skeptical. "Boyfriend?" she asked. "You clearly don't know my sister."

"Sure I do," the man said, retreating to his corner, and lounging on the mossy floor like a king on his throne. "Pretty girl. Silk dress. Stuck out in a shithole tavern, I can tell you."

Betsy's eyes widened. "What color was the dress?"

The old man licked his chapped lips. He had the shifty look

of a person who knew precisely what the shade would be called, but was resisting saying it for fear of diminishing his manhood. "It was sort of a lass's color," he said, gruffly. "My old lady had a dress just like it before I lost everything, including her. Lilac, I think she would've called it."

Her heart thudding painfully in her chest, Betsy surged forward. She gripped the old man by his shoulders. "She went back to the ship? Is it still here? *Is it still here?* How long ago?"

The old man stuck out his lower lip and thought about it. "'S hard to tell," he mused. "The days sort of run together in this place. But it was before the hurricane."

"Would the ship still be anchored in harbor?"

The man gave a nasty grin. "You better hope it's not, after the story you just told. You have to know who's upstairs."

Betsy was about to ask, "Who?" but the return of her arresting officer rendered the question pointless. He stood outside the cell bars, bouncing on his heels like a dandy, and said with obvious delight, "Admiral Lang would like to see you, miss."

Betsy was escorted up to the marble finery of the main floor. The door to Admiral Eden's office was flung open by a sentry, who acknowledged her with a curt nod of the head. The admiral was a very handsome man: middle-aged, with cool brown skin and close-cropped, prematurely gray curls. He stood, his hands clasped elegantly behind his back, and inclined his head graciously to Betsy. For her part, she tried to drop into an appropriately deferential curtsy but found it awkward with no skirts to grip. "Miss Young, I presume?" the admiral asked, gesturing to the open seat before his desk.

"Yes," Betsy said, rushing to take the offered seat, but all the while twisting around looking for Lang, as if the woman would pop out of a closet somewhere to give her a good fright. Seeing Lang nowhere, she turned her attention back to the man in front of her. "You are Lady Ruza's brother-in-law, if I've heard correctly?"

Admiral Eden gave her a stern, yet somehow curious, look. "You have. I was very relieved to find that Ruza had escaped her troubles with Jack Copeland relatively unscathed. And from her account, we have you to thank for that."

Was this what good luck felt like?

"How did you know," Eden said, his brows furrowed, "that Ruza is cousin to her imperial majesty?"

Betsy almost choked on her own spit. "Pardon?"

"You told the pirates that Ruza is the grand-queen's cousin," Eden said. "Well, second cousin, anyway. And that was what saved her. But she hadn't confided that in you, so how could you have known?"

"I didn't know," Betsy said, shocked into honesty. "I made it up. It was a lie."

Amusement dawned over Eden's face. "A damn believable one. So believable it was actually true. Well played."

Despite herself, Betsy felt a smile pulling at the corner of her mouth. Her curses may have sunk ships, but at least her fibs could make royalty of a friend. Maybe her intent could work miracles, as well as bring catastrophe. It was almost enough to make one believe in magic.

The admiral suddenly seemed to compose himself, wiping the

traces of admiration from his face. "But of course," he added, "you understand the seriousness of the charges being brought against you and your sister."

Betsy opened her mouth to rebut, but no sound came out. She cleared her throat and tried again. Softly, she managed, "My sister would never mutiny, sir. She only joined the navy because she wanted to prove herself."

A rather sad look softened the admiral's stony face. "And meeting you, I believe you think that. I suppose you would have to, to go to such lengths to protect her. But . . . I'm afraid you misjudged the girl."

Betsy's lip quivered. She felt a chill run up her arms. "I don't know what you mean."

Admiral Eden sat on the edge of his desk, as if exhausted by formality. "At this very moment," he said, not unkindly, "my colleague, Admiral Lang, is receiving the crew of the *Bluesusan*, your sister's ship."

Betsy nodded.

"And," the admiral continued, doggedly, "your sister is not among them. I'm afraid she attempted an insurrection. She murdered the captain, and the first mate as well, and tried to install herself at the head. The crew discovered her scheming, and her true name, and well . . . she was formally executed."

The admiral kept on speaking, describing how Ophelia was thrown into the sea, but Betsy didn't quite hear it. All she heard was a dull roaring in her ears. At first, she saw Ophelia washed up on a beach somewhere—her hair tangled with seaweed, her eyes wide open. But then, she saw Ophelia lying in her father's bed.

She felt her sister's cold, stiff hands pressed in her warm ones.

The door to the office reopened. Admiral Lang entered, alongside a young man in well-tailored blue coat. They stopped speaking immediately upon seeing Betsy, still as marble in her chair.

"Miss Young," Lang said. Her voice seemed distorted, as if Betsy were hearing it through water. "Miss Young, I'm afraid this didn't end the way either of us wanted it to. I must express my deepest sympathies—"

"Miss *Young*?" the young man asked, his voice equally far away. His features swam before Betsy's eyes. "Surely, she's not— it can't be!"

"She certainly is, Captain Ludlow," Lang was saying. "This is the real Elizabeth Young."

The man, Captain Ludlow, drew back from Betsy as if she were a poisonous snake.

"There, there," Eden admonished the younger officer. "None of that. Have some compassion. This girl just lost her sister, and besides all that, she's had a run-in with Jack Copeland."

Betsy slowly became aware how tightly she was gripping the arms of her chair. The room was coming back into focus, if only marginally.

Ludlow let out a sharp laugh. "Has she now? It seems we have something in common."

Lang nodded. "It seems that on its way back to port, the *Bluesusan* apprehended Jack Copeland, floating helplessly in a dinghy not far from the wreckage of his ship. Unfortunately, Fiona Wall had already escaped—so we won't see her reach justice just yet. But at least we have him in custody now."

In another life, Betsy would have cared to hear someone insinuate that Fiona was still alive. But now the words just rung dully in her ears. Ophelia was gone. Nothing else mattered.

"It was really nothing," Ludlow said, with the air of someone who thought it was really everything.

Eden gave a tight smile, crossing the room to clap Ludlow on the shoulder. "There are great things in your future, my boy. Take my friend Lang here—she was a commodore three months ago. Then she captured the pirate queen and secured her promotion to admiral. You seem likely to equal her record, with time."

A greedy glint flared in Captain Ludlow's eyes, like a still burning ember tumbling out of the fireplace and threatening to set the house ablaze. He gave a courtly bow in Admiral Lang's direction. "It would certainly be a fine legacy to match. What officer doesn't want to catch a Cray or two? And you know, I'm quite ready go right back out and sniff out Fiona. I tend to have very good luck with these sorts of things."

"If that's your mission, I won't stop you," Eden said, and laughed. "Is there anything we can do to repay you for your service?"

Ludlow straightened the panels of his uniform. "I would love permission to speak with my old friend, one more time, before she is court-martialed. I believe she is being held below?"

"We can manage that," Eden said. "She'll be easy to find. We only have one cell."

Lang gave Betsy a gentle tug upward, bringing her unsteadily to her feet. "Perhaps you might be so kind, Captain, as to escort Miss Young back down as well? Now that she has heard the news of her sister." She gave Betsy a helpless little pat on the shoulder, and, her face showing a hint of emotion for the first time in Betsy's memory, said, "I am sorry, you know."

Admiral Eden now showed a trace of concern. He objected to Lang's suggestion. "I am not entirely comfortable with sending the girl back downstairs, to share a cell with *him*."

"I understand your concern, which is right and proper," Ludlow said, his hands folded neatly behind his back, "but my crew who escorted him to the brig assured me that Copeland is both bound and unconscious—and likely to remain so. Surely there can be no harm? But, of course, I yield to your discretion. If you would prefer the convict stay up here, then it shall be so."

Lang shook her head. "That would be against protocol. She hasn't been cleared yet—and were she to make a run for it, which she has been known to do before . . ."

Eden's jaw hardened as he realized he had few options. "I suppose Admiral Lang is correct. We must follow procedure, and if Copeland is unconscious, there is no danger." At that, he took Betsy's hand, giving it a gentlemanly kiss. "I thank you, for the help you gave Ruza. We shall not hold you or your friend much longer. I owe you that for your bravery. I just need to appeal to my superiors, and see your charges dropped. It will be done, and quickly."

Then Ludlow steered Betsy from the room, back down the long flight of stairs. He laughed quietly to himself. "I suppose I'll have to take their word that you two are sisters, because frankly there's no family resemblance I can see."

"Leave me alone," Betsy said, voice flat and distant. "You executed her. I don't want to talk to you."

Ludlow gave a light chuckle, smugness plastered across his blandly handsome features. "How uncivilized. And when I'm such a charming conversationalist."

"I hope you drown," Betsy spat.

"On second thought," Ludlow said, smiling an odd, crooked smile that was thus his first physical imperfection. "I can see your sister in you now. You're both uppity chits." He redoubled his grip on Betsy's arm, unlocked the screeching iron door, and threw her bodily to the cell floor. Betsy's shoulder cried out in agony, having absorbed the shock of impact.

She tried to stand up, but a long shadow fell over her. The shadow of a large, familiar man—who was grinning down at her with one cracked tooth.

Horror broke through the fog of Betsy's grief, slowly at first, like a hammer chipping away at a marble slab, until suddenly it was shattered by the reality of who was standing above her. "He's—he's not unconscious."

"No," Ludlow said, feigning mild surprise. "I suppose not. I suppose that when my bilge rats dragged him down here, he was faking." Jack sprang forward to the open door, but Ludlow slammed it shut with finality. He wagged his finger at Jack like a disapproving tutor. "I don't think so, Copeland. Your freedom is not in our deal."

"Deal?" Betsy choked out, struggling to sit up.

Ludlow grinned a grin so wide that it could have allowed her to count each of his perfect teeth. Jack was grunting, his hands raised to the iron bars as he rattled them as best he could with his wrists tied together.

It was then that Ludlow theatrically withdrew a silver blade from his jacket sleeve. "Yes," he mused, turning it over in his hand, "I suppose Jack faked being unconscious. I also suppose he must have concealed this blade somewhere on his person, and my bilge rats were idiotic enough to miss it when they searched him." He started to chuckle, lifting his chin to an invisible superior officer and furrowing his brow in mock concern. "I suppose, Admiral Eden, that Jack stopped pretending to sleep and cut himself loose from his bonds not long after I deposited the girl. I suppose he massacred everyone in that cell with him." His playfully sorrowful tone dropped away, becoming flat. "Tragic."

Ludlow turned the blade over between his fingers. "Jack will have to hang for it, of course, but that's no great loss, because Jack was always going to hang. And no one will be surprised—it's not like you can expect a killer not to kill. No, it's the bilge rats who'll ultimately need to be punished, for their sloppy search work, missing that blade. For shame." He smirked. "I'll have them keelhauled for their incompetence, as a way of making amends with Admiral Eden. But he won't be angry with me, in the end. It was Lang who insisted you be sent down here, after all, when I was perfectly amenable to you remaining upstairs. Of course, whether the bilge rats are flogged or dragged behind my ship, it won't matter much to you. You'll already be dead and beyond caring of such things. Bad luck."

Someone behind Betsy was breathing heavily, as if too angry to form words. She vaguely thought it must have been Ravi, but she couldn't tear her eyes away from her sister's killer for the spare moment it would have cost her to check. "You're a monster," Betsy said, her teeth gritted against a wave of tears.

"Perhaps I am," Ludlow said, smiling sweetly at her. "But don't weep, young lady. Trust that I'm doing you a favor. Admittedly, you're about to die. But you won't be alone in the Cities of Death long. I'll be sending your sister to join you there any day now."

Betsy was confused. "Ophelia? But—but she's already—you said!"

"Unfortunately," Ludlow drawled, "she got away. There was a little snag in the plan, and some strange women in a sloop plucked your cocktease sister out of the waves before she had time to drown. Her reprieve won't last long, though."

Betsy's heart thudded against her rib cage. "Not? Dead?"

He was taunting her—it couldn't be true, and yet. She was certain that it was. After all—Ophelia Young? Killed by a splash of water? It sounded false.

Ludlow's terrible grin grew wider, and he spread out his hands like a painter trying to visualize the wide expanse of a landscape. "I believe it was fate's gift to me, sending them to save her like that. Now I know they're real, and that Cray Island is real too, and it's presented me with a remarkable opportunity. I will be the man who stamps out every last Cray on the Emerald Sea. I'll turn over every speck of their treasure to boot. I'll be made the youngest commodore in history for that. I just need to catch up with your sister and spill a tad more of her blood." He tipped his hat to Betsy. "Pity you'll be too dead to witness it. It'll be quite the show. My grand finale."

He turned his gaze on Jack now. "Remember, Jack," he said,

his voice light and taunting, "I will be just upstairs, and I still have your lady stashed away on my ship. If I cut you loose and you don't follow through on your end of the deal and kill who I need killed, I'll renege on my end, and throw Fiona to the sharks. Her freedom, for their lives."

Jack nodded gravely, pounding his bound wrists against the bars. Ludlow licked his lips, and then sawed through the ropes with the silver razor. The bindings fell away to the cell floor, and Jack gave a feral grimace.

Ludlow pressed the blade into his palm, and now, the Violent Bastard was armed with his favorite weapon once more. "Kill who I need killed," Ludlow repeated, slowly, as if to someone he thought very thick. "Or Fiona will suffer." He gave a light shrug. "But beyond that, I don't care what else you do, or how you do it. As long as nothing is traced back to me. Just kill *Josephine* first."

Then he turned his back to them, and was gone.

Jack Copeland pulled his arm back into the cell, unsheathing the razor and admiring its shine. "My Fiona used to shave my beard with this," he growled, "before you ruined her."

Betsy was frozen with fear. Jack crossed over to her in two quick strides, straddling her prone body.

"No!" Ravi cried out. He threw himself over toward the pirate, but Jack was too quick for him. He caught Ravi in the throat with his elbow, and Betsy watched her defender sink to the ground, clutching his windpipe and gasping for air.

Jack gave a shuddering sigh, as if of pleasure. "I'll slide this blade into your gut, girl," he promised Betsy. "But I need to get rid of another bitch first."

It was then that Betsy realized the "Josephine" Ludlow had referred to was in the cell with them now. She stood near the back, her wide shoulders slumped, a fringe of black hair falling into her eyes. She was red-faced with rage, and taking shallow breaths that shook her whole body.

The woman held out an arm to Copeland, gesturing him in close, and said, "Kill me then, if you think you're man enough."

TWENTY

Ophelia smelled the land before seeing it through the mist. Even the most inexperienced sailor could recognize the oncoming shore this way. Back when they anchored in Orana, she had smelled an odd combination of wind off the fishmongers' row, chimney smoke, and freshly turned farmland, which had been not entirely unpleasant after weeks at sea. Now the smell dancing out from the invisible island was a tantalizing mix of citrus and wet grass. Soon, the prow of the boat cut through the mist, revealing the hazy outline of a thick jungle.

Phe was sitting backward on the rail, the tail of her red coat swaying out over the side. "Magnificent, isn't it?"

"Where are we?" Ophelia asked, touching her fingers to the necklace at her chest.

"The middle of the Boiling Sea. About fifty miles off the coast of Carthay. Small island. People tend to miss it."

"And you really call it Cray Island?"

Phe shrugged. "That's what Mum called it."

Cray Island, in its color, was almost indistinguishable from the color of the sea. It was not a particularly large expanse of land, but it gradually ascended out of the ocean, the summit of its tallest hill like a wave at the peak of its height, about to come crashing down again. Thousands and thousands of emerald-leaved banyan and palm trees rose from the sea. Only the beaches—as white as those in Orana—stuck out against the vibrant green of the water.

The sloop glided around the backside of the island and into a sheltered cove, where Ophelia counted ten—no, eleven—ships harbored there, hidden from external view. After the sloop bobbed to a stop and Phe had dropped anchor, Ophelia heard the click of a gun echoing off the shining obsidian walls of the cove. There was an ugly pause, in which only the dripping of water could be heard.

The barrel of a gun prodded Ophelia between the shoulder blades. "This is our stop," Cordelia said. "Best get off, and keep your hands where I can see them."

"Is that really necessary?" Phe asked, sliding off the rail and onto solid ground.

"I'm taking precautions."

"Precautions against what?" Phe sneered. "She's got a set of cracked ribs and water in her lungs. What's she going to do—fight us off single-handedly, and sail the sloop away with no gun and no crew? Stop being insufferable, Cord."

Ophelia felt the metal of the gun fall away from her back, as Cordelia stifled a deep, throaty laugh. "Oh, I'm insufferable, am I? Hear that, new girl? Our fearless leader says I'm insufferable."

Cordelia raised her chin high, slinging her shotgun up to rest against her shoulder, and began to stalk away. Ophelia's mouth dropped open so far that her jaw clicked painfully. She was overcome with the idea that looking at Cordelia, with those bone-familiar mannerisms, was like looking at her own reflection in a darkened shop window.

"Come on," Phe said, roughly, but not entirely unkindly. "We'll take you home." She then vaulted off the sloop and bounded down the length of the cove with all the power and agility of a leopard. Ophelia followed her slowly, making note of each ship she passed. The red-sailed sloop they'd arrived in was by far the smallest among the Cray fleet, the contrast in size reminding her absurdly of her father's miniature ship in its glass bottle. Something troubled her, though—most of the other ships had cannons for firepower, while the sloop clearly had none at all.

"Why wouldn't you sail out in one of the armed ships?" Ophelia asked. The sea was dangerous, and who should know that better than the daughters of a pirate? The sea was dangerous— *and they were meant to be the most dangerous things on it.* They had ceded that advantage by taking the sloop, instead of almost any other ship there.

"Stupid question," Cordelia gave a snort. "If we had the crew to man a larger rig, we would." Ophelia thought of the pirates her own crew had slaughtered. They all swore allegiance to Captain Cray. But surely there were others, weren't there?

They emerged from a fissure in the back of the cave into the verdant jungle canopy. Golden sunlight shone through the fiber of the leaves overhead, casting thin shafts of glittering light across the rough-hewn path. Her ears were filled with a symphony of parrots squawking, monkeys chattering, and cicadas crowing. The earth smelled rich and wet beneath her boots, like a garden in the height of spring. Shade from the thick leaves overhead left the air cool and pleasant against her skin. Stepping into that jungle felt like she was diving beneath the emerald waves again, except she could breathe freely, and she wasn't afraid. Everything around her seemed to vibrate, from the sprawling roots of the surrounding trees to the crystalline-winged insects, all buzzing with energy and life.

It was not like Ophelia had imagined Cray Island would be, if only because she had never allowed herself to try imagining what her mother's home would be like. She had only ever imagined herself as a Lang, a stoic hero—guessing at what it would be like to stand on this island would've been too close to an admission of weakness, of longing. But that was why she hadn't thrown away the necklace, wasn't it? Because she was weak. Because she had desired this place, as much as she had denied it to herself.

And if she had tried to imagine it, she still could not have conjured up a place in her mind's eye like this. It was sacred. Holy. What right did she have to anywhere as sublime as this?

"How long have you both been here?" Ophelia asked, a strange tingling beginning from the center of her chest, stretching all the way to her fingertips. She felt warm and invigorated. She had forgotten about the pain in her ribs.

Phe grunted, "Me about nine years, Cordy about seven."

"Frankly," Cordelia crooned, "you're a late bloomer. We each found our way here at the age of twelve."

"You . . . *found* your way here?" Ophelia asked.

"Of course," Cordelia responded, tone sharp now, as if daring Ophelia to object. "The island called us home."

"I wouldn't say that," Phe countered. "I'd say things were too shit to stay where we came from, and it was pure luck we landed in the right place at the right time. I'd run away from home, was catching a ship to Cornwallis to start a new life there, when Mum showed up, pistols blazing to sink our rig and collect all our valuables. Thank the gods she was vain enough to see her own face in mine. She took me in hand and I never looked back."

"Well the island called *me* home then," Cordelia sneered at Phe, clearly delighting in some sense of superiority. "I was from Carthay originally. One night, a voice called to me. I stole a fisherman's dinghy and rowed until my palms bled. And then I washed up here. The island is the reason Mum became a pirate, and the reason I did too."

Ophelia's tone was hesitant. She was intrigued, but her pride wouldn't allow her to make it obvious just yet. "How can an island be the reason someone became a pirate?"

She had barely let the words escape her lips when pain blossomed on her right side. Cordelia had slowed down to hip-check her. "Don't say 'pirate' like it's a dirty word," Cordelia said. "Like it's something you stepped in. It's your blood."

Ophelia fixed Cordelia with a measured stare, unwilling to back down. "On the island where I come from, everyone has crime in their blood. They don't all make it the family business."

To her side, Phe snorted, and swatted an overhanging vine.

"Really," Ophelia said, a mocking edge to her voice now. She could not let herself be lured in by the delights of this island so easily. She had to push back—or prove the crew of the *Bluesusan* right about her. "If I'm so ignorant of your ways. Tell me. Explain yourself. Explain how you can sleep at night."

Phe's eyes flashed, but she sent a smirk in Ophelia's direction. "With the help of rum, pretty soundly. But you do know Mum used to be in the navy, don't you? To hear her tell it, her captain was a particularly brutal bastard. He drove the crew hard and took all the glory for himself. Once, their rig was caught in a storm, and they had to anchor on this island to ride it out. The place was completely unsettled—but when they spread out to look for food and water, they found . . ."

"Found what?" Ophelia prompted.

"Gold," Phe said. "Mountains of it. Just stacked up toward the sky in great big bars. It was all Lalithan quality. The best, the purest there is. And Mum saw an opportunity—no more toiling away for a navy who paid her piddling wages and always promoted useless rich boys to officer positions over her." Phe's tone had become very pointed, and Ophelia found she couldn't meet her eyes.

Phe kept on, saying, "Mum knew that if she let their captain make the call, he'd hand all the gold over to the navy, get promoted to their glittering upper brass, and the crew wouldn't see a single coin of the profit. So, she gave her fellow sailors a choice—join her in seizing the ship and the gold, or keep getting stepped on." Phe gave a wide-toothed grin. "Every sailor in a beige uniform chose not to be a stepping stone that day. And those crew members, and some of their children, ran with us for decades. Mum used the gold to buy ships, which she used to make back the gold's value for her crew tenfold."

Ophelia's stomach jolted as she remembered that old man in Orana.

One day, I'll find me another crew! I'll find some good men, and we'll sail to your rutting island. I will take what is owed me!

She had not liked the man. He had grabbed her, tried to hurt her—even when she'd done him no harm. She had felt guilty then, that her mother had wronged him. Now—her ribs screaming with pain, her lungs burning with salt water—she was happy that he had been put in his place. She would not mind seeing Edgar similarly brought low. She understood the inclination to mutiny now, for the first time.

Ophelia was so busy—happily imagining Edgar being forcefully drowned—that she only just broke out of her reverie in time to duck and avoid smacking her head on a low-hanging branch. When she straightened up, she found Phe studying her face. It was obvious that Ophelia's bitter expression had been as plain as the roses in an embarrassed Betsy's cheeks. Her dark eyes alight with shrewdness, Phe said, "But enough about Mum. Tell us about you. Who in your family was the criminal, to be sent to a penal colony?"

Ophelia blinked, a little surprised by this change in direction. "No one," she said, suddenly defensive. "My father was born there. His father was a highwayman back in Cornwallis. He was the one sent to Peu Jolie."

"Interesting," Phe mused, her face inscrutable. "Personally, I don't see the difference between a highwayman and a pirate, do you? But obviously, Peu Jolie must be a very forgiving place, for a robber's son to become such a successful businessman."

Ophelia felt completely blindsided. How did Phe know anything about her father? Wrong-footed, she began mumbling something about Eliza's family having had money, but she didn't have time to finish before Phe cut her off.

"Tell me—did you find Peu Jolie quite as welcoming to you as they were to your father?"

Blood pounded in her ears. Phe was taunting her with questions she already knew the answers to. Ophelia was overwhelmed by the desire to lie, to grab Phe by the shoulders and stare her down and cry out, "Yes! They loved me! I was everybody's friend! They threw flowers at my feet when I passed!"

But Ophelia knew by now that she was no good at lying. "They hated me," she said, feeling her half sisters' eyes on her. "They thought I was cursed."

"Were you?" Phe asked.

"Hard to tell. They never really gave me a chance to not be cursed."

At that, Cordelia let out a soft humming sound, a noise of gentle agreement. This almost startled Ophelia. She wouldn't have imagined such a sound coming from Cordelia—who had been so hostile to her thus far—if she hadn't witnessed it herself.

"That's more or less what Mum said," Cordelia said, a lulling cadence to her voice now, "about society on land, I mean. That everything that happens out there happens because they believed it would. She said they forced us to the sea that way, but we still have a powerful will of our own."

For a moment, only the whites of Phe's eyes were visible, because she had rolled them so far into the back of her head. Luckily, Cordelia was several yards behind Phe, taking up the rear of the group, which meant that Ophelia was the only one to notice the oldest sister's skepticism.

It was then that trees around them began to thin. Speeding ahead, Phe slipped through a break in the tree line and emerged into a small clearing that contained only half-collapsed tents and the cold remains of a campfire. Cordelia swanned forward, her arms outstretched, her skirt fanned out behind her. "This is it," she called, "the pirate queen's great manse. Behold, ye mighty, our fortress."

Ophelia counted eight tents. "Where are the others?"

Phe sank down onto a split log and began unlacing her leather boots. She turned the right boot upside down and allowed a few pebbles to fall out. "No others," she grunted. "We told you. The only ones left went out to find a mark a few weeks ago. It's just us until they come back."

Staring upward into the branches of a great nearby banyan, Ophelia noticed several wreckages of wood, half-formed shelters, in its upper branches. Broken, rotting planks littered the ground around its roots. "What are those?" she asked. The hair on her arms stood up. She sensed a tragedy.

"We used to live up there," Cordelia said. "Until the most recent hurricane. A few months after Mother swung. But we haven't got building materials so we're pretty much stuck on the ground." She glared up at the ruined treehouses as if she blamed them for being weak, rather than the storm for tearing them apart.

"We'll rebuild when Norris comes back with supplies," Phe told her, gruff and dismissive.

"Please," Cordelia snorted. "Norris isn't coming back. He and the crew have screwed us over for the last time. No honor among pirates."

Phe's rage erupted like a volcano that'd finally had enough. "Don't you dare doubt them. You never knew them like I did. Spent too much time hanging on to Mummy's skirts and listening to her stupid fairy tales about island magic."

"So, you just want to wait around for rescue?" Cordelia sneered, jabbing a finger in Phe's direction. "At least I'm communing with the island. At least I'm *trying* something to protect us. When Mum died, she left you in charge. But what have you done but whine and moan about the dreadful burden of responsibility?"

"Oh go talk to your mists!" Phe said, waving Cordelia away. "Put your faith in Mum's ridiculous stories. I'll put my faith in my crew." Ophelia's head was swimming. She felt out of her body. Nothing these sisters were saying made any sense to her— what was this about mists?—but she could tell in an instant that they were both doing their best to cut the other to her core. It was like she was back on the sand at Peu Jolie, watching herself bite and snap at Betsy. Expending every effort to make her only friend hurt. And her only friend doing the same in return.

Cordelia's laugh was high and derisive, but as she began to spit back a retort, Ophelia raised her voice. "Stop it!" She let out a painful gasp at the pang in her bruised ribs. "I've just come from a different island, fighting with a different sister. Since then, I've been whipped, shot, and drowned. Trust me when I say: You don't know how good you've got it."

Somewhat chastened, the older girls quieted. "I'll catch us some dinner then," Phe mumbled, picking a sharpened stick up from near the campfire.

"And I'll pick some oranges," Cordelia said. Without another word, they turned their backs on each other and walked in opposite directions out of the clearing.

TWENTY-ONE

Jack charged at the stout woman, howling like a wounded dog. She charged at him in return. He slashed at her throat, but only managed to nick it before she kicked him in the gut. He staggered back but was unperturbed. He darted in again. She seized his wrist, trying to drive the blade toward his own stomach. But their strengths were equally matched. Neither could break the other's grip.

Betsy clambered to her feet. She didn't know what she could do—if only she had her lighter, she could set Jack aflame. But someone else got there first. The ragged old man had leaped up from his corner, come up behind the woman, and added his strength to hers as she pushed on the razor.

Jack gave a soft cry, like the hiss of air from a bubbling pot. The blade slid into his stomach, and was lodged there.

He stayed upright for a moment, his expression a bit pinched, as if in mildly exerting thought—and then collapsed. His leg twitched. His hand dug at the wound, yanking the blade out of his flesh. Blood spurted from the gash in the absence of a knife to stop up the leak.

He died, right there on the floor.

After a brief moment of contemplation from all considered, the stout woman looked around at her cellmates and said, "So, that's settled, then." She stepped out of the pool of blood and scraped the tip of her boot on the rough-hewn wall. "I'm Jo. As you may have noticed, Ludlow isn't too fond of me. I was cottoning on to his scheming and he didn't want me to speak up at my court-martial. Engineered this whole damn thing with Copeland to kill me before I could cause problems for his naval career. Since you were all almost collateral damage, only seems polite to introduce myself. Who are you lot?"

The old man dropped into a bow to Jo, his shabby uniform looking rather elegant in motion. "The name is Abel Sherry, ma'am. Former captain of the Imperial Navy, now a drunken layabout, awaiting my vengeance. And may I say it is a pleasure?"

"You may," Jo said.

Betsy helped Ravi climb to his feet, and he extended a trembling hand to Jo. "Ravi Randawa," he said, indicating Betsy. "We—she and I—we sort of burned Copeland's ship. That's why he wasn't too pleased with us."

Betsy's mouth was very dry, partly from fear, and partly from the fact that she hadn't drunk any water for nearly a day. "I burned his lady too."

Jo looked impressed. "I saw the job you did on her. Not bad."

"You saw her?" Betsy asked.

"Aye," Jo nodded. "Ludlow's telling people she escaped, but it ain't true. She was too injured to get away on her own. He's setting her free in exchange for Copeland doing me in."

Betsy wrinkled her nose, thinking. "He told the admiral upstairs that he was going to find her and bring her to justice."

Jo shrugged. "Maybe he's gonna double-cross her. Wouldn't be a first for him. But what do I call you?"

"Betsy Young."

Jo crossed her arms. "Is that so? I believe I know your sister."

Ravi laughed out loud, a high-pitched, breathless sound. He was staring at Jack's body bleeding out on the floor. He looked about ready for a nervous breakdown. "You know her sister? Along with everyone else on the Emerald Sea, apparently."

Jo had already begun inspecting for weaknesses in the door hinges. "We need to get out of here," she said. "You don't know Ludlow like I do. I'm starting to realize—he's far more dangerous than I ever gave him credit for. I should have known: Emily is a spot-on judge of character. He wants your sister dead. He wants all the Crays dead, after they pulled her out of the water. Someone needs to warn them." A shadow crossed her face. "And I need to find Emily. I don't know what he's done to keep her quiet. But he didn't send her here to die with me, so I'm plum worried he's got something worse in store for her."

"How do we find the Crays?" Betsy asked. She knelt to pick up the bloody razor, thinking perhaps they could use its flat blade to remove screws from the door.

"I suppose they'll be on Cray Island," Jo said. "But we'll cross that bridge when we come to it."

"Cray Island?" Ravi asked, laughing wildly again. "You mean the pirate outpost no one is sure exists? Let me tell you—I know something about looking for islands in a vast sea, and it requires a little more than improvisation. No one knows where it is, if indeed it is real."

"It's real," Sherry said. "And it's fifty miles off the coast of Carthay, right smack dab in the middle of the Boiling Sea. Weather patterns mean it's frequently shrouded by mist—but I discovered that island, back in my prime. Ophelia Cray mutinied so she could take it from me. I could navigate there with my eyes closed."

Betsy blinked at the old man. "Pardon me. What?"

A shout of fear split the dusty air. An officer had come, rather too late, to inspect the racket from the brawl. He now saw Betsy standing, with a bloody razor in her hand, over the dead body of Jack Copeland. "Murder!" the officer shouted. "Murder!"

She was being dragged from the cell. The razor fell from her hand, clattering to the floor in the hall. "No!" she cried out, all priorities lost. She couldn't do this now! She needed to hear Sherry's explanation.

"Wait!" Betsy screamed. Her voice cracked like shattered glass. The desperation in her voice must have been palpable because the guard indeed paused for a brief moment.

"Wait for what?" he asked, dully.

Betsy didn't have an answer. So in lieu of a reply, she head-butted him.

The guard reeled back, yelping in pain. He went to draw his gun, but Betsy took advantage of him being off-balance, charging him and knocking him to the ground. The officer shouted, twisting as he fell face-forward to the floor. Betsy knelt with her knee in the small of his back, pinning him. "Drop the pistol," she growled, "and your keys as well. Just stay down."

The officer gave an obedient squeak. He slid his gun away from him, and Betsy stooped to take it. She kept the pistol trained at the officer as she stepped backward toward the door.

"So you *are* a pirate, and not a lady," the officer mumbled to himself.

"I have sunk two ships in as many weeks," Betsy said as she slipped away, "so if that's what makes a pirate, I suppose I am."

Betsy tossed the keys through the bars to Ravi, who unlocked the door from the inside and allowed Jo and Sherry to shuffle out. Handing Jo the gun, Betsy said, "I hope you know what to do with this."

Jo cocked it. "I do."

They burst out from the stairs into the sunlit hall, but they only met a single other guard on their way out the front door, a scrawny, mostly decorative sentry in the front lobby. At Betsy's instruction, the sentry turned his back to them and placed his hands against the wall while Sherry collected his pistol.

Then they were out on the street, and Sherry was hollering, "This way! Follow me, to the docks!"

They followed.

Sherry led them, his shabby boots pounding against the cobblestones, until they had gone off the city roads altogether and were whipping through the white-sand dunes. As he slowed down, clutching at a stitch in his side, Betsy couldn't help admiring the delicate circular patterns of the sand—what she wouldn't do for a bolt of lace like that.

Sherry gestured toward a rickety dock, clearly for fishing boats and nothing grander than that. "This—this way," he said, gasping.

"Gods almighty," Ravi said as they stepped onto the dock, which creaked disconcertingly. Bobbing in the water, tied to a pole, was a small schooner, its two masts bare, but tall.

"This is my beauty," Sherry said, wading out toward the schooner to tap its hull. "Brand-new and all. Never breached an emerald wave. Been saving up since the day I was fired. I call it the good ship *Redemption*."

Betsy was standing up to her ankles in the water, gaping up at the ship. "I thought you were arrested for being a drunken nuisance."

"Aye," said Sherry.

"How does a drunken nuisance happen to own a boat?" Betsy asked.

Sherry gave Betsy a look that suggested she was stupid. "I'm a navy man. A navy man doesn't go without a boat, whatever his relationship to alcohol might be."

Betsy and Ravi exchanged a look.

Jo gave an awe-inspired whistle. "Can't fault him."

Betsy pointed at the *Redemption*. "With this boat, you can take us to Cray Island to find my sister?"

Sherry nodded, and then inclined his head at Jo. "I can if you two are willing to pull your weight, and with an able seaman like this one. The Crays have done me wrong, but the hangman won't get me my honor back. I was marooned. My fellow sailors called me cursed: unlucky. No one would sail with me. You'll be the crew that redeems me, and I will get what I'm owed."

"Good chap," Ravi said. He hauled himself up into the *Redemption*, grinning broadly down at Sherry. "I don't know if the Crays will be willing to share, but consider me a backup plan. Lucky for you, I have a lead on a tremendous amount of gold."

"Wait," Betsy said, grabbing Ravi's arm. "This is your chance to go. Be free. You almost died on the *Bloody Shame*, I won't put you in danger again."

"Elizabeth Young," Ravi said, with an almost piratical grin. "We're headed to a secret island. Isn't that what I've been searching for all this time? I'm a hair's breadth away from earning my ship and completing the quest that's hounded my family for generations. If I walk away now, it doesn't matter if I live to the ripe old age of ninety-three. I'll always regret not seeing this through. Sometimes you've just got to take a risk . . . Just look how far risk-taking has already taken us." He extended his hand to help hoist her up. "Let's push our luck a bit farther."

Betsy's heart fluttered. She took it.

TWENTY-TWO

Before settling down to sleep, Phe gave Ophelia a pillow to hold against her chest, to ease the pain of her cracked rib if she had to cough. She slept surprisingly soundly in one of the abandoned tents, until Cordelia prodded her awake. "Get up now if you want to eat," she said. "Phe only caught two fish to split between us all this morning, and personally, I don't mind eating your share."

Bleary-eyed, Ophelia obeyed, squirming from the tent's opening and into bright sunlight. She shuffled to where Phe sat, squinting at the pan over the campfire. If she had thought she'd be able to guess the type of fish that Phe had caught, she was wrong. Very little was left of the creatures after the others were done eating. Ophelia pulled a face at the fried tails sitting in the flat of the pan, crispy and curling toward the sky.

"Can you afford to be so picky?" Cordelia sneered.

"Sure she can," Phe said. "You never met her father, Cord.

One of the wealthiest men on Peu Jolie. Bet she's never gone hungry a day in her life."

"How do you know anything about my father? Who told you that?" Ophelia asked, both bristling at the implication that she was some spoiled brat and absolutely flummoxed at how Phe could have private knowledge of her life.

"Who do you *think* told me that?" Phe said, slurping up the end of a fish tail.

Heat rushed to Ophelia's cheeks. Her mother. Her mother had spoken about her. She'd told the others about the daughter she had abandoned on Peu Jolie. Ophelia had assumed that in the time between dropping her on her father's doorstep and seeing her at the gallows, the pirate queen would not have thought of her twice. She'd obviously assumed wrong.

Cordelia stood up, straightening the skirt of her gauzy dress. "I'm off to the beach," she said. She glanced at Phe, eyes wide. "I'll let you know if I spot the crew coming back."

There was a long pause before Phe nodded, her lips softening into a grudging smile. "And I'll try climbing the banyan," Phe told Cordelia. "See if we can stretch the nails we have to fix at least one treehouse. I'm tired of sleeping in tents too."

"Thank you," Cordelia said, simply.

"Say hello to the mists for me," Phe called after her.

Ophelia hadn't known them long, but after their argument the previous evening, she understood this was their way of apologizing without saying the words. She felt a pang of guilt. When was the next time she would see Betsy? She had left a wound between them, and not lingered long enough to see it heal.

Phe stretched before pulling on her red coat, which had been previously strewn across a nearby rock. Ophelia noticed, with a little bit of envy, how well-muscled her uncovered arms were. She supposed that a full life of sailing did that. Ophelia's own muscles had grown quite a bit in the short time she'd been working the bilge, though unfortunately not to such a grand effect. With a glance at Ophelia, she said, "You fit enough to try scrounging up some lunch? Some oranges, a rabbit. Whatever you can find. Just step lightly in the underbrush."

"And what would you have me do with the rabbit once I'd caught it?" Ophelia asked, her brow arched. "You want me to kill it?"

Phe gave a tiny snort at Ophelia's obvious disgust. "You fancy islanders. Happy to eat food someone else killed for you. Just bring it to Cordy. She knows how to kill things."

"I don't doubt that," Ophelia muttered.

Moving slowly to accommodate her ribs, Ophelia moved to the tree line and reentered the jungle, ducking under overhanging branches and stepping carefully over knotted roots. Now walking through the thick greenery without a guide, she was much more attuned to every rustling of leaves behind her. What animals lived in this place? She supposed nothing truly dangerous, or her sisters wouldn't have let her wander, defenseless and alone.

However, it transpired that the skittering she'd heard in the flora was merely a large lizard with bottle-green scales. Neither edible nor predatory.

As she treaded farther and farther into the deep jungle with no recognizable paths, Ophelia longed again for her father's compass.

She thought she could trace her way back to camp, but where she was heading was another matter entirely. Eventually, a breeze rustled through the trees, carrying with it the smell of citrus, sharp and sweet. She followed the scent to an unfamiliar part of the shoreline, overhung with a number of short, squat trees, their branches heavy with fruit. Ophelia's mouth immediately began to water. She could taste them already. The bright oranges overhead looked lush, fat, and satisfying—but unfortunately, Ophelia slowly began to notice, there were not many of them left. The trees were starting to look distinctly overpicked.

Ophelia found a fallen branch in the sand and used it to playfully swat at a monkey trying to make a snack of one of the remaining oranges. The monkey made an idle, complaining sound before streaking back down the trunk. It circled Ophelia three times, then clambered up the side of her leg and came to rest on her forearm.

Ophelia's entire body tensed as she held the monkey away from her face. But he did not strike. Rather, it nuzzled her.

It seemed this monkey knew what the citizens of Peu Jolie had not: Ophelia was no threat. Ophelia loosened up, marveling at its shining black eyes and the sleek white fur that covered its head and shoulders, transitioning to its deepest brown farther along its spine. It let out a soft, keening sound and seemed almost to be smiling. Hesitantly, she reached out her free hand and stroked the top of its head.

It remained on her shoulder all the while that Ophelia used the branch to knock the remaining oranges down. When it was time to collect the fruit, she shook her hand at the monkey, gently shooing it away. It leaped off Ophelia's arm and scampered away into the mist that gathered at the edge of the beach.

Ophelia stared after it for a long while, until it was completely obscured by the swirling fog. Far in the distance, she thought she could hear a woman humming a lilting, melodic song. *Must be Cordelia*, she reasoned. But as her eyes unfocused, it seemed that the mist had solidified into the vague shape of a woman.

Ophelia's heart stopped as the mist rolled down the beach, bubbling and beckoning for her to follow. She did follow, without question. She did not know if this figure was friend or foe. But she knew she wanted to find out.

The ground beneath her feet sloped downward as the line of trees gave way to the rocky edge of a lagoon. The mysterious silhouette paused upon a great boulder, as if it were waiting for injured Ophelia to catch up. Ophelia lunged, grasping for the mist—expecting to find something solid beneath. But it dissipated between her fingers, leaving her holding nothing.

She fell to her knees on the boulder's flat stone, some ten or fifteen feet above the water's surface. At the opposite edge of the lagoon, a spring of water tumbled joyfully over their own boulder's twin, pouring into the pool below. Sunlight danced across the surface of the churning water, reminding Ophelia oddly of the glint in her father's eyes when he laughed.

Unlike the familiar green waters of the Emerald Sea, the lagoon was a shocking crystalline blue. And yet, it was also so clear, she could see the fossilized remains of ancient merfolk embedded in the stone beneath the lagoon's lapping depths.

Ophelia's eyes tracked to the thundering waterfall on the

opposite edge of the lagoon, which cast a rainbow haze across the air where the stream met the pool. She watched in amazement as the haze gathered into the insubstantial form of the mist-woman, who now sparkled vivaciously.

Ophelia was relieved she hadn't left forever as a punishment for her trying to grasp her. She gestured imperiously for Ophelia to follow again, but her head was thrown back in eerily silent laughter at the girl's folly.

"Look, don't touch," Ophelia muttered to herself, her cheeks red. "I can understand that position better than anyone."

Ophelia made her shaky way to her feet, and followed. She knew she must catch up with the woman, but she felt an aura of intense foreboding. Visions of slipping clouded Ophelia's mind. Of being pulled beneath the water—of ancient, skeletal merfolk peeling themselves from the submerged rock and dragging her down, down, down. "Are you sure that this is a good idea?" Ophelia asked the mist-woman.

The woman did not answer, nor had Ophelia expected her to. She merely wafted behind the stream of falling water, slipping into a dark cave beyond. Ophelia let the water soak her as she emerged through the weeping curtain.

Much like the cave that served as the docks for the Cray fleet, this cave's walls gleamed obsidian. Unlike that cave, the ceilings were low, and the space much narrower. "Where are we?" Ophelia asked, the hair on her arms standing up like sailors at attention. "Why did you bring me here?"

The only answer was her own voice echoing off the rock.

As her eyes adjusted to the darkness, Ophelia saw a flat, sturdy shape in the distance. Her heart skipped a beat. A pirate's treasure chest! The mist-woman had taken her to her mother's hoard. The spoils from all her years at sea.

Ophelia paced forward, expecting stockpiles of gold coins, standing like mountains and flowing like rivers. Failing that, she had expected to see a trunkful of jewels, their dark colors glimmering menacingly in the scant light that shone into the cave. What she saw instead was a chest of wooden drawers, pushed back against the far wall of the cave, as if this were merely a bedroom in someone's new house, only half decorated, with its bedposts and wardrobe yet to be brought in.

Ophelia was not sure she was ready to see what was inside.

She almost turned back, but she felt the almost imperceptibly cool touch of the mist-woman's hand at her cheek. A phantom's caress. It urged her forward.

Ophelia approached the chest slowly, as if the drawers were the mouths of rabid dogs that might snap off her fingertips if she looked at them wrong. The only sound in the cave was the splashing of her boots as they disturbed shallow puddles. Not even her own breathing.

"Don't we need a key?" Ophelia asked, her growing dread being replaced with hope for some sort of delay. But the mist-woman would not have taken her here for no reason. She stretched out her hand to the first drawer, her mind running wild with theories. Pirates often kept physical trophies of their victories, in addition to the loot they stole. Papa had once, under the influence of a particular fine vintage, talked about how when Billy "the Brute" Burnham's ship was captured, they'd found a collection of sixty-odd human fingers in a box in the captain's quarters. It had made Eliza screech to hear it told at the dinner table. Back in Orana she'd even heard rumors of some new pirate gilly who wore a necklace beaded with teeth. Just what secrets was her mother keeping in the secret cave? And more important, were they *decaying*?

She squeezed her eyes shut and pulled the first drawer open. There was no smell of rotten flesh, no rattle of stray bones. She opened her eyes the smallest fraction and squinted down to find . . . letters. Hundreds and hundreds of letters, lined up with immeasurable care so that they would not be bent or otherwise damaged—although each with their wax seals broken. "What is this?" The words had barely escaped Ophelia's lips before her brain caught up to the answer. She had recognized one of the wax seals—that of Commodore Lang. A closer inspection made it clear that all the letters were from officers of the Imperial Navy, or else noblemen, bureaucrats, or high-ranking officials of the royal court.

Any of these letters might have been entrusted to the captains of the royal navy, for transport to some far-off corner of the continent. Despite herself, Ophelia felt a smile twitch at the corner of her mouth. Her mother, a former naval woman, would have known that these letters were crucial to the orderly function of the empire. That their loss would jeopardize the career advancement of any red-jacketed officer responsible for them. Her mother hadn't been content to lash out at the upper echelons of the navy with one mutiny—she'd made a game of destroying what Ames had declared their highest calling: efficiency.

Ophelia began to laugh. She couldn't stop. Tears poured from the corners of her eyes as she clutched at her shrieking ribs, doubled over in increasing hysterics. It had been sheer *pettiness*. The letters were worth nothing—except to someone who had dedicated herself to embarrassing the royal navy. Land-dwelling society would fumble, confused, without their timely arrivals, and the officers would risk demotion for losing them, but there was no monetary value in them at all.

She had wondered why it was that her mother had been captured while pregnant so many times, and only once when unburdened with a child. But it was obvious now that her mother, whenever carrying an immunity to the noose inside her, would go out of her way to pick a fight with any naval ship she spotted. Because no pirate in their right mind tries to seek out the people who are the greatest danger to them, when they could instead prey on merchant ships that likely carried more valuable cargo— unless they had a vendetta, and a collection of letters to expand.

Ophelia slid a handful of letters out of their place in the drawer. She sat down, cross-legged, on the rocky ground, not minding the way the dampness crept through the seat of her britches, and started to pull letters from envelopes. Their contents were the oddest mixture of the mundane and the lurid: storm predictions; crop yields; proposed legislation filled with dense, impossible-to-parse clauses in need of the grand-queen's signature—but also the news of a governor's daughter who'd run off with a female sailor, whose father was desperate for her to be found and returned to him. A tale of field-workers who had risen up to protest their low wages and long hours, and had thrown their foreman into a bog. And most common of all, there were arrest warrants, all adorned with the sneering faces of pirates and calls for information as to their whereabouts. These sketches had obviously never reached the street corners on which they'd been meant to hang.

"That's why the other pirates called her their queen," Ophelia said aloud, a soft smile on her lips as she peered at a sketch of man with a broken front tooth, "because she protected them all."

She could feel the mist-woman still lurking behind her, but Ophelia did not turn to look at her. It was like an itch she refused to scratch. Because she was starting to realize just who this mist-woman might be.

Ophelia carefully placed the letters back into envelopes, and returned them to their drawers. She peeked through the remaining drawers but did not examine more letters—until she saw one envelope, in the bottom drawer, sticking up oddly from the pack. This was unusual, considering the care with which the others had been placed. She glanced inside this envelope and found that it did not contain naval missives but rather a collection of newspaper clippings and other scraps of paper. The first was an obituary for a little boy from Peu Lorraine, Milo, who had caught the Mosquito Fever at the age of six. The second was an engagement announcement from Peu Ankirk, saying that Ophelia Newsome would marry a wealthy, respectable banker at the end of the month. There was an advertisement for a fish shop in Carthay, newly opened, owned by a young man named Hector. A notice from Peu Toulouse that a barmaid named Portia had disappeared after her shift. Beneath that, a note in looping handwriting, sent from the Beaugrand province, which merely said,

I had to leave. Don't look for me.

And there was a short letter, dated five years previous— written in a hand that Ophelia knew well. She had seen that scratchy, hopeless mess logging profit margins in her father's ledger books all her life.

Ophelia's hands shook, rattling the paper so hard she could hardly read it.

Dear friend,

Our daughter is growing taller every day. She is whip-smart, and brave, and never stops talking—even when it would be better for her to stay quiet, just for a short while. She has your teeth but my smile. You would be proud of her, and perhaps a little afraid of her too. I know I am. I simply cannot keep up. Soon she will outstrip me entirely and realize what a dolt her papa truly is. I hope you are keeping the picture I gave you in a safe place, where no water will damage it. I only had one, but I gladly entrust it to you. After all, I have come out on top in this deal. You have her likeness, and I have her.

~Nate

Fixed to the letter—with the sort of pin Betsy would have used while adjusting a hem—was a sketch of herself at no more than four years old. Her curls were tied at the top of her head with a ribbon, and she wore a frilly dress that exposed dimpled knees. Her eyes were bright, directed at someone to her left—as if a parent were holding candy from just behind the sketch artist and promising it to her if she would only sit still for a while longer.

She knew in an instant this sketch had been drawn the very same day and place as the sketch of Betsy and Eliza. Her father had not chosen to forget her, after all. Eyes wet as the waterfall beyond her, Ophelia held the letter and the sketch to her chest, which suddenly hurt very badly. She cursed herself for ever thinking badly of her father. She wanted to see him. To hear his voice. To apologize for not saying goodbye, and for writing him off in her head.

There would be time for that, she promised herself. She had not gone to her grave at sea the day before, and that was miracle enough to prove anything possible.

Ophelia jumped to her feet, swinging around to find the mist-woman. "Mama?"

But there was no one at her side. The mist had blown away.

Ophelia stumbled through the rest of the afternoon, eyes raw from crying, looking under every leaf in the jungle for another sign of her mother. What was it she'd said in that letter? *"Force of will is magic, my child."* Could it be that her mother had willed it so much to see Ophelia again that she was able to pay her this last visit? Could it be Cray's will that protected this island? If so, then Ophelia wondered why she was gone. Had the last spark of her mother's consciousness on this plane been used up, so many months after her death? Would she ever see her again?

Just before the sun went down, she heard a rustling and spun around, expecting her to have returned as the wind in the trees. But instead she found a rabbit, and with a heavy sigh, reached down to gather it in her arms.

She emerged from the trees onto the beach where Cordelia had spent most of the day re-knotting the broken strings of fishing nets that had been torn during the hurricane. Ophelia, usually so steady, had been feeling her emotions swinging wildly since her arrival on Cray Island, and she laid a tiny kiss on the rabbit's head, and whispered a quick apology before handing him off to Cordelia, who took the ball of fluff into her arms, whistling to herself.

"The island always provides," she said.

Unwilling to watch the rabbit be made into dinner, Ophelia turned back to fetch Phe from the campsite. While she'd announced her intention to spend the day rebuilding the tree-house, when Ophelia reached the base of the banyan tree, she did not hear the banging of a hammer against nails. She saw Phe, leaning against the side of the house, one leg dangling off the damaged platform and swinging like a pendulum. Her face was melancholy and terribly still.

Ophelia suspected that the building supplies had run out long ago, and Phe had opted to stay in the air for several hours to maintain some peace and quiet.

Pretending she had seen nothing, Ophelia dropped to her knees and busied herself by retying her bootlaces. "Dinner's cooking!" she called, making a distinct effort not to look up at Phe's sad, quiet face.

Phe jerked into motion so quickly she must have been

embarrassed by her lack of occupation. She dropped down from the tree, clapped Ophelia with a grim, steady hand on her shoulder, and steered her back to the beach.

Cordelia had made swift work of carving away the rabbit's fur, and she already had it roasting on a spit by the time the others returned. Ophelia noticed she was talking to herself.

"Yes, that will do well enough. Don't you think?" Her dark eyes glanced skyward, as if she were speaking to the swirling eddies of mist that enveloped the island. "I mean," Cordelia continued, chuckling harshly, "they won't serve it at the grand-queen's table, but it's not tragic. We're going to hold out for a little longer yet." She turned the spit, eyes cool as she watched the rabbit's flesh singe.

"Aren't you going to say thank you?" Phe drawled. "Mum was always polite with the mists."

"I'm a damn sight nicer to the mists than you are," Cordelia muttered under her breath.

Phe chose to ignore that particular shot from Cordelia. She twirled a finger in a circle next to her head, indicating to Ophelia that her sister was absolutely out of her gourd. "Mum," Phe began, and as she leaned in to whisper, Ophelia smelled alcohol on her breath, "used to believe that the mists were our friends. That they magically guarded the island from detection by the unworthy. She spoke to the mists quite often to thank them for this kindness, and Cordelia used to think it was as idiotic as I do. But when Mother swung, she took up the cause herself." She directed her next statement at Cordelia, her voice raised dangerously, "But it cannot work, you see. Because Mum actually believed it, and Cordy's just faking. And the belief, as Mother said, is the thing."

"Phe," Cordelia said, straightening up. "Button your trap or I will sew it shut."

"Try it, sister," Phe countered. "I dare you."

Cordelia's lip curled. "You're drunk."

"I've had some rum," Phe admitted with dignity, pulling a flask from her red greatcoat.

"Well," Cordelia grunted, holding out a hand. "Give it here."

Phe loosed a transparently delighted laugh, and shared the flask. Cordelia took a long swig, sighed contentedly, and looked upward through the mists at the gathering stars. Quietly, she admitted to no one in particular, "I am just trying to do what Mum would have wanted. She told us that things are as we believe them to be. If you think you're cursed, you are. If they think we're something to be feared, that we're magic—then we are. She said that she believed the mists protected us, so they did."

"Too bad we're both faithless," Phe said, reaching back for the flask.

Cordelia refused to return it, drinking deeply again. Ophelia took this as a silent acknowledgment that Phe was speaking the truth and Cordelia knew it.

They sat down for a meal around the campfire Cordelia had built, Phe instinctively passing Ophelia the flask for a swig of her own. The smell and taste of it could have peeled paint, but with no whippings or superior officers to fear, Ophelia let the rum fill her belly and render her thoughts hazy. The sky above was like an oil painting, all gray and yellow and midnight blue. The cicadas hummed, their wings strumming like the string section of an orchestra. The air was warm, and the white sand soft as a feather bed. Eventually, Cordelia stood, her arms snaking above her head in a slow, wistful dance. She waltzed around the fire, her gauzy dress billowing behind her, and Ophelia could almost swear the mist swirled all about Cordelia to play her partner.

She thought about telling her sisters about the mist-woman she'd seen today. Cordelia would probably see it as proof she was right about the island's magic. Phe would probably see it as a sign Ophelia'd had too much to drink.

But she said nothing. The wound of the day was too fresh to let anyone else poke at it now. She'd keep her memory of her mother private, a secret treasure buried in her heart.

Ophelia put a hand to the necklace at her collarbone. The metal was pleasantly warm against her skin. She liked the way it reflected the firelight. But still, she had seen the way Cordelia's eyes were drawn to it during meals. She wondered if Cord hadn't been right—back on the sloop. That Ophelia didn't deserve it. She wasn't a true daughter. Not least because they didn't know what she knew. That she had already betrayed them, by killing the crew whose return they still awaited.

And if she didn't deserve the necklace, she certainly hadn't deserved her mother visiting her. Maybe that was why she'd vanished. Because she had sensed Ophelia's unworthiness.

Phe had been watching as Ophelia studied the necklace. When Ophelia looked up, Phe quickly averted her eyes from her. Determined not to look at her dancing sister either, she stared into the flames and admitted, "I do not know how to be Mother.

I am not capable of it. I would not be capable of it in the best of times, and we are far from that. We need a leader, and I . . ." She trailed off, her eyes moving from the burning logs to the waves, spilling onto the shore just beyond them.

She didn't need to finish. Ophelia knew that Phe wanted an escape. That she wanted to put her hands on the wheel of a rig and sail far away, emerald-green water beneath her and cornflower-blue sky above. She'd longed for that once too.

In her next circle around the campfire, Cordelia seized Ophelia's hand and dragged her up to join her in the dance. A throaty laugh burst out of her as she slipped in the sand and Cordelia steadied her. She threw her arms wide, and spun, her face lifted toward the mist and the peak of the jungle mountain above. Her secret guilt seemed to wing away from her, even if just for the length of the dance. It seemed that if she could just keep dancing, it might never return at all. She felt her father's letter, and the sketch of her own face, like a heartbeat in her breast pocket. Her parents had both loved her. They had wanted her to find this place, and these sisters. Phe might have wanted to depart, but Ophelia? She was finally content to stay.

TWENTY-THREE

They were sailing smoothly across an ink-black sea. Betsy wasn't sure when they had left Orana. She wasn't sure of much anymore, except for how sluggish she felt, and how hot and dry her tongue was. Sherry had stored a small cask of water on the ship, and they had passed it around and drunk greedily—but still. She and Ravi hadn't drunk nearly enough to make up for rowing to shore under the baking sun.

Betsy sat cross-legged on the deck, her back against the rail. Ravi had settled beside her. She wanted badly to sleep; her eyelids kept getting heavier. But she needed to stay conscious. They had to stay sharp in case they needed to change directions suddenly. She would have liked to look up at the stars, but none were visible. The clouds weren't about to break open just yet, but a storm was coming soon. When she listened really hard, she thought she could hear thunder in the distance.

Betsy reached out to put her hand on top of Ravi's, and he

moved closer to her, resting his head on her shoulder. "Don't let me fall asleep," she said.

"How shall I keep you awake?" he asked, teasing.

"Talk," she said. "Tell me about your family. Are they happy?" She wanted to hear about someone, anyone really, who was out in the world, living their lives—not wasting away in a lonely house, locked in a coffin, or lost in a storm.

Ravi spoke softly. He told her of a gleaming house along a river, where he and his younger sisters had played along the banks. He told her about his mother, who kept her garden in neat, meticulous lines. He talked about his father, who had been so excited for Ravi to go to sea and learn about the business firsthand.

At the mention of his father, Ravi exhaled deeply. "He really thought I would be one to find that lost gold. 'An auspicious beginning,' he called it." He ran his thumb across the back of Betsy's hand. "My father is superstitious in the way all the sailors from his generation are. Lalithan wayfarers believe that the outcome of your first voyage will set the tone for all the ones that follow." A wry smile crept across Ravi's face, and it was clear that he couldn't bring himself to verbalize the irony.

"Do you believe that as well?" Betsy asked. "If so, I can't imagine you'll ever come back to sea. This was hardly a promising start."

"I've never thought of myself as the superstitious type," Ravi admitted. "I'm hoping not to start now."

"That's where you and I differ," Betsy said. "I believe in it all. Curses, jinxes, blessings. All of it. My Papa didn't hold stock in it. Nor Ophelia. But they would if they felt the way I do all the time. Like the world is out to get us."

"I believe we make our own luck," Ravi said. Betsy studied his face. It was impassive, calmer than it should have been. His eyes were almost vacant, in the way that eyes often looked right before someone dozed off.

"It's a nice thought," Betsy said. She prodded him in the ribs. "Stay awake, now."

Jo was pacing the deck, wound as tightly as Eliza had ever been before an onslaught of guests. She kept glancing at the sky and muttering threats to the gods of the sea. Finally, she lifted her pointer finger to the clouds and shouted, "Don't screw with me!"

From his place at the wheel, Sherry gave a snort. Betsy noticed that even when the old man wasn't talking to himself, his jaw was always moving. She supposed he was working on a piece of chewing tobacco, or worse, his own tongue. "Never have I seen," Sherry called out to Jo, "good luck coming from a sailor antagonizing the fates. Keep your mouth shut, woman."

Jo scowled, jabbing her finger in his direction too. "What would you know about luck? You're not just any fool who got fleeced by Ophelia Cray, you're the first fool. You claim you know where we're going—but we've been sailing for hours and we're still in the center of the Boiling Sea, with no island in sight. If that bastard Ludlow beats us to its shores because of your shitty navigation, I swear by my ten fingers and nine toes, I will beat you raw for raising my hopes."

"Nine toes?" Ravi muttered.

Jo raised her fist to her mouth, resting her knuckles against her lips. Her brassy voice lowered to a whisper. "Do you think he still has Emily? He kept her aboard when he sent me away to take the fall. But do you suppose he's gotten rid of her by now?"

Betsy slowly rose to her feet. She didn't know if there was anything she could say or do for this woman. But she crossed to Jo and took her free hand, squeezing it. Jo turned her head to not look Betsy in the eye but didn't pull her hand away. "I'm sorry, lass, but this isn't about your sister for me. She's a decent sort, and we were friends, but I need her as a witness. I need her alive, coming back to Orana, to testify that Ludlow's sneaking scum. As long as I'm alive to speak the truth, and Ophelia can back up my story, he can't afford to arrange an accident for Emily. At least I hope he can't."

"We'll find her," Betsy promised. "We will."

"Cut out that womanly sentimentality," Sherry drawled, his elbows resting between the spokes of the wheel. "Let's stay in a fighting mood, shall we?"

Jo ripped her hand from Betsy's at last, affecting a loudmouth, tough-guy drawl. "Big talk for a man whose old bones are as brittle as sea salt!"

That was when Ravi jerked to his feet, undistracted by the conversation. He pointed past them, beyond the ship, in the direction they'd come. "We've got trouble!"

Betsy swung around to see what kind of trouble could follow them so far across the sea. She quickly felt stupid to have been surprised at all. This was the logical conclusion.

A naval ship had emerged from the darkness, illuminated only by the lanterns along the edge of its hull. Betsy's throat was dry. She tried to swallow, but that only made it worse.

"Ravi," she asked, voice hoarse. "You don't suppose that ship's hull says *Bluesusan*, does it?"

Ravi pushed his glasses up on the bridge of his nose, clearly desperately hoping that his eyesight would clear up and suddenly the ship's name would be anything but what it looked like. Finally, he admitted, "I suppose it does."

"Rut me running," Betsy whispered, a phrase so vulgar that Eliza used to shriek when she heard Nathaniel use it in front of the girls.

Jo let out a dreadful roar. "Everyone, move your asses! We've got navy on our tail, and we need to make moves!"

"Put out the lamp!" Sherry ordered Betsy. She rushed to the deck lantern, licking the pads of her thumb and index finger to snuff out the flame.

Ravi and Jo had manned their stations at the rigging, and while moments ago she could see them by the flickering light, with the fire gone, they winked away in the darkness. "Pull!" Sherry cried, and the schooner lurched sharply to one side, sending unprepared Betsy tumbling to the deck floor.

Gasping, Betsy sat up, listening for the sounds of her comrade's groans as they pulled at the lines. She stumbled toward the ropes she usually manned and began to pull when Sherry instructed her to. Betsy still didn't have a damn idea what any of these ropes did without someone else's instruction, and she guessed that Ravi didn't either. As a novice sailor when his maiden voyage was interrupted, the only ship he knew how to operate required two oars.

But they were turning, and turning fast. She could hear angry shouts from the *Bluesusan* in the distance—they'd lost sight of them in the pitch-black.

The lights on the *Bluesusan* were the only things Betsy could see now, and as they became smaller and smaller in the distance, she breathed easier. If they could escape the naval ship's sight line before losing the cover of night, they might just elude them entirely.

She wondered how they'd tracked them so far—though in the end, it didn't matter. They'd been tracked all the same. The rising sun was their truest enemy now, but as the *Bluesusan*'s threat shrank behind them and the sky turned pale orange, the sun still graciously allowed Ravi to spot an emerald-green *something* in the distance.

"I see it!" he cried out. "I see it! The island, there!"

Betsy laughed, long and free and loud. There it was! Cray Island, exactly where Sherry had said it would be, with its tree-covered peak mirroring the color of the sea below!

"Yes," Sherry said, his voice choked. "There it is. Finally, I've returned."

He swung his body around, his gun raised at Betsy's chest. Whatever vestige of the old-man frailty that had plagued him throughout their voyage was gone now. "And this is where I leave you."

"What?" Betsy and Jo both shouted.

Sherry shrugged. "I came here for redemption. And I'll only get that by wiping out the Cray menace root and stem. I doubt you're interested in helping, so I have to leave you behind now."

Jo reached for her own pistol, but Sherry had already dived into the sea.

"No!" Jo roared. She threw herself to the edge of the rail,

firing down at the white wake where Sherry had gone under.

"Did you get him? Did you get him?" Betsy asked.

"Not a chance," Jo growled. "That old bastard can swim fast." She pointed outward, and indeed, Sherry was making fast headway toward the island's shore.

"It's fine!" Ravi shouted, rushing to the ship's wheel. "It's fine! We'll just follow him!"

"I think we've got bigger problems," Jo said.

She was right, again. Betsy's heart stopped. In all the fuss, they had almost forgotten the true danger waiting behind. The *Bluesusan* was gaining on them, and quickly.

A high-pitched male voice rang from the navy ship's deck. Betsy looked up to see a weedy ginger boy calling out to her across the waves. "Present Elizabeth Young! The captain says that if she turns herself over, we needn't blow your ship out of the water."

"Your captain, huh?" Betsy said, wild with frustration. She lumbered to the other rail, to glare up at the deck of the approaching ship. "You mean that piece of shit who tried to murder my sister?"

Ludlow appeared at the ginger's side, leaning carelessly against the rail. "Your sister was a mutineer and a witch. I did what any upstanding naval man would do. Surrender now, and I'll treat you as chivalrously as I do all my prisoners." He gestured behind him, beckoning someone forward.

The ghostly figure of a woman came forward; every inch of her skin, including the face and scalp, was wrapped in thick white bandages. She walked hesitantly—her arms outstretched in front of her, clearly afraid she would fall. Ludlow stretched out an arm in a perverse show of gallantry, linking his elbow in hers. She leaned away, as if his touch pained her. But he didn't appear to notice. "I promised Fiona's beau that I would escort her somewhere safe, in exchange for services rendered," Ludlow called out. "But you four ran off so quickly after slaughtering him like a pig, that I just didn't have time to make the drop-off. I'm sure you two have a lot to catch up on."

Ludlow unlinked his arm from Fiona Wall's. His smile had fallen away. "Fiona and Jack gave me another swell idea, you know. They mentioned your boy: how he was navigating them to a lost island. I realized I had someone who could do that too."

"You didn't—" Jo cried out, smacking herself in the face. "The pirate captain!"

"You always were a clever one, Jo," Ludlow said. He was playing with a brass compass as he spoke, opening and shutting it carelessly. "Yes, the pirate captain. I persuaded him I'd commute his sentence if only he betrayed the Crays and led me to the island."

"The Imperial Navy doesn't bargain with criminals!" Jo roared at him.

Ludlow laughed. "That's why the top brass doesn't know. Why should they care about my methods as long as they get results? And anyway," he gave a lazy shrug. "I won't need him much longer. Once I have the Crays, I'll dump his body in the sea. Yours too, Jo." He grinned again, this time at Betsy. "But perhaps not you, Miss Young. When I'm done with your bastard sister, I may leave your death to Fiona. She wants it so badly, and a gentleman is always accommodating."

Betsy had never known fear like this before. The sensation was not unlike falling into the shaft of a well—the light fading into a smaller and smaller pinprick the deeper down she went. She had completely lost all awareness of her own body; it was as if she had already died in that moment.

She felt a hand at her elbow. *Ravi.* Betsy's heart was pounding, thundering like the steps of a mare in gallop. They were going to die. She was going to die, somewhere right between two of the people she loved most in this world; Ravi at her side, and in a straight line across the water, her sister.

Ravi's hand squeezed at her elbow again. His lips moved as he mouthed to her. "We jump. Now."

He pulled her by the hand, and they leaped over the rail.

TWENTY-FOUR

Ophelia woke before dawn to the sound of the island birds making a racket. Cordelia was already awake, dragging her mended fishing net off the great rocks and into the sand. She slung it over her shoulder and made her slow way up the beach, in the direction of the hidden cove and the fleet. Ophelia supposed that even now in Peu Jolie, other fishermen were heading out from their beds to their little skiffs too.

Once up, Ophelia couldn't fall back asleep. Only Phe, who had consumed more of the previous night's rum than anyone else, slept on undisturbed.

But it was all right to sit quietly for a bit, because Ophelia spotted the tiny shells of infant turtles dotting the beach as they made their halting way toward the waves. She drew her knees to her chest and hugged them as she watched nature take its course. One by one, they slipped into the embrace of the sea, off to untold adventures. "I understand," she whispered to them. "You want to see the world. I did too."

The turtles had all successfully fled the land when Cordelia reappeared from the jungle, eyes wild, her net nowhere to be found. Ophelia's stomach growled. "No fish for breakfast then?"

"Better!" Cordelia announced. She knelt to shake Phe awake, not at all gently. "Get up! There's a ship on the horizon."

Phe sat up, groggy and rubbing at her eyes. "Is it Norris and the others?"

"No," Ophelia muttered, not able to help herself. "It's not." She knew it couldn't be. They were all dead, except the captain in the *Bluesusan*'s brig, who was probably this "Norris."

"It's the next best thing," Cordelia said, her grin predatory. "A mark. Some little rig, not much bigger than the sloop. Called the *Redemption*. Stupid name, isn't it? I saw them when I was out on the skiff, but I don't think they saw me. It was still dark then. And here's the cream of it: There aren't more than four sailors on that boat. Let's say we grab the guns from camp, sail out, and go take what's theirs."

A slow smile crept across Phe's face. "Yeah, Cord, yeah. Let's do that." She waved at Ophelia. "You'll come with us. They're probably idiot tourists to the Carthay coast who got lost in a storm. We can scare 'em easy."

Ophelia felt cold down to her bones. "But, why? They haven't done anything to us."

Phe and Cordelia gave her an exhausted look. "They don't need to," Phe said. "We have to eat, sure as anyone else. You don't see the mainland clamoring to give gainful employment to Ophelia Cray's bastards, do you? That's why we're all here instead of living the easy life ashore. This is what we have to do to survive. Now, are you with us, or *are you with us?*"

"Usually," Ophelia shot back, "people end that sentence with the 'against' option."

Phe snorted. "Please, gilly. You haven't had an option all your life. None of us have. Why would you start being offered them now?"

Ophelia tried to protest, "Maybe—"

"Get a grip!" Cordelia snapped. "No maybes. We're sailing out. We're robbing them. And lucky for those tourists, we ran out of bullets weeks ago, so at least we'll leave them alive. Don't pout, don't argue. Every second we stand here arguing is a second that rig might get away from us, its supplies with it! The island called them here to provide for us. If we don't take what they've got, we're all dead in a month."

Phe stood hastily, checking for the pistol in her holster. Still, she couldn't help checking her sister's negativity. Her voice was surprisingly tender and comforting. "Cord, we're gonna be fine. We'll take that rig, but Norris will come back with supplies. Trust me, we are not going to die here."

"Do you honestly think that?" Cordelia asked, her voice dangerously sharp.

"I do," Phe said, eyes narrowing in a challenge.

"Please," Ophelia said, gripping the mass of her hair and knotting it at the top of her head. Guilt gnawed at her. "Let's not argue. Let's just go. It's fine, I'll do it."

"No need to argue," Cordelia said, flatly. "Just as soon as Phe gets it through her thick skull that the crew has either abandoned us or they're already dead."

Phe stilled, a tiny, understated gasp sneaking from between her lips. She looked like she had been knocked backward a decade, suddenly resembling a child in her look of unguarded betrayal. She couldn't summon words.

Cordelia pressed a hand to her mouth, as if she could pull her rash words back inside her jaw and trap them there. "I'm—I'm sorry. I shouldn't have. I'm sure they're not dead . . ."

Ophelia swallowed, her throat like dry sand. "They are."

Her sisters redirected their focus onto her, their postures straightening like pistols being reloaded and cocked.

"What did you say?" Phe asked, her voice having dropped several octaves.

"They are dead," Ophelia repeated. She owed her sisters the truth. They shouldn't sit around praying for a rescue that wouldn't come. "The *Bluesusan* fought them. They killed them."

"Don't say *they*," Cordelia snarled, baring all her teeth. Though she'd been the one arguing that they wouldn't return, her fury surpassed even Phe's. She was livid to be proven right. "When you mean *we*. You helped kill our family." She launched herself toward Ophelia, bringing her painfully down on the sand. Cordelia's fists connected again and again with Ophelia's stomach as Ophelia tried to squirm away.

At first, Ophelia didn't even try to fight back, despite the pain, which was unspeakable. Despite her lungs crying out for air.

Cordelia was right. She had killed their family. She had watched their mother—her mother—die, and it had meant only a little to her. But it must have meant the world to them. She had rescued them both from lives of misery on land. It would have been as if she had lost Papa, and then three months later, someone had slaughtered Betsy and Eliza and even Valois for good measure. They had lost everything and everyone, and it was her fault.

Phe tried to pull the screeching Cordelia away, but Cordelia threw her elbow hard into Phe's face, sending her older sister tumbling backward. "I'll kill her!" Cordelia shrieked. "Don't try to stop me—she killed our family, and I'll kill her right back!" Cordelia's hand reached out, grasping for something. At first, Ophelia thought she was just going to punch her in the gut again, but no—Cordelia had withdrawn the silver blade from Ophelia's holster. She was ready to cut, to stab, to slash any inch of Ophelia she could find. She gripped the hair at the back of Ophelia's head and pulled her close, pressing the blade against the soft flesh of her neck.

A harsh voice. "No!"

Cordelia landed sideways on the beach, with a dull thump. She was breathing, and still conscious, though a small amount of blood trickled from a spot beside her ear. Phe stood beside Cordelia with a rock in her hand. "No more fighting amongst ourselves," she ordered. "I'm the captain here, and what I say goes."

Ophelia seized her moment to wrench the knife from Cordelia's hands. Cordelia blinked up at her, her eyes so full of hatred she might have been a resident of Peu Jolie.

"Get off our island," she said, "Get off our island, and never come back. You're not one of us. You're a navy stooge and a traitor."

"You're right," Ophelia said, struggling to her feet. "You're not my family, and this isn't my home. I only have one home."

Peu Jolie. With despair, she realized Betsy had been right all along. Peu Jolie, as much as it loathed her and wished her dead, was her only home. And as much as she'd wished for it, there was no better one to find. She didn't *deserve* a better home. Ophelia's fingers scrabbled at the back of her neck, loosening the gold chain of her mother's necklace, until it fell away. She chucked it onto Cordelia's stomach, hoping the impact bruised her as Cordelia's fists had bruised her own skin.

"Here, take it. You wanted it so badly. You're her real daughters, after all. It's yours."

She turned on her heel and sprinted down the beach. A plan began swirling in Ophelia's mind, picking up speed and strength, like a burgeoning hurricane. She would go to the cove where the fleet and the one-man fishing boat waited. She would steal it, and row out to the ship *Redemption* and beg them to take her along with them as they sailed away. And from there, who knew? She would have to find her way back to Peu Jolie somehow, to Betsy and Papa and Eliza.

As she ran, Phe shouted her name and tried to follow. Cordelia merely sat in the sand, fastening the necklace around her throat. She waited for a moment, and then stood, walking into the jungle—away from the others and toward the camp.

TWENTY-FIVE

Betsy had never been a strong swimmer. Her head went under and she immediately felt the sharp sting of seawater as it flowed into her mouth. She bobbed to the surface, coughing. Ravi had his arm around her waist. "Kick!"

A massive splash to Betsy's left. She shrieked. Her eyes were closed—she didn't want them stung by the water too, and she was almost certain that Ludlow had fired the cannons on them.

But it was Jo, jumping behind them into the sea. "You unreliable bastards!" she spat, launching into a well-practiced stroke. "You could at least warn me when we're jumping!"

They were propelling forward, but Betsy could hardly think why they were bothering. They were just people being buffeted around by cruel waves and crueler fortune. Ludlow had a naval ship at his command.

Behind them, Ludlow seemed to be having a similar thought. "You're fleeing?" he asked, almost politely puzzled. "I could crush your bodies beneath this ship, you know!"

But luck—for this brief moment—returned to their side. The *Redemption* lay between them and the *Bluesusan*, an obstacle in Ludlow's path.

"Captain," the ginger boy at the rail pleaded, "we have to sail around the schooner."

"No!" Ludlow was snarling. "Through it! Through it or you'll taste the cat!"

In a matter of moments, Betsy heard the crunching, creaking sounds of the *Bluesusan*'s bow slamming into the smaller ship's hull, breaking it apart as easily as if it were made of glass. And she, Ravi, and Jo were kicking, kicking, kicking. They were moving with the tides now, being pushed forward and spat up on the island's shore.

Betsy gasped for breath, pushing wet hair from her eyes and scrambling to her feet. White sand clung to every inch of her. "Come on!" she roared, pulling Ravi up from the beach. He was even more spent than she was, having helped her while swimming.

"My glasses!" he cried, "I've lost my glasses!"

Betsy glanced behind her, back at the waves, but she knew this instinct was pointless. "There's no time," she said, shaking from head to toe. "Can you see at all?"

"Not well," Ravi said, blinking water out of his eyes and looking like a lost little boy. "I can't see two steps ahead of me. You have to run, now. Leave me behind."

Betsy's response was immediate, harsher and louder than her voice had ever sounded before. "Not a *chance*, Randawa. If you can't see, I'll have to be your eyes." She waved her arm at Jo, gesturing toward the rocks at the edge of the beach and the line of trees beyond it.

They scrambled up the beach, an ungainly four-legged creature. It did not matter to Betsy a whit that they were moving slower than she could alone. She could only see death in her future—and she would not spend her last moments betraying the boy who'd kept the feeble spark of her hope burning.

Betsy's right boot slipped out from under her as she tried to climb up the slick surface of a boulder. She cracked her knee against the rock, hissing as her pant leg split open. She could feel blood trickling down her leg as she regained her balance, but she ignored it. She had plenty of blood to be getting on with—for now, anyway.

They slipped under the cool green canopy of the jungle. Betsy narrated every obstacle as they encountered it. "Tree root. Lift your leg. Branch, duck now." She didn't know where they were headed, exactly, but in a way, wasn't that a good thing? Staggering aimlessly around in the wilderness like this, at least Ludlow couldn't track them as easily.

And then, before her, Betsy saw the trees thinning. She heard a strangled cry.

She was running. Ravi was shouting in confusion, trying to keep up with her, but she didn't have time to explain. She knew that voice. She *knew* who was crying for help.

They emerged into the streaming sunlight of a clearing. Less than thirty feet away, she saw Sherry in his red jacket, crouching over the limp body of a young woman with a mass of dark curly hair. He was choking the life out of her.

Betsy dropped Ravi and he collapsed to the ground. "So sorry!" she cried back to him, sprinting toward her helpless sister. She launched into Sherry's side with the force of a hurricane, knocking him well away from Ophelia. She was hitting Sherry as she had never hit anyone. Nothing made sense but to keep striking him.

Behind her, Ophelia was gasping for air. "Who—" she croaked out, extending her hand to touch Betsy's back. "Who are you?"

Betsy stopped hitting Sherry, who had by now gone wheezing off into unconsciousness, and turned to face her sister. But this wasn't her sister. This woman's face, gone all purple, may have looked like Ophelia's. Her curls might have been Ophelia's curls. But this wasn't Ophelia. This was her sister's double, a woman in a linen gown and brilliant red marks at her throat where Sherry's hand had pressed a gold necklace into her skin. Betsy's jaw dropped. She remembered that necklace.

The double staggered toward Betsy, her face distorted with rage and pain, her hand resting at her injured throat. She seized Betsy by the shoulder, demanding, "Are you with this man? I'll kill you if you've touched my sisters."

Betsy shook Ophelia's double off. "I haven't seen your sisters, I swear. I'm just here looking for mine."

The woman drew herself up to her full height, her shoulders arching, haughty and beautiful. "I'm Cordelia Cray. Who are *you*?"

Betsy blinked, and stuck out her hand. "Elizabeth Young. I think I'm your sister's sister."

Cordelia looked thunderstruck. Her jaw hung open, and she

was gesticulating madly at Sherry's prone body. "And who is *that*?"

"That's the captain who found this island. Your mother took his ship, I think."

Cordelia's lip curled as she looked down at the old man. "Pity."

"Listen!" Jo cried out. She was the one supporting Ravi now. "We need to get moving. They're hot on our trail. Where's the girl?"

"What does it matter where she is?" Ravi muttered. "We have no ship. No way of getting away when we find her."

Cordelia's sharp eyes were darting back and forth between Betsy and her companions. Betsy could almost see the gears turning inside her skull. "That's not strictly true," Cordelia said. "Help me find my sisters and we can all get away. Now, who's chasing—"

A shot was fired, waking birds from their sleep and scattering them into sunrise-orange sky. Two beige-uniformed men emerged from the trees, the taller one holstering his pistol. They both carried unlit torches. "Hey look," the shorter of the two said, a wolfish look on his plump face as he looked Cordelia up and down, his eyes lingering on her curves. "It's one of them pirate girls. Looks awful like our old captain. Maybe a bit more . . . *mature*."

"Hey!" Cordelia snarled. Then she shook her head out like a wet dog, clearly trying to remember her priorities. "Who are you? We've broken no laws. I demand to know why you are trespassing on our island."

"Oh," the tall sailor said, ambling toward Cordelia. "Your island, is it? You have the proper documentation for that? Besides, your mother was Ophelia Cray. Our captain's got orders to bring you all in, and we're happy to oblige."

Cordelia's face split into a grin that revealed the same gap teeth as Ophelia. "I'm sorry to tell you," Cordelia said, clearly not sorry at all, "those orders are going to be a bit tricky to carry out." She reached for a gun at her waist, raising it at the men. But at the last second before firing, she seemed to remember something. "No bullets," Cordelia muttered. She began cursing under her breath. "Perfect."

"Not gonna be so hard, I think," the tall man said.

"There's still four of us and two of you, Allan," Jo snapped. She made to pass Ravi off to Betsy, but Allan held up a hand. "And I could take you and Weber handily by myself."

"Rest easy, Jo. We're not going to fight you."

"Nah, certainly not," the short one, Weber, said. He produced a hip flask, and started shaking its contents onto the sulfur tip of his torch. "That's the great thing about rats. They run from fire."

Jo inhaled sharply. Her eyes glanced toward the others for the briefest moment before she ordered, "Run!" Betsy didn't have a moment to tell if Jo was entirely serious, because Jo was already off and running, weaving her way through the trees.

Betsy threw Ravi's arm back over her shoulder. "*Come on*," she cried out to Cordelia. "To the beach!"

"*To the beach*," Weber mocked in falsetto, giving Sherry's unconscious body a hard kick as Allan started dousing his own torch in alcohol. They disappeared as Betsy dipped behind the vines and branches.

"But my sisters!" Cordelia protested, following Betsy as they darted through the trees all the same. "I need to find them!"

"Neither of you can find your sisters if you're dead!" Ravi shot back. His practicality won both girls over, and they quit protesting. Betsy could feel the sweat pouring down Ravi's back. He was breathing heavily, his footsteps faltering more easily now. "I can't see," he whispered, almost to himself.

"Oh, get it together!" Cordelia said. She crouched down to take the spot beneath Ravi's other shoulder, and now she and Betsy were halfway carrying him, but moving faster. Together, they made a quick-footed but ungainly monster.

By now, Betsy knew the smell of fire like she knew the contents of her sewing box. She felt it burst into life behind them, bringing heat that was as suffocating as the accompanying smoke. This fire was not of her own making. It was not her friend. It was coming to eat her alive.

She didn't have time to wonder if she deserved to burn to death. If this end would be oddly poetic. She was too busy running.

They burst out of the trees in very nearly the same spot they had entered, onto a glorious white beach. Jo, who had come out ahead of them, already had her hands raised in the air. Fifteen crewmen, armed with pistols, were waiting to collect their fleeing rats.

"Where is Emily?" Jo snarled as they bound her arms, dragging her toward the water. "Where is she? I know you know. *Bastards!*"

The fire setters emerged from the jungle behind Betsy. The flames they had created were now truly engulfing the trees at the island's heart. The short one was breathless, not only with the exhaustion of outrunning his creation but also with laughter. Allan came forward, shoving his gun into Cordelia's face, and pulled her from their tight-knit pack. Cordelia scratched at him and swore colorfully, but it was no use. She had no working weapon, hadn't had time to grab anything that might have saved her.

More sailors rushed forward, bent on tearing Betsy and Ravi apart now. A primal screech ripped its way out of Betsy's lungs as she fought to hold on to him. "No! *No!*" By the time her grip failed her, they had already been dragged down to the water's edge. Waves lapped at Betsy's feet. When she finally let go of Ravi's arm, her boots slipped out from under her. She collapsed into the soft, gray sand that had been worn down by the tides, which ordinarily felt so much like a bolt of silk.

Not today. Today, Betsy's palm seared with pain. She looked down and found that her hand, in absorbing her fall, had been driven into a pair of glasses that had washed up on shore. One of the lenses was shattered, its broken shards digging into her skin.

The sailors hauled Betsy to her feet, and she quickly scooped up the glasses and shoved them into her wet apron pocket. She could pass them to Ravi. He could die with a fraction of his eyesight. It was the least she could do, after getting him wrapped up in her family's curse.

The sailors began to take her out to the cold embrace of the waves, and the *Bluesusan*.

Betsy prepared an elegy for herself. She was going to die, and she knew it. What she didn't know was how long it would take for her mother to find out. Days, months, years? How long would Mama sit by the parlor window, waiting for her daughter to come down the street? Betsy had betrayed her mother by leaving, and she compounded that sin now by dying.

She tried to pass the glasses to Ravi as they were hauled aboard, but she couldn't quite reach him. His fingers scrabbled uselessly against empty air. *Here lies Elizabeth Young, who broke her mother's heart.*

Ludlow swaggered forward across the deck, swinging a length of iron chain as if it were an umbrella. He looped it tight around her neck. The metal smelled of sweat and felt like it could cut to the bone. He grabbed her upper arm tight, pinching its padded curves so hard his fingers sank through to muscle, and hauled her upward to stand on a stool top. *Here lies Elizabeth Young, who covered her eyes when Ophelia Cray swung, but would die the same way.*

Captain Ludlow wore a wide, mad smile. He patted her roughly on the cheek, chuckling to himself. "I want to thank you," he said. "If you hadn't escaped to this wretched island, I might never have had my brilliant spark of inspiration as to finding it. Ophelia could have lived out the rest of her days here in safety. Isn't that the most delightful thing?" *Here lies Elizabeth Young, who let her sister down a million times, and then a million more.*

A hot tear trickled down Betsy's cheek, burning the skin Ludlow had touched. He leaned in toward her, whispering so no one else could hear. "I suppose there's something else I should thank you for. Your name. Without that name, Ophelia wouldn't have ever made it into the navy. She wouldn't have fought that duel for me after I convinced Ronan to murder our drunkard captain. She was so easy to manipulate, that was the gift of it. Didn't you folks love her enough at home? You must not have. She threw a tantrum like a squalling babe, and that's what turned the crew against her in the end. Without Ophelia to blame for it all, I couldn't have heroically thrown her overboard and become captain so effortlessly. And I tell you this, of course, because you're about to die. Fiona will be so put out with me." He tipped his captain's hat to her, winking. "Have a lovely drop."

He turned his back to her, crossing to the rail of the ship. He idly consulted the face of a brass compass, and with a jerk to her stomach, Betsy realized to whom the compass had once belonged. At least, once she hanged, she would be able to see Papa again. But before she swung, she had to do one last thing. She had to let Ophelia know she wasn't alone. Because that was the thing Betsy did at hangings. She provided company.

TWENTY-SIX

Ophelia's fingers fumbled as she unknotted the fishing skiff from the rock. "Stop running!" Phe shouted, doubling down to catch her breath as she reached the shade of the cove. "Cordelia tries to murder you *once*, and you run like a coward? If I had a gold piece for every time Cord tried to murder me, I could buy a title from the grand-queen."

"You are not my family," Ophelia insisted. Her hands were shaking violently. Her face was shamefully wet. "You are not my family." But they were *not her family* only because they didn't want her. And they were right not to want her. She had done a terrible thing that could never be forgiven. But then, she had done many terrible things—to her family on Peu Jolie as well. Stealing Betsy's name, not bothering to say goodbye. What if she got back home and they wouldn't forgive her either?

"We are your family," Phe said, her scar-bisected eyebrow raised in defiance. "We're just not perfect, that's all."

Ophelia let out a strangled sob, but couldn't answer.

"I don't think—" she began, but stopped, sniffing the air. There was something funny about the scent. It was not wet earth and citrus, as it usually was. It was something else, almost too faint to recognize at first. She turned to face the mouth of the cove and noticed something even odder. A great three-masted ship in the distance, just inside the shroud of mist at the island's shore. "That is not the ship Cordelia said she saw."

"Smoke," Phe said. "Why do I smell smoke?"

Ophelia barely registered that she had jumped from the skiff, wading into the water without regard for her boots. Phe ran too. Within an instant, it seemed, Ophelia and her sister were peeking through the opening in the rock face. The smoke was black and thick now, billowing from the treetops and blotting out the newly rising sun. Smoke coated Ophelia's lungs. She gave a hacking cough that made her fractured rib cry out. The scent burned her nostrils: not the smell of a small brush fire. This was the smell of torches, made with sulfur and lime and doused in rum.

Then came the columns of fire, twenty feet high—devouring whole trees, dissolving them instantly like sugar candy on a child's tongue. If Ophelia's judgment was right, they were springing up from around the clearing with its array of tents and the cold logs that would probably no longer be cold.

"Cordelia," Phe said, in soft disbelief. "She went back for the guns." She staggered toward the trees, but Ophelia seized her arm.

"No," Ophelia said, her throat burning, thick with ash and glowing embers. "We need to get out of here. Someone's coming, and they want us dead."

Phe considered this, turning backward to look at the sloop beside the fishing boat. It was bobbing in the water, which was now alternatively its natural green and flickering with the reflection of the orange flame. "Get in," she ordered.

Ophelia got into the sloop without argument.

Phe gave the sloop a mighty shove, propelling it off the cove's natural incline. She vaulted over the rail as it glided outward and took her place, as captain, at the helm. As they left their hiding place, Ophelia craned her neck, getting a better look at the other ship's hull. A thrill of terror went up her spine. Yes, it was the *Bluesusan*. That was her ship that had burned her island; the island that was almost home.

"What's the plan?" Ophelia demanded.

"I don't know," Phe said, throwing all her weight behind the wheel so that the sloop could turn away from the hulking shadow of the naval rig. "But I know we can't just leave Cordelia out there to burn!"

"How do we find her?" Ophelia asked.

Phe's hands slipped away from the wheel, and instinctively grasped at her own head. "*I don't know!* Aren't you listening to me? I don't know! I'm not Mother, alright? I don't know what to do!"

"Okay," Ophelia said, battling through an encroaching panic. "Okay. But we have to do something. We could round the island, send up a signal somewhere—"

"Send up what kind of signal?" Phe asked, laughing breathlessly. "A fire? I think Cordelia might miss it somehow, don't you?"

The mist danced around the sloop, brushing against Ophelia's skin and raising goose bumps. She watched a glimmering tunnel of air particles streak out toward the water, and Ophelia knew there was something the island wanted her to see.

Ophelia had never felt her limbs so still, her mind so perfectly clear. To her back, her island was a blooming mass of black smoke and spluttering flame. Ahead of her, a cool, beckoning mist, and her ship. *Hers*, its sails billowing and full and starch white. There was no turning back. There was no sailing elsewhere—the *Bluesusan* would catch up. "I know what to do," Ophelia said. "If Cordelia is alive, she's on the beach or on that ship. Either way, the *Bluesusan* has come here for a reason, and we can't outrun it. Best to meet it head on, don't you think? Perhaps we can negotiate."

"Negotiate with what goods?" Phe spat. "We can't afford bread. Our only valuable was Mother's necklace, and that's around Cordelia's neck."

"Not strictly true," Ophelia said. "You have a fleet of idle ships in that cove."

Phe snorted. "We're not trading away Mother's ships! They were her treasure."

"You were willing to trade away her necklace," Ophelia pointed out.

Phe's arms were crossed, her face petulant. "You can't sail a necklace."

Ophelia's eyes were fixed on the *Bluesusan*. "We can't sail those ships either," she muttered. "Not without a crew. A fleet without sailors is every bit the decoration a necklace is."

From the look on her face, Phe must have felt as if Ophelia were suggesting she carve out her own still-beating heart. But at last, she conceded. "Fine." They locked eyes. "Do you really think you can negotiate with them? Get them to go away?"

Ophelia took the helm, turning the wheel firmly back to starboard, back toward her lost ship. "I'm not sure," she admitted. "But it's the only thing we can try. And Edgar—the new captain—well, he's criminally ambitious. He might be convinced to take the fleet and present it to his higher-ups as an addition to their forces. It would be a feather in his cap. Ten free ships for the navy."

"Eleven," Phe corrected, her eyes gaunt. "We had eleven ships."

Ophelia had hoped that the *Bluesusan*'s crew wouldn't immediately see their tiny sloop. An element of surprise would not necessarily be a tactical advantage, but it would have given them a sense of dignity. Unfortunately, almost as soon as she set course toward the frigate, cutting quickly through the water, she heard a gleeful tenor ring out across the waves.

"Lucky Teeth! You never fail to be civilized, do you?"

Phe lowered the sails just in time, so that the sloop did not drift directly into the shadow of the great ship. They came to a stop, and Ophelia looked upward to see Edgar, his arms resting carelessly on the rail, twisting her father's compass through the fingers of his right hand, like he was doing a coin trick. His smile was so wide that the elusive dimple had formed in his cheek again. Quieter now, more conversationally, he greeted her again. "Hello, darling. A thousand apologies for the mess." He indicated the burning island. "But we had to let you know you had guests. You didn't have a door knocker, you see."

"Hello, Eddie," Ophelia said, coolness etched into every syllable.

"Oh, don't be like that," Edgar said, still smiling blandly. "Not when I'm so happy to see you. We're still friends, aren't we?"

Ophelia laughed, hardly believing he would have the nerve. "Do you drown all your friends?"

Edgar grimaced, shrugging. "If my friends commit fraud, yes. 'Tis the law, you see. But I'm quite pleased to see you made it out. And I'll remind you, we didn't sentence you to *drown*. We consigned you to the ocean. And you survived, lucky you. So there's no reason to assume that your legal punishment hasn't been technically fulfilled."

Ophelia blinked up at him, wary. "What are you saying?"

Edgar's response was instantaneous. "I'm saying there's no reason we shouldn't be allies again. You've proved it yourself, coming over here all sensibly instead of attempting a futile escape. We have a rapport, you and I, and we both have something the other wants. Why shouldn't both parties leave satisfied?"

"You have my father's compass," Ophelia said, raising an eyebrow. "I wouldn't mind having that back."

Edgar shook his head, turning the compass over in his hand. "I wouldn't waste your bargaining chip on this old thing. I've got something much more valuable to you."

"And what's that, pray tell?"

Edgar's smile became oddly crooked. "Your sister."

Behind her, Phe, who had been standing in rapt attention,

burst into a gasp. Ophelia swung around to share a glance with her. "I knew Cordelia would be on that ship. I knew it."

She didn't bother to explain that the mists had told her—Phe didn't believe in island magic anyway.

Ophelia could see her own reflection in Phe's wide, glassy eyes as the older girl gave a firm nod. "Make the trade. Get her back."

Ophelia returned the nod. She pivoted back to make eye contact with Edgar. She kept her voice steady, not too eager or relieved. "You have Cordelia Cray?" she asked. "Prove it."

Edgar gestured to someone behind him, and an officer shuffled forward, pushing Cordelia toward the rails. Her hair was wild, her face bruised, and her hands shackled—but she was otherwise unharmed. She raised her chin to stare out at her sisters in the sloop below. "Careful," she warned.

Edgar flung out a hand in front of Cordelia, and the officer pulled her backward and out of sight again. Edgar called down to Ophelia. "You can see she's not dead, anyway."

"Fine," Ophelia said. "Do you remember the Cray treasure we discussed?"

Edgar's interest was obviously piqued. "I'm always rapt during our conversations. You know that."

Ophelia kept her gaze hard. "I'm prepared to offer it to you in entirety in exchange for Cordelia's freedom, and that of ours." She indicated herself, as well as Phe.

"And what's this treasure, exactly?" Edgar asked, canny. "Gold? Jewels? Bearer bonds? You'll need to be specific."

Ophelia looked back at Phe, conferring. If she said "ships" too soon, he might refuse to give Cordelia back, and take the ships anyway. It would surely not take too long for them to track down the cove. Phe gave Ophelia a sharp shake of the head.

"We can't tell you that," Ophelia said, facing Edgar. "It'll have to be a matter of honor."

Edgar let out a peal of laughter. "A matter of honor? With pirates? I hadn't realized you were funny, Lucky Teeth. I can hardly take your word that you have valuables. Your so-called treasure could be anything. It could be old rags or counterfeit bills for all I know. Even if it were valuable once, it might be ash now that we've set fire to the whole damn place!" The smile slid off his face, and his expression became very still. "No, I'll take what I can see with my eyes. Hear this, Ophelia. If you want your sister back, you need to give me the other one."

Ophelia snorted. What sort of deal was that? Give up Phe in exchange for Cordelia's freedom? Surely if he knew his captive's personality better, he would never have thought this a tempting deal. "I'm afraid I'll have to pass, Edgar. You don't understand, you're not playing with a full deck. By all accounts, you've got my least favorite sister up there."

Edgar looked pleasantly puzzled at this statement. "Oh, is that so? I was led to believe you were rather fond of Miss Young."

Ophelia didn't know what he meant. "Miss Young? That's not Cordelia's surname."

"I believe if you remember my exact words," Edgar hissed, "I didn't say Cordelia was the sister I was offering back to you. Certainly, I would never. She's a pirate. She needs to face justice. I was offering you the other one." Here, he reached into his breast pocket, where his handkerchief usually was, and withdrew a piece of paper. He uncreased it, reading aloud, "Elizabeth Young. Born in Port Jolie, on the island of Peu Jolie, on the eighty-seventh day of the dry season." He folded the birth certificate up again, putting it back in his pocket. Then he tilted his head behind him, toward the mainmast. "Give us a shout, Betsy!"

"Ophelia!"

Ophelia was given over entirely to primal fear. She threw herself toward the rail, a shout ripping out of her. *"Betsy! Betsy, where are you!"*

Edgar put his hands neatly behind his back. He made a *tsk* sound. "Struck a nerve, I see."

Ophelia's breath was coming heavy and fast. Her rib ought to have been killing her, but she hardly felt it now. "How did you—why did you? She hasn't done anything wrong!"

"Not strictly true," Edgar said. "She's broken a few laws now, in pursuit of getting you out of the mess you made. Shame. If she had just stayed home, you would all be fine. I pursued her here, you see. She wanted to find you before Lang's noose did."

Words were lost on Ophelia. There was nothing she could do. Betsy was up there. Her Betsy, her frightened sister, had followed her across the sea? Even after how they'd left it?

"Give me both pirates," Edgar said, a smile haunting his mouth, "and I shall let poor Betsy go free. Come on, Lucky Teeth, this shouldn't be a hard decision. You don't know these criminals. They're not your family. They're not your charitable cause. A week ago we planned to cleanse the seas of their kind. We still can. Bring in the Crays, and no one will doubt your loyalty to the empire ever again."

Ophelia's heart stopped. Edgar kept crooning like a snake charmer.

"I'll pull strings for you. Get you amnesty. I promise you I will—I am nothing if not generous. Our days of fighting are at an end. I've gotten what I needed. I'm a captain now, and poised to rise higher and faster than anyone can imagine. I'll pull you along with me. We were made to be a team."

Ophelia looked down at her palms, flexing her fingers. Why were they so numb? She needed to get to Betsy. She needed to save Betsy like a drowning victim needed air.

"How they'll cheer for you in Port Jolie," Edgar said.

She could see it. *The multicolored shawls waving like banners in port as her ship rolled in. Hands extended to reach out to her as she passed—not to pull, or tear, or tweak. To show respect. They would line up for miles when they heard she would be landing, standing on the roofs of the candy-colored houses to catch a glimpse of her. They would hoist their children up on palm trees to get a better look. She could hear it. The booming crowd. Their deafening roar, like crashing waves in a hurricane. The throng screaming her name: "Young! Young! Young!"*

Never witch. Never Cray. Her curse would be lifted at last.

Edgar had been right, after all. It wasn't a hard choice.

Phe reached out to comfort Ophelia, to take her hand. A foolish move. Ophelia twisted as deftly as the wind, seizing Phe's wrist, twisting it behind her back. She drew Cordelia's knife again, back to her older sister's throat. "Let's start negotiations," she said.

"You conniving bitch!" Phe spat out.

"I sure am," Ophelia said, gritting her teeth. "But I told you. You're not my family. And I'd never let anyone hurt Betsy."

Ophelia glanced up at Edgar, who was obviously delighted by this easy turn of events. He sent some of the bilge rats down a ladder, where they swam to the sloop. In the brief time they had left, Ophelia whispered to her sister, "I'm sorry, Phe. But I need to take this shot. It's just bad luck for you."

Phe didn't flinch. Heedless of the blade at her throat, she raised her chin in an unbearably Cray gesture. "I wouldn't have thought you had it in you," she said. "Maybe you *are* cursed."

Fitz was among the bilge rats' number, and Ophelia found that he couldn't meet her eyes as he went about their work. Her former crewmates restrained Phe with rope, and Fitz was the one who bound her hands. Phe didn't fight; instead surrendering gracefully, her dark eyes locked on Cordelia on the deck above them.

Ophelia didn't release the knife from Phe's neck until the bilge rats dragged her into the waves, and up the ladder to the *Bluesusan*.

Ophelia leaned against the sloop's rail, willing herself to leap back into the waves that had tried to suffocate her so recently. She had to get through them to reach Betsy. "Maybe I am cursed," she muttered, agreeing with Phe's assessment. Fitz lingered on the sloop with Ophelia. He looked pale, from his freckled face to his feet. His hands were held stiffly behind his back, and he kept opening his mouth to try to say something to her, but no words came.

"*What?*" Ophelia snapped. Even now—even now when she

had handed over her own flesh and blood—he treated her with suspicion. What had she ever done to deserve this boy's ire? She had only held the rigging steady for him, brought down the sail to save their ship from the storm. *"What?"* she said again, prowling toward Fitz like a jaguar surveying weak prey. "Do you still think I'm a witch? Are you still afraid of me, positively shaking in your boots?"

The jerk of Fitz's head was so quick it almost looked like a mistake. "N-no, I'm not afraid of *you* anymore," he said, his eyes flicking significantly toward someone on the deck above. He pulled something from the pocket of his breeches and showed it to her: a perfectly normal hammer, with a steel head and claw, attached to a wooden handle. "I have this," Fitz said, his eyes wide and fixed on Ophelia's, as if trying to silently communicate something important. "*Please* remember I have this."

A tiny, strange laugh escaped Ophelia. Was Fitz threatening to knock her brains out if she got too close? A very bold, almost overconfident claim. But still, that he could hate her so much, a boy who was almost her friend, well, it hurt.

She hardened her jaw. This changed nothing. In fact, it reinforced how necessary it was for her to abide by her plan. Without another word to Fitz, she dove into the waves.

The cold water didn't affect her. Even with her cracked rib, Ophelia scaled the ladder with a kind of ease that could only be accomplished by someone who was beyond caring about physical pain. She was only staying alive from second to second so that she could look Betsy in the eyes and see her freed.

The deck seemed unusually crowded at first, so Ophelia

couldn't find Betsy right away. The entire crew was assembled, and they were buzzing with discontent to see Ophelia standing on their vessel once more. There were her Cray sisters, side by side and fuming together. Their hands were bound, their shoulders held by blue-jacketed officers.

Fitz climbed up the ladder a little way behind Ophelia, and when he appeared on deck, Clovis—who had been restraining a tall Lalithan boy Ophelia had never seen before—shoved his captive in Fitz's direction. "You hold him," he grunted. Clovis's glare held Ophelia's attention for a long moment, and then the large man broke eye contact, reaching for a flask on his belt. He took a long drink, then wiped his mouth with his forearm.

Fitz, wincing, took the boy by the shoulders and led him to stand beside the Crays, fitting him into the group directly beside—Jo, of all people. Jo didn't smile when she saw Ophelia. Her mouth was a grim line. She pointed to the mainmast, and Ophelia swung around, following the gesture.

Ophelia's brown eyes found Betsy's gray ones almost instantly. It was so very odd, seeing her here. Betsy stuck out violently, a remnant of her home thrown haphazardly onto the sea. It was as if Ophelia was looking at a burlap sack that someone had embroidered with silk.

But then—Ophelia took it all in. Her mind had briefly refused to accept the horrific scene, the joke of it all. Betsy was standing on the top of a stool beside the mainmast. A length of iron chain was looped around her neck like a makeshift noose, and it extended all the way up to the yard. Betsy was mouthing something at her, but Ophelia couldn't tell what.

A hand on her shoulder. Edgar had come to greet her. "Welcome back, Lucky Teeth. You made the right choice, you know."

"I know," Ophelia stepped forward, letting Edgar's hand fall limply away. She walked steadily forward to where Betsy was restrained, and unable to reach the rest of her, took Betsy's hands. She kissed every finger, the way that Eliza would do for them when they were small and troubled by bad dreams. "This will be over soon, Bets," she said. "I promise."

"Don't trust him," Betsy whispered back, and now Ophelia knew what she had been mouthing. "Don't trust him a minute."

Ophelia closed her eyes, trying not to be overwhelmed by tears. "I'll do whatever it takes to get you out of here. It's my fault. It's all my fault. I never should have left. You were right—"

"No, I wasn't." There was a steely note in Betsy's voice that Ophelia had never heard before. It made her eyes snap open instantly. Yes, Betsy was wearing an iron noose for a necklace, but there was something else different about her.

Betsy swallowed heavily. "I was wrong, in every way. I should have listened back then, when you tried to tell me—but I'm here now. I'm just glad you're alright. *It will all be alright.*"

Ophelia nodded. Hearing an off-key execution band in her head, she faced Edgar. "Let her go now," she said, sounding more powerful than she had thought she would, under the circumstances. "I gave you what you wanted."

Edgar shrugged, juggling her father's compass from hand to hand, like a bored schoolboy. "Not everything. But that can be fixed well enough." He tossed the compass to a waiting officer. He waved Ophelia forward. "You fulfilled your half of the bargain, but if we're to work together again, I'll need more assurances than that."

Ophelia's nostrils flared. He needed assurances? She was the one who had been thrown overboard. "Like what?"

Grinning, Edgar held out his arms and suggested, "Why not seal the deal with a kiss? Do that, and all will be forgiven."

Ophelia took a ragged breath, and pain exploded in her rib again. The numbness from the water and the shock was gone, and she felt completely alive in her body. She tilted her head toward Betsy, who kept whispering, "No, *no*."

"Remember," Ophelia said, her voice hushed. "I'm doing this for you."

The death rattle. The drum roll. Entirely in Ophelia's head, but no less terrifying. She made her gallows walk across the deck she had meant to be salvation. Above her, a gray line of clouds on the horizon. Hurricane season was retreating—but she wasn't quite beyond the storm. Her boots thudded rhythmically as she walked toward Edgar.

"Why not?" she said. He was so close she could smell his breath.

He put his hand on the back of her neck. "That's what I like to hear."

Edgar pressed his mouth, *hard*, far too hard, against Ophelia's. His lips opened, becoming a wet, gaping void, like a cavern where a sea monster would live. Ophelia did what she had come to do. She opened her mouth against his and snapped her jaw shut just as quickly, biting into his lower lip until she tasted blood.

She didn't let go until she felt the solidity of her two front teeth meeting her lower set.

To say Edgar yelled would be not quite accurate. His howl of agony was wordless, yet somehow still eloquent—almost as illustrative as the warm blood bubbling up between Ophelia's lips, tasting of copper. He tried to push her away, but she was already ahead of him. She had released his lower lip and swung around to twist his left arm into a painful knot behind his back. Cordelia's knife, for the third time in an hour, was pressed against the soft flesh of a neck.

Ophelia spoke softly in Edgar's ear. "You always said my teeth were lucky. Didn't know how right you were." Ophelia allowed herself a grin at her former crew, showing her blood-adorned teeth. "I didn't have much to bargain with before," she announced. "But I reckon I do now. Your captain was very stupid to let me back onboard. Release my sister from her noose and let all the captives go free, and I'll trouble you no more."

Murmurs came from the crew. Murmurs of duty, mixed against superstition. But Ophelia knew their worries now, and how to play on them. *It is their fear of us that gives us our greatest strength.*

"I wouldn't waste my time standing around if I were you," Ophelia said, raising her voice, letting it ring like pounded steel. "You will not win. I will cut into your captain's throat like butter. I'll shear through the bone, until he's headless. You only know a portion of what I can do. I can survive drowning, and shootings, and all manner of storms. Don't test my power or my temper. I am the Curse, and nothing can stand against me."

TWENTY-SEVEN

Ophelia's pronouncement echoed impressively across the deck. No one dared to move, it seemed.

Betsy let out a tiny laugh. Ophelia was a miracle, she really was—still trying to talk her way out of trouble. That had always been Betsy's card, but Ophelia was playing it well.

"Cut his throat, then," a large sailor called out. He was leaning against the captain's cabin, and taking another swig from his flask. He looked weak with pain. He wore no shirt, and his whole torso was wrapped in bandages, as if he'd been recently whipped. "Personally, I'd consider it no great loss. But that's just one mutineer's opinion."

Betsy's stomach lurched as she watched Ophelia lick blood from her front teeth. It was rather theatrical but impressive nonetheless. Ludlow was whimpering, twisting slightly, this way and that, but she held him tight. Now Ophelia whispered, greeting the troublesome sailor by name, and the whisper floated across the deck like the creeping mist beyond, sending a chill like death across Betsy's skin.

"Very unwise, Clovis," Ophelia crooned. "On her gallows, my mother promised the world a thousand curses to repay the empire for the wrongs that were done to her. I'm only one of them. Don't make me invoke the rest."

Murmurs. The crew was scared. But Betsy knew that talk alone couldn't solve their problems. Action had to be taken. Ophelia needed backup, and even chained by the neck, Betsy wanted to provide it.

Her hands were bound in front of her, a foolish mistake of Edgar's that allowed her to dig her fingers into her apron pockets. What did she have? There had to be something that could help. No lighter—that was taken from her in Orana. No pistol—she had given their only pistols to Jo and Sherry. She had kept a spare needle there before, but it had washed away in the tides. That left only Ravi's shattered glasses behind.

And that meant—well, it meant only one thing. Betsy was about to die. She had not attended a hanging since Ophelia Cray's, but she was determined to go to this one a little more bravely. So Betsy pulled Ravi's glasses from the apron and gripped them for courage.

Pain. Not just in her sliced palm, but on the back of her left hand. It startled Betsy, as if she were being roused from a deep sleep. She squinted down, and saw a red, stinging mark below the unshattered lens of Ravi's glasses. She tilted her head, following the gaze of the rising sun, as it peeked through the hurricane season clouds just now passing away.

Betsy tried to reposition the glasses. Could she bend the sunlight to hurt Ludlow somehow, like a vicious child burning ants? No, the angle wasn't right. She shuffled herself a little to the left, feeling the heavy iron chain pinch at her skin as she angled herself toward the mob of crewmen opposite Ophelia. She fidgeted her hands, twisting her wrist painfully to get the glasses in the right position. She chewed at her lip in concentration, ripping off a fine layer of skin and feeling a sting that was more invigorating than painful.

She found her angle and caught the sun. Her narrow beam of light fell just on the exposed hand of a pimple-faced, anxious-looking officer. He was holding the oldest Cray and staring at Ophelia with such horror that Betsy was half-convinced he might piss himself then and there. She wouldn't have blamed him. She knew the feeling.

She willed the sunlight into a piercing flame. And if there was any magic left in the world, Betsy knew *intent* was it.

The officer shrieked like the famous howling goat of Peu Lorraine. He began falling all over himself, holding his hand as if it might simply fall straight from the bone. "I'm on fire!" he screamed. "The witch has lit me on fire!"

Betsy smiled, showing all her teeth, though no one was looking at her. *A witch has lit you on fire, silly man. Just not the witch you're thinking of.*

And spinning outward from Betsy's newfound curse, chaos reigned. The Crays had seized their moment, as Betsy had hoped they would. The oldest one had taken advantage of her freedom by launching herself at the officer holding Cordelia, and

Cordelia had in turn smashed the manacles that bound her wrists together into the mouth of another captor. Many of the superstitious sailors had retreated—unwilling to fight directly against foes with witchcraft on their side. A few huddled fearfully at the rail; Betsy thought she saw some eyes drifting hopefully toward the lifeboats.

Now all three Cray daughters were moving: kicking, snarling, knocking skulls together—wreaking unholy havoc upon those sailors foolish enough to still battle them.

But Edgar had seized upon the distraction too. He'd somehow knocked the knife from Ophelia's hand, and now they were both rolling across the deck, trying to strangle the life from one another. But they were at a different angle than before—Betsy thought now she might have a chance to burn Ludlow. She pivoted again, fixated on her target, her pink tongue sticking out between her lips.

But—it happened so quickly. First he was on his feet, and rushing toward her stool, kicking out. And then she was—

Falling.

It was like having the wind knocked out of her. A punch to the gut. And that was just the sudden fall. Her neck—it was no longer her neck at all, but the fractured neck of a wine bottle her father had dropped.

She was not instantly dead, and Betsy thought that was a pity. She had, of course, hidden behind her fingers for the majority of Cray's slow demise, but Betsy had never forgotten the last kick of the pirate queen's boots.

She was the one convulsing now. *Here lies Elizabeth Young, who could not breathe.* A fire had begun behind her eyelids, not unlike the one still raging on the nearby island.

A flash of memory: a miniature ship pressed forever between her father's cold hands. Proof of both joy and sorrow. Physical evidence of a life well lived.

But she had something like that too. As Betsy Young died, she tried to focus on the one thing that seemed to still matter: She would not drop the glasses. She would die with them in her hand.

TWENTY-EIGHT

etsy's boots began to jerk. She was dancing the gallows' jig. Edgar was laughing, blood gargling in his mouth. He had kicked the stool out from beneath Betsy's feet. A pair of male voices were screaming, "No! *No!*"

Ophelia's own legs had given out from under her, her kneecaps hitting the deck with enough pain that she might have taken a bullet in each. There was her sister—her face purpling, eyes bulging—dying right in front of her. And there was nothing she could do.

Suddenly, the tall Lalithan boy, who had been restrained by Fitz, staggered out across the deck. He didn't appear to be able to see very well, but he located Betsy's kicking legs, lifted them from the knees, and hoisted her up on his shoulders so that the noose was no longer tightening around her neck.

Betsy gave a tremendous, rattling gasp, drawing in a lungful of air. Ophelia let out a sound that was half scream, half laugh. Betsy was still alive, still blessedly alive. It was only then that Ophelia realized that her face was wet with tears.

Edgar roared, drawing his saber, as if ready to launch at the Lalithan boy's back. Phe, demonstrating the fearsome competence she had inherited from their mother, had somehow slipped from her bindings and wrestled the cat-o'-nine-tails from Allan, charging up to stand between Betsy, the boy, and the angry crowd. "Whoever wants to knock this girl down again shall go through me!" she roared, striking the air impressively with the lash.

Even with Phe standing in defense, Ophelia knew she had to take Edgar down permanently, or he would never rest until Betsy had the life choked from her. But she had no weapon.

Silver glinted in the corner of her eye. The knife that had been knocked from her hand, lying perhaps ten feet across the deck. She lunged for it, ready to gut Edgar like a fish dinner. She reached the knife at the same time as Fitz. The young boy's face was pale and shocked. He seized the knife by the blade and offered its handle wordlessly to Ophelia. She stared at him, just for a moment, and realized the truth. Fitz had been the other voice screaming. He had let the Lalithan go willingly.

He had not been threatening Ophelia on the sloop at all. He had not been afraid of her. He'd been on her side since the moment she arrived.

Fitz showed her his hammer again, glancing up at the mainmast, where Betsy's noose was anchored directly above the sail. "This should break through the chain," he said, "but we'll need someone else to help me steady the rope if you're ever to reach the yard. Hold him off. I'll find Emily." And Fitz was gone, weaving through the battling crowd of sailors and Cray daughters, and disappearing down the hatch.

Ophelia spun about, diving at Edgar. She met the saber's downward thrust with the flat edge of her knife. She held it at both ends, trying to keep it from breaking. Silver wasn't strong enough to hold its own against steel, and she could already feel it warping.

Edgar's expression was twisted with rage and exultation. Ophelia's weapon was inferior enough that he already knew his victory was certain. But he didn't have the ability to announce it—his broken lip had seen to that. In a desperate attempt to throw off his concentration, she said, "Where's the gloating, Eddie? I would have expected better from you."

A vein throbbing in his temple, Edgar's face was growing increasingly red, until its shade matched the jacket he was wearing. He choked out a word that was probably "bitch," but Ophelia had barely heard it over the sound of her knife breaking in two. She groaned, ducking, and levied a kick at Edgar's right knee, bringing him stumbling to the deck.

"Ophelia!" Fitz had returned, his skinny chest heaving with shallow breaths. He folded the end of a hammer into her palm, and his eyes drifted up the mainmast, to the yard where Betsy's noose was anchored. Edgar seized Fitz's leg, growling like a wolf, but Fitz shook him off—the heel of his boot striking Edgar's forehead. Ophelia knew what she had to do.

"I can't find Emily," Fitz gasped. "She's gone. Ain't no one but that burned lady down there, and I'm not going nowhere near her. I can't hold that rigging by myself. You won't be able to climb safely."

Ophelia didn't know who this "burned lady" was, but that didn't matter. She squeezed Fitz's shoulder. "Just do your best, and so will I." She glanced down at Edgar, stirring feebly on the ground, and moved toward the towering mast.

She seized a handful of rigging. It felt rough and sturdy in her hands. And she hoisted herself up, lifting her boots to climb up the side of the mainmast. Fitz was right. He wasn't strong enough to hold the line steady for her by himself. Yes, Fitz was a bilge rat, like her. Yes, his arms had grown stronger from pulling the iron line, but he was just fourteen, and you could only expect so much.

The line shook, wavering as if they were in a storm, making her bones rattle. Fitz was leaning back quite far, nearly horizontal on the deck in an attempt to make his body weight the anchor Ophelia needed to move upward. It would not last long, Ophelia knew. She needed to make progress quickly if she stood any chance to reach the top of the iron chain and free Betsy.

Ophelia's palms burned. Her lungs were empty. Her ribs were so damaged she could barely expand her chest to draw breath. And she would fall, almost certainly, when Fitz's strength failed him. But that was all right. It would be worth it if she could reach the yard first.

The last time Ophelia had climbed this mast she had been dizzy from fear. She was still afraid now—but the fear only spurred her to ascend. Inch by inch. Second by second. If there were sounds of the battle going on below, Ophelia didn't hear them. She had gone to another place.

Betsy's eyes shining with rage. "He was rude. He should be punished."

Betsy inside a tent of sheets, lifting a bottled ship into the air to ride an imaginary wave.

Betsy, her arms shielding her from a crowd that was out for blood.

Betsy, sitting in the corner of the parlor, embroidering and letting out a contented hum.

She had reached the yard. Ophelia wrapped her right elbow around the wood, and with her left hand, withdrew the hammer from her back pocket. She struck a link of the iron chain that wrapped twice around the yard and heard a satisfactory *clang*. She hit it again. Again. She laughed. She felt good. She could breathe again, because now, even if she fell on the way down, she would make damn sure Betsy would live.

Clang. This was for Papa. *Clang.* For Eliza, who must be so worried.

Clang. For her island, her almost-home. Reduced to cinders.

Clang. Ophelia struck harder now, a white-hot pain burning in her aching palms. This was for her neighbors on Peu Jolie, who would never love her. But what did it matter? She had Betsy.

Clang. For Lang, who perhaps had been right in saying no.

Clang. For her mother! Whose hanging Ophelia had never thought to protest.

Clang. For her Cray sisters. She hoped they would forgive her.

Clang. For Betsy. *Clang.* For Betsy. *Clang.* For herself.

The chain broke, unraveling like a dying wind, and falling to the deck. Below, Ophelia heard a thump, as Betsy and her hero collapsed to the ground.

Ophelia laughed again, long and loud. There was a storm beneath her skin, and it had miraculously cleared, yielding to blue skies. She took hold of the rigging again, shouting to Fitz, "Get ready! I'm coming down!"

She began to heave her weight back against the mast, but midway through the shift, she felt the rope slacken, slipping away from her. Ophelia shrieked and threw herself clumsily back to the sturdy yard, now too far from the mast for her feet to steady her. A shot fired, a crack like thunder above the fray. A bullet whistled just under Ophelia's kicking legs, blowing a hole into the mainsail.

Edgar was on his feet again. He was usually a crack shot, but the blood loss and Fitz's blow to his head had unsteadied his aim. He let out an inarticulate roar, but Ophelia knew what it meant. It meant death. It meant a reckoning and bloody vengeance.

Another shot. Another narrow miss. She had to get down. She was a sitting duck up here, dangling from the yard. But if she let go, the fall would kill her. Ophelia stared dumbly at the hammer still clutched in her hand. She drove its claw into the sail where the bullet had punctured it, and let go of the yard.

She fell, the hammer tearing through the cotton sailcloth, slowing her descent only marginally. It was lovely and terrifying at once. The ripping sound was almost as satisfying as the clangs. Ophelia hit the ground on her feet, but the pain of striking the deck was so intense that both her ankles immediately rolled over with horrid twin *cracks*. Her face struck the wood, and with a dawning horror, she wondered why her cheek was wet. She couldn't stand; her ankles were broken. She rubbed a palm against her cheek, and found crimson clinging to her skin. She flipped onto her back, gasping, expecting to see Edgar leering over her with a gun. But as she turned, she saw only Fitz's unconscious body, splayed out on the deck as if he were sleeping. He was lying in a bed of his own blood.

She cried out, but her scream was lost in the sound of the ongoing battle. "Somebody, anybody! Help!"

While Ophelia fell, Jo had seized her opportunity to launch herself at Edgar. Ophelia sat up, not sure if her ankles would accept her weight again, and saw Jo beating Edgar mercilessly in the face, her blows punctuated by shouts. *"Where? Is? Emily?"*

Edgar grunted a single word, and Jo must have understood it, because she stopped hitting him, sprinting away into the crowd. Ophelia crawled toward him, her hand sticky with sweat on the handle of her hammer. She straddled him, placing the ball-peen at his temple, already a bloody mass from Jo's fury. "Give me a reason," Ophelia growled. "Just one."

Click.

Ophelia felt the barrel of Edgar's gun against her stomach. He tried to grin, but it was more of a grimace. It was clear that even smiling was agony for him now.

Ophelia closed her eyes. "Do it"—she took a breath—"end it already."

But Edgar's shot didn't come. There was no reason for it not to come. She was almost angry that he was dragging this out. He had already fired on her twice. Why was he too cowardly to finish the job?

And she realized. Edgar had used his first bullet on Fitz while Ophelia was still hammering at the noose. The only reason Edgar hadn't emptied his bullet into Ophelia's stomach was because he didn't have a bullet left.

He barely struggled as she raised her hammer, ready to strike true and strike lethal—

Bang! The sound of another gun, from behind Ophelia, firing into the air. An echoing baritone commanded the attention of every soul on the deck. "Stop! And I mean everyone!" Ophelia heard the man's gun cock again, and he ordered, "You too, Young. Stand down, or I'll blow you to pieces."

"Don't do it!" The cry came from Betsy, though her voice croaked like a frog. Ophelia was surprised she could make any noise at all after what she'd just gone through. "Don't hurt my sister!"

Although Ophelia couldn't, Edgar must have been able to see the man's face, because his gray eyes filled with terror. Ophelia yielded, lowering her weapon. She tried to stand, but her ankles betrayed her, and she ended up collapsing in the growing sea of Fitz's blood.

"Has anyone noticed—" Clovis began, everything about his manner steady. He was addressing not only Ophelia and Edgar but the entire crew and the captives as well. Everyone had gone terribly still. "—that the boy is gutshot?" Clovis indicated Fitz's prone body. He jerked his head to Ophelia. "This girl ain't got a gun. Nor has any of the other captives. *They* didn't shoot him. Our captain did." Clovis's deep voice was sepulchral, ghoulish. "So quit your squabbling and find our ship medic. Emily has got to be somewhere, unless our venerable captain killed her too."

No one moved.

Clovis took three deep breaths, and then let out a roar, the tendons in his neck stretching like rigging in a storm. "Find Emily now! Or would you rather keep fighting children? I didn't come to the navy to hang little girls or to watch lads die in front of me. Go!"

Lawrence, who had been sprawled on the deck, being kicked in the ribs repeatedly by Cordelia, scrambled on his hands and knees away from her, toward the hatch below. Several other members of the bilge rats followed him, keen to find someone who could save their smallest, best-loved comrade.

Clovis offered Ophelia his arm. Hesitant—she took it. He lifted her near bodily to her feet, and when he realized her ankles were broken, held her upright so that they wouldn't absorb her weight. "I don't like you," he said.

Ophelia blinked. "I know. You're right not to. I wouldn't like someone who lashed me like that."

"But I never lent Ronan that gun," Clovis said, unblinking. "Ludlow framed me. Surely you knew that?"

"No," Ophelia said, almost inaudibly. "I didn't know."

Clovis jerked his head in the direction of Edgar, who was stirring feebly on the ground. "He stole my gun, let Ronan out, and gave my gun to him. After all, who has the keys to the brig but the first mate? Then he let you punish me so harshly that the crew would turn against you. He was always working the angles. We just have to make the rest of the crew see 'em too."

Ophelia groaned. It was so obvious.

"I don't like you," Clovis repeated. "But I hate him more." He supported Ophelia a few steps across the deck, and laid her back down beside Fitz. Ophelia ran her fingers through his ginger hair. He shivered, his eyes nearly vacant.

"You're going to live," Ophelia lied. This time, she hoped she was convincing. She hoped she could believe it, like her mother and the mists. She hoped she could will it to be true.

There was a low rustling of talk from the crew. They seemed split as to how they should proceed—Edgar at last seemed to have exhausted any trace of the crew's remaining goodwill, but as much as they had soured on him for what he'd done to Fitz, it was clear they were reluctant to trust Ophelia or the Crays. "She destroyed our mainsail!" Allan called out, spit flying from his mouth as he gesticulated at Ophelia, still kneeling beside Fitz. "We'll likely starve to death in this spot because of that! She brought this bad luck on us. She can't just get away with it."

Clovis moved to stand between Ophelia and Allan. "You're right that our mainsail is ruined. You're right that we won't be able to move. But I'll be damned before I let a fool like you hurt the lass." A slow, clever smile began to creep across Clovis's wide face. "Because she's the only chance we've got to replace that sail. We're in the domain of the pirate queens. Who else would have one to lend?"

Ophelia looked up at her giant ally, blinking in confusion at him. But luckily, someone else seemed to realize what he meant.

Phe, who had had her strong fingers wrapped around Weber's neck and had not removed them as long as Clovis had been speaking, now took her hands away. She cleared her throat dramatically. "As your mainsail is unusable," she said, magnanimous and grand as she offered a boon—the Emerald Sea's newest pirate queen. "Perhaps we could give you one of ours, as a gesture of goodwill?"

TWENTY-NINE

Betsy was still gasping. The soft skin of her throat had been sliced open by the iron chain. She wasn't cut so deeply she would die, but she expected to be scarred. Blood flowed down to the collar of her shirt, staining the rough material. Across the deck, Ophelia was crying over the body of a young boy. Betsy crawled on her knees to hold her sister in her arms. "It's going to be alright." Betsy had always been a better liar than Ophelia, but she was not sure if this one was altogether convincing.

Jo came bursting up through the hatch, crowing in triumph. She jabbed a thumb at Ludlow's direction, where he was being held in a headlock by Ravi, who seemed to be rather enjoying himself now. "You tricky bastard! You wanted to play mind games—make us so wary of Emily we wouldn't go near her."

She offered a woman her hand, leading her up the ladder. Betsy gave a strangled cry. It was Fiona Wall! In all the horror, she had forgotten about the woman she had burned and scarred. The woman who wanted her head.

Fiona picked her way up the ladder, her skirts hitched, every inch of her skin wrapped in bandages. "Don't get near her," Betsy moaned to Jo. "She's dangerous."

Jo wagged a finger at Betsy. "That's what Ludlow wanted us to think." She peeled back a layer of bandages from the woman's face, revealing a smooth cheek—completely unmarred by burns. Realization began its slow creep through Betsy's body. Fiona couldn't have escaped that fire without skin damage. It wasn't possible. Jo stripped away another layer, exposing another impossibility. There was no way that fire—as transformative as it was—could grant Fiona Wall a better set of teeth than she'd had before. The bandaged woman's teeth were clean, relatively straight, and lined up one after the other in their normal numbers.

This wasn't Fiona.

Finally, the woman's eyes were revealed, and the top of her head. She was perhaps five years older than Fiona, and maybe a bit taller too. Her eyes were deep brown, carrying shadows beneath them. Her head had clearly been shaved so that her lack of auburn hair wouldn't give her identity away.

Ophelia gasped, beaming at the woman through tears. "Emily! Oh, thank the gods!"

Emily was shaking like a leaf. "Is it over?" she asked.

"Aye, lass," Jo said, kneeling before Emily as if she were completely at her command. "It's over. You're alright now. Though I can't say the same for the ruined woman Ludlow disguised you as. Where'd the wretch go? I saw her climb aboard the ship, but she's not here now."

Emily was tugging the bandages away from her hands now. "I think Edgar let her off the ship when we moored in Orana. I don't know where she went, or even if she could live long after all those burns." She started scanning the deck for Edgar, pale and trembling with rage. "Where is he? I want a piece of him myself."

"Already pummeled," Jo said, proudly.

"Not pummeled enough!" Emily said, words fracturing. "He told me his plan, the gloating goat! Once you were dead at Jack's hand, he was going to light me on fire. Burn me to a crisp and hand what was left of me over to the navy as Fiona Wall. He said no one alive would know the difference."

Jo made a strangled, choking sound. The crew rumbled with increasing displeasure toward their captain—now that his multifarious cruelties were making themselves known. *Too little, too late*, Betsy thought.

"Let's hang the bastard now!" Jo roared, and the rest of the crew answered with approval. Ravi released Ludlow from his grip and let the bloodied man flop, pathetic, to the ground.

"Stop!" Ophelia shouted from her position kneeling on the deck with Fitz in her arms. "We've got to focus on what's important now. Ludlow's *not important*." She directed her gaze toward Emily. "I'm sorry to say, but you've got a patient."

Emily's eyes widened, noticing the wounded boy for the first time, and she hurried to examine Fitz, using the bandages from her hands to stem the blood flow as best she could. Two burly crewmen helped her carry him into the captain's cabin, leaving Betsy and Ophelia sitting alone in the wide, red pool.

It was utter disgust for their captain that ended the war

between the *Bluesusan* crew and their captives. Cordelia was released from her heavy shackles, which she had been using to brain people all throughout the fight, and those manacles were put on Edgar instead. Betsy had thought that he would be dragged to the brig, that his betrayed crew would jeer the way her neighbors had done at Ophelia Cray's execution. But it wasn't like that at all. The sailors who brought him below to his cell were a sober escort, quiet and grim. Ophelia's reminder about Fitz being the priority, and their fear for his life, had snuffed out all their energy.

Still, Betsy had to hope that Ludlow *would* suffer one day. Even if it was just from the memory of Ophelia calling him "not important" echoing in the corners of his mind.

Clovis, stepping up as interim captain, declared that they would accept the kind offer of a replacement sail from the Crays in exchange for their freedom. After all, the oldest Cray girl had been right. The mainsail was unusable now, and without coopera-tion, the navy crew would never go home again. You got nowhere on the sea without the wind.

But Betsy couldn't calm herself. Her face grew hot, her lungs ached. "Fiona can't have gotten away," she muttered, shaking her head repeatedly until she wasn't sure if she could actually stop, though her neck was bruised beyond imagining. "It can't be like that. She's murderous, sadistic! We can't just let her go free."

Ophelia squeezed her shoulder. "Someone will find her."

"Maybe," Betsy said. "Who though? You, I suppose?"

"Not me," Ophelia said. "Definitely not me. We're going home, you and I."

Betsy squeezed her eyes shut, blocking out tears. "Not if you don't want to. I'm done trying to force you to hide in the dark with me."

"You're not in the dark now, are you?" Ophelia said. "Betsy, home isn't just one place. It's wherever you and I are together. And for at least a little while, I want us to be home together in Peu Jolie. We deserve a rest."

Betsy pulled her into a tight hug which Ophelia returned tenfold. At last, Betsy asked, "Where are the Crays going to go now?"

"The only place they'll be accepted," Ophelia said. "That is, if you and our parents will take them."

Betsy stared open-mouthed at her sister. "Y-yes," she said. "Of course we'll take them. But——" The weight of their father hung between them. Ophelia still thought she would find him at home. Betsy pressed her lips together, and decided she would tell Ophelia on the voyage home, when they felt a little more secure. What wouldn't she give, after all, for a few more hours with a living father? "You'd better go tell your sisters that—that we can't wait to get to know them."

Ophelia's smile would have shamed the sun. "Thank you, Bets. I love you and I'm sorry for——"

Betsy waved a hand. "No apologies. Save those for your new sisters. You might have some groveling to do after that hostage trick. For what it's worth, though, I'm sorry too."

A brown hand was extended down to Ophelia. "Let me help you with that." Betsy grinned up at Ravi, her savior. Ophelia leaned against Ravi's chest as he helped her across the deck to where her two sisters sat, checking each other for wounds. When she was kneeling beside them, Ravi doubled back, and he and Betsy went to sit with their backs against the rail.

She leaned her head against Ravi's and opened her palm at last. "Your glasses," she said.

"My gods," Ravi said. "I think I'm happier to see those than I'd be to find the family gold."

Betsy laid her head back against Ravi's warm neck. "You saved my life."

"Well, it's only fair. You did save mine."

They stayed that way, wrapped in each other's embrace, for a long time. Emily came to offer Betsy a strip of bandage for her neck. A sail was recovered from the Cray cove, and hoisted up to occupy the *Bluesusan*'s mast. Eventually, Cordelia's shadow loomed over them, blocking their patch of sunlight. She was scowling. "I am to understand," she said, sighing, "from that loud woman, Josephine, that your boy came to sea looking for some Lalithan gold?"

Ravi's head perked up. He squinted at her through his unshattered lens. Cordelia tapped the golden necklace at her throat. "Sorry to say, this is the last of it. We spent it all on ships years ago. I would give you the necklace, but frankly . . . I don't want to. It looks best on me. But how would you like a ship, in the interest of fairness? We've got a few to spare."

Cordelia turned on her heel, and went away before Ravi could stammer out a thank-you.

Betsy felt . . . sad, somehow. But she tried to put on a cheery, supportive face.

"You really did it," she said, almost in disbelief. "Completed your quest. You found the island and earned your ship. I suppose you'll want to go home now. Show everyone what you've done."

"I suppose I will," Ravi said.

Betsy let out a laugh that was almost a sob. "And this has been one hell of an auspicious first journey for you, hasn't it? I mean—captured by pirates. Thrown in jail. Held at gunpoint. Your treasure long gone. I'd imagine that with the precedent this trip set, your family won't want you sailing anywhere else, ever again."

Ravi's smile faltered. He reached up to push his glasses up on his nose and gave a satisfied sigh to have his fingers touch metal. "I think you're looking at this the wrong way, Betsy Young. You're being awfully pessimistic. Almost . . . me-like. I was captured by pirates—but not killed. I was thrown in jail—but I escaped. I was held at gunpoint—but not shot. I call that lucky indeed."

"Huh," Betsy said.

"And what's more," Ravi fumbled on, "as far as the treasure is concerned, I think my family would be agreed that I found a different kind—" He half grimaced, half smiled, becoming bashful. "Well, don't make me say it. It'll sound silly if I say it out. Overly sentimental. But—you know—I found something better." He reached out for her hand.

Betsy ducked her head to hide her blush, before remembering that he probably wouldn't mind seeing her cheeks go red. She let him take her hand. "So, you're not planning on going back to Lalitha?"

Ravi burst into a peal of laughter. "Of *course* I'm going back to Lalitha. I've been missing for months. I need to show my family I'm not dead." But then his voice grew solemn, as if making a vow. "But," he added, bringing Betsy's hand up to his mouth for a gentle kiss, "if you wouldn't be opposed . . . after visiting Lalitha, I thought I'd conduct some business on Peu Jolie."

A slow smile crept across Betsy's face. "I've heard there are a lot of opportunities for economic growth there."

EPILOGUE

It took three months for her ankles to fully heal. When they did, Ophelia Young chose a fine, warm day to stride across Port Jolie's main square. A pack of boys watched her warily from the stoop of a nearby home, eyeing the way her embroidered red coat flapped out behind her.

"Witch!" a boy called out from the steps. He stood up and made to follow her across the square.

Ophelia smirked, but ignored him.

"*Witch!*" he cried again, louder. "We don't want you here!"

Ophelia laughed so long and loud that the boy clamped his mouth shut and backed up several paces. "That's too bad!" Ophelia said, still walking away. "You're stuck with me!"

In a matter of minutes, Ophelia was standing in the lobby of the naval base, opposite the powder-haired sentry. When he saw her enter the main doors, his lips immediately puckered, like he was restraining the urge to ask, *You again?*

Ophelia turned left, sweeping by him. "I know the way."

"You certainly should by now," the sentry muttered.

At the end of the long hall, Ophelia rapped on the door to Lang's office.

"Enter," Lang's voice called.

Ophelia stepped into the office, pulling two items from the coat Phe had given her: a letter tucked inside a blue envelope and her handkerchief. She gave a respectful bow. "Good morning, ma'am."

Lang stood up from her desk, and returned the bow. "Miss Young. I hope you and your family are doing well."

Ophelia's smile faltered, and she felt the beginning of tears burning at the back of her eyes. She blinked them away. In the months since her return home, she'd had to face the stark reality of a house without her father in it. And while she had been getting better about allowing herself to cry around the people close to her, mostly Betsy and Eliza, at this moment Ophelia wouldn't give in. She wanted to leave Lang with a certain image of her: stoic, graceful.

She faked a smile again, swallowing the lump in her throat. "We're doing about as well as can be expected. Luckily, we have some new faces in the household now, as you probably know. Makes the place feel alive. Less empty."

"I am happy to hear that," Lang said, gesturing at the seat opposite the desk. "Please, sit down."

Ophelia sat, and slid the envelope across the desk's lacquered surface. "I'm sure you've anticipated the reason for my visit. My resignation letter. I wasn't sure about whether I should even write one, at first, given the circumstances of my enlistment."

Lang raised an eyebrow, smiling. "Yes, rather unusual circumstances. I'm sure you're happy that your sister's friend, that Carthay noblewoman, carries such sway with Admiral Eden."

Ophelia bowed her head. Lady Ruza had indeed negotiated her brother-in-law into granting amnesty for Betsy, Ophelia, and the remaining Cray sisters. He'd even made good on Edgar's unscrupulous deal with Norris, the last of the Cray crew. It had not been his fault that he'd been offered his life in return for betrayal.

"Yes," Ophelia said. "We're very lucky."

Lang picked up the letter but didn't open it. "Yes, you really are."

Ophelia clasped her hands together and fiddled her thumbs. "But not as lucky as I would like. You didn't do anything about Edgar. Not you, or Admiral Eden, or anyone."

Lang bristled uncomfortably—Ophelia's words had struck a nerve. "He has been court-martialed and dishonorably discharged from service."

"He killed a boy," Ophelia said, flatly.

"There is little more I could do," Lang responded.

Ophelia gave a harsh smile. "Because his father is rich. Because he bought his way comfortably into the navy, and he bought his way comfortably out. He should have been hanged. You hanged my mother. If the navy were just, it would have hanged him too."

The words fell heavy between them, making the polished desk feel as wide an expanse as the great Emerald Sea. Lang did not counter Ophelia's claim, and though she said nothing to confirm it, Ophelia knew that meant she was right. She was finding her moral compass, after all. It just didn't align with that of the land.

In a conversational mercy stroke, Ophelia broke the silence. "But I've come to tell you something else," she said. "Not just that I'm leaving the navy."

Lang leaned back in her seat, tapping her fingers on the desk. "Oh? What's that?"

Ophelia lifted a handkerchief—stained ugly brown with blood—off her lap, unfolding it to reveal Lang's Star of Merit. "You were right all along. The navy was never meant for me. I shouldn't have lied, to you or anyone. That wasn't legal, but more important, it wasn't right. And it also didn't get me what I wanted. Because I didn't *know* what I wanted. I was trying to win people over. People who are stubborn, superstitious, and set in their ways. But instead of a fanfare, I got shot in the head and thrown overboard, so it seems I set myself an impossible task. I am tired of proving myself to people who want me to fail."

Lang's lips got a bit thinner. "So you're abandoning the straight and narrow?"

"No," Ophelia said, lifting her chin. "I wouldn't say that. I'm just not going to let other people tell me what the straight and narrow is anymore. I can navigate myself."

Lang glanced down at the handkerchief and brought the medal up close to her face for a brief examination. "I thank you for returning this to me," she said. "But as I've said, it was a gift, not a loan. And it's earned through service. You fought mutineers, at risk to yourself. I think that for serving as Captain Young, even briefly, you deserve a medal of your own."

Ophelia didn't know what to say. She did not want to be praised by an institution that let Fitz Durant die and Edgar Ludlow live. "Thank you. But there's someone else who deserved it more. Could you get this to the Durant family, in Peu Nadal? I think they'd like to know their son got to be a hero, even if it was just the once."

This was the fatal blow. The victory that was not worth the cost.

Lang nodded, and she accepted the medal back at last.

Ophelia quickly stood up. She brushed at her eyes, pretending she was scratching an itch. "Now I'm afraid," she said, drawing herself up to her full height, "that I have to be going. I have another appointment." She blinked, then made eye contact with Lang one last time. "Thank you. I wish you the best."

After returning from sea, Betsy had tried to commission a re-creation of the *Moonskimmer* from a local artisan, but the trouble was, the original model had been buried in her father's hands, and she couldn't recall quite what the rig looked like. She requested a model of the *Bloody Shame* instead, thinking that if there was to be a model of a sunken ship in her house, it ought to have been sunk by her doing. She placed the new model on the mantel in her bedroom. That morning, while Ophelia was visiting Lang at the naval office, Betsy found herself lost in thought, turning the new bottle over in her hands and running her index finger along the place where a hairline fracture ought to have been.

This ship also served as a dark reminder to stay vigilant: With Fiona Wall still unaccounted for, such things were necessary. Was she dead? If not, where was she? It had been months since Betsy's own name had been cleared with the navy—but still no one had laid eyes on the Temptress of the Red-Flame Hair. Was Fiona perhaps in hospital somewhere, too injured to move, or even be identified? Or worse, was she perfectly fine, and out there plotting revenge?

Betsy heard the door creak open, breaking her out of her reverie. Ravi entered, holding an unlit cigar. "Valois said you might want this," he said. "For your nerves before the meeting?"

Betsy grinned. She crossed to her window, cracking it open. "Yes, but let's try to keep the smoke outside, shall we? Keep Mama happy." She dug a new silver lighter from her apron and set the cigar's end aflame. She took a drag, then exhaled a perfect smoke ring out into the balmy autumn air.

Ravi straightened his glasses, watching the ring dissipate as it floated out over the cobblestones below. Betsy passed Ravi the cigar, and he too brought it to his lips.

Absentmindedly, Betsy traced her fingertips across the thick, ropelike scar that now stretched across her neck. It seemed to warm itself, like a beating heart, when she was anxious. "Do you know how Mama is doing today, actually?"

Ravi shrugged, passing the cigar back to her. "She said she doesn't want to see him. She's staying in her room."

Betsy sighed. Mama had claimed, upon her and Ophelia's return, that all was well between them again, but it clearly wasn't so. Since Papa's death she had retreated into the master bedroom and rarely came out.

Ophelia's voice called out from the foyer, floating up the stairs. "Betsy, where are you? He'll be here any minute!"

Betsy crushed the cigar's glowing embers into the ashtray on her desk, and smoothed out the front of her dress. She waved Ravi out of the room ahead of her. "Go on, I'll meet you." She made her way out of her bedroom and shouted down the stairs. "We're coming!"

Ravi descended the stairs, but Betsy cast a glance back to the darkened master bedroom. The door was ajar, and her mother was peering out of it, wide-eyed and pale.

"Mama?"

She looked down at the rug beneath her slipper-clad feet. "Put on some lily water before you go below, won't you, dear? I *can* smell that cigar." The door shut again, and she disappeared behind it. Betsy swallowed heavily, and ignoring her mother's advice, she followed Ravi directly downstairs.

Down in the foyer, Betsy found Ophelia adjusting the sleeve of her red coat, pulling on a loose thread. "I can fix that for you tonight, if you want."

The kitchen door swung open, and Valois came bustling through it, balancing a teapot and a set of rattling porcelain cups. He made that prissy teeth-sucking noise. "You're honestly telling me we're going to play host to that wretched boy again? We ought to put poison in his tea, that's what we ought to do."

"Valois, you're getting more piratical by the day," Ophelia observed.

"Call it the influence of our house guests," Valois sniffed.

Ophelia said, lifting the teapot off the tray, "Let me help."

She followed Valois into the parlor, and Betsy entered behind her.

"So we're ready?" Betsy asked, her hand on her chest, trying to exhale all her anxiety out of her body. "We're really, really ready?"

In the corner of the room, Cordelia and Ravi strategized beside Papa's mahogany desk—which had been recently moved down from his office on the second floor and placed in the parlor. In all honesty, the move had been necessary simply so Ophelia and Betsy could work on the company's ledgers without being distracted by the memories of their father in every inch of his office. But now that Cordelia had gotten more comfortable with the bookkeeping aspects of the Whitman-Young Company, Ophelia and Betsy were working with the numbers directly less and less. As it turned out, all those years of scrimping and saving to provide for the inhabitants of Cray Island had made Cordelia something of a managing genius.

"We're ready," Cordelia said, snapping the company's ledger shut. "As long as Randawa's ready."

Ravi pushed back his new glasses and assured Betsy, "I'm ready."

Betsy smiled, crossing the room to squeeze his hand. He grinned at her, and she marveled again about how different that smile had become since he'd gotten false teeth to replace the ones that Fiona had stolen. "Then we are definitely ready."

As if on cue, the doorbell rang. Betsy took a deep, shuddering breath. "Oh gods," she said, as Valois exited into the foyer to greet their guest.

"It will be fine," Ophelia said, locking confident eyes with Betsy. "I promise."

Betsy nodded. "I know."

Ophelia gestured to Cordelia and Ravi. "Take a seat, both of you. Or he'll take the most comfortable one for himself. I can promise you that." Cordelia took this advice straight to heart, sinking into the green armchair that had once been Papa's favorite.

Ravi also sat, though Ophelia and Betsy had previously decided between themselves to remain standing—the better to make the most of their height. Valois reentered the room, ushering in Matthew Whitman behind him. Valois helped their guest remove his jacket and hat, then bowed, departing the room.

There was a moment of heavy silence as Matthew regarded Ophelia and Betsy, and as the sisters regarded him in return. No condolences were offered on either side.

Betsy hadn't seen Matthew since the day he and Ruza had paddled away from the *Bloody Shame*, and she was curious to see how he had changed. In all honesty, he didn't look too different from the boy she had met six months earlier—although now he had a set of fake ivory teeth and a pair of shadows beneath his eyes.

Betsy broke the silence. "We're so happy to have you visit our home. It's been awhile since we saw each other last, and under very difficult circumstances. I hope your family is well, and your voyage was uneventful?"

Matthew winced visibly behind his glasses, and glared at her. "My ship didn't sink this time, if that's what you mean."

Ophelia raised her eyebrow, sharing a significant look with Betsy, and crossed her arms. "I'll let you take the lead on this one," she said.

"Happily," Betsy told her. She pointed to the last remaining chair in the room, a stiff-backed wooden one. "Please, Mr. Whitman. Have some tea, and take a seat. Our apologies if it is uncomfortable, but I'm sure you won't be too inconvenienced. You won't be sitting in it long."

Matthew accepted his offered chair, but made a scoffing sound and waved off the cup of tea that Cordelia stood to pass him. "Won't I?" he asked, his voice dripping with disdain. "I thought I'd made the trip so we could discuss business."

"You have," Betsy told him. "But unfortunately, sir, your part in this conversation won't take more than a few minutes."

"Oh?" Matthew said, but he didn't seem to quite follow.

"No," Betsy said. She gestured to Ravi and Cordelia. "Because you're not going to be our partner in this venture for much longer."

Matthew immediately jumped out of his chair as if he'd been struck by lightning. "Excuse me? I own half the shares in this company. You can't just push me out!"

"Certainly we're not pushing you out!" Ophelia said, breaking into the conversation with a derisive laugh. "*We're* not dishonorable." She let the uncomfortable implication hang low over their heads, and then she paced to the room's edge to lean against the doorframe, obviously pleased with herself.

Betsy gave Matthew a tight smile. Her hands were shaking, but when she spoke, her voice was surprisingly steady. "No, sir," she said, "We're not pushing you out." She motioned for Cordelia and Ravi to step forward, each holding out a ledger. "We're buying you out. Allow me to introduce you to Miss Cordelia Cray, and Mr. Ravi Randawa. We think that together we have accurately estimated the approximate worth of your shares in the Whitman-Young Company. Mr. Randawa, our newest investor, is prepared to offer you that value today, with additional compensation, of course."

Matthew had sunk slowly back into the stiff wooden chair, his mouth agape. "But—"

Ravi strode forward to stand at Betsy's side. "You might be familiar with my father's corporation? The Randawa Company? We do a lot of business on the continent's western coast, but my father has always wanted to expand toward the String Islands— or even as far as the northeastern provinces. I believe you hail from Cornwallis? Long journey, to be sure."

"Yes," Matthew said, looking down at his lap and blinking rapidly. "And you don't know the northeastern lines. That part of the business will collapse without my family involved."

From the door, Ophelia's voice sounded like a purr. "That's a risk we're willing to take. My sister Phe has quite a lot of sailing experience. She is currently captaining a voyage to Gordon as we speak, and she would be happy to oversee our business on the northern lines. Don't you worry about us."

"What's more," Ravi said, looking back at Betsy with an admiration shining behind his spectacles, "as my fiancée mentioned, I'm willing to compensate you at more than your shares are worth. You won't get a deal that fair again—and certainly not a deal that will end your necessity to travel by ship so frequently." He cast a kindly smile onto Matthew. "I too ran afoul of Jack Copeland and Fiona Wall. It's enough to make anyone want to abandon the sea, especially if you have a weak constitution."

Matthew Whitman's eyes were just about bulging out of his head, and he seemed to have barely registered the majority of Ravi's words. "Fiancée?"

Betsy ignored him. She took the ledger that Cordelia offered her and withdrew a contract. "Sign here, and then here, and initial here, Mr. Whitman. That way, there will be no more pirates in your future."

Matthew Whitman took a pen, his hand shaking, and meekly signed his name. Cordelia crossed over to explain certain important clauses and the legal rights he was now waiving.

Betsy turned her back on their former partner and crossed the room to where Ophelia stood against the wall. She reached out to take her sister's hand, then leaned in to whisper in her ear. "You *really* think we're ready to run this company on our own?"

Ophelia gave a full-toothed smile and whispered back, "Come on, Bets. When have we really been ready for anything?" She shrugged. "We'll fake it."

Betsy couldn't hide the flush of excitement in her cheeks at the suggestion. "And what if the curse comes back?"

"Let it," Ophelia said. "From now on, we control our luck. And damn anyone who tries to stand in our way."

ACKNOWLEDGMENTS

It takes a village to raise a child, and a small city to write a book. Writing might be a solitary activity, but no one does it alone. Especially not me.

First and foremost, I have to thank Mom and Dad. This book is about good luck, and being born to such loving and supportive parents was the first and best piece of luck to ever come my way. Everything I am and everything I ever will be is because of you. There are no words for what you mean to me.

To my sister, Kathy: I still remember you asking to read my very first story and helping me with the grammar, the two us sitting together on the guest bed in our grandparents' house. On that day and on every day since, I have been grateful for you.

To my agent, Laurel Symonds, who signed me for this book nearly six years ago: A lot of people might have given up on me, on Ophelia and Betsy, but not you. You believed in us so hard. Thank you.

To my editor, Tamara Grasty, who is in many ways the fearless captain of this ship. Thank you for seeing the potential in this story and guiding me to make it the very best it could be. I am so glad to have gone on this journey with you.

To the entire team at Page Street Kids, and anyone who helped this book along the way: Emma Hardy, Meg Palmer, Rosie Stewart, Juliann Barbato, Shannon Dolley, Sossity Chiricuzio, Cas Jones, Hayley Gundlach, Lauren Knowles, Lizzy Mason, and Lauren Cepero.

To my extended family: aunts, uncles, cousins, and especially my grandma, thank you for believing in me and cheering me on for so many years, ever since I was the little kid reading books at the dinner table. It's meant the world to me.

To those wonderful friends who have suffered in particular with me on this publishing journey (aka the ones who've listened to me ramble about plot issues, or whom I've leaned on to read my drafts and point me in the right direction): Joanna, Alyssa, Elizabeth, Abby, and Jessie. The support and interest you've shown in my writing buoyed me in the years where the waiting felt endless. Thank you from the bottom of my heart.

And to all the many, many friends who kept me sane in those waiting years by being wholly unconnected to publishing, checking in on me through the process, and always making me laugh even when I was down: Marielle, Kathryn, Jen, Dana, Kendall, Emma. You are cherished. Book deals come and go, but you are forever.

To the history department at Lafayette College, who advertised a class on Colonial America in the course catalogue, without specifying that the only topic of focus would be colonial *piracy*. Best mistake I ever made.

To my workshop class who was with me in the early stages of this book's creation: Victor, Anya, Shelby, Will, Theresa, Fajr, Sasha, Michael, and Kanya.

To everyone who's ever read a draft of anything I've ever written, and most especially: Mara F., Alex B., Jen G., Annemarie P., Tashie B., Andy P., Elle T., Meryn L., and Bridey M. It would be so lonely in the trenches without other people in there with you.

In case there's anyone I've forgotten, let me just say this: For every friend and family member who has touched my life with your kindness, thank you. I have been blown away by the support and outpouring of love I've experienced—not just since getting this book deal, but every day I've been alive. Becoming an author has always been my dream, but that's in large part only because you all made me believe I could. I love you all.

ABOUT THE AUTHOR

Christine Calella lives in a place she refers to as "New York City–adjacent." She spends her spare time singing showtunes in the shower, drinking more chai lattes than are strictly necessary, and either over- or under-watering an unfortunate string of houseplants named after sitcom characters.